RITA® award winner for Best First Book

"A tense, gripping adventure set in a future world where courage and love might not be enough to save you…"
—*New York Times* **bestselling author Sophie Jordan**

"Engaging and electric with heart-pounding suspense. Pintip Dunn's gorgeous storytelling makes this an incredible read. Be prepared to stay up all night turning the pages."
—**New York Times bestselling author Kristin Cast**

"Breathtakingly creative and powerfully written."
—**New York Times bestselling author Kristan Higgins**

"*Forget Tomorrow* grabbed my heart and left me breathless at the end."
—**Brenda Drake, author of** *Thief of Lies* **and** *Touching Fate*

"This gripping read is sure to have you on the edge of your seat."
—**BuzzFeed.com**

"A page-turner full of adventure and danger."
—*USA Today's HEA*

"A YA adventure with ethereal prose and appealing characters."
—*Kirkus Reviews*

"VERDICT: Recommended for avid dystopian fans."
—*SLJ*

"With a cliffhanger ending that somehow still packs a powerful punch of hope, *Forget Tomorrow* is a top pick for readers who love action and themes around fate and the future."
—**YA Books Central**

PINTIP DUNN

REMEMBER YESTERDAY

Entangled Publishing, LLC
2614 South Timberline Road
Suite 109
Fort Collins, CO 80525

Entangled Teen is an imprint of Entangled Publishing, LLC.

Visit our website at www.entangledpublishing.com.

Edited by Liz Pelletier
Cover design by L.J. Anderson, Mayhem Cover Creations
Interior design by Toni Kerr

ISBN: 9781633758322
HC ISBN: 9781633754959
Ebook ISBN: 9781633754942

Manufactured in the United States of America

First Edition September 2017

10 9 8 7 6 5 4 3 2 1

*For Antoine. I'll love you
for the rest of this time
and all of the next.*

1

My sister Callie didn't kill herself so I could risk my future pulling stupid stunts. Yet here I am, hanging upside down over a cage of mice, while my best friend, Ryder Russell, anchors me with a rope and pulley as he squats in the air duct.

"If you drop me, I'll tell Mikey you snuck out of the compound last weekend," I say, too softly to set off the sensors inside the lab but loudly enough for Ryder to hear.

"If I drop you, my dad will be the least of our problems."

I stretch my fingers toward the metal cage, making sure my shirt stays tucked into my pants. I have a unique, blobby-hand birthmark at my waist, one I'd like to keep hidden from the security cameras. "A few more inches, and that should do it," I say.

Ryder grunts, and I fall half a foot.

My heart bounces as if it were attached to a bungee cord. But he won't drop me. He never has. This is our fourth time breaking into a lab, and we haven't made a mistake yet.

I swing my arms and reach for the cage door. Ryder and I bicker like brother and sister, but we're a team. From the time we were six years old and he gave me "first turns" with the mud puddles. He's like a cloud of gnats—always annoying and yet endearingly loyal. I'd never be able to do this without him.

One last swing, and I grab the latch. The cage is so big it runs the length of the counter. Inside, hundreds of white-furred, pink-nosed mice climb over one another, wriggle under the straw, and run through a three-level maze with bells and doors.

Below the latch, taped to the counter, is a photo ID. Even upside down, Tanner Callahan's straight brows and barely curved lips look cocky.

Of course they do. Tanner's sixteen, like me, but ever since he was a kid, the Technology Research Agency's been training him to become one of them: a scientist. I've heard rumors that his parents died in an accident, and he's grown up as an orphan within the walls of TechRA, adopted for all intents and purposes by a government organization.

Exaggeration? Maybe. But that doesn't mean he has to swagger around school like he's some kind of genius. Even if he kinda is.

I pry open the gate, setting off the silent alarm. The countdown begins. I have exactly one minute before the guards burst into the lab.

The mouse closest to me sniffs the air, as if testing the smell of freedom, and then clambers out of the cage. Another follows. And then another. Pretty soon, an avalanche of mice pours out of the opening and disappears behind the computer equipment and nests of wires.

Go on, little mice. Wriggle your way to a better life. Anything's better than being imprisoned here, day after day, at the mercy of scientists who treat your brain like a Petri dish.

I should know. That was me, ten years ago. Strapped to a reclining chair, hooked to a million sensors, forced to inhale chemical-laced fumes. If Callie hadn't broken into the Future Memory Agency, if my sister hadn't sacrificed herself to save me, I might still be there today.

Never again. If I can help it, no other living creature will be subject to the scientists' whims, either.

"All set," I say to Ryder. "Get me out of here."

The pulley creaks, and I inch up, up, up toward the ceiling. Victory, sweet and heady, floods my veins. We did it. We freed another cage of mice. There are dozens more cages just like this one, but at least these mice won't be studied. Will no longer be tortured. There's success in that.

I'm halfway to the ceiling when I notice him. A mouse, with his foot caught in the grating, half in, half out of the cage. The other mice scamper over him, their claws digging into his head as though he were just another obstacle.

The mouse pulls and tugs, but he can't get his leg loose. As the cage empties, his movements become more frantic, as if he realizes this is his last chance to escape. When he's the only one left, he flips his body around and attacks the caught leg with his teeth.

I suck in a breath. This must be one of the hypcrintelligent mice I've heard about. He understands. He calculates. He weighs morality and makes decisions, just like us.

"Stop, Ry!"

The upward motion halts, and my teeth click together.

"What is it?" Ryder asks.

"A mouse is stuck. Lower me so I can hclp."

The rope jiggles. "The guards will be here in thirty seconds."

"He's about to gnaw off his leg. We have to help."

No response.

"Do it, Ry!"

I fall through the air so quickly I bump my head on the counter. I grit my teeth, ignoring the throbbing. I reach for the mouse instead. He turns and bites my hand, his teeth breaking through my glove and sinking into skin.

Ow. Lightning streaks across my brain, and I waste several moments blinking away the pain. This isn't the first time a mouse has bitten me. In fact, my gloves are all scratched up from the scrape of teeth. But it's the first time a bite has broken through their thick, protective material.

"Twenty seconds," Ryder says above me. "Come on, Jessa. The mouse isn't worth it. Leave him."

No way. I press two fingers on the mouse's jaw, wrap my hand around his torso, and pull.

Maybe I yank too hard. Or maybe the mouse had already gnawed through too much of his flesh. Whatever the reason, the leg *separates from his body*. And stays in the grating.

Shocked, I drop the mouse, and he hobbles away, his three legs scratching against the counter.

I stare at the detached leg. Furless, pink. The size of a matchstick. The skin is loose and bunched, the toes disproportionately long. Nausea roils in my stomach. My mouth dries, and I'm light-headed, but that could be from hanging upside down too long.

"Ten seconds," Ryder says. "Are you ready?"

I take a shuddering breath. Retreat first. Mourn later. "Yeah. Pull me up."

I fly through the air as if I'm on a zip line. Ryder grabs me under the arms and hauls me into the air duct, just as the lab door opens and half a dozen guards in navy uniforms spill into the room.

The ceiling panel is still uncovered, but a mechanical "spider" sits at the edge of the hole, projecting a holographic image that makes the surface appear smooth and uninterrupted.

I pull my knees to my chest and will myself not to move.

Not to breathe. Not to look at the tiny severed limb stuck in the cage.

Oh Fates, I didn't mean to hurt him. The last thing I wanted was to rip off his leg. I was only trying to help.

In the dimness of the chute, I meet Ryder's eyes. His six-three frame is folded like origami, and the smooth darkness of his skin blends into the shadows. I read in his face the same emotion that compresses the walls of my throat. He saw the limb, too.

Below us, a strong voice cuts through the din. Through the holographic screen, Tanner pushes his way through the guards. His tousled black hair falls into his eyes, and he wears his bad-boy-scientist uniform—dark thermal shirt and cargo pants. Clothes just as appropriate for running lab experiments as for racing around on a hoverboard.

Here it comes. Tanner Callahan, boy genius, is about to throw a fit that will blow the spirals off this steel and glass building.

But he doesn't. Instead, he crouches in front of the cage and studies the leg. And then, with a gentleness even a precog couldn't have foreseen, he wiggles the limb loose and wraps it in a piece of white gauze.

I gape. He's not actually…sad…about the amputated leg? He can't be. They're not pets to him. The only person—or thing—he cares about is himself.

No. I can't start imagining things that don't exist. This is the boy who plays holo-images of himself across the inside of his locker, for Fate's sake. And if that's not enough, he's declared his loyalty to the scientists, who have only one goal. Under the direction of Chairwoman Dresden, their purpose is to discover a way for people to send memories back to their younger selves, so that our society can return to a time with no guesswork and only guarantees. A time when every seventeen-year-old knew exactly what his or her future held.

I wrench my eyes from Tanner and hook my fingers through the harness strapped across my torso. All of a sudden, I can't wait for the guards to leave so we can crawl through the air ducts back to our secret entrance in Mikey's office.

Callie died in order to prevent future memory from being invented. She killed herself so the horrendous vision she saw of our world would not come true.

Anyone who seeks to undermine my sister's sacrifice is automatically my adversary. And I will never, ever forget who my enemy is. No matter how sorry he might feel for a mouse with three legs.

2

"You should've seen the leg," I say to Logan a couple of hours later. I'm back in the Harmony compound I call my home, and we're balancing a rowboat over our heads as we make our way through the twenty or so individual family houses. "It was so small. It might have even been moving." My heart thuds behind the black tourmaline pendant hanging around my neck.

He turns, and we lower the boat to the moving sidewalk that weaves through the compound. Even though we aren't walking, the projected holos, the transport tubes, and the metal gardens continue to zoom by. Logan's ten years older than me, the age my sister would've been if she had lived. In the last decade, his swimmer's build has gotten even broader, and the lines around his eyes and jaw have hardened.

And yet, he's still good-looking, still the boy Callie fell in love with as a teenager. Still the friend who whisked me away from FuMA after my sister injected herself. Still the protector who looked out for me all those years the psychics were on the run from the government.

"Why didn't you use your precognition?" he asks. "You could've seen what was about to happen."

I let go of the boat and grab my necklace. "You know why I couldn't."

Callie. It all comes back to Callie. When she stabbed the needle into her chest, she took away more than her life. She also took Logan's heart—and eventually my desire to use my psychic abilities ever again.

"Besides, I don't think my precognition is that powerful," I say. "It's good for simple physical events just a few minutes in the future—or the will of one or two people. Not so accurate for complex situations with so many independent minds. You need someone with real precognition for that."

He frowns, as though remembering his last brush with a real precog—and the vision of genocide she showed him and Callie. "You've got to stop breaking into labs. First, it was cliff-diving, and then parasailing, and now this. Do you have a death wish, Jessa?"

"No more than you," I retort. "Look at you, spending all your time in the water. I don't think you'd ever surface for air if Angela didn't make you."

"At least I'm not hell-bent on being a rebel." The moving sidewalk curves around a corner, and he leans along with it. "You need to put aside this risky behavior. Start focusing on the future. Now, more than ever, employers are returning to the old ways of evaluation, like they used to do before future memory. School is important. Your grades are important. How are you going to get a job if you don't start applying yourself?"

I don't lean, just to be contrary, and as a result, I'm almost knocked off balance. "Easy for you to say. You always had your future memory. You always knew you were going to be a gold-star swimmer."

"We've been given a chance for a new start, Jessa," he says

softly. "Don't mess this up."

We certainly have been. After Callie's sacrifice, Logan and I fled civilization to join Harmony, a wilderness community governed by its own laws. We were on the run for six years before the Committee of Agencies, or ComA, realized that without the psychics, their research into future memory came to a standstill. So they offered a deal to the Underground, the covert organization made up of psychics and their families. It wasn't easy for them to find our leaders. After all, the identities of the Underground members are kept secret for a reason. But a few well-placed whispers got the message to the right people. ComA was desperate, and they were willing to compromise to get back their psychic citizens.

Compromise they did. They granted the people of Harmony amnesty for breaking the law and legislated that we would no longer be coerced into experimental testing. They promised us the luxuries of every normal citizen and even our very own compound. That way, we could continue living as the same tight-knit community we were in the wilderness—just transported to Eden City.

ComA said the compound was a perk, but we all know better. Really, it's just a way for them to keep an extra-careful eye on us, so that they can quell any rebellious uprisings before they begin. The other members of the Underground were invited to join us, but they would be stupid to do so. ComA can say whatever they want about no longer hunting down the psychics. No one's about to announce that he or she has special powers.

Still, the treaty was a chance for us to stop running. To live back in civilization once again. So we took the deal, and our leader, Mikey—Logan's brother and Ryder's adopted father—oversaw the construction of the compound.

We came back. But I'm not sure I'll ever be a normal citizen.

Logan gestures to the rowboat, indicating we should pick it up again. "If they catch you breaking into their labs, all bets are off. You know the scientists have been salivating to get their lab gloves on you. ComA's treaty will be cheerfully ignored once you're in detainment."

Guilt coats my throat like thick slime. I knew I was risking more than myself by breaking into the labs. But his words, and the mild reproach in his tone, make me want to slit a hole in the cosmos and disappear.

In a different future, Callie and I held the key to the invention of future memory. She took herself out of the equation, but I'm still here. My brain is still fertile ground to excavate. And yet, since she and I were a Sender-Receiver pair, the scientists can't discover anything without her. Right?

"I couldn't leave the mice to the whim of the scientists," I say, not looking at Logan. "It's cruel the way they're treated."

"Not as cruel as genocide."

He doesn't have to remind me.

We don't speak as we step off the sidewalk and exit the compound. We walk into the woods—an almost entirely different world. Here, in this small, dwindling-by-the-day patch of forest, there's no metal or technology. There's just vegetation and rocks and the smell of rich, damp soil. If there was ever a place for peace and relaxation, this is it.

Problem is, when we reach the gurgling river and push off in the rowboat, Logan still isn't talking to me. I don't know if the silent treatment is just the way our friendship is—or if he's annoyed at me.

We lived in the wilderness for six years, where the sky was our ceiling and the grass was our floor. Those first few months after we left, in those days when I didn't talk, and not even Ryder and his mud puddles could draw me out, Logan would take me on the water.

He would row until we reached a pool of still water, and we'd sit in silence for hours. I'd look at the fish swimming below the surface and the water rippling in concentric circles, and the knots inside my stomach would slowly unwind. As though I could finally stretch after crouching too long in the restrictive box of grief.

This was how we mourned Callie, in the first months after her death. And even though Logan's busy with his swimming career and I'm busy with school, this is how we mourn her still.

I drag my oars through the river, and drops of cold water sprinkle on my forearms. Logan's face is clenched in concentration, the way he looks before one of his swim meets. Yep, definitely mad.

I try to think of something to say—and then a prickly sensation converges on my brain. I drop the oar and clutch my head.

"Are you okay?" Logan grabs my oar before it slides into the water. "What's wrong?"

Whispers rumble at the edge of my mind, digging their sharp talons into my scalp. It's not painful, exactly. Just uncomfortable. Like an insect has crawled into my head space and is buzzing around the empty cavity.

"It's probably nothing," I say through gritted teeth. "I bumped my head on the counter when Ryder was lowering me, and I have a migraine. That's all."

Even as I say the words, I look at my hand, which throbs where the mouse bit me. Where his teeth broke through the glove and pierced skin. The marks are red and swollen, and angry streaks radiate from the bite.

I swallow. Could I be reacting to it? Nah. These are lab mice. It's not like they have rabies.

"Please don't be mad." I take the oar back from Logan, changing the subject. "Even if I were caught, even if the scientists experimented on me, they wouldn't find what they're looking for. Not with Callie gone."

He takes a deep breath and holds it so long he might be doing one of his underwater exercises. "What if she's not gone?"

I jerk. "What?"

"We never saw anyone take away her body." He stares at his fingers. "We never watched it burn in the incinerator. She had no pulse, but we escaped down the laundry chute before we saw if an antidote revived her. Someone could've entered the room after we left. Someone could've saved her. We don't know."

My heart knocks against my ears, and I can't breathe. Because this was my biggest fantasy as a child. This was the dream that took years of "talks" with Angela for me to let go. Callie, still alive.

Angela knew Callie for only a short time, during the couple of weeks that my sister ran to Harmony to escape her future, but she loved her. If Callie had lived, if she had married Logan like I imagined, Angela would've been her sister-in-law, since she married the other Russell brother, Mikey.

And I would've still had my twin.

Callie and I were conceived from the same egg and sperm, although my embryo was removed and implanted eleven years later. What's more, we were linked through a psychic bond, making us closer than sisters. Maybe even closer than regular twins. But that bond didn't survive her death.

Oh, for a long time, I thought it did. For years, I would've sworn I still felt her, somewhere on the other end, barely holding on. But as one year flowed into the next, and I received no other sign, Angela convinced me that it was nothing more than wishful thinking.

"She's gone, Logan," I say gently. "Think about what you're

saying. According to your scenario, someone would've had to inject her with the antidote seconds after we left. Nobody even knew you were there."

He holds up his hand. I realize he wasn't staring at his fingers after all, but at a jagged cut running across his palm. "I did this at practice the other day. This cut was in my future memory. The one where I'm warming up for the Gold Star competition and I meet Callie's eyes in the audience. The one where I feel an overwhelming sense of belonging."

He traces the cut, almost tenderly. "When she plunged the needle into her heart, Callie sent out ripples that impacted a lot of people. Half the memories people received wavered and then faded like sound waves traveling away from their source. Because those memories no longer belonged in our time. Callie changed our future. She picked up our universe and moved it to a different timeline."

He looks up. Our boat has drifted to the shoreline, and his face is bisected by shadows cast by the leaves. "My memory didn't fade. It's just as vivid now as it was ten years ago. That's one of the reasons I still get endorsements, even though most of the other swimmers' revenue streams dried up a long time ago. They've had to get other jobs, while I could focus on my swimming.

"And now, with this injury, it seems like my future memory is coming true, at long last. Only, how can that be if Callie's gone?" He picks up the oar and pushes us off the shore, away from the shade. "Unless she's not."

The sun beats down on my skin, but suddenly I'm shaking, shuddering, shivering inside.

Unless she's not.

That sentence is too big, its implications too familiar. This hope will bury us alive if we let it.

"You have to let her go," I say around the mass in my

throat. "Mikey, Angela—we're all so worried about you. You can't stop living just because she has."

He laughs, a short, sharp sound that could cut glass. "Fates know, I haven't stopped dating these last ten years. In fact, I'm seeing a girl right now."

"Yes, but you're never serious about them. You haven't had a real girlfriend since Callie died."

An expression of immeasurable sadness crosses his face. I reach out to touch him—but pain sears across my head, and I fall forward to my knees. The whispers are back, scrabbling at my brain, searching, searching for a crack or chink, slicing me with tiny, quick jabs. I press my hands to my temples, but no matter how hard I push, I. Cannot. Make. It. Stop.

"Owwww," I whimper. "It hurts, Logan. It hurts so much."

"Hold on. I'm rowing as fast as I can. I'll get you back to the compound. I'll get help."

I keep squeezing my head as the boat speeds over the water, keep applying pressure as Logan lifts me in his arms and runs back to the compound. My teeth chatter against one another as first my mom's and then Ryder's and then Mikey's faces pass in front of my vision. Fine tremors erupt along my skin as Mikey lifts my hand and squints at the bite marks.

"Yep, she's been infected," he says.

And then I pass out.

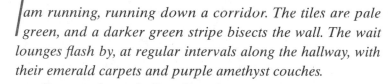

3

I am running, running down a corridor. The tiles are pale green, and a darker green stripe bisects the wall. The wait lounges flash by, at regular intervals along the hallway, with their emerald carpets and purple amethyst couches.

Green and purple. Purple and green.

These colors mean something to me. Something important. Something I need to remember.

I just can't figure out what.

Sweat drenches my back, making my shirt cling to my skin. I pump my legs, as steady as a piston, and gasp at the air, not as steady, not as sure. No one is chasing me, and yet I have to run as quickly as possible. Along the corridor, make a left, through the double swinging doors, bypass the elevators, open the emergency exit, down, down, down an endless set of stairs, until I dead-end in front of a door.

A metal door, locked up tighter than a tomb with its blinking-purple-light security system, its pale-green box of personal identity scans.

Green and purple.

I'm here, exactly where I'm supposed to be. I don't know where "here" is. I don't know how I knew to follow this particular path. I don't know why this door is so significant.

All I know is this is where I'm meant to be. I was born to fulfill this destiny.

When I wake, my mother is running a cool washcloth along my heated skin. It takes me a moment to figure out where I am—in my bed in the little cottage behind the Russells' home, in the Harmony compound. Not running in a purple and green hallway I've never seen.

I shiver, and immediately my mom brings her hand to my forehead. "Your fever finally broke after forty-eight hours. Are you cold?"

I shake my head and rise onto my elbows. "What happened to me?" I croak.

"A mouse infected you." She glides the cloth down my arms.

I sink back onto the pillows. My bones slosh around my limbs like water, and my head pulses with lights. Still, I could sit up if I really wanted to. But I'd rather have my mom keep taking care of me a little longer.

Ever since I came back from the wilderness, our relationship has been...strained. We were both to blame. She didn't want to leave her home and move into the Harmony compound. She said it was too dangerous for us to be affiliated with the Underground, but I don't buy that excuse for a second. I was already on the run with them. I'd say I was already associated. So I went on a hunger strike until she let me live at the compound with Mikey and Angela. I'm not proud of it, but what did she expect? I hadn't seen her for six years, and it was hard enough for me to move back to civilization. I didn't want to be ripped away from my community, too.

Our relationship never recovered, even though she comes by the cottage to see me every day. It's like she can't forgive me for choosing another family, and I can't forgive her for letting me go into the wilderness by myself.

Except when I'm sick. For some reason, my mom drops her guard then. She even lets herself be affectionate, and I can fool myself into believing that she loves me. The way Ryder's adopted mother, Angela, loves him.

"Mikey says you should go back to normal once the poison passes through your system." She smooths my hair and tucks it behind my ear. I keep my eyes closed. Pretend I'm drifting to sleep so she won't withdraw her soft hands. "Except, that is, for the enhanced powers."

My eyes fly open. "Powers? What powers?" And do they have anything to do with a green and purple hallway?

Aw, fike. I spoke too strongly, sounded too healthy. In front of my very eyes, she retreats into herself. Her spine gets straighter; her chin lifts higher. She drops the washcloth like it cooked too long in the Meal Assembler.

"Don't know." Even her voice is cooler. "Whatever powers the mouse had. We won't know until we speak to the administering scientist."

"Mikey's going to talk to Tanner?" I ask hopefully. It's not out of the question. When we came back to civilization, Mikey returned to his first love—science—and took up a post at TechRA. A scientist in name, but definitely not one of them.

"No, *you're* going to talk to Tanner." She crosses her arms across her chest. "You're the one who got yourself into this mess. You clean it up."

"But then he'll know I let his mice loose!"

"Should've thought of that before you broke into his lab." She tosses back her shoulder-length hair, ready for battle. "Besides, isn't Tanner your classmate? Strike up a conversation with him. Maybe he'll spill about the mice without you having to confess anything."

I make a face. Yeah, right. I'm as excited to seek out Tanner Callahan's company as I am to take her advice. At least that's what I've always thought. Unbidden, an image of his gentle hands wiggling loose the mouse's leg floats across my mind. Is it possible Tanner isn't the self-absorbed jerk I always assumed?

Before I can decide, the floors vibrate, and an image of my front stoop appears on the wall screens. My mom puts her hands on her hips, and my heart rate triples. We have a guest.

I can't see the caller's face. Her silver hair, a shade brighter than my mom's, is pulled back in a sleek chignon. She wears a navy uniform, its lines so sharp it looks like it came straight out of the air press, and a pair of transparent shoes, whose heels might double as icicle daggers.

Chairwoman Dresden. This isn't her first visit, and it won't be her last.

"Does she know about my infection? Did she find out…" I force the words out of my throat. "I broke into the TechRA labs?"

"I don't think so. She's probably just here to make you another proposition." Mom moves to the wardrobe and tosses me a jacket, the kind that will mold itself to my body upon wearing. "Here, put this on."

"I'm not changing for her."

"You can't wear your pajamas to receive the head of FuMA, Jessa."

"She's the head of a now-defunct agency," I correct her. "The chairwoman title is merely honorary. What's more, she's a future dictator responsible for genocide, our very own post-Boom Hitler. I'll wear whatever I want."

"Just do it." My mother clicks her tongue. Maybe she's as sick as I am of our constant arguing. Maybe she, too, wishes we could go back in time and fix yesterday's mistakes. But too many years have passed. Too many resentments have piled on too many hurts. Even if I wanted to start over with my mom, I wouldn't know how.

The floors vibrate again. My mom shoves my safety pads and hoverboard gear into the closet and then looks right into my eyes. "Just remember, Jessa. I don't need the stars and moon. The only thing I need is you."

Right. I don't even dignify her lies with a response. My family situation is pathetic, no question. I never knew my father, and my sister killed herself in front of my very eyes. My mother chose to stay in her home, wrapped in the comfort of Eden City, rather than venture into the woods and risk hardship to be with her daughter.

She *says* she's acting as an anchor for my father, who time-traveled into the future. She *says* if she leaves, he will forever be lost in time. But he's already been gone for twenty-three years, with scant hope of every returning. For all we know, he's dead, and the time-travel experiment was a miserable failure.

That's what all his cohorts believe—everyone except my mom. The experiment was never sanctioned by ComA in the first place. Instead, a group of Underground scientists did the research and built the time-travel machine themselves. When my dad disappeared, they all but abandoned the project. It was just too risky, and no one was keen to lose another loved one.

In contrast, I'm right here, right in front of her. And she still prioritizes her absentee husband over me. What else am I supposed to conclude other than that she doesn't love me?

And yet, you know what's even more pathetic than a woman who doesn't love her daughter? Underneath the eye rolls and the bratty behavior, I love her. The woman who deserted me.

And I would give anything if her lies could be truth.

4

My mother leaves the room to answer the door. I stick my arms into the jacket, and the heated rubber molds around my forearms and biceps. What's it going to be this time? My very own self-driving car. More credits than I could spend in a lifetime. Admittance into the top uni programs for... what, exactly? Do they have university degrees for rappelling or, I don't know, parkour?

I sigh, remembering Logan's words about applying myself. For a moment, I wish I were part of Callie's generation. They, at least, weren't plagued by the unknown. They didn't have to choose an area of study—because their future memories chose one for them.

Just as quickly, the envy disappears. Future memory was great when it worked. But when it didn't...well, that's exactly why I'm in this predicament today. With Chairwoman Dresden making me offers I can't turn down—and me turning them down.

I zip up the jacket over my pajama top just as Dresden strides into the room, her icicle heels clinking against the tile.

My mother isn't with her. Figures. She's been conveniently absent during all my conversations with the chairwoman.

She doesn't blink at my attire. "Jessa, so good to see you," she coos, as if we're great friends and this is a social visit.

"The answer is no."

"You haven't heard the question."

"Doesn't matter." My voice is steady, even though my knees, my fingers, my shoulders shake. "The answer is still no."

"You might want to hear me out, Jessa." Her tone turns as clipped as her shoes. "I'm giving you the opportunity to do something selfless for a change." She walks overs to my desk and plucks up one of my black chips. No doubt it contains vids of a hoverboarder performing tricks. Dropping the chip, she turns and crashes right into the transport tube that delivers packages to the cottage. I snicker. The tube's made of clear plastic and is as wide as I am. There's no way she should've missed it, but I guess even the chairwoman makes mistakes.

She straightens slowly. "It seems a position has opened up for a medical assistant, and we think your mother would be perfect for the job."

"Oh, really?" I could mention the crash—in fact I'm dying to—but I don't. "Even though she hasn't worked in that position in two decades?"

"Through no fault of her own. There was no one better at her job than your mom. But then these young upstarts showed up with data chips revealing successful futures as medical assistants. Your mother couldn't compete, no matter how competent she was. She had no data chip, and back then, no future memory meant no job."

"You don't have to tell me about my mother's life," I say.

"I'm reminding you." She walks forward, her eyes more intense, her figure more menacing with each step. "Reminding you why your mom is stuck working as a bot supervisor, a job that gives her migraines from being around machinery all day, a job that chews up her soul and spits it back out. This is a unique time in our society, one you should take advantage of. Half of our employees no longer have their future memories, which means the hiring process is pure chaos as people are scrambling to figure out what to do, how to hire. All of a sudden, there's an opportunity for someone like your mom, a good worker with a solid basis of knowledge. Don't you want your mother to have the career she trained for? A career she would love?"

"Of course I do." I close my eyes so I don't have to look at Dresden anymore. Mistake. Because what I see, instead, is the way my mother sinks into a chair, massaging her temples, when I drop by her house. I see her turn off all the lights and lie flat on the tile floor when she doesn't know I'm there.

Whatever her faults, my mother works hard. She may not love me, but she's made a point to see me every day for the last four years. That's something, right?

If I turn down Dresden now, how am I any different from my mom, when she chose her personal desires over me?

"One word from us, and that medical assistant job is as good as your mom's," she continues. "In fact, I'll do you one better than that. I'll make her a memory." Her eyes glitter, as deep and black as jewels. "In the past, there was no way to manufacture future memories because it was impossible to make one that seamless, that real. A fake could be spotted in an instant. But now that the memories are deteriorating, it's made room for a black market. It won't be perfect, but your mom can just claim that her future memory is fading, and her employers would be none the wiser. A fading memory may not be as valuable as a pristine one, but it's still better than nothing."

I open my eyes and see the crisp navy suit, those

transparent icicle heels. That uniform used to taunt me as it wove among the white lab coats. Of course Dresden is talking about fake memories and unethical conduct. I've known for ten years that's what she's about.

They...they tortured me back then. Strapped me to a chair, made me live memories that weren't mine. Nightmare after nightmare of all the phobias known to man. Falling from a cliff, drowning in the ocean, being buried alive in a coffin. Over and over, until they found the one phobia specific to me. The one horror that made me scream louder than the rest.

They played that memory, again and again, until I curled into a fetal position and whimpered. Until, at six years old, I wished my life were over.

It was ten years ago, and my time with the scientists lasted only a few days. But I still live that memory they gave me, the one they played over and over again. The one of me betraying my family, of the shock and hatred on their faces. Of the bloody knife in my hands and the bodies at my feet.

The memory isn't mine. They took it from a hardened criminal tripped out on fumes. I could see his long, ropey limbs; the hands holding the knife were calloused and masculine. And yet, several nights a week, I still jerk awake, drenched with sweat, and know how it feels to be a traitor.

That's why I won't work with the scientists. They can dangle whatever they want in front of me. I won't cave. It's the principle of the matter.

"No," I whisper. "I don't work with scientists who torture children by giving them fake memories. Not now, not ever."

"Only a few of them were involved in that project," she says smoothly. "The vast majority of TechRA didn't even know about it. I can assure you, we no longer undergo such...experiments. The only fake memories we deal in these days are the innocuous ones. Would you really hold the shortsightedness of a few against an entire agency?"

"Yes," I say evenly. I am quite certain who authorized such "experiments," as she calls them. "I believe I will."

"Oh, really? Maybe this will change your mind." With a smirk, Dresden lifts her hand and presses a few buttons on her wristband. And then a holo-vid starts playing in the air.

I don't want to look. I'm loath to do anything the chairwoman asks me to do. But like a spectator to a hovercrash, my eyes are drawn to the vid.

A prison cell is stuffed with teenage girls in dirty school uniforms. At one end, a brunette roars and leaps onto a redhead's back, grabbing her hair and yanking until it detaches in clumps. Another girl in the corner sings at the top of her lungs. Her head lolls around in a pile of feces, streaking her once-blond hair with brown.

I swallow hard. It's not like the memories the scientists made me live. Instead of experiencing the memory across five senses, I'm merely watching the scene — and yet, it's so vivid, so intense that I almost feel like I'm there.

Two people appear at the end of the hallway. They converse briefly, and then the tall one walks toward us. She wears a navy uniform and has silver hair cut closely to a well-shaped head. The face is more lined, but the features are unmistakable. Chairwoman Dresden.

She strides briskly to the cell and stops in front of one of the prisoners. "Mom," a young female voice says. "You have to call off the execution."

"I told you, Olivia," Dresden says. "You knew the price of receiving a mediocre memory, but you wouldn't listen, would you?"

"My future self sent me a happy memory," the girl says. "In it, I held my newborn baby and felt at peace with the world."

"It was mediocre! You of all people should've known what

was coming." A muscle ticks at the corner of Dresden's mouth. "It was your vision of the future that showed us what we could become. A race of superhumans."

My mouth goes dry. Dear Fates. This isn't a memory but a vision of the future. The vision, in fact, that the six-year-old Olivia showed Callie. The one that made her stab a needle into her heart. Logan's recounted it enough times for me to recognize it. Why is Dresden showing it to me now?

Dresden wraps her hands over the girl's on the bars. "I know you've got talent, Olivia. You're my daughter, aren't you? Why didn't your future self send a better memory? You could've chosen any memory. One that showed off your superlative skills as a violinist. One that illustrated your mathematical genius. Why did you send this one?"

"I don't know why she did it, Mom," Olivia says. "Maybe my future self thought it wasn't right to execute ninety-nine percent of the population on the basis of their memories. Maybe she knew this was the only way to get you to listen. To show you there's more to humanity than pure talent. There's also happiness. And love."

Dresden drops her hands from the bars. "Not in this world, I'm afraid. We can't allow any mediocre genes to contaminate the breeding pool. The execution has been set. You and the other Mediocres will serve your sentence in two hours."

She turns and strides away, her heels clicking against the floor, toward the person with whom she entered the hallway.

"Mom!" Olivia calls. "You can't do this. I'm your daughter. Your daughter!"

"No. No daughter of mine is mediocre."

The vision should end here. That's where Logan always concluded his telling. But it doesn't. I tilt my head, squinting at the vid. The worms wriggling around my stomach begin to crawl up my throat. Something's about to happen. Something...

bad. Dresden is showing me this vision for a reason, and it's not just to satisfy my morbid curiosity.

Dresden flings out her palm and knocks to the floor the handheld device her assistant is carrying. The device smashes into a million pieces, and the assistant gets to her knees to retrieve them.

MK Rivers, I'm guessing. The chairwoman's assistant back then and, ten years later, her assistant now.

She stretches to retrieve another piece, and her shirt gets untucked from her pants. It lifts up and reveals the splatter-paint birthmark at her waist. One that consists of a splotch that radiates in five directions. Just like the fingers of a blobby hand.

I can't breathe. The air gets stuck somewhere between my lungs and my windpipe, and no amount of pounding will dislodge it. No. *No.* That can't be my birthmark on that girl's waist. I would never be on Dresden's side, let alone be her assistant. Never.

And yet, there's no erasing the image. That birthmark like a splatter of paint. The splotch that radiates into five fingers. That's my birthmark. Mine. With me since my birth and catalogued into ComA's records of identifying characteristics.

"You might as well stop fighting the inevitable." Dresden crosses her arms, smirking. "Now we both know you'll be working for me someday, after MK gets promoted."

I'm trembling, my knees, my arms, probably even my hair. But I shake my head forcefully. "No. You're wrong. This is just one possible vision of the future. It doesn't have to come true. Callie proved that."

Dresden's eyes flash. "You can tell yourself that. But we both know this vision is more than just a prediction. It originates from your very genes, Jessa. Why do you think, as a child, you reacted so strongly to the memory of betraying your family? Somewhere, in your chemical makeup, you already know this is going to happen. This is who you are. Accept it. Perhaps your sister was able to fight Fate. But you will never be able to fight your very nature."

A weariness descends on me, one that goes beyond my bones to the molecules themselves. Maybe it's from the infection. More likely, it's from this guilt I've been lugging around like the hydration packs sewn into my hoverjerseys.

She's right. This is who I am.

My sister ended her life to save mine. But never once did she stop to consider whether my life was worth saving over hers.

Callie was the strong one, the noble one. She's the one everybody loved. Logan's heart ripped in two when she injected herself, and my mom walks around like she has some essential organ missing.

All I have to do is look into their eyes to see how they really feel: The wrong sister died. The one who lived is nothing but a girl who can't get along with her mother. Nothing but a slacker whose only goal is to find another cliff to fling herself off.

If I could go back to the past and undo my sister's decision, I would. But I can't. So all I can do now is thwart my sister's enemy. As long as I live, I will never betray my family.

Even if I'm as unworthy as the chairwoman says.

Squaring my shoulders, I stare down Dresden. "The answer is no. No matter how many visions you show me, I will never, ever be on your side."

5

Magnificent in its swirls of color, the ramp is part of a system of banks, half-pipes, and undulating waves that make up Eden City's best hoverpark—and Tanner Callahan's favorite hangout.

My heart pounds like I'm on the last leg of a marathon, and I'm burning up under all this padding. I swallow, tuck the stray hair under my helmet, and swallow again.

Not only do I have to go down that ramp, but I have to do a heel-flip trick as my entrance. Without falling on my head. In front of a growing audience of hoverboarders.

Maybe this is my punishment for defying my future. Maybe, after conquering skydiving and cliff jumps, I'll fall and break my neck on an incline that rises a mere twenty feet off the ground.

A guy with stringy brown hair nudges his friend, and they both look at me, broad smiles on their faces. Of course they're happy. The crowd loves to watch boarders land cool new tricks. They like it even better when we crash against the concrete.

But this is all part of the plan. After Dresden left, I

decided my mom was right. As much as I hate the scientists, I need to talk to Tanner. I have to find out what infected me.

I catch a glimpse of Tanner now next to a girl in a white tank top. His lips rest against each other in a straight line, and he stares at me, his eyes dark and unfathomable. He's got a hoverboard balanced against his hip. Like everyone else, he's waiting for the show.

I swallow hard. Despite myself, little pinpricks of awareness sprout all over my body. It's like my every nerve has come alive because of his presence—which is just ridiculous. I can't stand the guy. I only want to pump him for information.

Exhaling slowly, I square my shoulders. I've already been standing here too long. Much longer than my allotted twenty seconds. I either need to put down my board or move aside.

That's part of the plan, too—I need time for the crowd to gather. Time for Tanner to become interested in watching me.

I take one more breath and hop on my hoverboard, balancing on the balls of my left foot at the back end, the toes of my right foot just peeping over the front edge.

"Make sure you get enough air," the girl in the white tank top shouts.

"Timing is everything," the guy with the stringy hair says.

"I've already got the medics on the line." His friend smirks.

And Tanner? He watches me with the same attention he gave the mouse's severed leg and says nothing at all.

Go time. I slide my front foot forward, catching the edge with my heel and flipping the board. For an infinitesimal moment, I hang in the air. *Don't worry about the ramp. Just think about landing on the board.*

That's all I have to hit. That's all I have to hit. That's all I have to—

My feet catch the board in midair, and then the magnets below the concrete latch on. I bend my knees, and all of a sudden, I'm racing down the ramp. The wind rushes over my ears, and my eyes water with the speed.

I laugh, wild and reckless and free. I did it! I landed the trick, and now I'm flying. This is what I love best about extreme sports. The adrenaline pumps through my body; my senses jumble together; and for a single, untouchable moment, I feel like I can do anything at all.

Even the impossible.

I charge up the opposite ramp and jump off the hoverboard. Ryder gives me a high five, thinks better of it, and then sweeps me up in a hug. "You killed it! On your first try, too."

He sets me down, but the hoverpark keeps moving, a kaleidoscope of colors and movement and people. "I had a good teacher."

"Damn straight," he says, grinning. "Too bad Rat Boy's not impressed. He's leaving."

I whip my head around. Sure enough, Tanner's setting his hoverboard on the edge of the coping.

"He can't leave yet," I blurt. "He's supposed to congratulate me on a job well done."

That was the whole point of the trick. I had to impress him, to give him a reason to approach. Because if *he* takes the initiative, then he won't suspect me of pumping him for information. I have to stop him. But how?

Before I can come up with any bright ideas, Tanner puts his foot down and charges away, locking onto one of the racing circuits that circles the hoverpark. Great.

"Father of Time," I moan. "Only, like, five people in this park could've landed that trick. What do I have to do to get him to notice me?"

Ugh. I gag just saying the words. It kills me that I'm even trying to get his attention. In any other situation, I'd rather pull out my nails, one by one, than talk to him. Prop open my eyelids with toothpicks and read the history of the pre-Boom era, over and over again.

And now, I'm stooping to tricks in hopes of getting a single word of congratulations? I think I'm going to throw up.

"Dude, Rat Boy doesn't care about tricks. He's the best wind sprinter we've got, but he won't touch the vert walls." Ryder adjusts the magnifying goggles on his head, the ones he wears everywhere in case he needs to examine the cellular structure of something. "Don't worry. He'll be back. He's probably just nervous, and who can blame him? I'd be scared of me, too."

I smirk, but he has a point. In spite of his techno-geekiness, Ryder looks like he could kill large animals with his bare hands.

Underneath the tough exterior, though, he's not so scary. Once upon a time, when we were kids, I caught him lining a homemade coffin with acorns so that a squirrel would have something to eat in its afterlife. That was the moment I decided I wanted him as my best friend.

Good thing, too. A few seconds later, Tanner comes barreling back down the circuit, just as my best friend predicted. Ryder gives me a little shove. "Quick, do another one of your tricks."

My mind whirls. "Which one?"

"Does it matter? Just go!"

Moving fast, I set my board on the coping. But when I push off, my balance is wrong. The board doesn't feel glued to my feet. Instead, it slides right out from under me.

Keep loose! I hear Ryder's voice in my head. *Roll.*

Ooommmpppphhhh.

I hit the concrete with my shoulder, keeping my elbows tucked in. I roll with the fall, spreading out the impact. I do everything right, but curse the Fates, it hurts. *A lot.*

"You okay?" a voice says from above me.

I squint against the sun, and my eyes travel up over a pair of baggy cargo pants. I hit the low-slung waist, and my breath—what little there is left of it—catches. Because the light gray thermal shirt hugs his abdomen, and I can see every line, every ridge of his six-pack. My gaze continues up, and I see a broad, well-defined chest and long, ropey muscles. I swallow hard. Whoever my rescuer is, he's hot. Really hot.

Almost in a hurry now, I drag my eyes farther up. Surely his face will be as pretty as the rest of him. Surely he'll have the kind of eyes that will pierce right through me. Surely—

I see a lean, chiseled jaw and soft, kissable lips. Tousled black hair brushing up against dark eyes framed with thick lashes. But the eyes don't pierce right through me. Instead, they're...laughing...at me.

Oh, good Fates. Was I actually checking out Tanner Callahan? What in Limbo is the matter with me?

He holds out a hand to help me up. "You know, the six-inch curbs are over by the entrance. Maybe you should master those before you attempt a real drop-in."

My cheeks flame. "I'm not a beginner. I've been dropping in practically since I could walk."

"Oh, really?" His eyebrows rise, so that they disappear under his fringe of hair. "Could've fooled me."

I stare at him. This is not going the way I expected. Not at all. "Did you *not* see me land the heel-flip trick? That's the sickest stunt of the day."

"Guess I must've missed it." He smirks. Did I think those lips were kissable? More like smackable. Of course he saw me land the trick. He was standing *right there.*

Ignoring his hand, I push myself to my feet, even though my elbow stings and my knee burns. What a condescending ass. He's just trying to get a rise out of me. No wonder everyone says he thinks he's Fate's gift to the world. He's just like every scientist I've ever met.

I glance up the ramp, and Ryder gives me a salute, his shoulders shaking with laughter. He's watched me fall on my ass dozens of times. Maybe even hundreds. Now that he sees me on my feet, he's not the slightest bit concerned.

When I turn back around, however, the smirk has dropped off Tanner's face. He narrows his eyes, taking in each of my movements, and his hands hover in the air, as if he wants to pick me up and spray my wounds with antiseptic. "Are you okay?" he asks, his voice gentler now. "You had quite a fall there."

"I'm fine," I say brusquely. I twist my arm gingerly to check out the ramp burn. I hiss in a breath as a cool breeze hits the scrape. *Ow*, it stings. I look like I got tangled up with a vegetable peeler. But I've had worse.

"Oh, good," I mutter. "It matches the scars on my other arm."

"I have them, too." He pushes up his sleeves to show me the blemishes on his forearm, and his bare skin brushes ever so slightly against mine.

I go perfectly still. Maybe Tanner's not so bad after all. Maybe we just got off on the wrong hoverboard...

"Go sit down," he orders in a tone that suggests he's the game master and I'm one of his carved pawns. "Over there on the bleachers, where it's quieter."

My mouth drops open. Maybe not. "You don't get to tell me what to do."

"I do when you're acting like an idiot. You had a bad fall. You need to sit down."

"*You're* the one acting like an idiot. Tell me, does that actually work for you? Bossing people around like you're a ComA official?"

He smiles, slow and wolfish. "It's been working so far." His tone is so silky it reaches out and caresses me. "Maybe the fall is an excuse. Maybe I just want to spend more time with you." He looks at me, his gaze long and liquid, and my stomach executes a slow ollie. I will my body to behave. He might be attractive if you were looking at a frozen still of him. But once he opens his mouth, all those good looks slide down the ramp. All the turtle-shell abs in the world can't make up for his typical scientist arrogance.

He takes my uninjured elbow, his grip firm and strong, and I let him lead me to one of the long rows of metal bleachers. I'm not stupid. I don't buy his act for a nanosecond, but this is Plan B. I need to ask him about the mice.

We sit, and I find my voice. "Why would you want to spend more time with me? We don't even know each other."

He looks out at the hoverpark, at the boarders zipping past, a blur of speed and color. He stares so long I think he might be timing wind sprints, but then he turns to me. For the first time in this conversation, his expression is uncertain. "I know this is going to sound strange. But do you get the feeling we know each other? From before, I mean."

"Like from when we were kids?"

"I was thinking more like a past life." He leans forward, his tone urgent. "I can't shake the feeling we're meant to be in each other's lives."

I burst out laughing, partly because he's so hokey and partly because I'm relieved. I wasn't sure what to do with this earnest side of him. "That's the worst line I've ever heard. Maybe someone might've fallen for it, back in the pre-Boom era. But these days? You're better off telling me you saw your future, and I was in it."

An expression I can't read crosses his face. "I'm not hitting on you, Jessa. Trust me, you'd know it if I were." He leans his elbows against the bleachers. "You're not exactly my type."

"Oh, really?" I bristle. I shouldn't. This guy means less than nothing to me, and I don't need anybody to make me feel okay about my looks. Why should I care if he's not attracted to me? And yet, in some tiny, bruised corner of my mind, I do. Pathetic, but there it is. "Well, that makes two of us, then, because you're the *opposite* of my type."

"How so?"

"First of all, you're a scientist. I don't date scientists. I don't even like them."

"One of your arbitrary rules?" His tone is mocking.

I give him a steely look. "More like a life lesson I had to learn the hard way."

"I feel sorry for you." He lifts his hand and grazes his fingers against my cheek. "You have no idea what you're missing."

I slap away his hand and then have to sit on my own so I don't do something worse. Fates, this guy is something else. His ego is so large I'm surprised the hoverpark's magnets can hold him up.

But I have to play nice. I take a deep breath. As much as I can't stand the guy, he still has information I need. So I push down my irritation and paste a bright smile on my face. "Doesn't mean I don't enjoy hearing about your experiments. So tell me, Tanner. What kind of projects are you doing at TechRA?"

"I'm not." He tilts his head, as though considering me in a new light. "Three days ago, someone broke into my lab and set my mice free. Would you know anything about that?"

6

My heart grows wheels and about rolls out of my chest. *Clack-clack-clack*. He can't possibly know it was me. Right?

"Why would I know anything about that?" I ask faintly.

He shrugs. "No reason. It feels like a prank, and I thought you might've overheard one of our classmates talking, that's all."

I relax. "Oh. I haven't heard anything." Which is technically true. "If I do, you'll be the first to know." Which is blatantly not true.

"I also found a mouse's leg stuck in the cage," he says. "One of them must've severed its leg escaping. Seeing that… it messed me up a little."

I blink. Why is he talking about this? Admitting any kind of vulnerability? It doesn't fit with my image of him. "Why do you care?" I struggle to keep my breathing even. "TechRA will just get you new mice."

"That's not in question. TechRA would do anything for me. I'm their one bright hope for the future. *Everyone's* hope for the future, really." His tone is even, matter-of-fact. No surprise there. But for the first time, I catch a hint of sarcasm in his voice, too.

"But aside from the fact that I'm not a total monster, I care because even TechRA can't breed my mice any faster. It'll take me a year to recreate five generations of mice with the proper genetic enhancement. Which means I won't be able to go to uni next year. No program in the country would accept me without a completed core thesis these days. Another fallout from a world with no future memory. No one's willing to take a risk on anything."

Wait…what?

In spite of the late-afternoon sun, in spite of my fingerless gloves, my hands turn ice-bucket cold. I didn't know. I thought I was freeing the mice. I thought I was getting back at the scientists. I didn't know I was jeopardizing Tanner's future.

What does it matter? a voice inside me grates. *He's one of them. He's your enemy.*

But it does matter. Tanner might grow up to be the cruelest scientist who ever lived—but right now, he's just a guy with goals and aspirations. And I'm not in the habit of destroying other people's dreams.

"I'm sorry," I say, even though I know the words are inadequate.

He shrugs. "Their loss. The world will just have to wait another year to be graced with my brilliance."

I take a shaky breath. His arrogance gives me an easy out. No need to feel guilty when he *deserves* to be cut down a few billion molecules. The world will thank me for it. But there's something else here, too. Something below his breezy words.

Not your concern, Jessa. Get on with it.

I clear my throat. "What exactly are you breeding the mice to do?"

"To run the maze."

I wrinkle my forehead. "Haven't they been running mazes for centuries?"

He looks at me like I'm a small child inquiring into grown-up matters. "Do you think you'll be able to understand the explanation?"

"Oh, I don't know," I say drily. "If you use itty-bitty words no bigger than two syllables, I just might."

His lips quirk. "I did give a presentation to a group of five-year-olds the other day."

"You're a big jerk, you know that?"

"I've been called 'big' by lots of other girls." He lowers his voice silkily. "But I don't think they were talking about my personality."

"Um, that's gross."

He shrugs. "It's the truth."

"Truth is relative. You should know. You're in the business of manipulating other people's truths." The words slip out. I don't know if he knows that a select few scientists used to torture kids by making them live through horrific memories. All I know is that it was a condition of the treaty that I never go public with it.

He gives me a sharp look. "Do you want to hear the explanation or not?"

"I'm nearly breathless with anticipation."

He shakes his head, but he's also smiling. Just a little bit. Which—Fates help me—makes *me* smile.

"I've always been fascinated by animal migration," he says. "The monarch butterflies, for example, migrate twenty-five hundred miles to the same mountains, year after year, generation after generation. Even though each individual butterfly has never traveled there before. Scientists have offered a bunch of explanations—instincts, the magnetic pull of the Earth, the sun used as a compass. But what if it's more than that?" He takes a breath, as if gearing up for his next sentences. "What if the butterflies are communicating with each other—across time? What if one generation is able to send a message to the next generation, telling them where to go?"

The smile falls off my face, skitters down the ramp, and disappears into the hoverpark. Because this research he's doing? It sounds an awful lot like future memory.

"I injected my mice with a genetic modification that enhances their natural Sender-Receiver abilities," he continues. "And then I run them through a maze, which they figure out through trial and error. Pretty soon, they're memorizing the order of doors by their shapes and colors."

Sweat gathers at my hairline. The corridor with the green stripes and purple sofas flashes across my mind. The feeling of running, of being compelled to go down a certain path. Of being born to do it.

"Green, purple. Purple, green," I murmur.

"What was that?" he asks.

"Nothing." I lift the damp hair off my neck and twist it into a ponytail. "Please go on."

"As I bred the mice, the Sender-Receiver abilities got stronger. Or at least, each generation of mice figured out the maze a little quicker than the one before it." His words come faster now, as if they're racing the maze alongside his mice. "Guess how many times it took the fifth-generation mice to figure out the maze?"

"How many?"

"One. Each mouse ran the maze correctly on the very first try."

I rock back on the bleachers. I was the Sender in my relationship with Callie, but I also have a small amount of Receiver abilities. We all do. When the mouse bit me, could my natural abilities have been enhanced? Could my dream of running down a corridor be some kind of message someone's trying to send me?

Despite the sweat, a chill runs up my spine. All of a sudden, I'm sure someone's trying to communicate with me. Just like the mice.

But who? And why?

I can't dwell on these questions for long, however. Because Tanner isn't finished. "I have to believe the Sender parent mice are sending messages to their Receiver children. I have to believe this discovery is the first step toward the discovery of future memory." He looks at me, his eyes bright with knowledge. "Your sister delayed the invention of future memory, Jessa. But she didn't stop it."

"You don't know that," I say quickly.

"Of course I do. Think about it. Future memory hasn't disappeared from our world altogether, so we know that sometime, at some point, it will be invented once again. Besides, nobody can halt scientific innovation. One way or another, science will find a way. All the scientists in my wing are running similar experiments, with different formulas and different mice. Sooner or later, one of us will discover the link to future memory." He straightens his spine and looks directly into my eyes. "And I will do everything in my power to make sure that it's me."

7

The next morning, I'm in the eating area of the Russells' home, where I eat breakfast every morning. It looks like a baked goods café exploded in here.

Every available surface is covered with cookies. Chocolate chip, almond lace, pinwheel, peanut butter. Sugar cookies and snickerdoodles, macaroons and pecan cookie balls. Angela pops the next tray into the Meal Assembler as soon as the previous one comes out.

I snatch up a still-warm cookie and put it into my mouth. The sweet and bitter chocolate tingles my taste buds, and the gooey center explodes over my tongue. Molten magma cookie. Yum.

This is what I need right now. Something to warm me from the inside out. Something to help me forget that somewhere out there, someone is sending me a message to compel me down a path I've never seen, toward a destination I'm not sure I want to find.

Even now, sweat slicks over my skin, and my legs ache with the need to run. My nerves vibrate, faster and faster with each passing hour, getting more and more antsy, because I'm not moving, not acting, not galloping down a purple and green hallway.

My body begs me to listen to this compulsion, but I can't. I don't even know where this hallway is.

The Meal Assembler dings. Angela takes out a tray of madeleines and swaps it with a package of coconut snow. Her hair, arranged in a thousand braids, is pulled off her face in a low ponytail, and everything about her is smooth. From her creamy brown skin, to the gentle but capable hands, to the long, stretchy fabric wrapped over her shoulders and midsection, with the tiny face of a six-month-old peeping over the edge.

"You think Remi's old enough to eat a cookie?" I pick up a bunny-shaped treat and wave it in front of the baby's face. "Why'd you make so many, anyway?"

"It's called nesting." Angela looks at the piles of cookies and laughs wetly, like a saturated sponge about to overflow. "Although I suppose I've already had the baby."

I put down the cookie and whisper a finger over Remi's face, marveling at the lashes that lay like thistles against her cheek. She turns toward my finger and tries to bite it. "And she's wonderful."

"I know it. I've never been so happy in my life." She bursts into tears.

I pull my hand from Remi's face. "Angela, what's wrong?"

The air leaves her mouth in quick, breathe-in-a-paper-bag puffs. "What am I doing? I don't know how to take care of a baby. I have no idea how to keep her safe when she's learning to crawl." She presses the plastic wrap from the tray of cookies against her forehead. "I don't know how to keep her alive."

With each word, her body gets a little stiffer. The paralysis spreads a little more. Who can blame her? The fear stems not from normal new-mother anxiety but from her future memory, the one that foretold that her baby girl would crawl off a cliff and fall to her death.

It's taken the better part of a decade for Mikey to convince her the memory doesn't have to come true.

I wrench her hand from her forehead, plaster wrap and all. "You can change your future. Remember yesterday. If my sister did it, so can you."

And so can I. I don't have to fall in line with whatever future is shown to me. I don't have to become Dresden's assistant.

"Callie's the only reason this baby exists." Angela looks down at Remi, beyond smitten. Ready to sacrifice the world for a six-month-old. "Her courage showed me, showed so many of us, that we don't have to live in constant fear of tomorrow."

"You'll be fine. More than fine. You're a wonderful mother, Angela. This baby is lucky to be born to you."

I should know. For the six years I was on the run with Harmony, she was the only person who tucked me into my pine-needle bed and kissed me good night. Since she and Mikey adopted Ryder, and Ryder and I were inseparable, she was like my mother, too. And now that I'm living in the little cottage behind their home, sometimes I can even pretend she is.

She ruffles my hair. "I'm the lucky one. You and Ryder came to me fully formed. Six years old, the two of you, with so much goodness shining from your eyes I was slayed. I was fortunate enough to guide you a bit and love you a lot. That's all."

I drop my head, resting it briefly next to Remi's. She squirms, trying to twist free of the wrap, and holds her arms out to me.

I grin. Other than Ryder and her parents, the only person Remi will let hold her—the only person *Angela* will let hold her—is me. It's like a double seal of approval.

"Can I play with her?" I ask Angela.

"Well..." Even now, after I've held the baby dozens of times, Angela hesitates. "You have to make sure you don't put her on the ground. Or let her play with any small trinkets or beads. Or put a blanket too near her mouth. Or jostle her too violently. Or—"

"I've read the baby care manual along with you," I say gently. "Twice. You know how careful I am with her."

She smiles. "Yes. I do know that."

She unwraps Remi from the fabric and hands her to me. I hold her straight above me, her dimpled thighs dangling in front of my face. She squeals and coos, clapping her hands as if to say, *More! More!*

If it were any other baby, I might toss her in the air. I've seen Laurel do that with her son, Eli, and I remember his laugh of pure delight. But this is Remi. Maybe Angela's too protective of her, but I can hardly blame her.

I take the baby on a tour of the eating area, pointing out the various Meal Assemblers and the pantry of plastic-wrapped trays, and then give her back to her mother. Angela carefully places her back in the length of fabric. For a moment, I wish I were a baby again, so I could be as safe and warm as Remi.

"I don't know how I would've made it through those years without you and Logan," I mumble.

"You would've managed. You're a survivor." Calmer now, Angela tugs a plastic block out of the wall and begins to transfer the madeleines into it. "So is Logan, although sometimes I think you've adjusted better than he has."

I hesitate, not sure I should betray Logan's confidence.

But if there's anybody in the world who worries about Logan as much as I do, it's Angela.

"He still hopes she's alive, Ange. He thinks…he thinks his memory is going to come true, the one where Callie cheers him on at a swim meet. Last week, he cut his hand in the same way it was in the memory."

"Was it an accident?" She puts down the spatula, her voice as sharp as the metal corners. "Or did he cut himself on purpose? Is he so desperate to make the memory come true, he would do anything to help it along? Even hurt himself?"

"I…I don't know. I didn't ask."

She snaps the lid in place and fits the block back into the wall. A hose sucks out the excess oxygen, and the madeleines join an array of other airtight blocks, designed to maximize freshness. "I'll talk to him. It's not healthy for him to dwell so much on the past. We have to focus on today. And prepare ourselves for what tomorrow will bring."

The words are strong and sure, but her voice wavers. Like the ripples that expand from a single stone, the trembling gets bigger and bigger until her voice cracks. And I know she's no longer thinking about Logan.

I touch the soft black down on Remi's head. "Keep her away from those cliffs, okay?"

"Are you kidding?" Angela smiles, quick and ferocious. "She'll be lucky if she leaves the house these next eighteen years."

The door opens, and Ryder swaggers into the room. He does a double take at the cookies. Recovering quickly, he sweeps up half a dozen with one hand. "Who aren't you letting out of the house? Is that why you made so many cookies? Because we're stuck inside?"

Angela swats him on the shoulder, the way she used to when he was a little kid. Except now, he towers over her by half a foot, and he has to lean down to kiss her on the cheek.

"It's called nesting," she says.

"You should nest more often." He places a soft kiss on Remi's head, leaving cookie crumbs in her hair. "Except next time, maybe you could nest with red meat? Lamb chops, rib eyes, beef tartare. That would be epic."

"I don't think birds eat red meat," I say.

He raises an eyebrow. "Oh, because they eat cookies all the time?"

Angela giggles, and whatever else, I'm glad to see her happy again, if only for the moment.

"Get out of here, both of you," she says. "I need to figure out what to do with these cookies."

Ryder grabs another handful, and we leave the eating area.

I take a deep breath. "I have a mission for us."

He groans. "Another one? Jessa, your bite hasn't even healed, and if we break into another lab, Mikey will ground me for—"

"Not that kind of mission. No more labs. I just need to figure out where a certain purple and green hallway is. Are you game?"

He finishes the snickerdoodle and looks longingly up the stairs, as if wondering if he should've gotten out of bed this morning. Then, he turns back to me and sighs.

"For you, Jessa? I'm always game."

8

Ryder sends me upstairs to grab his magnifying goggles—can't leave home without them, even if we're just going to the storage shed—and I skip down the hall toward his room. On the way, I pass Remi's nursery, catching a glimpse of muscles and bare, glistening skin. I halt. Wait a minute, that can't possibly be... I double back slowly, certain I'm imagining things. But nope, there he is. Tanner Callahan in the flesh. Literally.

He's wrestling with a large plank of wood and foam padding. And he's shirtless. Before I can stop myself, my eyes rake over his torso, exploring every ridge and dip that my mouth watered over the day before, when I didn't know it was him. Now, I do know it's him—and it doesn't make a damn difference. My mouth's still watering.

I swallow hard. *Pull yourself together, Jessa. This is Tanner Callahan. You don't like him, remember?* My brain remembers that, all right. Too bad my hormones didn't get the memo.

"What in Limbo are you doing here?" I ask, more sharply than I intend.

He looks up, mopping his brow with a soft gray fabric. Dear Fates, is that his shirt? And if so, will he put it back on? I can't decide what I want the answer to be.

"Making a playpen for Remi," he says. If he's surprised to see me, he doesn't show it. "She'll be crawling in a few months, and she'll need a safe place to explore her world."

Wait—what? I shake my head, trying to compute the information. "How do you even know Remi?"

"Mikey's my boss at TechRA. One of them, anyway. When I heard that Angela was having a hard time putting her daughter on the ground, I offered to make Remi her very own maze. I design all the mazes for the mice, you know."

Oh. I look at the octagon-shaped frame he's already built. It spans more than half the room and yet fits perfectly in the space. The padding is covered with a sturdy tangerine material—Angela's favorite color. I can't help it. My heart softens. Remi will love playing in here, and maybe Angela will be eased into not having the baby constantly attached to her.

I open my mouth to thank him. But what comes out instead is: "You're not supposed to be inside the compound. There's an unwritten rule that scientists aren't allowed."

He picks his way around the raw materials to stop in front of me. His bare torso is now inches away, and it takes all my strength not to back up. Not to lower my eyes from his face.

"Mikey's a scientist," he says.

"That's different. He's one of us. We may have reached a truce with ComA, but that doesn't mean we have to be friendly with the likes of you."

He swipes his sweaty hair off his forehead. "So if this isn't a friendly visit, then where are my milk and cookies?"

"Come again?"

"I've been working for hours. The least you can do is fetch me some refreshments."

My jaw clenches. There's no longer any danger of me lowering my eyes anywhere because all I can see is red. "I don't *fetch* anything for anyone."

"No?" He inclines his chin toward the hallway. "Aren't you heading toward Ryder's room right now? To fetch him something, I presume?"

"It's called a favor," I say between gritted teeth. "For a friend. Not that you would know anything about that."

"Maybe I would." His gaze runs over my eyes, my cheeks, my lips. "If you'll let me be your friend."

Could I? For a moment, I look back on the half-constructed playpen. He can't be that bad, can he, if he's building a maze for Remi? If he feels sorry for an amputated mouse?

But then I remember it was his fault that the mice were locked up in the first place. I remember his vow that he'll be the person to invent future memory. He's as egotistical as the rest of the scientists—and that's their ultimate downfall. That's the quality that allows them to be okay with torturing little kids. Because it's all in the name of science.

"I told you already," I say, spinning on my heel. "I don't make friends with scientists."

A few minutes later, I'm still fuming as Ryder tugs the sheet off a big, bulky machine, scattering dust motes in the air.

"You could've given me a warning that Tanner was in your house," I say.

"I thought you might want to continue your riveting conversation from yesterday." He snickers, and I realize that's precisely why he sent me to *fetch* his goggles. So that I would run into Tanner.

"That's real juvenile, Ry. If you wanted to torment me,

there're about a hundred other things you could've picked."

"Hey, I was as surprised as you were to see him this morning," he says. "And you know what? He's not half bad. You know how much work he's saving me by building that playpen for Remi? Mikey totally would've made me do it if Rat Boy hadn't offered."

I sigh. Thinking about Tanner makes my skin itchy. And that's the last thing I need. "Can we not talk about Tanner anymore? We have a purple and green hallway to find."

We're in the storage shed behind the Russells' house, and I crouch in front of the doughnut-shaped computer screen that Ryder has just uncovered. It's the one that translates a memory to the viewer across five senses. I haven't seen one of these since I was six.

No wonder. When people stopped receiving future memories, these machines became largely irrelevant. They were good for only two things. Torturing victims like me with other people's memories. And reading the visions a precognitive received. There's been only one real precognitive in our nation's history—the chairwoman's daughter, Olivia Dresden. And no one's seen or heard from her in the last decade.

The vision in my head might not be a glimpse of the future, but Ryder had the bright idea of scanning it with the doughnut screen, so that we have a physical image with which to work.

"How in space-time did Mikey score one of these?" Just seeing the machine makes my heart race, but I'm being silly. The scientists aren't chasing me. No one's going to strap me down and torture me.

Ryder flips a row of switches in front of the terminal. "When FuMA shut down, these machines went to a storage room at TechRA, collecting dust. So Mikey snagged one for our house."

"So that it can sit here, collecting dust?"

"Something like that." He flashes a you-know-me-better-than-that grin. If this doughnut screen is like any of the other relics Mikey's lugged home, Ryder would have taken it apart, studied it, and put it back together within the first week.

"Sit." He gestures to a storage crate and holds up a metal contraption that looks like a cross between a helmet and a headband. "Put this on and open your mind, the way you've been taught." He squints at the terminal hooked up to the doughnut. "The memory will come to you."

"What are you talking about?" I adjust the contraption on my head. Is it supposed to feel like it's falling off? "I haven't been taught anything. The meditation core hasn't been part of the curriculum for years."

"I know." He smirks. "I'm just reading the script they included for the administrators. Hello, my name is Ryder. How are you this fine day? Would you like a meditation aid?" He pretends to hold up a tray, Vanna-bot style. "Flickering candle? Scents to sniff? No?" He mimes throwing the entire tray over his shoulder. "Good. None of this hocus-pocus stuff works anyway."

I giggle. "The script does not say that."

"Okay, you're right. But do you feel more relaxed?"

I nod.

"Good. I bet that's part of opening your mind." He arranges two more crates behind me. "Just be...comfortable. Maybe the vision will show up."

He puts on a less bulky helmet and ducks into the hollow middle of the doughnut screen.

I take a deep breath and ease myself down. The second my back hits the wooden slabs, the swords are back—hundreds, no, millions of them, jabbing at every corner and seam of my brain, peeling back any layer they can grasp.

I want to give them access. I try to open my mind. We're working toward the same thing here, the swords and I, but we…just…can't…connect.

Panting, I sit up. Sweat plasters my hair to my forehead. "I don't get it. Why is this so hard?"

"How did the vision come to you last time?"

"I was sleeping. There wasn't any kind of struggle. I just fell into it, like a dream."

He frowns. Only his head sticks up in the middle of the screens. "What else was different?"

"What I'm wearing." As soon as I say the words, I know the answer. Of course. I can't believe I didn't think of it before. Reaching up, I grasp the black-tourmaline pendant hanging around my neck. "My necklace. My mom took it off when she changed me into pajamas."

He shakes his head. "Most people would kill to have your powers. I don't know why you would voluntarily stunt them."

My fingers trembling, I take off the pendant. Back when I lived in the wilderness, I never used to bump into anyone, ever. Never lunged in the wrong direction when I was trapping a fish. Never got caught without shelter during a freak thunderstorm. My precognition didn't extend more than a couple of minutes into the future, but I used it as unconsciously as my eyes or my ears.

Then, we moved back to Eden City, and I let my psychic muscles atrophy. I bought this tourmaline pendant, so that the stone's natural qualities could shield my abilities.

"Why, Jessa?"

I shake my head. It's not something I can talk about, even with him. Especially because it's him. Ryder brings flowers to my mom as well as Angela on Caregiver's Day. He thinks she didn't accompany me to the wilderness because of circumstances beyond her control. I can't bear for him to know what I suspect is the truth. That she chose not to join me. That she wishes it had been me who died instead of Callie.

When we returned to civilization and I saw how cold my mother was, I never wanted to use my psychic abilities ever again. She blames me for my sister's death, and if I could've gouged out my powers with a knife, I would've. Wearing the tourmaline stone—and in essence shutting down my abilities— is the next best alternative.

I put the pendant down on a crate, ten feet away. "Let's try again without the necklace."

Ryder turns back to the screen, and I lie on the crates once more. The wood scratches my shoulders, and I shift until I find a more comfortable position. I breathe in. And out. In. And out.

This time, when I open my mind, I fall into the corridor like a kitten tumbling into a bucket of cream. Fast, unprepared. And then I'm drowning in the vision.

I am running, running down a corridor. The tiles are pale green, and a darker green stripe bisects the wall…

I run past the wait lounges, the purple amethyst couches, pumping my legs, gasping for breath, past the elevators, through the emergency exit, until I reach the metal door with the purple-light security system.

I stand before the door, certain that I was born to fulfill this destiny. And then the vision fades.

This time, instead of being jerked to consciousness, I open my eyes slowly. Ryder's already out of the doughnut screen and gawking at me.

"Holy Fates, I felt like I was in there with you." He swipes an arm across his forehead. "No, I *was* you. The vision was happening to me."

I nod, my clothes sticking to me in wet patches. "That's how it felt when the scientists made me live those memories.

Except they weren't nearly as benign as running through a corridor."

"No wonder Callie killed herself." Ryder's voice is hushed and a little spooked, like he's seen a ghost from the past. Or maybe a flicker from the future. "She saw those girls moments before Dresden sent them to their execution. Their death was imminent—and Callie felt it. She would've done anything to save them—and you."

I swallow, but I can't dislodge the mass in my throat, the ache like a hole in my heart. I miss her; that's always been true. But at this moment, I'm so sad, so sick about what she had to live through. The guilt over a murder she never committed. The responsibility she felt for all those Mediocres in prison. The final inevitability of her choice.

I need to make it up to her. Somehow, some way, I need to make myself worthy of her sacrifice. Maybe it starts with this vision.

"Did you recognize the corridor?" I ask Ryder.

He moves to the terminal. "No. But give me a few minutes. I'll grab several stills and run them through the system, using Mikey's security clearance."

His fingers dance over the keyball, and I pick up my pendant again. Instead of slipping it on, however, I stick the black stone in my pocket.

Something tells me I'm going to need all of my abilities to figure this one out. For better or for worse. I lie on the ground and prop my black high-top hovershoes against the wall. And wait.

Half an hour later, Ryder looks up. "Got it. The corridor's right here in Eden City." He pauses. "It's one of the basement floors of the TechRA building, where the FuMA offices used to be located."

Of course. The information should be a revelation, but

it doesn't surprise me. It's like I've always known it. Like my name. Like the path down the purple and green corridor. Somehow, I knew this was all connected.

"Now," I say, "all we have to do is follow that path."

9

"What if Dresden's daughter sent you that message?" Ryder whispers the next day as we're waiting for our turn through TechRA security. "She's got sick abilities, and no one's seen her in ages. I'd bet my hoverboard she hasn't been at some boarding school for the last decade."

My eyes widen. "You mean Olivia? You think she's been held captive all these years?"

"Shhh, keep your voice down." He looks around the glass walls, but there's no one else in the waiting vestibule. The guy in front of us has already stepped through the security arches.

"It must be because of the vision of genocide," I say, warming to the theory. "Dresden's hiding Olivia because she doesn't want anyone to know about the vision. Maybe Olivia sent me the message as a cry for help."

"If that's the case...we should abort," Ryder says darkly.

"What? No." My voice rises. "If it is Olivia, she needs our help. We can't just abandon her."

"Why not? I thought you said she was a brat."

"She was six. Think who her mother was. You'd be a

pain, too." I reach into the past. Most of my pre-wilderness memories are a blur, and most of them center on my mom and Callie. But I remember Olivia. "She was my friend."

"You didn't even like her!"

"That's not true. She talked to me, Ryder. She sought me out when all the other girls shunned me. Because of her, I know how it feels to ride on the seesaw pods." I blink, my eyes suddenly wet, which doesn't make sense. "Maybe that sounds stupid, but it meant something to me."

"It doesn't," he says, softening. "But that was ten years ago. People change in ten years."

He's right. But I can't shake the image of the little girl I used to know—the big brown eyes and the straight-cut bangs. I keep hearing Dresden's cold, cruel voice: *No daughter of mine is Mediocre.*

I know all too well how it feels to be forsaken by your own mother.

"You and I, we know how it feels to lose a parent or two," I say. "But we had each other, and we formed a new family. If Olivia's been imprisoned—or worse—then she doesn't have anybody. How can we ignore her cry for help?"

He sighs, and I know I've got him. This is the guy who collected acorns for a squirrel's afterlife, for Fate's sake.

We walk through the security arches, and the guard runs a scanner over the chip embedded under my wrist. My identification pops onto the screen, along with a list of locations I'm cleared to visit.

"Bots along the wall. Find one to escort you," he says in a monotone.

We select the first bot, a squat one with a copper spiral at its belly, and are keying in Mikey's office when the guard calls us back. "Forget the bot. It says here you have a human escort."

I exchange a nervous look with Ryder. A human escort?

But how? Nobody even knows we're here.

Wrong.

A few minutes later, a man approaches the guard. He's broad and good-looking, with eyes that notice everything and a mouth that can either be stern or smiling. His hair is tied back with a piece of rawhide—a leftover habit from our days in the wilderness. Mikey.

We are so busted. Fike, fike, fike.

He gives us a quick, cutting glance and slaps the guard on the back. "I'll take it from here, Rinaldo."

Mikey turns and wraps an arm around each of us. The loving father, the trusted friend. How many times can I say *screwed*?

"I programmed the system to send me an alert when one of your IDs was scanned." His voice is even and pleasant, as mild as a clear blue sky—that's about to split wide open. "According to the logs, it seems you've visited me dozens of times in the last two months. Too bad I've been away at a meeting each of those times."

I know better than to respond—not out here in the main corridor. In fact, none of us says another word until we walk into Mikey's office.

Every surface area is covered with artificial limbs. A hand here, a foot there. So realistic it looks like a dozen bodies got blown apart. Mikey is the foremost expert on the connection of neural pathways to prosthetic limbs. One of his fake arms responds nearly as well as a real arm to orders from the brain.

"Well? What do you have to say for yourselves?" He moves a hand from his chair and sits down. "It's bad enough you've been breaking into labs behind my back. But then Jessa gets herself bitten, and you're back here for more?"

"You were the one who showed us how to access the air vents," I burst out. "You gave us the holographic spiders. What did you think we were going to do with them?"

"I wanted you more involved with the Underground. To see that there was more to life than your crazy stunts." His eyes flit first to Ryder, then to me. Not being officially adopted has never saved me from his lectures or his expectations. "You're sixteen now. Old enough to understand why we accepted the treaty with ComA. Sure, the comforts of modern living are convenient, but that's not why we came back to civilization. There's work to be done. A future of genocide to prevent. It's about time you two joined the fight."

It's not the first time Mikey's lectured us about our civic duty. And not the first time I tune him out. Truth is, I couldn't care less about his political agenda. I have no interest in joining his fight. Callie took it upon herself to save the world— and look what happened to her. I'll stick with helping my mice, and maybe a childhood friend or two, thank you very much.

Even if it means I inadvertently delay someone's entrance into uni for a year. I flush guiltily. Tanner glossed over his ruined experiment with a few careless words, but how does he really feel? Is he sad that he won't go to uni next year? Is he…devastated?

My stomach clenches. I don't want him devastated. He might be my enemy, but the thought of his lips trembling rips and tears at my heart.

"You have to think." Mikey's voice gets louder. "In order for a resistance movement to be successful, it has to be carefully orchestrated, precisely planned. You can't just go on your own unsanctioned raids because you feel like it. You were almost caught; Jessa was infected. This kind of action shines an unnecessary spotlight on us, attention that could jeopardize the entire mission. From now on, neither of you acts unless I say so. Got it?"

We both nod. We have no choice, really.

Mikey sweeps his arm through the air, indicating the jumbled-up piles of body parts. "As punishment, you two will clean my office. I can't find a damn thing in here, and you might as well make yourselves useful."

Ryder groans, poking a leg as if it might grow teeth and bite him. "That'll take weeks! You can't walk in here without a limb clobbering you."

"Then you'd better get started." Mikey's com unit beeps. "I have a meeting. I'll be back in a few hours."

"You mean you're going to leave us here alone?" Ryder asks incredulously.

His dad lifts his eyebrows. "Is there any reason why I shouldn't?"

"Not at all." I step forward and give him my best you-can-trust-us smile. "We'll have your office all cleaned up by the time you get back."

With one last scuff against Ryder's shoulder, Mikey leaves.

The door bangs shut behind him, and I jab Ryder in the chest. "That was really smooth. You might as well have told him we were going straight into the air vents as soon as he left."

"Are we?" my best friend asks, looking troubled. "He let us off easy this time. But he won't be nearly as forgiving if he catches us again."

"Of course we're still going! Olivia needs us."

He huffs out a breath. "Right."

We look at the smooth expanse of the south wall—that's not really a wall. Rather, it's the holographic projection of a solid surface created by a "spider," and it leads to air vents that wind all over the TechRA building.

I reach inside the wall and flip a switch. The hologram disappears.

I gasp. As expected, the plaster ends abruptly. But instead

of a gaping hole, metal slats seal off the opening into the air vents.

"That's why he left us," I moan. "He wanted us to snoop and find out that he closed our access to the vents. He's telling us he'll always be one step ahead of us."

Ryder slips on his goggles and peers at the black box sitting next to the spider. "They're not closed permanently. The slats are retractable—and they're keyed to a set of biometrics. Probably Mikey's. So if we want to get into the vents, all we have to do is ask."

"What are the chances he'll approve this mission?" I ask faintly.

"Oh, I don't know." He picks up a prosthetic hand and scratches his back. "Probably about as likely as you joining forces with Dresden."

10

My lungs feel like a vacuum has sucked out all the air. "Now what?"

Ryder slides the goggles off his face. "Plan B."

"We don't have a Plan B."

"Of course we have a Plan B. What kind of delinquents would we be if we didn't have a Plan B?" He grins with enough confidence for both of us, and I know that in spite of Mikey's warning, we won't abandon our mission that easily. "We've got to convince an unsuspecting TechRA employee to let us into the lower floors of the building. And to do that, we need to use the full extent of our abilities."

I freeze. Because he's not referencing my quick thinking or poise under pressure. This has nothing to do with my hoverboard skills or my fling-myself-into-open-space courage. He's talking about one thing alone: my precognition.

"I know you believe your psychic abilities somehow killed your sister," Ryder says gently. "It's not true. Even so, if you use your powers to help Olivia, maybe you'll feel like they led to something good."

He's right, of course. There's no good reason I'm blocking my abilities. I saw it as atonement for Callie's death, but in my practical moments, I know that it won't bring her back. Nothing will.

I pick up an artificial limb. It's nice to have something to hold. "Okay. What did you have in mind?"

I grip the handle of the picnic basket. People swarm around me, traveling between the industrial-sized Meal Assemblers and the long metal tables, carrying trays of food with mouthwatering smells. Silverware clinks together, and meal packets are tossed through the air. Bots roll around, picking up trash, and a thousand conversations blend into a dull roar. If anyone notices me in the chaos of TechRA's cafeteria, it would be a miracle.

That's exactly what I'm counting on.

"Check it out." Ryder scans the labels on top of each Meal Assembler, his eyes wide. "Seafood risotto with head-on prawns. Blue cheese and fig ravioli. Pappardelle with braised short ribs. Have you ever heard of this stuff?"

"Sure," I say. "But I've never actually tasted them."

Our Meal Assembler at home doesn't get this fancy. We have the basic model, the one that produces standard fare — rotisserie chicken and beef stew, pot roast and spaghetti squash. Upgrades for each additional cuisine cost an entire year's credits, and my mom and I never had the kind of money — or appetite — to warrant the purchase.

"You never tasted them? Then how..." Ryder trails off. "Gotcha. Your sister's digital journals, right?"

I duck my head, squeezing the basket handle until I feel

the straw digging into my palm. Everything I know about Callie comes from three sources: my own scant memories, Logan's stories, and the school's mandatory journals. Problem was, Callie wasn't much of a writer, and so her journals were filled more with recipes than her personal thoughts.

"She wrote about pappardelle," I say. "About making the pasta and cutting it by hand. When you did it just right, she said, the taste was to die for."

"I'll ask Mikey to bring some home next time he goes to the cafeteria."

"You don't have to do that. I could eat the same meal from the Meal Assembler every day, and I wouldn't notice."

"Don't discount it," he says. "Food is a way for you to be close to your sister, so it matters. Just don't go pigging out and refusing to share."

My heart compresses, and I squeeze his hand. Ryder's my best friend for a reason. A million reasons, in fact, and this is just one of them. "Thanks. You're the best."

He grins. "Don't I know it? Come on. Let's find our mark."

Nodding, I scan the crowd, looking for a person who fits our profile. A romantic who isn't too strict about following the rules. Someone young enough to remember the zero-gravity flight of first love.

"What about her?" Ryder inclines his head toward a brunette retrieving a lychee fruit slushie at a Drinks Assembler. Her eyes are as shiny as a new circuit board, and her shoulder-length hair curves at the ends in a familiar question mark.

I let out an explosive breath. "Fates, no. That's MK Rivers, the chairwoman's assistant."

"Yikes. Okay, moving on." He zeroes in on a guy with leopard spots dyed into his tawny skin. A potential rule breaker. "Him?"

I flash forward into his future and see him walk right

past a girl sprawled on the floor, her belongings scattered everywhere. "Nah. Too cool to help others."

We consider and reject three more candidates, and then I see her. A woman with perfectly outlined lips and hair as bright as a cardinal's tail. She wears a ring on her finger and beams as though she's single-handedly responsible for feeding the entire cafeteria.

I flash forward and hear her gushing to a friend about her boyfriend waking her up with a daybreak proposal.

"Perfect. She just got engaged this morning with a data-chip ring. If anyone's going to support geeky young love, it's her."

"Okay," Ryder says, trusting me implicitly. "To our places."

I take a deep breath. *Please, Fates, let me have picked the right one. Olivia's future depends on the kindness of this cardinal-haired woman.*

Five minutes later, I'm in the loading deck of elevator capsule nineteen. The handle of the picnic basket is slippery under my palms, and my heart marks nanoseconds of time. Two-dozen capsules line the cafeteria lobby, but the cardinal-haired woman will choose this one. I can just see it—literally.

Ryder is in the lobby, hiding behind a plant statue with gold and silver leaves and a twisted copper stalk. He was able to hack into the electronic screen and display an X on top of capsule nineteen, indicating that it is out of order. When the red-haired woman approaches, he'll turn off the X, only to switch it back on after she enters the loading deck, thus ensuring our privacy.

The plan is foolproof…in theory. But because it involves too many independent decisions, even my precognition can't tell us how it will play out.

"I hate that I'm not in there with you," Ryder says into my earpiece.

"We have no choice." My voice echoes in the tight chamber of the loading deck. "You need to make sure no one else enters this capsule."

"I know. Doesn't mean I like it—" He cuts off abruptly. "She's coming, Jessa. Get ready."

I take a deep breath, reach into the picnic basket, and remove a hand. One of Mikey's prosthetics, with long, elegant fingers, cut off below the wrist.

"Five steps, Jessa... Three, two..."

I run the prosthetic hand over the sensor, again and again, as if I'm trying to scan an ID embedded in the wrist.

The door clicks open.

"I don't get it," I mutter, loudly enough to be overheard. "It worked before. Why isn't it working now?"

I hear a gasp and spin around, hiding the prosthetic hand behind my back. My face is hot, my movements jerky. Good. At least I don't have to fake my anxiety.

The red-haired woman gapes at me. "What is that? Don't tell me... Oh Fates, are you trying to swipe the sensor with a severed hand?"

Up close, I can see why her lipstick is so perfect. The color's been tattooed on.

"Oh, no, this isn't a real hand." I hold the prosthetic out to her. She touches it gingerly, and her shoulders visibly drop.

"My boyfriend's a scientist here," I say, my voice warm and confiding. "One of the interns, in the prosthetics department. My birthday was last week, and he gave me this as a present. Can you imagine?" I laugh girlishly, even though I'm not girlish. I rarely laugh. And I never confide in strangers. Fates, I don't even talk to strangers. "He put a duplicate of his data chip in the wrist, thinking it would be romantic, and he couldn't understand why I wasn't more excited to get a fake hand."

She smiles, as I knew—hoped, prayed—she would. "My boyfriend—I mean, my fiancé—is the exact same way. He just proposed this morning." She holds up her hand with the ring. The square black-colored chip, with metal prongs lining four sides, gleams in the light. "Most girls get diamonds or rubies. I get a data chip."

"This is so much better," I say. "Anybody can give a silly old stone. He's asking you to share in his data stream. In the true blood that courses through his life." I pluck the lines straight out of the future conversation she has with her friend, detailing the proposal.

Her smile widens. "That's exactly what he said. The rest of my friends don't get it. They think he's too cheap to spring for a real gem, but I think it's sweet. Besides, we're saving our credits to buy a house, and I like that he's thinking about our future."

"I think that's beautiful," I gush. "And your ring is so unique. No one will have one like it."

"Thank you so much." She looks at the severed limb. "So, um, why are you trying to scan a prosthetic hand?"

I exhale. This is it. The moment where she falls for my ruse—or calls security on me. "Our meetiversary is today, and I wanted to surprise him." I move my shoulders. "I was able to scan the wrist to get up to the cafeteria. I don't know why it doesn't work now. I never should've stopped for the chocolate-covered strawberries." I look at her pleadingly. "You won't tell, will you? I know it was wrong to use the data chip, but I wanted this date to be perfect."

She twists the ring on her finger. Is she buying my story? Oh Fates, what if she works for Chairwoman Dresden? Any moment now, I could find myself in electro-cuffs...

"I won't tell," she finally says, and the air whooshes out of my body. "But you have to promise you won't try this again. It's sweet of you to surprise your boyfriend—but our security protocols are here for a reason."

I nod and flip open the cover of my picnic basket. Plump strawberries covered with silky dark chocolate gleam up at us, along with wrapped sandwiches and a glass bottle of milk. "We met at lunch a year ago, and I've recreated the entire meal—peanut butter and guava jelly, chocolate milk, and strawberries. Standard school fare. Not gourmet by any means, but I thought it would be cute. I guess it will just have to be cute at dinner."

She twists the ring again. The air feels full, saturated with my anticipation.

"Oh, what the Limbo?" She blows the cardinal hair out of her eyes. "I suppose there's no harm, and you two should eat your meetiversary meal. Peanut butter and guava sandwiches, huh? That's so sweet it makes my enamel ache. What floor is he on?"

"He's working on a subterranean floor today. B-23." Inside my shoes, my toes contract. The lower the floor, the more restricted. *Please don't ask what an intern is doing so far beneath the surface.*

But she doesn't even blink. She swipes her wrist over the sensor and keys in the right floor. "Go. Have fun. Give him a big kiss for me."

"I will. Thank you."

My legs shaky, I climb into the capsule and strap myself in. The doors slide closed, and a huge grin spreads across my face. I can't believe it. The plan worked!

"I'm in," I murmur to Ryder. Before he can respond, the capsule is propelled through a series of tunnels. I can tell the moment we're underground because my earpiece cuts out. It's part of the security of the subterranean levels—no communication via the normal channels. Like it or not, I'm on my own.

The capsule lurches to a stop, and the doors open. I can't see anything at first but black stars and bright lights, and then my vision clears.

I step into a corridor with pale-green tiles and a darker green stripe bisecting the walls.

Just like in my vision.

11

The moment I step into the hallway, something clicks. The vision rushes over me, layered on top of my reality, and I'm flooded with a feeling of rightness. A magnetic force pulls me forward, sucking me into this path. I must run this maze. Not because the vision tells me, not because it's in my genes. But because sometime in the future, I already did.

Callie felt this way. On the last day of her life, Logan told me how she talked about Fate's invisible hand, urging her forward.

She may have changed the future. She may have proved that an infinite number of parallel universes exist, and it's up to us to determine which world we live in. But she had to walk into my room, with a syringe in her hand. Because this was her Fixed.

Mikey posited—and I believe—that some moments are lived more strongly than others. These sequences of actions happen in every world. The Fixed, he called these moments. You can change your future all you want, but you will never get away from walking certain paths.

The blood roars in my ears. My heart attempts to lap itself in beats. Somewhere inside my soul, too honest for artifice, too deep for excuses, I know this is my Fixed. However I choose to live my life, in whatever world parallel to this one, I will always end up here, at this moment.

Metal clatters down the hall, and I snap to attention. I scan the corridor and duck into a relief room, heart pounding in an entirely different way.

I take a deep breath, count to one hundred, and then slip back into the corridor. Nobody. Good.

Of their own volition, my feet start moving. There's no question which way to go. Even if I hadn't dreamed about the purple and green corridor every night, there's that invisible hand, tugging me in the right direction.

I'm not going quickly enough. Something pushes between my shoulders, urging me faster, faster. I start trotting and then break into a full-out run, holding the picnic basket tightly. My sneakered feet slap loudly against the pale-green tile, but I'll risk the extra noise. I have to. The hand of Fate won't allow otherwise.

The wait lounges flash by, and sure enough, I see emerald carpets and purple amethyst couches.

Green and purple. Purple and green.

By now, it no longer seems strange that the combination of colors feels so familiar. That it resonates so deeply inside me. Sweat drenches my back, making my shirt cling to my skin. I make a left, go through the double swinging doors, bypass another set of elevator capsules, open the emergency exit, and descend down, down, down an endless set of stairs.

And then, I enter a hallway and stop dead in my tracks. Stretchers line the wall, holding people. No, not people. Bodies. Corpses, with their hands clasped across their chests. All lying perfectly, deadly still.

The hair stands on my neck, and my bones melt into fluid. Where am I? Did I stumble into a morgue?

I rub my arms. The air is chilly, at least ten degrees cooler than above ground, and smells too clean, too sterile. Like the entire hallway was doused with sanitizer.

This isn't right. I must've taken a wrong turn because these corpses weren't in my vision. And yet, I continue walking down the hallway. Because that unseen force is still here, still tugging me down the path.

I see it. A door. Just like the one in my vision.

It is metal, locked up tighter than a tomb with its blinking-purple-light security system, its pale green box of personal identity scans. Two long strips of green and purple, twisted together, bisect the walls on either side of the door. The exit signs flash purple; the grating over the lights is green.

The message couldn't be clearer. *This is where the colors lead. This is where you're meant to be. This is the place to which you've been called.*

I'm here. I found it. Now what?

I look up the corridor, my breath erupting in pants. I don't know what I expected. Fireworks, a symphony orchestra? Instead, it's just a hallway. Just a door. Locked, with no way for me to get inside.

Clearly I'm not going to turn around and go back. My only choice is to find a spot and hide. Stake out the door and wait for something to happen. But where?

There's nothing else in the hallway. No twisted metal plant, no laundry carts, no trash chutes. Could I conceal myself underneath the stretchers? I crouch down and examine the crisscrossing metal rods. It wouldn't hide a three-legged mouse, much less a person.

Frustrated, I stand. That's when I notice some of the stretchers hold more than one corpse. The bodies are crammed together, side-by-side on the narrow mattresses, as if the administration ran out of beds and thought the corpses wouldn't mind.

I shiver. A sick feeling starts in my stomach and climbs into my throat, all acidic and sharp and burning. Not just because of the cavalier treatment of the dead bodies. But also because I've realized there's only one spot for me to hide. One spot where I can stake out the door and remain concealed.

On one of the stretchers, snuggled against a dead body.

breathe too fast. I gulp the air as if I'm storing up for a famine, and it's still not enough. Faster and faster. Pant, pant, pant.

Slow down, my brain screams. I can't hyperventilate, not now. I have a mission to accomplish.

I focus on a single detail—the hourglass insignia edging the white sheets. The old symbol of the Future Memory Agency. Weird. I thought FuMA didn't exist anymore. I thought all of their old equipment was stowed away or trashed. So what are their sheets doing here?

I don't know the answer, but thinking about the anomaly slows my breathing enough for me to scan the faces of the corpses closest to the locked door. In the third stretcher, I see a girl about my age, with black hair arranged in a tidy braid. She looks like she has a mixed heritage, like me, with a smattering of freckles across her nose and cheeks.

For some reason, these details are important in choosing which corpse to share a bed with.

Taking a deep breath, I pull a stun gun from the picnic basket—something else I swiped from Mikey's office—and stow the basket under the stretcher. Then, I close my eyes and jump. Only I launch myself too hard and sprawl across the stretcher. Skin touching the corpse's skin.

Ew. I leap off her, and my foot smacks into the wall, sending the stretcher careening across the corridor and disrupting the precise line of hospital beds.

At that moment, I hear a loud swoosh of air rushing through a tunnel, signaling the arrival of the elevator capsule. Hurriedly, I push the stretcher back into line and lie down on the mattress, pulling the sheet over my body. My shoulder brushes against the girl's. Even through our shirts, I can feel her coldness. The smell of formaldehyde winds into my nostrils.

I scream inside my head, and my stomach lurches. The nausea climbs up my throat, and I'm gagging, gagging, gagging. I'm touching her. A dead girl. In a straight line from shoulder to waist.

I turn my head to the side and breathe shallowly. Oh Fates. I've got to get ahold of myself. They'll be here any moment, and I can't mess this up because I'm being squeamish.

Sweat breaks out on my neck, and I grip the gun tightly against my thigh. I have only a small window to act, and I need to be ready.

The capsule arrives, and I hear voices. Male and female, businesslike and authoritative, discussing a report that hasn't been filed. Good. They're scientists. At least one of them is. Scientists won't be carrying weapons like the guards. They won't be expecting me to force my way into the room. They're more likely to succumb to the threat of electrocution.

I close my eyes, feel the reassuring weight of the gun at my side, and try not to move. Try not to breathe. Try to appear dead.

The voices get closer, and the argument becomes more spirited. I crack open my eyes and peek at them.

The woman wears a crisp navy uniform, which means she's

an official, not a scientist. A high-ranking one, too, if the metal bars pinned to the shoulder of her suit are any indication. She has brown hair that falls to her shoulders before curving out like a damn question mark.

Just my luck. MK Rivers.

"Bottom line, the chairwoman wants the reports on her com, first thing every Monday morning," MK says. "I don't care what you do to make it happen. Just ensure that it does."

"With all due respect, MK, I don't report to the chairwoman," the man says. His name tag says PRESTON, and he has black hair, eyes that come to a crease at the corners, and a square jaw. Scruff on his chin that reminds me of Mikey, but maybe that's because he's approximately Mikey's age, somewhere around thirty.

He looks familiar. I know this man from somewhere. Is he one of Mikey's friends? A covert member of the Underground? Or maybe that's not it at all. Maybe he looks familiar because I've glimpsed him at Dresden's side in the news feeds, and one day, he'll destroy us all.

"The chairwoman is consulted heavily on all TechRA projects. For all intents and purposes, she is your boss." MK's voice is low and surprisingly gentle. She doesn't sound like I expected, given the bars on her shoulders. "If that's not enough, you know this is personal for her. This girl means everything to her. The reports would ease her mind, and frankly, she'll be a better boss for me. Maybe she won't yell as much if she's consistently updated."

My heart thrums against my ribs, so hard I worry my body is vibrating the stretcher. Olivia. They have to be talking about Olivia. My old friend is ensconced behind that locked door, and she's calling to me for help.

"What's this?" Preston says suddenly, his voice coming directly above me. The stretcher beneath me moves.

Fike. I must not have realigned the stretcher properly. *Don't wiggle*, I order myself.

"What's the matter?" MK asks.

"Nothing. I don't think."

I feel the scientist's eyes like a solid object, pushing and prodding my face. I lie as still as possible. Not twitching. Not breathing. But he stands over me too long. The pressure in my lungs builds too much. Climbing, climbing, climbing. When I can't bear it anymore, I take a tiny sip of air.

Oh Fates. My chest rises. He must see it. I'm done for.

But he doesn't say anything. I hear a small sound that might be a gurgle in his throat, and then, the security system beeps. The door clicks open. "Coming?" MK asks impatiently.

"Right away," he says.

I feel a light pressure on my arm above my elbow, and then he walks away, his footsteps pattering the ground like raindrops.

My heart jumps into my throat. Did he squeeze my arm? He must know I'm not one of the corpses. And yet, he didn't turn me in. Why? Who is he?

As I debate the possibilities, the door closes. MK and the mysterious guy are gone. I've lost my chance to threaten them. Lost my chance to get inside. Lost my chance to rescue Olivia.

Disappointment floods me. I should've jumped from the stretcher; I should've acted. But the surprise at seeing MK rendered me useless.

I flex my fingers around the stun gun. Next time, I'll be ready.

13

lie back on the stretcher and wait.

Twenty times, I brush against my bedmate's arm, and twenty times, I cross my arms over my chest, vowing not to touch her again. Twenty times, my mind drifts, and twenty times, my arm drops. Her skin presses against mine, disturbingly cold, and I yelp, silent and desperate, inside my head. Then the cycle starts all over again.

MK and the scientist come back out. I hold my breath, bracing for another signal from Preston, a meaningful throat-clearing or a touch of his hand, but there's nothing. When they reach the elevator capsules, I hear MK's voice. "So, it's settled. You'll file that report next Monday, like we discussed. The chairwoman is *very* anxious about the girl's condition."

The man's answer is lost in the whoosh of the capsules.

Two hours later, my legs are hot, my neck is sweaty, and the hand wrapped around the stun gun is sticky. I was more comfortable hanging upside down over a cage of mice.

Dear Fates. How did I end up in this situation? There's no telling if anyone else is coming today. How long am I going to wait? I could be at home, drinking a tall glass of gingerade, eating spaghetti from the Meal Assembler and dreaming that it's pappardelle.

And my legs would still ache with the compulsion to run down a particular hallway. Olivia Dresden would still be trapped, wondering why I haven't responded to her call.

I have to stay. Who knows if I'll be able to sneak down here a second time? I owe my old friend at least this much.

I readjust my grip on the gun, and then I hear it. The whoosh of the elevators. Someone's here. Finally.

My muscles bunch like I'm about to swim one of Logan's meets. I've got this.

The capsule doors open, and a figure walks out. He's dressed in cargo pants and a thermal shirt, and his hair falls over his eyes.

All the breath and resolve flee my body. My bones turn to water, and the determination encasing my heart trembles. Wouldn't you know it? Tanner Callahan. Exactly who I don't need.

My mind whirls, trying to process this twist of fate. I can't exactly follow through now. I already ruined his experiment. Can I threaten him with bodily harm, too? What will he think of me? Does it matter? It shouldn't. This isn't about him. It's about Olivia. Right?

I need about a year to puzzle this out, but time doesn't have the good manners to slow down. Tanner marches right by me and strides to the security system. In a matter of seconds, he'll disappear inside the room. I have to act. Now.

My plan hasn't changed. Threaten to stun the scientist, get inside that room. It makes no difference that the scientist happens to be Tanner. None.

Quickly, before I change my mind, I launch myself off the stretcher and point the stun gun at his back.

The stretcher crashes into the wall, and he turns at the noise, his eyes widening. "Jessa? What are you doing here—"

"Get me into that room, or I'll stun you."

He looks at the gun and lifts his arms slowly into the air. But instead of backing away like he's supposed to, instead of breaking into a sweat and fumbling with the security system, he walks toward me.

Fike. This is so not in the plan.

"Stay where you are! Don't come any closer!"

"Or you'll do what? If I'm lying inert on the floor, you won't get into that room."

I tighten my grip. Damn him and his logic. It's not like I haven't considered the dilemma. I was just hoping I wouldn't have to resort to the second part of my plan.

"There's another setting on this gun—the tort mode." My voice shakes as though *I'm* the one being threatened. "It will focus the electricity on a single part of your body. You won't be knocked out, but you will feel excruciating pain."

"The tort setting?" He lifts his eyebrows. "Don't you mean torture? Torture of a living thing. Of another human being. You're not going to tort me, Jessa."

"I will if you don't do what I say."

He stops in front of me, close enough for the metal barrel to brush against his chest.

Close enough to kiss me.

"I don't believe you," he whispers. The way his eyes capture mine, it's like he sees all the memories stuffed inside my body. From the time I watched my sister plunge a needle into her chest to now, when I stand before him, a torture device in my hands and trembling in my heart.

"You can't even bear for lab mice to be confined in their cages," he says, his voice steady and sure.

My mouth falls open, and it takes two tries to push out

the words. "What…what do you know about the mice?"

"I know you broke into my lab, Jessa." He moves closer, even though I would've sworn there weren't any more steps between us. "I know you opened the cage and let my mice loose."

I think about denying it, but there's no point. The problem with Tanner Callahan is that he thinks he's always right. The bigger problem is that he usually is.

"How did you know?" I look at the computer-embedded tiles, unable to meet his gaze.

"It was when you did the heel-flip trick. Something about the arch of your body felt so familiar. I went back and re-watched the vids. Sure, your hair was hidden and your face was covered. But you can't change the shape of your body. You can't disguise the way you move. It was you."

My face burns. He knows the shape of my body. What does this mean, exactly? Is he talking about my overall height and form? Or, um, something more specific? Something… having to do with my curves? "I thought you didn't see my heel-flip trick," I manage to say.

He smiles smugly. "And I thought you weren't attracted to scientists."

I try to speak, but my voice is lost somewhere in the recesses of my heart. When I find it, I can't be sure it's the right one. "If you knew it was me, why didn't you turn me in? Dresden would've rewarded you handsomely. Forget the mice. She would've gotten you into any uni you wanted."

He blinks. "If I turned you in, you would've been stuck in a lab chair for the next decade. The treaty doesn't cover lawbreakers."

"Why do you care?"

"I don't have to like you to care, Jessa."

A laugh rattles out my throat, but it tastes like the tears

on my lips—hot and aching. "I can't stand you, either."

Shakily, I lower the weapon to my side. I haven't given up on saving Olivia. But I can't tort Tanner, not now.

Doesn't matter. I have something else he wants and needs. Something he won't be able to turn down.

I let the breath flow out of my lungs. What I'm about to offer him crosses a line I never thought I'd approach. I hold up my arm, the inside of my elbow out, so that he can see the purple-blue veins through my skin. "If you get me into that room, I'll give you my blood."

His brows crease together. "Why would I want your blood?"

"Your mouse bit me. You saw that on the vids. What you don't know is I was infected. I developed the same powers as your mice. Someone sent me a vision of a maze, a path I was compelled to run, and I was led here." My breath hitches. "So it seems you haven't lost the fifth-generation strand of your virus after all. It's flowing through my blood. A sample should give the lost data back to you."

His jaw works, gnawing on nothing. "You destroyed an entire year's worth of my work. You jeopardized my entrance into uni. And you don't tell me about the virus in your blood until just *now*?"

I wince. Of course he's pissed. I'd be steaming, too. "I couldn't tell you. I didn't know if you would turn me in."

"You're not the girl I thought," he says, his voice hard.

"And who was that?" I shoot back. "All you've done since we talked at the hoverpark is order me around and insult my intelligence." I take a deep breath. It sucks that I didn't tell him. Agreed. But it's done. Fighting about it isn't going to help either of us. "It's a good trade. We both get what we want. The virus worked. I was able to get the vision, even though I'm not a Receiver. Like your mice, I ran the maze.

Are you going to walk away from your experiment, just as you're about to get it back?"

He smiles wryly. "So I guess we've finally discovered what we are to each other. Just a means to an end. Is that right, Jessa?"

"We can help each other." I lick my lips. "That's better than being enemies."

"You might change your mind when you go inside that room."

A chill snakes up my spine. "Why?"

He doesn't respond. Instead, he steps forward to have his eyes scanned, which is all the answer I need.

Whatever is inside that room, I'll find out soon enough.

14

Insects flit around my stomach. Not just annoying gnats, either, but giant moths that fly around, crash into one another, and rip up their own wings.

Tanner presses his palm against the sensor and sticks his finger into a machine that takes a prick of his blood. Once his biometrics are verified, the door clicks open.

He steps aside to let me go first, but not out of politeness. Oh, no. His stiff jaw tells me he's still angry. But there's something else, too. An alertness to his stance, a readiness in his eyes. As though he wants me to go first so that he can catch me if I fall.

Ridiculous. The only feeling Tanner Callahan has toward mc is disgust.

I lift my chin and try to channel Callie. Try to be as brave as she was. As brave as a girl worthy of her sacrifice.

I walk into the room.

The space is dark, with low lights set into the ceiling. I can't see much at first, but I have the sense of being in a vast room, a massive underground cavern whose walls disappear into the shadows. A slight wind blows against me—an oscillating fan, perhaps, to keep the air moving. I shiver and rub my arms.

And then, my eyes adjust. I see row after row of rectangular pods rising out of the ground. There's a stretcher in each pod, surrounded by blinking machines. A person lies on each stretcher, but unlike the bodies in the hallway, each chest rises up and down. These people are alive.

I swallow hard. "What is this place?"

"TechRA's best-kept secret. The hot spot of our scientific innovation. We call it 'the dream lab.'" He places his hand lightly on a bed rail. "This is the place in between, where the people are neither dead nor alive. Their bodies are in a coma, but in this suspended state, their minds work. They dream, floating through an endless, dark night. You wouldn't believe the number of breakthroughs that have come from studying their minds."

His words are a sledgehammer to my knees. I stumble forward, my mind shooting in so many directions it can't form a coherent thought. "These people—oh Fates—trapped here—forever— The mice—fike—this is so much worse than the mice—"

"They volunteered." He pulls back his hand. "Once it became clear the end was imminent, they signed a directive donating their brains to science. They knew exactly what would happen to their bodies, and they chose to benefit science rather than let their brains go to waste."

"So who are the people in the hallway?" I whisper.

"TechRA no longer has use for them. Their bodies are in the hallway waiting to be transported to another sector of the building. And then they'll be…disposed of."

My eyebrows climb toward the ceiling. "Disposed of? You mean killed."

"I suppose," he says. "But I repeat: For the most part, they donated their bodies to science. What else are we supposed to do with them when we're finished?"

"For the most part? That means at least some of them didn't have a choice."

The pause is so long you could stack a row of pods inside.

"Yes," he finally says.

My nerves turn to rage. Olivia. The only true precog of our generation. Her brain is a gold mine. Rather than letting her live, her mother's trapped her here this last decade, so that the scientists can excavate her mind, day after day. And when they're done with her, they'll dispose of her like last week's garbage.

Well, not anymore. Not if I have anything to do with it.

"Where is she?" I ask.

He grimaces. "Maybe this isn't such a good idea after all."

I round on him. The stun gun's still in my hand, and I point it at him, as though shooting him is a possibility. The way the anger pulses inside me, maybe it is. "She sent me a message, Tanner. A vision that led me down a purple and green rabbit hole to get me here. That means she's not dreaming in there. That means, to some extent, she wants out. So tell me now. Where is she?"

He places his hands on my shoulders, and a burst of electricity zips through me, tangling with the anger, leaving me unsettled and confused. Blindly, I grope for the future, searching for something—anything—that will get me back to solid ground again.

The vision crashes over me, almost knocking me down. In the near future, I weep, sobs racking my body. Strong arms wrap around me, pulling me close to a muscled chest covered by a thermal shirt with a tight weave. Tanner's shirt. Tanner's chest. Moments from now, Tanner Callahan will hold me as I soak his shirt with my tears.

"No!" Back in the present, I wrench away from Tanner and race down a row of pods, running from him and my vision. I don't want to be comforted. Don't have time to cry. I've got to find a girl.

I scan the faces in the stretchers, searching for those telltale brown bangs, trying to extrapolate how Olivia might've aged in the last ten years. Not a little girl anymore, but a teenager like me.

I finish one row and turn down the next. In my wake, the machines start beeping and flashing.

"Slow down," Tanner says, jogging behind me. The bastard, he's not even breathing hard. "These monitors are very sensitive. They detect the slightest change in the vital signs, and you're making too much noise. The bodies are reacting to your running."

"So they *are* aware."

"In the same way that a plant turns toward the sun. They react, but that doesn't mean they feel. You're making the machines go crazy. Stop running."

"Tell me where she is." I slow down, but I swivel my head, continuing to search. Olivia's here, and she's counting on me. I'm not going to desert her. Not the way I was deserted.

He sighs. Even with the incessant beeping, I hear the soft whisper of air. "Last row. The pod all the way at the end. She was our very first suspension."

I run to the back of the room and fly down the row, setting off even more alarms. But I don't care. Because for the first time, I'm about to do something that might make me worthy of my sister's sacrifice. I've waited ten years for this moment. I'm not about to delay it a second longer than necessary.

When I reach the last pod in the row, I freeze. The girl on the stretcher doesn't have brown bangs. Her face is nothing like the little girl I remember from my memories.

It's not Olivia Dresden.

When I stare into the girl's face, I feel like I'm looking in a mirror. The same high cheekbones, the same sparse eyelashes, the same swoop at the end of each eye.

I'm lying on the bed. No, not me. She's thinner than me and older. Ten years older.

My legs buckle. Deep, deep in my soul, I scream, a scream that started ten years ago and hasn't let up since.

It's not me lying on the bed, but my other half. My twin, my sister, my soul.

Callie.

15

Callie. Here. Not dead. Not alive, maybe, but not *dead*. How is this possible?

My head feels strangely light, like a balloon about to detach from my body. I sway, and the ground rushes up to meet me. Suddenly, I'm on my hands and knees, with no clear idea how I got here. I crawl forward until my hands hit the rectangular pod, until I'm sitting inches below my sister.

My sister.

This can't be real. It has to be some weird vision, not from the future or the past, but a hallucination created from my dearest wish, my most fantastical desires. The dream lab, Tanner called this room. That's what this is. A dream.

"She's not here. She's not." But I say the words in a whisper, because no matter what dreamland dimension I'm in, I don't want to break the spell.

I pull myself to my feet and drink in Callie's face. The beige skin with the yellow undertones, the barely there lashes. As a kid, I used to watch her experiment with eye tints, but she never bothered with false lashes, and I was glad. Falsies would've blocked her eyes. I saw my entire world in those eyes. I'd give anything to see them now.

"She is here," Tanner says. His voice is gentle, too gentle. Like he's pushed his anger aside because he feels sorry for me. "Who did you think it was?"

"Olivia." I can barely get out the syllables. "I thought Dresden had locked her up, and she sent me the vision as a cry for help."

"No. I thought you'd guessed. Your sister's always been here. From the day she injected herself ten years ago. She was brought straight to this room and has been here ever since."

I should be angry with him for not telling me earlier. I should be absolutely furious. But he had no more reason to trust me than I had to trust him. So I guess we're even, in a twisted sort of way.

Besides, I can't shake the wonder that my sister is actually alive. A feeding tube trails from her mouth, and an IV plugs into her wrist. Automated metal braces wrap around her limbs in order to move her muscles and prevent them from degenerating. "How did this happen?"

"Somebody rushed in after you escaped. They injected her with the antidote around the two-minute mark. Soon enough to preserve her mind but not in time to save her body. She slipped into a coma and has been in that state ever since."

"Does this mean…" The words get stuck in my throat. "Does this mean she might someday wake up?"

"There's no way to know for sure." His words are noncommittal, but his tone is hesitant—even hopeful.

It's the hope that does me in.

The ocean roars in my ears, and I collapse onto the floor. My breath rushes in and out, as useless as if I've punctured my lungs. No matter how much air I gulp, it's not enough.

Tanner wraps his arms around me, pulling me off the floor.

I am trapped against the wall of his chest, surrounded by the bands of his muscles. I sob. Tears pour out of me, the ones I couldn't shed as a child. In the year after Callie injected herself, I didn't cry, not once. I held both my tears and my words inside, close to my chest, even as Logan and Angela and Mikey worried. I didn't talk, and I refused to cry, and they thought I would never recover from my sister's death.

They were right. I never recovered. I could never express the deep, deep sorrow of my other half being ripped from me—until now, when she's been given back.

"Shh…" Tanner whispers against my hair. "It will be okay. I promise it will be okay."

It's more than okay. Callie's not dead. She's been here, the whole time, in this realm, this dimension. In the same city, for Fate's sake. Just like the future, all I have to do is reach out and I'll be able to touch her.

My tears eventually subside, and the physical world seeps back in. Tanner smells like soap, fresh and woodsy, and his shirt brushes against my face. It's not rough, like I imagined, but baby-soft. The contrast of the texture over his solid chest makes me shiver.

I glance up, and his face is inches away. So close I can see the individual bristles on his chin, the creases like shadows in his lips. I lean forward to get a closer look.

He briefly tightens his hold on me. "I'm not going to kiss you."

I blink, not understanding. And then the words sink in. "Who says I'd let you?"

"I've been with enough girls to know when my kisses are wanted, Jessa."

"Well, you're w-wrong," I sputter, heat flooding my face. "I just found out my sister's still alive. The last thing I want is to kiss you."

"I've told you before. You're not my type." He smiles, still gentle, and smooths my hair back from my face, so carefully that I feel like a precious artifact from the pre-Boom era.

My mouth dries, and my pulse speeds as though it's approaching the final leg of a race. I wonder if he can hear my heartbeat—but it doesn't matter. Because none of this is actually about kissing. He's trying to pull me back from my despair, and he knows he can't do that by soft words and sympathy. He knows he has to make an outrageous statement to which I'll react.

Swallowing hard, I turn to the stretcher and Callie. She's just reappeared in my life, and already, she's protecting me. Saving me from awkward conversations and confusing emotions.

"What's wrong with her?" I ask.

He slides his hand down my arm to my waist, his thumb moving in slow circles. "She's suffering from a condition called Asynchronicity, which means her mind is not lined up in time with her body. It's the same condition that afflicts time travelers. The main reason they get lost is because their minds don't stay in the same time as their bodies."

I struggle to concentrate on his words. "Never heard of it. Is this a new disease?"

"Nah. It's been around since the beginning of time." His thumb continues circling, hooking under my shirt and lifting it. All of a sudden, the rough pad of his finger is pressed against my bare skin. I shiver, zips of awareness racing through my entire body. "But back then, when a traveler showed up, claiming to be from a different era, he was dismissed as crazy. It's been only in the last ten years, since time travel's been accepted as a possibility, that Asynchronicity was also recognized as a medical condition. There are a few reported cases in the European States, but Callie's our first patient in

North Amerie."

His thumb keeps moving; the zips keep shooting. Part of me never wants him to stop—and part of me wonders if he's deliberately trying to distract me. Is he telling me the entire truth, or are there parts he's continuing to hide?

I move back, and his hand falls from my waist. I don't know whether to cry or be relieved. "So how do I wake her up?"

"You can't. Or at least, we haven't been able to, not for lack of trying. You see, her body's here, at this fixed moment, but her mind floats through time, skipping from one period to the next, unable to distinguish what is real and now. We need to signal her, somehow, that this is the present, so that her mind knows where to land." Now that his hands are free, he holds them up, palms out. "That's the problem. Ten years have passed, and she's never been present in this time. So how is she supposed to recognize it?"

"But she sent me the vision," I whisper. "Of running the maze through the purple and green hallway. Did that corridor exist ten years ago?"

He shakes his head. "It was repainted last year. So you're right. The memory couldn't have come from a decade ago. Callie leaves this room twice a month, so that the medics can thoroughly examine her. She would've traveled along the exact path that you ran."

My pulse leaps. "That proves, doesn't it, that she's more aware of the present than you think?"

"I don't know," he says slowly. "Her eyes would have to be at least cracked open. She would've had to see the hallway and register it. Maybe it means her mind is starting to become more aware. But even then, it doesn't mean she recognizes the hallway as the present. She probably sent you that memory because it pops up the most often."

He pauses, as if he's not sure if he should continue. "Whatever the explanation, time's running out. Last week, she took a turn for the worse. With each day that passes, she gets weaker. Her hold on life gets more tenuous. She's been in a coma for ten years now. She can't hang on forever."

"No." I turn to my sister's body, wrapping my fingers on the railing. "I've only just found her. I'm not going to lose her again. Besides, she looks good to me. Not weak at all."

She's thin, but there's warmth to her cheeks and a glow to her skin, no doubt due to the sunlamp slung over the monitors. If I didn't know better, I could believe she was simply asleep.

Tanner comes up behind me, the quick exhalation of his breath caressing my neck. "You're right. She looks a lot better than she did yesterday. Maybe it's due to your physical proximity."

I can't breathe. It's like the air has turned to lead, and I'm trying to suck it up with a straw. Is Tanner right? Is Callie stronger because I'm here? More importantly, would she be stronger still if we resumed our natural roles and I were to send *her* a memory?

There's only one way to find out. I haven't exercised this muscle in years, but it's not something you forget, no matter how hard you try. I should know.

Hesitantly, I pick up her hand. It's so narrow, so limp. But warm. Alive. I sift through my memories and choose one from earlier this year, when my mom and I made dinner on the anniversary of Callie's supposed death. We hand-cooked a meal, even though neither of us has a fraction of her Manual Cooking talent. The eggplant Parmesan was too soggy, the chocolate cake too dense. Still, we lit a flame and remembered Callie until the candle burned down to a stub.

I send this memory to her now, pouring it into the psychic threads that still connect us. Into the bond that won't be severed, no matter how much time has passed. Even if I was led to believe that it was merely wishful thinking.

I pour the memory into my hand connecting hers, my body touching her body, my heart intertwining with her heart.

Come back to me, Callie. Oh please, come back.

I hold my breath, waiting and searching for the click. The same click I used to feel years ago, whenever Callie opened a message from me. It's like the memories I sent hovered in another dimension, waiting to be received. When she got the memory, the communication was complete. The universe clicked into place.

Come on. Where are you, click? I count down the seconds. One, two...I know it's here. It's got to be...seven, eight... any moment now...eleven, twelve...Oh Fates, the click's not coming. It didn't work...

And then I feel it. *Click.*

She jerks once, twice. Static erupts from the monitors hooked up to her body. A beeping fills the room.

My heart stops. It hangs in my chest, suspended, the beats superseded by the *beep-beep-beep* of the monitor. The noise surrounds me, swelling in my ears, filling the entire cavern of a room. Loud. Insistent. Accusing.

Oh dear Fates. Did I just kill my sister?

16

anner pushes past me to the computer terminal. He holds up his hands, and a keyball jumps under his fingers. A few swipes later, and mercifully, the noise—the recriminations—stops. "What did you do?"

"Nothing." I swallow hard. "I sent her a memory. I thought it would strengthen our connection." Acid climbs in my throat. "Did I…hurt her?"

His fingers skim over the keyball, and holo-reports appear in the air, one after the other, covered with numbers and notations I don't understand.

He sucks in his breath and sweeps his hand in a wide arc, clearing the reports from the air. The documents pop up again, slower this time.

I step closer to him. "Tanner? What do the reports say?"

He turns to me, his eyes glazed. "Her vitals have entered the safe zone. Her heart rate, oxygen levels, blood pressure—none of her numbers have been this strong since the first year of her coma." He puffs out a breath. "You haven't hurt her, Jessa. Quite the opposite. I think you may have just saved her life."

I stare at him, not willing to talk, hardly daring to move, in case the moment falls apart like a dream.

The security system sounds—short, staccato pings that pierce the air—and a broad figure strides into the room. Down the center column, and then along the final row toward us.

It's him. The scientist. The one who watched my chest move but didn't turn me in. What was his name? Something with a *P*. Oh, yes. Preston.

So that's why he stared at me in the hallway for so long. He must've recognized my resemblance to my sister.

"What's going on?" He peers at Callie and takes Tanner's place in front of the terminal. "Aren't you supposed to be some kind of genius, Callahan? Our hope for the future? I can't leave you alone for five minutes! What did you do to her?"

"*I* didn't do anything," Tanner says.

Preston turns slowly, as if just realizing I'm here. "You." His eyes widen and he takes a step backward, crashing into a machine. "How did you get in here?"

"I let her in." Tanner squares his shoulders, and I wait for him to tell this man, who is obviously his boss, that I bribed him, that I threatened him with a stun gun. Anything, really, to show he acted under coercion.

"It's not right she doesn't know," he continues, and I blink. What is he doing? "This is her sister, her twin. She believed Callie was dead all these years. That's not okay. Tell Dresden if you want. Take away my lab and experiments. I don't care. Jessa deserves to know the truth."

My heart beats funny, and my face feels hot. He's taking the fall for me. But why?

Preston looks from me to Tanner. The air shivers, just like the moment when he saw me breathing in the stretcher. The moment of indecision. Will he report us or let our transgression pass?

The seconds tick by, and he makes no move to call Dresden. He doesn't even seem interested in continuing to lecture. Instead, he stares at me as if I'm a creature dredged from a black hole.

"Are you going to tell Dresden?" Tanner asks hesitantly.

"I don't see how it's any of her business. My experiments, my responsibility."

I breathe a sigh of relief, but I can't relax. Not yet.

Preston's eyes are still glued to me. I don't think he's even blinked. "How did you find this place? How did you know she was here?"

There's no reason to hide the truth. If he's going to turn me in, he already has ample ammunition. "Callie sent me a vision. A maze that led me to this place."

Briefly, I explain how I was infected and developed the same abilities as the lab mice. I tell him how I found Callie and sent her a message, which made the machines start beeping.

Preston blinks at me for several seconds. And then he lurches to the computer terminal. "This is amazing," he mutters. "We were so wrong, so completely off base. I can't believe I didn't see it before."

"See what?" I glance at Tanner. He shrugs, as if to say he doesn't know, either.

"Callie has been more or less stable for ten years," Preston says. "And then last week, her condition worsened. Her vitals flirted at the edge of the red zone, and her brain waves became erratic, irregular. We didn't know what it meant, but we assumed it couldn't be anything good."

He drums his fingers against his cheek. "Now, it sounds like Callie's memories have been firing all along, and when you became a Receiver, one of those memories found a home. Her brain started to wake up—that's what accounts for the irregularity. Her body went haywire because it was searching, searching, searching for a hold, and it couldn't find one. Here, take a look."

He presses some buttons on the keyball. Images of Callie's brain appear in the air, pictures that must've been taken from the sensors on her scalp. Dots of lights in varying colors and brightness pulse in different lobes. He zooms out, and I see a vertical figure standing next to Callie's horizontal body. Me. A string of light connects us, ropes upon ropes of overlapping braids, twisted together to form our bond.

My mouth drops. Every doubt I've ever had of our psychic link evaporates. There it is, right in front of my eyes. A visual manifestation of our connection.

"You see what I'm seeing?" he asks Tanner.

Tanner's breathing is shallow. "We never guessed it could happen this way. We thought the experiment failed."

"What experiment?" I ask. "What are you talking about?"

"Before now, Callie's mind was tied to this time by a mere thread." Preston wipes away the holograms. "She was connected with the present only because her body was in it. Over the years, as her mind zoomed off to different times, the thread became more and more frail. Then you came here." His voice is full of awe and something else. Something that sounds very much like fear. "And her mind found something to latch onto."

My mouth goes dry. "What do you mean?"

"You are her connection to this time. She's twined her consciousness with yours, and the link between the two of you is stronger than the fragile bond she had with her body. By sending her that memory, you woke up her Receiver abilities, powers that have laid dormant inside her for a decade."

"I don't understand." My mind whirls, trying to piece it all together. "If I could become her link with the present, why didn't you ask me to send her a memory years ago?"

"Oh, believe me, we wanted to. But we had received reports, in no uncertain terms, that you had tried and failed."

It's true. I remember sitting on a rock in the woods, feeling as lost as a balloon floating away in the sky. I had tried to send Callie a message, and there was nothing. No click. An emptiness that took my breath away, a blankness that stabbed me right in the chest. Because there was supposed to be *something*.

I admitted, then, that Angela was right. The bond I thought I still felt was nothing more than wishful thinking.

I continued believing that until just now.

"You held her hand while sending the memory," Tanner muses. "Maybe it's the touching that made the difference."

"Of course." Preston nods briskly. "Touching always amplifies the psychic connection between two people."

I swallow hard. "So now that Callie and I are reconnected, what's next?"

"You'll send her a memory every day, and we'll hope. Your bond will get stronger with every memory you send. Maybe someday, the bond will be strong enough that Callie will be able to follow the thread back to the present and wake up."

"What are we waiting for?" I blurt. "I'll just send her a thousand messages right now."

"That's the worst thing you could do," Preston says. "A new psychic connection is like a newborn baby. It must be nurtured. You have to allow it to grow on its own terms. You can't make a baby grow any faster by stuffing it with food, and by the same token, you risk endangering the bond by feeding it too much. At the same time, you have to nourish the connection daily."

He looks at Callie's face and then lifts his eyes to mine. "I cannot impress this upon you enough. You are Callie's only connection to this time. The only thread keeping her mind from flying into oblivion. You must come here every day. You must send her a new memory every day. Otherwise, the connection will wither and fade. And if that breaks, Callie will be gone from us forever."

I nod, my heart roaring in my ears. "Anything. I'll do whatever it takes to keep Callie safe."

17

I run toward the Harmony compound, my feet a blur underneath me. I feel like I'm flying, and I don't even have my hoverboard. Callie, here and not dead. Vitals in the safe zone. And maybe, just maybe, she'll wake up and come back to me someday.

It's just as likely she won't.

My heart contracts so abruptly it hurts. I can't tell what I'm feeling anymore. Joy or sorrow. Anxiety or anticipation. I'm tiptoeing along the razor's edge of hope; one wrong step in either direction and I'll fall on the blade again. Only this time, it will be worse. Losing Callie once sliced my heart into ribbons. If I have to mourn her a second time? The ribbons will be fed through a meat grinder, and I don't know if I'll recognize what comes out the other side.

I take a breath and let it out slowly. Let's hope I won't have to try.

As I approach the compound, I see a lone figure sitting on the ten-foot wall, his long legs dangling against the stucco. The sky has turned purple with the dusk, and a spotlight shines on my best friend's oversize feet, leaving the rest of him in shadows.

I smile. Two years ago, Angela ordered the branches of the nearby trees trimmed, but that didn't stop Ryder and me. Very little does.

I break into a run, getting in four nice strides before I strike the wall waist-high with my foot and vault myself up. I grab the ledge with both hands, scrabbling my legs beneath me until I get a sneaker on the wall. From there, it's a simple matter of hauling myself up.

It took me six months to learn this trick. And I'm still pretty impressed with myself.

"I think I'm ready to try a twelve-foot wall," I pant.

But Ryder doesn't grin at me, and he doesn't make fun of my form. I plop onto the wall facing him, my legs hanging on either side.

"Where have you been?" He swings his leg around so that he's facing me, too. The moonlight glints off his goggles, but he's close enough that I can see the worry lines in his forehead.

"You'll never believe it," I burst out. "It wasn't Olivia sending me that message after all. It was my sister! She's alive!"

With run-together words, punctuated by gasps, I tell him the entire story. Ryder's eyes widen, and he grips the wall as though he might be in danger of sliding off.

"I remember her," he says wonderingly. "When I was a kid. She came to Harmony and stayed with us. I didn't know her well, but I thought she had a pretty smile. I can't believe she's still alive."

I kick my feet against the wall. "I can't wait to tell everybody. They're going to go crazy."

"Maybe Mikey will even forget to be mad."

My feet stop mid-swing. "Mad? Why is he mad?"

"I'm sorry, Jessa. I didn't know where you were. I didn't

know if you were hurt or in danger." He ducks his head. "I had to tell Mikey everything."

Aw, fike. We deliberately disobeyed him. He warned us, and we broke into the lower floors of TechRA anyway. Mikey's not going to be happy.

"He's convinced you're a bad influence on me," Ryder says quietly. "I'm grounded from seeing or talking to you for the next month. This is to be our last communication. I'm under strict instructions to bring you to the house as soon as you show up. Your mom's waiting there with Mikey and Angela."

I barely hear his last sentence. Not see or talk to my best friend for a month? I've never gone so long without Ryder's friendship before. What am I going to do?

All of a sudden, his wrist com flashes white and then red, bright alternating lights that can't be ignored. I shield my face, while he lifts his wrist to shut down the alarm. "That must be Mikey now."

I check my own com unit. I turned it off when I climbed into the stretcher and forgot to switch it back on. The dial spins, counting off the messages with each rotation and emitting the corresponding light. Violet, blue, green, yellow, orange, red.

My stomach sinks to my toes. Someone's left me six messages, each with an escalating level of priority. From violet — "where are you?" — to red — "even if your country is under attack, hear me *now*."

"Which message should we listen to first?" I ask weakly.

"Doesn't matter." Ryder squints at his com. "Same ID code. The security vids outside the compound must've gotten a picture of us."

He hits play, and Mikey's voice fills the sky: "I can see you two on the wall. If Jessa isn't here in the next two minutes, I will personally take apart both your hoverboards and send them on the next trash shipment to space."

I wince. "I guess he's not a fan of our hoverboards?"

Ryder sighs. He flips on the light on his wrist com and holds it under his chin. "Take a look at this handsome face, Jessa. There's no telling when you'll see it again."

The wave of Mikey's anger almost knocks me over as soon as I enter the house. I wish Ryder were still with me. We always faced Mikey's disappointment together, always received our punishments together, from the time we lived in the wilderness. Somehow, scaling fish by the bushel was easier when Ryder was by my side, making fun of my technique or flinging fish guts at me.

But he's not here. And he won't be for the next month.

"This is not a game." Mikey slams his foot down as I approach, and a red and yellow splotch appears on the pressure-sensitive floor. Behind him, the tile shows blue and green footprints walking between the couch and the wall screen, where my mom and Angela are standing. "I made it clear you were no longer to snoop around TechRA, and you did what you wanted the first chance you got. I don't know how else to get through to you."

"These agencies are doing things they don't want the public to know about." Angela bounces Remi in her arms. "It's not safe."

"You don't know what you're doing." Both my mother's voice and expression are pinched. "You're going to mess everything up." *Just like always*, I could've added for her.

The voices come at me from every direction, the concern and anger and disappointment blending together, and I let their words wash over me. In a moment, everyone's world will tilt off its axis. All because of a girl who used to be at the center of all our lives. And then wasn't.

"I saw Callie," I blurt out. "She's not dead like we thought. She's in a coma—she's been in a coma these last ten years—and she's being kept in one of the basement levels of TechRA."

It is so quiet you could hear a bot reboot. My mother turns pale, the color of a chicken before it goes into the Meal Assembler. Her hand moves to her throat, kneading and squeezing, as if she can massage out the words that are stuck there.

My insides twist. "She's back, Mom. Actually, she never left us. She's been here all along. She might...come back to us still."

My mother's eyes well up. "I hoped she was still alive. Something...in the past...made me believe she might be. But as the years passed, and there was no sign of her, I began to lose hope. My little girl...my baby. How is this possible?"

For the second time in half an hour, I repeat the story. You'd think I would get bored of the retelling, but I could talk about this—I could talk about Callie—for the rest of the night. Maybe even the rest of the week.

My mother's openly crying now, and she moves forward and hugs me, in a way she hasn't since I came back to civilization. I close my eyes, feeling the warmth of her embrace, the solidity of her arms and chest. This is how it would feel if she loved me. This is how it would be if we were a true family.

"Your true daughter, your firstborn," I murmur. "The one you actually love."

I don't know why I say it. Swear to Fates, it just slips out. I want to snatch the words from the air, stuff them back in.

But it's too late. She drops her arms and backs away from me. I reach out, but before I can touch her, she cries out and runs from the room. Blood-red footprints decorate the floor in her wake.

Stupid, stupid, stupid. What is wrong with me? This is the closest I've felt to my mom in years. Why did I have to ruin the moment with my insecurities?

Angela squeezes my hand. Her eyes are red, and she looks like she's been crying herself. "She's emotional, and who can blame her? I can only imagine how I would feel if my daughter were returned to me." She drops a kiss on Remi's head. "Don't you worry. I'll go talk to her. She may want to be alone now, but in a few minutes, she'll be glad for the company."

Shooting me a sympathetic glance, she and Remi leave the room.

And then it's just Mikey and me.

Except he won't look at me. His eyes flit from the magnificent mountains on the wall screens to the retractable coffee table to the water-filled massage chair. Anywhere but at me.

He's not crying, either. In fact, he doesn't even look surprised.

All of a sudden, I remember him coming to my room, in the early days after we relocated to Eden City.

"Callie's been gone six years, and you're still grieving her," he said. "It might give you closure if you resurrected your bond and sent her some memories."

"I already tried." I hugged a pillow to my chest. "Almost every day the first month we escaped, and nearly every week since. It doesn't work anymore. There's no click."

"Try again," he suggested. "For me. Try it one more time, right now."

Because I never had a father, because I was barely speaking to my mother, because I loved him as much as I've ever loved any parent, I obeyed. Nothing happened.

Looking almost as disappointed as I felt, Mikey left the room, and I pushed the incident out of my mind.

Until now.

Mikey works at TechRA. In fact, he's one of their head scientists. Is it possible that he's known this entire time?

"Did you know, Mikey?" I whisper. "Did you know my sister was still alive?"

He finally meets my eyes. And then he nods.

My knees go weak, and the room spins around me. I trusted him. He taught me to hunt, even though I didn't talk. When we came back to civilization, he let me live with his family in the cottage behind their house, when my mother refused to move to the compound. He was like the father I never had.

"You lied to me," I say.

"You have to understand," he pleads. "Every day, I wanted to tell you. I wished every single day that her condition would improve, so that I could come home and tell you the good news. But what good would it have done for me to tell you that Callie was in a coma? It would've killed you to see her lying there, day after day, and not be able to do anything to help her."

"I could've sat by her side. Held her hand and sent her my memories."

"I was trying to protect you." He walks to the water recliner and flops onto it, covering his eyes with one hand. "Both you and Logan. I had no guarantee she would ever wake up. And I didn't want the two of you to bury yourselves in that room until you might as well be dead." He lifts his hand, and it's like he's pulled back a curtain. As blank as his eyes were before, they're full now. Of a long-ago wound that's never healed. Of a pain so deep it's carried in his soul. "Turns out, I was right. She took a turn for the worst last week, and even I had to admit that my hope was foolish. It's only a matter of time before she leaves us once again."

"No, you're wrong, Mikey." I shake my head. "Today, her vitals entered the safe zone after I sent just one memory. All I had to do was touch her for the transmission to work. Preston thinks the only reason her brain was behaving erratically was because it had woken up and couldn't find a hold. But now that she's latched onto me, she's stable. More stable than she's been since the first year of her coma."

"Oh, thank the Fates." He closes his eyes briefly and then opens them. "You can't tell Logan. You have to promise me that."

"What? Why not? You just said you were waiting for good news before you told us. This qualifies as good news."

"Normally, I'd agree with you," he says quietly. "But when I believed we were going to lose Callie for good, Angela and I redoubled our efforts. We took turns talking to Logan every night; we invited him and Ainsley out to dinner at a Manual Cooking establishment. Angela even let Ainsley play with Remi, so that Logan could see what a good mother she could be. And then, a couple days ago, we finally seemed to get through to him. After all these years, my brother is finally on the verge of moving on. Of being happy."

"He deserves to know—"

"He deserves to live," Mikey says, his eyes blazing. "I'm glad Callie's gotten a new hold on life. I want her to wake up nearly as much as you do. But that may still never happen."

"Logan has a right to know," I say fiercely. "A right to live his own life."

"I can't let him do that! I can't lose him, too."

I stop, not sure I heard him correctly. "What do you mean? Who else have you lost?"

He pushes against the floor with his foot, and the recliner rocks beneath him. For a moment, I don't think he's going to answer. And then he sits up and rests his elbows on his knees.

"Most people know I was the first member of Harmony," he says. "What they don't know was there wasn't even a Harmony back then. I was just a sixteen-year-old kid who managed to escape from the TechRA labs. I didn't go into the woods, but up into the mountains, where a primitive community lived, one that had been together since the pre-Boom era."

A smile ghosts across his lips. "The mountain people thought I was strange, with my pockets full of gadgets and my talk of psychic powers, but they were kind and they accepted me. There was a woman there. Sierra. Just as I arrived, her little boy, Jonas, was about to step on some sharp rocks, and she swept him up just in time. He laughed, not understanding the danger he was in, and she covered his face with kisses. I fell in love with both of them in an instant. Sierra was the sister I never had, and Jonas was the nephew I never knew I wanted."

His words are quiet and halting, as though he's not used to the rhythms of this story. "I'd been there only a couple months when tragedy struck. A snake slithered into their tent and bit Jonas. The poison spread fast. By morning, he was dead."

I gasp, bringing my hand to my lips. But he continues as though he doesn't hear.

"We buried him under a mound of loose rocks." He looks at the wall screen, and I know he's not seeing the rotating images of the majestic snowcaps. He's seeing the mountains he knew. The ones where he lived and loved. "Sometimes, I wonder if it would've made a difference if I hadn't piled on so many rocks. Other times, I know this is my Fixed. The event that defines my life so thoroughly it would be the same in every world."

"What happened?" I whisper.

"An alarm sounded that night. A rockslide was coming, and we had to clear out. There should've been plenty of time.

But when the supplies were loaded into the wagon, I realized Sierra was missing. I found her at the rocks." His voice breaks and he drops his face, his shoulders shaking, shaking, shaking.

My mouth falls. Is Mikey…crying? The leader of our community. The man who makes the toughest decisions without flinching. I've never seen him teary before, much less sobbing.

I fall to my knees and inch closer to him.

"She was trying to dig Jonas out. Oh Fates, Jessa, she wouldn't leave him. I pleaded with her, I begged. I even lifted her and tried to drag her away. She fought me like a wild animal, and then she manacled herself to a tree. She said if Jonas couldn't leave our campsite, then she wouldn't, either. And then the rumbling started." He looks up, then, his eyes as dull and black as coals. "Leaving her was the hardest thing I've ever done." His voice breaks. "But if I hadn't, I would've been buried there with her and Jonas. My sister. My nephew. They weren't my first family, nor my last. But not a day goes by when I don't think of them."

He stands, scrubbing a hand down his face. Erasing his tears and the moment much like he clears holo-docs from the air — with a single swipe. "If I had to do it again, I would make the same decision, every time. I will always choose life over death. And that's why you aren't going to tell Logan about Callie. Because I won't have him burying himself in the past when he could be living in the present."

I don't speak. I can't. I'm sorry for Mikey's tragedy, but Logan would want to know. Just like me.

"Would you want him to end up like your mom?" Mikey continues. "Holding onto what could've been. Pining for someone who may never come back. She hasn't been able to let go, and that's caused her to make decisions that have hurt the people around her. That have hurt you."

I freeze. My knees become so weak I'm afraid they're going to spill on the floor. Would I wish my mother's fate on Logan? Would I wish *my* fate on Logan's future children? I imagine a future where Logan is married, where he has kids — but he's unable to give his family his full heart because he's hung up on a girl who lies in a coma.

"Give it a few weeks. Your connection with Callie is so new, we don't know what will become of it." His gaze pins me against the wall screens, up high on a precipice with no rope and no water. "What do you say, Jessa? If you care about Logan at all, promise you won't tell him. At least not yet."

It's not my place to decide. But Mikcy's right. I can't bear to think of Logan winding up like my mom. I can't bear to think of his children winding up like me.

Besides, what can a few weeks hurt? He's already waited ten years to learn the truth.

"I promise," I say. And hope to the Fates above that I've made the right choice.

18

manage to avoid Logan for the next seven days. I focus my energies instead on my clandestine visits to Callie, on the memories I send into her mind. I choose only the good ones. Like the moment I returned from the wilderness and saw my mother for the first time. I barreled down the hall and took a running leap into her arms. She was laughing and smiling and crying, all at the same time, and I was certain I had never seen anyone so beautiful in my entire life.

Like my first date with a boy. It was the anniversary of the Underground's truce with ComA, and he took me to dinner at a Meal Assembler café. I chose a café that served different varieties of tartare, thinking it sounded sophisticated. My dinner turned out to be a mound of raw beef—with a raw egg on top. I tried to eat it, I really did. But the texture was too much for me, and when I looked up, I saw that my date had hidden half of his dinner under a lettuce leaf, too.

Like the time I dove off the cliff behind the TechRA building into the roaring river below. Ryder and I inspected the area carefully, and we dipped a chain in the water to measure the depth. I even brought along a first aid kit. The most thrilling part was the jump itself. I stood erect at the edge of the cliff, my knees bent and my arms overhead. I swept my arms down and out, driving forward with my legs. Gravity pulled me into a vertical position, the wind rushing along my body, and I felt for one infinitesimal moment that I was with Callie once again.

I send all of these memories and more, and my sister's vitals improve with each one. The memories distract me from the needle that Tanner plunged into my arm, drawing a vial of my blood. They distract me from the fact that my mom's retreated further into herself and our relationship is more strained than ever, in spite of the fact that she accompanies me on every other visit to see Callie. The memories distract me from my promise to Mikey.

But at the end of the week, the first person I see when I return to the compound from a visit to the TechRA building is Logan.

And he's not alone.

In the long straightaway running through the middle of our compound, a woman balances on a board hovering a few inches off the ground. Logan has a hand on her hip, steadying her, while he gestures in the air with his other hand. She leans over to kiss his cheek—which sends the board shooting out from underneath her. She tumbles into his arms, and they both fall to the ground, a tangle of limbs.

I dislike her on sight.

Logan's eyes are lit with laughter. He looks...happy. Oh Fates, I want him happy. There was a time I would've given up all my safety gear if only he would snicker at one of my jokes.

But now, seeing him with this girl, while knowing Callie is still alive, feels like a stake through my heart.

Logan glances up and waves. I wave back, but I don't go

over to them. I can't. I'm just not up to meeting my sister's replacement right now.

Logan says something to his date, and then he jogs over and gives me a big hug. "Hey, there. How's my favorite girl?"

"Okay." I shrug. "Keeping busy, you know, with school and all." Not a lie, but not the whole truth, either.

"I'm glad you're here." We walk down the straightaway. The concrete is gray and smooth, and interlocking tracks of magnets lay underneath it. I'm wearing my hovershoes, with flecks of metal mixed into the soles, and each step fuses me briefly to the ground, before I break the suction with my next step.

"I've been thinking about what you and Angela said," he says, shortening his stride to match mine. "And you're right. My memory's not much proof that Callie's still alive." He pauses, and I know he's come to a big decision. One I'm not going to like, even though I encouraged it myself a couple of weeks ago. "I think…it's time to start living again. I like Ainsley. I've known her for a long time, and she has a kindness in her, an inherent goodness you can't fake."

We walk a few more paces. Step, stick, wrench out. Step, stick, wrench out. A regular rhythm, but not a comfortable one. Kinda like my heart. Kinda like my life.

"I will never forget Callie, and I will never stop loving her," he bursts out. "But she isn't here anymore, and she hasn't been for a very long time. I think she'd want this for me."

"Of course she would." I study my high-top sneakers, the silver laces, the special soles that help me stick a landing. That's Callie. That's always been Callie, thinking of others first.

He takes a deep breath. "I'd like to have your blessing to be with Ainsley."

"Wha—?" Shock cuts the word in half. "Logan, don't be ridiculous. You don't need my blessing for anything."

"I don't need it. I would like to have it. You're the closest thing I have to Callie herself. It would mean something if you approved." His voice drops. "It would mean that Callie would've approved, too."

I fight to relax the muscles around my eyes and mouth. *Oh, Logan. She's not in another realm. She's lying here, only a few miles from where we're standing. You could be holding her hand in thirty minutes. All you'd have to do is go to your brother. All I'd have to do is tell the truth.*

But the infinite sky above me is the same one that covered Jonas. It heard the escalating rumble of the rocks, it smelled the dust kicked up by the horse's hooves. It understands the dangers of loving someone too much and for too long. And now that Mikey's told me his story, it's become part of my life, too. I can't forget it any more than my arms and legs. I can't let Logan turn into my mom, not if there's something I can do about it.

"What do you say, Jessa? Do I have your blessing?" He sounds so sincere, so earnest. So much like the brother I never had, so much like the sister I had for too short a time. In a way, he's both those things for me—brother and sister. Maybe even parent, too.

I grab my temples. The sun blinds me, and my head spins with all this endless blue. I don't know what to say. I don't know what to do. Who is right? What is wrong? What would Callie do?

My breath comes faster and faster. I see spots in my vision, and my fingers begin to tingle. "Sure, Logan," I blurt out before I hyperventilate or faint. "Whatever you want. Of course you have my blessing."

It is the coward's way out. I have not so much made a decision as delayed it. But it's like what Mikey said. Give it a few weeks. There's no hurry.

In this case, time is on my side.

...

ogan goes back to Ainsley, and I walk along the wall of the compound, trying to clear my head. As I pass the gate, I catch a flash of black hair and a white lab coat over a thermal shirt and cargo pants.

I do an about-face and open the door. "Tanner, is that you? What are you doing here?"

He steps over the threshold, his eyes steady, his lips resting against each other. He's not frowning, but he's not smiling, either. "I offered to walk you home. You refused."

"So you followed me?" I ask, outraged.

"It's not like it was my choice," he says evenly. "Preston's orders. Now that we're asking you to come to TechRA every day, he feels responsible for you. Wants to make sure you get home safely."

Oh. I flush. That's sweet of Preston, even though I'm the last girl who needs an escort home. I lived in the wilderness for six years without a parent, and I've been getting myself around Eden City for the last four.

"Sorry I'm such a burden," I mutter, not looking at him.

He puts a finger under my chin and tilts it up, so that I'm looking into his eyes. They're dark and intense — and so damn-the-Fates inscrutable. Just once, I'd like to know what he's thinking.

"I never said you were a burden, Jessa."

For a moment, my heart stutters, suspended somewhere between beats. But he doesn't continue. He never said I was a burden, but he doesn't say I'm *not* one, either. He doesn't say he likes me or enjoys my company. Probably for one good reason. It's not true.

"Well, you've confirmed that I'm here, safe and sound. So

you can go now."

"Actually, I wouldn't mind having a tour of the compound." He looks over my shoulder, taking in the orderly rows of units with their shiny solar panels and the moving sidewalk that winds between them. "When I was here last time, Mikey met me at the gate at the crack of dawn, and he marched me straight to his house. Guess he didn't want anyone to see me."

I chew on my lip. On the one hand, I know exactly why Mikey took him straight home. The Harmony community doesn't allow in many outsiders, particularly scientists— Mikey's position notwithstanding. We may live in civilization now, but there's always been a clear "us" and "them."

On the other hand, Tanner was here to do Mikey a favor. To build a playpen for his daughter. It sucks that he was made to feel inferior—even if he is the most superior person I know.

What's more, I remember the look in his eyes when he found out I'd been withholding information from him. Information that might be able to salvage his experiments. He'd been pissed, sure. But there had also been a sliver of hurt, an edge of betrayal. I'm not that girl who thinks only about herself. Who offers to help others only when there's something in it for her.

At least I don't think I am. I may not be as selfless as Callie, but I'm not a terrible human being, either.

For some inexplicable reason, it kills me to think he might believe otherwise.

Unfortunately, I'm pretty sure that's exactly what he thinks. He's barely spoken to me all week—and when he did, it always consisted of polite civilities.

Except once.

Two days ago, we passed the cardinal-haired woman in the hallway, the one who helped me get into the elevator capsule. She twisted the data-chip ring on her finger and mouthed,

He's cute. Immediately, I lunged into Tanner, wrapping myself around him. His torso was solid and warm — and pressed against mine. My mouth went dry, and my heart fluttered in my chest like a butterfly caught in a cage. I lifted my eyes, and they locked with his gaze. We stared at each other for what seemed like forever — and then the woman giggled and walked away.

He raised one of his eyebrows.

"I…uh, tripped," I blurted out. "Sorry about that."

"If you wanted to grab me, all you had to do was ask," he said.

That was the first time he'd said anything personal to me all week. This is the second.

Without another word, I step to the side so that he can walk farther into the compound. Immediately, he zeroes in on Logan and Ainsley, still messing around with the hoverboard, and I know he must've seen my conversation with Logan.

"Who's that?" he asks curiously. "Your ex-boyfriend?"

"Fates, no." Why is he asking? Would he care if Logan were my ex? Would it matter if I were dating someone right now?

No, of course not, I tell myself sternly. I'm not his type, remember? And he's not mine. I'm not interested in scientists, even if they build playpens for sweet babies. Even if their hands are remarkably gentle when they comfort you after a crying fit. I'm not.

I don't think.

Aw, fike. This line of thinking isn't going to get me anywhere. "Logan's way too old for me," I say. "Besides, he's like my family. He was…my sister's boyfriend."

"Ah. I thought his name sounded familiar." He opens his mouth, as if to say more, and then snaps it shut again.

"It's not like he's forgotten about Callie," I say defensively. "I didn't tell him she was in a coma, and he's moving on. He's finally happy. I can't ruin that for him."

I turn to stomp away, but he catches my hand.

"Hey," he says softly. "There's no judgment here. I was just asking."

Our eyes meet. I still can't figure out a damn thing he's thinking, but for the first time since the mouse bit me, my stomach stops sloshing and my nerves become still. He makes me feel, in this one infinitesimal moment…not safe, exactly, but understood. And that's about as safe as I can feel in a world where Chairwoman Dresden has power.

"Slumming with scientists?" A voice intrudes my thoughts.

I look up. For the first time, I notice that passersby on the straightaway are shooting us—and, in particular, Tanner's white lab coat—dirty looks. The guy who spoke is a couple of years older than me. I don't know him well. He wasn't part of the original Harmony but is the son of a woman who was.

"Come on, Jessa. I expected better from you," the heckler continues.

I flush and pretend I don't hear him. And hope to Fates Tanner doesn't, either. "You sure you still want this tour?"

Tanner grins, and I realize that he has a dimple right in the middle of his chin. "Of course. Unless you're scared?"

"S-Scared?" I sputter. "Fates, no."

I get to decide with whom I spend my time. Not this heckler I barely know. If I want to hang out with a scientist, then I will.

To my surprise, I actually *do* want to hang out with Tanner.

Since Ryder's been grounded from seeing or talking to me, I've been a bit lost. Floating around my cottage, going from one room to another as though my best friend will magically appear. It would be nice to have company for the afternoon.

"Come on," I say. "I know the perfect place to begin our tour."

19

Halfway up the observation tower, Tanner's legs begin shaking. The tower is five stories tall—nowhere near the highest structure in Eden City. We have skyscrapers ten times that height. Difference is, we're usually inside the building, protected by steel and glass, instead of outside, clinging to a chain-link ladder that sways in the wind.

A particularly strong gust buffets us, and the ladder swings back and forth. Heights don't bother me—they never have—but even I have to pause a moment to swallow.

Above me, Tanner tilts his head skyward, either to pray to the Fates or to avoid looking down. Maybe both.

My lips curve. Okay, I *am* a terrible person. I really shouldn't be enjoying anything about his obvious discomfort. But it's not every day I get to see the great Tanner Callahan out of his element. Somehow, it makes him even hotter. His muscles are just as lean, his profile just as handsome. And yet, while I could push his attractiveness to the back of my mind before, now, my eyes are practically glued to the boy above me. I don't know if I could look away if I tried.

"You okay, Tanner?" I call.

"Fine." The verbal answer is quick and immediate; his physical response is not.

In fact, he stops climbing completely, gripping the rungs so tightly I can see his white knuckles from five feet below. The gust dies down, and the ladder steadies. Still, he doesn't move.

My amusement turns to guilt. I wanted to knock him down a few quanta, and I knew he didn't exactly love heights. At least, that's what I'd assumed when Ryder said he avoided the vert walls. But I didn't know he would be this paralyzed.

"We can go back down," I say. "It's no big deal. We'll start the tour somewhere else."

"I'm fine." He pants the words, as though the oxygen's thinner two and a half stories up.

"You don't sound fine."

"I am," he snaps, and I hear a glimmer of the old Tanner. Miraculously, he starts climbing again. Hand, foot, other hand, other foot. Somehow, he powers through the next two stories, and then we're at the top. Although not yet on a solid surface. A five-foot gap separates the ladder and the central platform.

"Um, Jessa?" He licks his lips twice. "How do we get to the platform?"

"We jump."

"Jump?" His mouth drops open. "What if we fall? Or worse?"

"What could be worse than falling?"

It's the wrong question because it makes him look down. Through the mess of spokes and slats to the concrete sidewalk five stories below. At the tiny, ant-like figures of Logan and his girlfriend, still playing around with the hoverboard. At soft-spoken Zed, walking through the compound with a bucket and a set of pre-Boom fishing poles. At the flurry of bots in front of an open truck, unloading prepackaged meals and transferring them to the transport tube.

Sweat breaks out on Tanner's forehead. "Please don't make me talk about what's worse than falling."

"Listen, we don't have to do this. We'll just go back down and—"

"We're already up here." He closes his eyes briefly. "I...I don't think I can brave the ladder for at least another hour."

My throat tickles. I slap a hand across my mouth, but it's too late. The laugh bursts out like a machine gun. "I'm sorry!" I gasp. "I'm not laughing at you, I promise. It's just..." *You're adorable when you're scared. Who would've guessed?*

"I remember the first time I climbed the tower," I say out loud. "I was nervous, too."

He narrows his eyes. "How old were you? Twelve?"

"Something like that." My lips vibrate, and I clamp them together. "Listen. The platform measures twenty feet by twenty feet. As you can see, there's nothing up here. Just an old telescope and a pile of ratty blankets. No one's used the tower in any official capacity for years. So you can't miss the platform, and you won't land on anything sharp, either. Easy as assembly pie."

He doesn't respond. The wind whistles across my ears, and two butterflies circle our heads and land on the far edge of the platform.

"I'll go first," I say. "You can jump into my arms. I'll catch you if you slip."

"You know, you're really not helping. I'm not a little kid."

"No," I say, my mouth quirking. "A little kid would've been across five minutes ago."

He looks pained, and I can't help it. My laugh comes roaring out again.

"Sure, laugh now. We'll see how funny you think this is when they're sprinkling my ashes along the river."

He takes a deep breath, mutters something about mutant babies of time, and then jumps. He crashes onto the platform, scaring away the butterflies.

I leap after him, ballerina-style. "That wasn't so bad, was it?"

"Show-off." He pulls his knees to his chest and tucks down his head. "Don't mind me. I'm just going to curl into a fetal position for a few minutes."

I sit cross-legged in front of him, patting him on the back. Partly because I feel guilty for making him come up here. And partly because I like him like this. When he shelves his ego for a few minutes and acts like a real person. "Who would've thought the great Tanner Callahan was afraid of heights?"

He lifts his head and pulls a water tube out of his shirt collar to take a few swallows. "Whoever said I was great?"

"You did. In everything you say and do. I mean, you even have holo-images of yourself playing across the inside of your locker!"

"That's not me," he says quietly. "That's my dad, when he was young. If you watch the slide longer, you would see my mom, too."

His dad? Oh.

All of a sudden, I remember the gossip about his parents being killed when he was young. Of course he would have a feed of them playing in his locker. Fike.

"I can't handle more than a few inches off the ground," he continues. "That's why I stick to circuit racing on my hoverboard."

"Since when?"

"Since the time I was six. My parents died in an accident, and I went to live at TechRA."

So the rumors are true. He did grow up as an orphan in the care of the scientists.

He offers the water tube to me. Normally, I don't share tubes with anyone, not even Ryder. The common cold is one of the few diseases the scientists haven't cured, and sniffling and coughing puts a crimp in my extreme lifestyle. But for some reason, I lean forward and take a sip.

"They…they made me afraid of heights," he continues.

I freeze, my lips still on the tube, the water just squirting into my mouth. "What did they do?" I whisper, even though a part of me already knows. The part that still wakes up screaming from my nightmares. The part that never left my six-year-old self's past behind.

"They strapped me to a chair and made me relive memories that weren't mine," he says. I've said these words. To Ryder and Angela. In my own head. These are my words, my experience, and he's taken them straight out of my soul. "Every last inch of me covered in cockroaches. Witnessing my parents' pod accident. And my personal favorite: walking on a tightrope over a ravine before plummeting to my death. Every day for six long months."

I feel like my lungs are in a vise. Dear Fates. That's why he's afraid of heights. And I made fun of him for it. What in Limbo is wrong with me? "I'm so sorry, Tanner. I endured their torture for a few days, and I've had nightmares about it ever since. I can't even imagine. Six whole months. And you were six years old…"

"It happened," he says stoically. "I survived, with the help of an angel who appeared in my life. I don't know who she was. Maybe a medical assistant or one of the FuMA employees. But she held me in her lap and told me none of this was my fault. She told me that as alone as I felt in that moment, one day I would be valued and loved. And I believed her."

My heart contracts until it's the size of a pebble. I never thought I'd meet anyone who could relate to my childhood.

And here, Tanner endured the same torture I did—except much, much worse.

No wonder I felt he understood me. Somehow, some way, he must've recognized the scars of his past in me.

Those few days formed my lifelong hatred of the scientists, but he had to continue living with them. He had no other choice. I didn't have my mom when I left civilization, but I had my adopted community. My adopted family. Logan, Mikey, Angela, and Ryder.

Tanner had nobody.

I lick my lips. "They made me live through those nightmares because they were trying to find out about future memory. Why did they torture you? Do you have some kind of psychic ability, too?"

"Nah," he says. "They were trying to make me answer a question I didn't understand. Explain a situation that was unexplainable. To this day, I still wouldn't be able to give them what they wanted."

There's something else here. Something he's not telling me. I lift my eyes to meet his, and I reach into the future—his future. The vision pours into me. The future Tanner grabs me and kisses me. Without warning, without hesitation. It is hot and searing and exquisite. And I like it. Oh, how I like it.

"No!" I fall out of the vision and scoot away from him, so far that I approach the edge of the platform. My pulse is thundering; my nerves are jumping. Oh, Fates. What's wrong with me? Is it because I don't want him to kiss me? Or because I want it too much?

His eyes turn watchful. "Come back here, Jessa. You're too close to the sky."

I look into the open space, fluffy with wads of cotton-ball clouds. I take a breath, hoping to inhale some of the sky's serenity. He doesn't know about the kiss. Why would he? In the vision, he acted impulsively, without premeditation. The desire to kiss me hasn't arisen in him yet. Maybe I can prevent it from cropping up altogether.

"Look, you don't want to kiss me," I babble, staying where I am. And hope I sound more reasonable than I feel. "It's only because we talked about kissing the other day. When you talk about something, you give it life. Make it real. Like an annoying song you can't get out of your head."

He creeps toward me, his eyes flicking between my face and the sky. "So you can't get the idea of kissing me out of your head?"

"I said it was annoying. Like a song. Not based on anything real."

He stops five feet from the edge of the platform. "So let me get this straight. You saw into the future and we kissed. Right?"

"Y-yes," I stutter, shocked that he guessed the truth so easily. "But it doesn't have to happen that way," I add quickly. "As my sister proved, we're in control of our own fate. We can make any future we wish."

"Unless this is our Fixed." His voice is low, rough. And yet, every syllable imprints into my memory forever. "Unless this kiss is so important, it happens in every one of our worlds."

"It's just a kiss. How can it be that important?"

His eyes glitter with the challenge. With one last look at the platform's edge, he crawls to me, slowly but steadily. "The path of our particular world might depend on this kiss. Would you risk our future just to be stubborn?"

And then, he's right in front of me. He rests his hands lightly on my back. They slide down to my waist, until his fingers brush against the strip of bare skin between my pants and top. I shiver, and my skin pebbles into a million goose bumps. He pulls me against him. So much of my body is touching his that I can't think, I can't breathe. All I can do is feel. His trembling breath. My hammering heart. His shaking hands—or hell, maybe that's me, vibrating against his touch.

Our lips are inches apart. Time blends together. You couldn't move me from this spot if the world were crashing down around us.

"I thought I wasn't your type," I whisper.

"You're not," he says. "But for the fate of our world, I'm willing to make the sacrifice."

And then, he closes the gap between us.

His lips tease mine, softly at first. Hesitantly. As though he's not at all certain his kiss is welcome. His mouth lingers, waiting for permission, and I feel the sweet ache all the way to my toes.

I kiss him back. I'm not entirely sure how this is done, but I move my mouth against his. I run my hands up his back, over his neck, and into his soft, silky hair. Am I doing this right? Does he like what I'm doing? Does he feel what I feel—

Oh. Dear. Fates. He's kissing me more assuredly now, and I didn't know. I didn't know it could be like this. He tastes like fresh mint. I'm flying down a ramp. My head's spinning in the air. I don't know which way is up.

This. The word lights up in my head, explodes at each of my nerve endings. This kiss. I've never felt anything like it. Every inch of my body is on fire. My heart's about to punch a hole through my chest.

A few minutes ago, I lived out the vision like it was the real thing. But it wasn't, and that makes all the difference in the world.

He eases me slowly onto my back. I feel the metal slats underneath me, separated by quarter-inch gaps. The air is tinged with moisture, on the verge of rain, and activity rumbles, long and low, far below us.

He shifts on top of me, and his weight is solid and welcome. The planes of his body press into me. Hard muscles. Soft clothes. Bristly jaw. So many textures. So unfamiliar, and yet so…overwhelming. Devastating. I'm not sure how I'll be able to sit up again.

Tanner Callahan thinks he's good at everything. Well, in this case, he is certainly, most definitely right.

And then, an alarm blares. I jerk in his arms. The sound is so loud and deafening that the platform turns inside out, upside down. I grab my ears and feel the noise deep in my bones.

"What. Is. That?" I shout to Tanner, but he can't hear me. I can't even hear myself. "Are we being invaded?"

He moves my hand and speaks directly into my ear. Or at least I think he does. I still can't hear anything other than the ear-splitting siren. And yet, he must have spoken, because the words appear in my head like a thought.

The alarm is from ComA. They have a big announcement.

And I know, from the grip of Tanner's fingers, that the announcement can't be good.

20

We descend the chain ladder as quickly as possible, given Tanner's phobia, and head to Mikey's house. My mom and I have made a deal to meet at the Russells' in case of an emergency. When Tanner and I arrive, she's already there, wearing an old sweatshirt of my dad's. Once upon a time, the sweatshirt might have been cozy and soft. Now, it is tattered, worn — sad, even. Kind of like our family.

Mikey and Ryder stand in front of the holo-screen, feet tapping, clearly impatient for ComA's big announcement.

I haven't seen my friend for a week, and I rush forward to give him a hug. But he only squeezes me briefly before looking over my shoulder at Tanner.

"What's he doing here?" he asks sharply.

"Tanner was making sure I got home okay from TechRA. And then the alarm sounded, so we came here." All right, so I might've skipped a few steps. A few touches and one really big kiss. If we'd been by ourselves, Ryder might have been able to pry it out of me. He is my best friend, after all. But we're not alone.

Angela rushes into the room, cradling a screaming Remi to her chest. "The alarm woke her up, and she won't stop crying. I tried to nurse her, but she was so upset, she wouldn't latch on."

As if understanding her words, Remi wails even louder, her little face turning bright red.

"Here." I reach for the baby. "Let me try to calm her down."

Angela hesitates a moment and then hands me her daughter.

Mimicking Angela's position, I slide one hand under Remi's bottom and the other behind her head, settling her against my shoulder. In the last six months, I've played countless games with her. Peekaboo, pat-an-assembly-cake, this little piggy went to the spaceship. But this is the first time I've tried to soothe her. Comforting a baby is strictly a mother's territory, but I'm hoping I can reach into her future and figure out what's wrong.

She squirms against me, finding my collarbone and gnawing. I suck in a breath. It doesn't hurt. Remi still has just gums instead of teeth. But this…this…tiny person is depending on me. I look down and count her eyelashes, each one black and thick but so small, so perfect. I've always adored Remi, but in that moment, I free-fall into love. Complete, boundless, gravity-free love.

Her cries slow, and then they stop altogether.

Shocked, my hands hiccup, and I almost drop her. "What happened? Is she okay?"

Angela brushes a finger through the fine down of Remi's hair. "Of course. You just made her feel safe enough to fall asleep."

I blink. "She's asleep? Already? But I haven't even reached into her future yet."

"She was just scared. All she needed was a little comfort

and a lot of love."

Tentatively, I move my hand from Remi's head and stroke her back. A feeling flashes across me for one searing instant. *I love you, dear heart. I will always protect you. I will go to the ends of time to keep you safe.* Just as quickly, the feeling disappears.

My mouth dries. My legs feel shaky, like I've just stepped off a simulation coaster. What was that? Is that how Angela feels all the time? The emotion is so intense, the love so consuming. How can she get anything else done?

I peek at my mom, hugging herself through her sweatshirt. Did she ever feel that way about me? Did Callie?

If so, then maybe I'm beginning to understand why my sister acted the way she did.

Before I can reflect further, the walls start flashing. Finally.

I pass the sleeping baby to Angela, careful not to wake her. She lays Remi in a portable crib, and the six of us drift in front of the screen.

It flickers, and then Chairwoman Dresden appears on the feed, standing at a podium in a public square, a crowd of people surrounding her. I can see the flyaway strands of her silver hair, the wrinkles that mar her chiseled cheekbones. She looks so lifelike she might as well be in our living area.

"Citizens of North Amerie," she begins, her voice low, controlled, and deceptively warm. "As you know, for the last decade, our world has been plagued by a crisis: our inability to invent future memory. We know this technology exists, because a lucky few of us still retain our memories from the future. Yet its discovery has proven elusive over the years.

"From the beginning, we knew that we were racing against time. With our worldwide partners in science, we have been working tirelessly to bring future memories back to our people. As a nation, we've fallen behind. While our competitors are forging ahead, we're wasting time reevaluating our loan structures, relearning our hiring policies, readjusting to a world where the future is not a guarantee. And with every day that passes, more memories fade. The recipients become foggier and more confused. Even those who seek to circumvent this loss by storing their memories in digital files have run into problems. The data gets corrupted or is 'accidentally' deleted. We in the administrative offices have seen this happen time and time again, and there are those who fear that if we don't discover this technology soon, future memory will disappear from our world altogether, and we will never catch up to our competitors."

She stops. Even though I know the pause is deliberate, even though she's obviously trying to heighten the suspense, it works. The hair stands up on my neck, and icicles climb my spine.

"We no longer need to indulge that fear." Her professional facade wavers, and for just a moment, she breaks into a gleeful smile. "Today, I am here to tell you that we have solved one of society's greatest ills. We will reinvigorate the allied nations of the world. We have discovered how to send memories back to the past. We have invented future memory!"

She raises her arms in a *V* of triumph, and thunderous applause fills the feed. Stomping, yelling, even crying. The noise wakes up Remi, and she adds her howls to the din.

My knees go weak. I collapse on the pressure-sensitive floor, sending streaks of red radiating from the impact. I can't believe this. I knew this day was coming—we all did—but I didn't think it would arrive so soon. I'd hoped it wouldn't happen in my lifetime.

I gulp at the air, but it leaks from my lungs as quickly as I fill it. My mother makes a small sound, and I meet her eyes. I don't even need telepathy to know what she's thinking.

Was Callie's sacrifice for nothing? Are we right back where we started?

"It will take time to get the infrastructure of future memory back into place," the chairwoman continues. "Luckily, many of the old protocols remain intact. Files that disappeared have miraculously reappeared. We aim to start facilitating the systematic receipt of future memory in two months' time."

She steeples her fingers, the image of serenity and control once again. "The time line is aggressive, but I will personally ensure that ComA puts forth every available resource to resurrect the Future Memory Agency. We are just as invested as you to return to a society that is efficient and productive, one that does not waste time on insecurities and what-ifs. We are just as eager to once again become a society where tomorrow is a given and today is worry-free!"

Once again, cheers break out. The chairwoman inclines her head and smiles as though she alone were responsible for the invention.

The feed shuts off. I look around the room. Ryder looks like he's spent too many hours fiddling with his machines. Tanner watches me intently. And Mikey. The leader of our community has paled to the color of a raw onion and teeters on his feet.

This was his life's goal. The entire reason the Underground came back to civilization. Mikey might've studied prosthetic limbs in his work for ComA, but his true purpose is to stop Dresden from achieving her vision of genocide. And the first step in stopping Dresden was preventing the invention of future memory. But now that it's happened, what do we do next?

I don't know how long we stand there, staring at each other. But then, a rock crashes through the window. I jump. Shards of glass sprinkle the floor like diamonds, and Angela picks up Remi and runs out of the room. My mother follows, presumably to help her find a secure spot for the baby. If there's anything secure in this world anymore.

Mikey picks up the flat rock and turns it over.

I gasp. A sewer rat is tied to the rock, a knife plunged into its round belly, drops of blood decorating its filthy gray fur. Three simple words march across the top of the rock.

Down with scientists.

"They blame me," Mikey says, his voice hollow. "I was supposed to protect them from this fate. I failed."

He walks to the window. I realize all of a sudden that the once peaceful night is now filled with shouts and people, chaos and anger.

Mikey rounds on Tanner. "You aren't safe here in the compound. The people are angry with me, but I'm one of them. You're the enemy. If they find you…"

"They already know he's here," I whisper, thinking about the glares from the passersby. The insults flung from the guy who heckled me. "They saw his white lab coat this afternoon when we entered the compound."

"You have to go, then." Mikey strides to an inside wall and slams his palm against the corner. The wall slides open, revealing the secret tunnel inside. Ryder and I have played in these tunnels for years, but I've never actually used one. Not for real. "Get him out of here, Jessa. Ryder and I will talk to the people. Settle them down before they do something they regret."

Footsteps stampede up the front porch, and heavy fists batter the doors. More glass breaks. Another rock lands in the middle of the floor.

"Go," Mikey whispers harshly. "I'll take care of this, but you need to leave. Both of you. You're associated with him now, Jessa. They'll think you're a traitor for cavorting with the enemy. I'm a scientist, too, but I've been their leader for longer. They'll give me a chance to explain myself before they attack. They won't be as forgiving if they find you."

Panic climbs my throat. Is he right? Am I one of them? A vision sprints across my mind. The one where my blobby handprint marks me as the chairwoman's assistant.

No. I will never be on her side. Never.

"I don't understand," I say weakly. "These are our friends — our community. They wouldn't hurt me."

Something crosses his eyes, something dark and ugly that suggests he's been here before. "Trust me, Jessa, you've never seen anything like a mob-fueled rage. These people have lost their minds to a riot. We have no idea what they'll do or not do. Go!"

We don't wait any longer. I grab Tanner's hand. We duck into the tunnel. And we run.

21

The tunnel leads to a metal pipe. We crawl along the cramped space on our hands and knees. A few inches of water, sludge, and who knows what else line the bottom, and the flashlight I attached to my forehead—one of the supplies we found at the mouth of the tunnel—cuts a swath in the darkness. Not that it matters. All I see is more tube, more water, and more sludge.

My arms ache, and my back hurts. With every forward motion, my palms sink into something wet and squishy, and the smell is almost unbearable. But I keep going. I keep crawling. If Mikey's right, Tanner and I do not want to be caught on the compound.

Above us, the ground rumbles, as though hundreds of feet are pounding across it. That doesn't make sense. We have only about fifty people living inside the compound. But people from outside Harmony must be joining the riot. Other Underground members and sympathizers. It's like a massive army is gathering. The thought makes me sway on my hands and knees. The Underground army. Mikey's army. I always feared that one day the Underground and ComA would declare war against each other. I guess that day's nearer than I thought.

"Jessa, you okay?" Tanner's voice echoes in the tube, and his hand closes briefly over my ankle. My skin is dirty, his fingers are probably dirtier, but the touch warms my heart and is enough to get me moving again.

"Only a little while longer," I say, sidestepping his question.

"Really? You can tell how far we've crawled?"

"No clue," I admit. "I was just trying to be encouraging."

He snorts, his fingers grazing my ankle again. A glow descends on me, dim and diffuse in the dark tunnel, but so warm that even the sludge and filth can't mar it. I could crawl forever, if he would touch me every few feet.

And then my hand slides out from beneath me, and my chest plops into the sludge, splattering drops all over my face.

Ew. I grit my teeth, wiping my face as best as I can.

You can do this, Jessa. You have no choice. With reserves I didn't know I had, I propel myself forward, knee after painstaking knee, until we reach an open crawl space.

A grate crosses over our heads, and the moon shines down on us. I switch off my flashlight, in case there's anyone outside the grate, and Tanner and I sag against the wall.

"Here." He lifts his shirt, flipping it inside out, and wets it with some water from his canteen—another piece of equipment we found in the tunnel. Cupping my chin, he carefully wipes my forehead, cheeks, and mouth.

His fingers accidentally brush against my lips, and we both go perfectly still. For a moment, all I can hear is the sound of ragged breathing. Mine or his, I can't tell. My heart pounds so hard I think it might break open my chest, and my whole world narrows down to his mouth inches away from mine.

The moment seems to stretch into eternity.

And then, he drops his shirt and backs away. "You look atrocious. And to think I kissed those lips before the siren interrupted us."

I flush. "You didn't seem to be putting up too much of a fight."

Even in the dim light, I can see his eyes watching me as if I'm just another specimen under his microscope. "You saw us kiss in the future. I wasn't about to defy Fate for something as meaningless as a kiss."

I blink. And blink again. He'd said almost the same thing right before he lowered his lips. But at the moment, I didn't think he actually meant it. "That was the only reason you kissed me?" I ask in a low voice. "Because you didn't want to send out ripples that would change our universe?"

He shrugs. "You never know how one small action might change the course of our future. If we hadn't kissed, who knows what state the world would be in now?"

"You can't seriously believe that."

"The future is a funny thing, Jessa," he says. "I saw exactly what your sister's action did to our universe. Let's just say I don't like messing with Fate without a good reason."

I rock back on my heels, my mind whirling. Everything he's saying is perfectly reasonable. If I'd stopped to think about it, I would've come to the same conclusion. And yet, and yet…I can't get over what he's ultimately implying. That he didn't want to kiss me.

He didn't want to kiss *me*.

When, in that moment, I felt like that was all I ever wanted.

Heat floods my body, followed by an icy flash of cold right to my core. It's stupid to feel hurt. It might even reach the level of moronic. Never once has he said he's interested in me. Quite the opposite, in fact. And if I'm dumb enough to have developed some sort of…feeling…for him, then that's my own damn fault.

I puff out a breath, annoyed at myself. *I will not be that girl*, I think fiercely. *The one who's going to worry about a boy when there's a mob after us. I won't.*

Gritting my teeth, I deliberately tilt my head toward the grate. It's quiet. No screams or shouts from outside. No rushing feet. Either the riot's died down or the people are all distracted elsewhere.

"We'll know once we've crossed under the walls of the compound because the pipe opens onto a river," I say, struggling to sound casual. As if the guy across from me didn't just reject me. "I'm guessing we're under the woods just south of the residences."

"Can we get out and walk?" he says, his even tone betraying no awareness of what he just did. Jerk.

I want to say yes. Oh Fates, do I want to. I wouldn't mind if I never touched a mud puddle again, and the sooner I get out of this tube—and away from Tanner—the better. But both my and his safety are at stake. And sometime during my week of visits to Callie, he stopped being my enemy. The guy might not be attracted to me, but he's become an ally of sorts. I certainly don't want him lynched by a mob. "Better not risk leaving the tube."

Before he can respond, I hear a hum, low and sustained. A few decibels louder than a vibration. For a moment, I think it's only my imagination, but then I look at Tanner. Under the layer of mud, he's gone pale. He hears it, too.

"That's the sound of a whisper-quiet machine," he says. "An invisible car, a perimeter force field, a blade to chop someone's head off."

Ah. Of course. "It's a stealth copter. Mikey acquired one for the compound when we moved back to civilization. We must be under the landing pad near the south wall. Which means we're close to the river. Really close."

This is our cue to leave. We need to dive back into the sludge and crawl our way to river water and safety.

Yet I don't move. Curiosity thrums through me—and a small part of me is grateful for the distraction. Mikey insisted on purchasing a stealth copter with the Underground's credits, but to my knowledge, it's never been used. He'd never get away with such a big loan these days, not with the financial system becoming tighter and tighter. At the height of future memory, getting a loan was as easy as assembly pie, if you had the right memory. Now that memories are fading—and therefore unreliable—it's almost unheard of to receive a loan that's more than a few months' credits.

So what stealth mission has this copter just run?

The moonlight becomes dimmer and dimmer, and then the copter lands with a thud, right above us. The crawl space goes black. I don't dare switch on my flashlight, but I reach out blindly and wrap my hands around the rungs of the ladder that leads up to the grate.

"I'm going to take a look," I whisper in Tanner's direction. "Stay here."

Without waiting for an answer, I clamber up the ladder. I reach the top and push aside the grate. Quietly, I hoist myself out of the hole and slither onto my stomach, my forearms scraping against the gravel and my head just brushing the underside of the copter.

Seconds later, Tanner's on the ground next to me.

What are you doing? I mouth at him, but it's too late to argue.

The hum shuts off, and the hatch door squeaks open. First one pair and then a second pair of heavy black boots land on the ground. The boots walk a few feet away from the copter, and I can just make out the shadowy figures of their owners.

By Eden City's standards, the first guy is tall, wide, and muscular. But the second man is arch-your-neck-to-the-sky huge. Two of me could fit across his shoulders. He must be pushing six and a half feet, and he carries a lumpy canvas sack over his shoulder as if it weighed nothing.

There's only one person I know who fits that description. Zed. One of Harmony's original occupants and a friend of Callie's. A big guy who saw a vision of his future self beating a girl—and ran into the wilderness in an attempt to avoid that particular future.

"How's she doing in there?" The first guy turns, and in the light of the moon, I recognize his red hair and freckles. Brayden. The guy I had a crush on when I first joined Harmony. He's much older than me, but he could read minds. I used to fantasize about growing up and marrying him so I would never have to say another word.

"Hasn't moved since we gave her the draught," Zed says. "Good thing, too. The screams were shredding my nerves."

That's when it sinks in what they're saying. Her? No way. Zed is a kind man, despite his size. He's quiet and steady, a person who gains the love and respect of everyone he meets. There's no chance he's a kidnapper.

But the evidence is right there before my eyes. I look at Tanner, my eyebrows trying to climb off my forehead. *There's a person in there*, I mouth. Or at least, I intend to mouth. It comes out more like a harsh breath, and I slap a hand over my lips.

Luckily, the two men are either too far away to hear or too preoccupied to notice.

Brayden runs a hand through his hair, spiking it up. "I really didn't like restraining her. I think we hurt her. You can't fake that kind of crying."

"Desperate times." Zed's voice is edged with fatigue, as

though he hasn't slept in a week. "I don't like this, either, but we all have to make sacrifices. Callie gave her life for the cause. This is the least we can do."

He adjusts the bundle across his shoulder, and they walk into the trees, presumably to the Underground cabin tucked near the landing pad. The cabin's used by Underground officials for board meetings, strategy sessions—and, apparently, middle-of-the-night kidnappings.

"Who do they have?" I ask Tanner as soon as they're swallowed by the night. "What are they going to do to her?"

"Someone like me," he says, his voice grim. "Another scientist. This is why Mikey wanted us gone. They have to punish somebody. They didn't find a victim at Mikey's, so they went and got her."

My stomach flips. "You mean they kidnapped her because of us?"

"Obviously, I don't know. But it seems that way."

A gust of wind blows under the copter, and I can suddenly feel each and every pebble pressing into my skin. This...this changes things. Oh, I wouldn't abandon her. No way. If I let Zed and Brayden take a prisoner, I would be no different than the scientists who tortured me. But this need for a scapegoat, any scapegoat, means I won't be able to circle back to get Mikey's help. There's no time.

I roll onto my side, so that I'm facing Tanner. "Listen. Just follow the tube and—"

"I know what you're going to say, so you can save your breath." He moves forward so that our noses are nearly touching. "I'm not crawling down that tube without you."

"I'm not leaving her."

"I understand that. What you don't understand is that I'm not leaving you."

I look into his eyes. Dark, discerning. So arrogant, so sure.

Once he makes a decision, he never second-guesses himself. I used to hate that about him—but now I'm beginning to see value in his confidence. Value in having someone like Tanner on my side. Even if I'm not his type.

"Okay, fine," I say. "Stick around if you want. Just don't get yourself killed."

22

The first moment I crawl from underneath the copter is the scariest. The moment when I'm out in the open, vulnerable. When I might be attacked by a person frenzy-whipped by the mob. When I'd make perfect target practice for anyone with a handful of electro-darts.

But nobody pops out of the bushes, and nobody shoots at me. I take a step, and then another, my pulse blending into one long beat.

The distance from the landing pad to the trees is approximately two hundred feet. It feels more like two miles. By the time we hit the woods, I'm panting like I just hoverboarded around the perimeter of the city.

"Where's the cabin?" Tanner squints at the dense woods ahead of us. "I don't see anything."

"That's because there're holographic spiders surrounding the perimeter," I say. "Projecting an image of the trees so that the cabin stays hidden. Walk another hundred feet, and you'll be able to see the cabin." I throw out my hand, hitting Tanner in the chest. "Five more steps, and the motion detectors will spot you."

"How do you know?" He swivels his head from left to right, as if to say every tree, rock, and bush looks identical in this place.

"I know about the cabin because Mikey's been recruiting Ryder and me to join his fight. And these woods?" I shrug. "This was my and Ryder's playground when we were kids. There's not an inch we're not familiar with."

I realize all of a sudden that my hand is still on his chest and snatch it away.

"There's no way around the motion detectors, not with our time constraints. I'm going to the front door."

His eyes dilate like a bot's. "Is that safe?"

"Mikey might be right about some Underground members getting carried away. But not Zed. I've known him since I was six. His broad back might look scary, but I know for a fact that it gives the best piggyback rides."

"Fine. I'm going with you."

"Zed will recognize you—"

"He won't." Tanner gestures to himself. "Look at me. I'm not wearing my lab coat, and I'm covered in filth. He'll just think I'm a regular guy. A friend of yours from school. Your boyfriend."

I freeze. "My boyfriend?"

He smiles slowly and turns me to face him. His hands remain on my shoulders, a tingling point of contact that sends waves of heat coursing through my body. "I'm sure we're good enough actors that we can be convincing, don't you think?"

"Let me get this straight," I say carefully. "You want us to pretend that we like each other, to flirt and touch and, hell, maybe even kiss, even if we don't actually feel that way?"

"I'm happy to practice now, if it will make you more comfortable." His smile broadens, and he slides his hands down my back, pulling me against him. Even now, it makes my heart beat a little faster. I kinda hate him for it.

I stare at his chest, the one I admired even before I knew it was him. The one — if I'm being honest — I still admire now. Tanner is hot. There's no denying that. But I need more than good looks in order to like a boy. He's already hurt my feelings once. I'm not going to let it happen again.

"Why would we want to do that?" I ask in a low voice. "So you can make a fool of me again?"

His hands still on my back. "Huh?"

I lift my eyes to his face. His brow is creased, and he looks genuinely puzzled. All of a sudden, I'm so mad that I'm trembling. "So you can string me along, and then laugh in my face when I think it's real?" I shake my head. "You don't get to do this, Tanner. I'm not playing these games with you. Everyone already thinks that the wrong sister died. Sorry if I don't willingly enter another situation that's just going to make me feel even more worthless."

"What?" he bites out. "Jessa, I never intended — "

I jerk out of his embrace. Backing away, I cover my ears with my hands. Whatever his excuses, I don't want to hear them.

I march straight through the motion detectors toward the first set of spiders. The log cabin will come into focus at any moment.

Not anymore. I don't need any more people in my life who consider me an inadequate substitute for the real thing. I've always been second best to Callie, and for the most part, I'm okay with that. Because she's first best in my life, too. I love her the most, too.

But just once since my sister died, I'd like somebody to care about me as much as I care about him or her. Just once, I'd like to look into someone's eyes other than Callie's — and know, without a doubt, that he or she believes my life is worth saving.

Maybe that will happen someday. And maybe it won't. But for now, I've got a girl to rescue.

A few minutes later, I press the button that will vibrate the floors of the cabin. Tanner has trailed after me to the door, but since I don't feel like talking to him, I keep my back turned away. I don't have to see him to feel his presence, though. His every movement, his every breath. It's like I've been cursed with my very own Tanner radar. Lucky me.

Clenching my jaw, I jam the button again, wrenching my mind back to the log cabin. This could go down one of two ways. Either Zed will clobber me over the head and drag me inside, true to Mikey's warnings. Or he'll shift his feet guiltily and pretend he hasn't kidnapped a girl.

I'm prepared for both, but betting my well-being—and Tanner's, the smug bastard—on the latter.

The door opens. Zed takes one look at me and falls into my arms, sobbing like I've brought the apocalypse.

My limbs turn to petrified wood. What happened? Only fifteen minutes have passed. In that short time, what could have turned a calm and controlled man into this blubbery mess?

Of their own volition, my eyes rise to meet Tanner's over Zed's back. *What in space?* he mouths.

I shake my head. I've never seen Zed cry before. Ever. It's as weird and awkward as the first time I realized my mom was fallible. When I finally admitted to myself that she was not always wise. Her decisions were not always selfless. She made mistakes, too. And maybe I never forgave her for it.

I regain control of my arms and wrap them around Zed.

But his back is too wide, and I only reach partway. "What's wrong, Zed? Talk to me."

"It's Eli," he gasps. "He's hurt."

My muscles turn to liquid. Eli. His gorgeous little boy. Curly brown hair like sprigs of parsley. Eyes as shiny as river rocks. Not quite four years old.

The last time I saw him, he bit into an orange slice, and his entire face lit up. "There's orange juice in here!" he exclaimed, as if he'd just discovered time travel.

"He and Laurel got caught in the riot," Zed says, his tone so heavy it pulls me to the floor. "She was carrying him, fighting her way through the crowd. And then, she was shoved from behind and fell. Eli rolled out of her arms. He only traveled a few feet, but she couldn't reach him, couldn't protect him with her body. The stampede was too great." He looks up, his eyes glinting. "They never even bothered to stop. By the time Laurel got to him, he had been trampled by Fates know how many feet."

My heart skips a lot of beats. Maybe an entire song. "Will he be…okay?"

Zed moves his big shoulders. "Don't know. They rushed him over to the intensive care at MedA."

He drops his face into his hands. I stand on my tiptoes, patting his back, and Brayden comes out the front door.

"Zed, my big man. You've got to pull yourself together." He gives the ginormous back a few slaps. "The draught's wearing off. She's stirring."

"Who's stirring?" Tanner asks. It's the first time he's spoken, and both Brayden and Zed turn to him.

The atmosphere shifts. The older guys straighten their spines, and an alertness leaps onto their faces, ready to fight, ready to defend.

"Who are you?" Brayden asks. Wars have been started

over less hostile tones.

I step in between them and back up until my shoulders hit Tanner's chest. "He's with me."

"You shouldn't be here, Jessa," Zed says in a shaky voice. "We've got Underground business. It doesn't concern you."

"I'm part of the Underground." I can feel Tanner's chest moving against my back. He wants to say something—his entire torso vibrates with the need. I take another step back, pressing harder into his body. "Mikey's been trying to get me more involved for years. You can tell me."

"Not a good idea." Brayden squints as though he's pushing his psychic tentacles at me, trying to read my mind.

I slam down my shields. I've blocked my own precognition for years; deflecting Brayden is assembly cake.

"For Fate's sake, it's just Jessa." The way Zed says my name, I can tell he still thinks of me as the little girl who showed up in Harmony a decade ago. The one who never talked and existed entirely in someone else's shadow—Logan's, for the most part, and then Ryder's, when he got older and bigger.

"Our world's rolling down a path we have to stop." Zed skips his eyes from my face to Tanner's and then back again. "Callie tried to derail this future, but the chairwoman somehow wrenched it back on track. We can't let her win, Jessa. We have to tell the people the truth. We need to show them exactly what our future will hold if we leave Chairwoman Dresden in charge."

He shifts in front of me. I don't wait. I dive around him and run into the cabin, tearing down the hall to the bedrooms in the back.

"Grab her!" Brayden shouts. "I'll get the boy!"

I don't pay attention. I have only seconds before they catch me, but that's all I need. I push open the first door. A bare room with seams in the floors and walls, where a bed and closet might be hidden. Second room, same thing. Third room—

Zed grabs my arm. "It's time to go, Jessa."

It's too late. I'm already in. A girl is curled in a fetal position on the floor, her long hair spread across her naked body. An oversize duffel bag lies next to her.

She looks up, through the curtain of hair. My thoughts jumble, tripping over themselves with disjointed images. A button nose. Straight-cut bangs. A sports cap falling to the floor of a racquetball court. Twin braids swishing outside the pod of a seesaw.

I haven't seen her for ten years, but I'd recognize her anywhere.

Olivia Dresden.

23

I wrench myself out of Zed's grasp and fall to my knees. I crawl to her, the girl who's haunted me most of my life. In my dreams, in my few, meager memories of her. She watches me with a swirl of emotions, fear and curiosity, shock and trust, each one battling the others to see which will dominate.

"Are you okay?" I whisper. I don't introduce myself. I don't need to. I feel the bond between us as if it were a physical thing, created all those years ago on the seesaw pods. Lying dormant until the moment we see each other again.

"I've been waiting for you, Jessa Stone." Her voice is soft and surprisingly fragile, so unlike the brash six-year-old who demanded answers from me a decade ago. "Every day, I reached into my future, wondering if you would be in it. This morning, you were."

"I won't let them hurt you," I say. But I don't promise. Once upon a time, my sister made promises to me, promises she couldn't keep. I learned the hard way that fate is something you can influence but never control.

I look over my shoulder. Zed waits by the doorway, but

Brayden and Tanner are nowhere to be seen. I'm not worried about Tanner's welfare. We're not dealing with a mob but two men who carefully weigh their decisions. Tanner's safe, at least for the moment.

"Why is she naked, Zed?" I stride to the seam in the wall and place my hand squarely in the middle of the panel. The wall slides open, revealing a storage closet. I grab a blanket and some oversize pajamas and hand them to Olivia.

He flushes. "We didn't touch her, I swear. Not like that. We were afraid TechRA embedded monitoring devices in her clothes, so we took them off so they couldn't track her."

"Really?" I cross my arms. "'Cause they usually embed trackers under our skin, next to our black data chips."

"Not Olivia. The chairwoman didn't want anything permanent inside her little girl. How else could she hide her daughter off the grid?"

Behind me, Olivia puts on the pajamas and wraps the blanket around her shoulders. Our eyes meet, and she nods once.

So Zed's telling the truth. Doesn't mean I'll stop the interrogation. "How did you find her?"

"The Underground has always known her location. From the beginning, we knew Olivia wasn't at a boarding school, like her mother claimed, but rather, hidden away because she was powerful. Too powerful. So powerful she crosses the line into dangerous."

"Doesn't make sense," I say. "If you knew where she was, why didn't you rescue her before now?"

He runs his fingers over his jaw, along a dark red scratch. The nausea climbs in my throat, and I know the answer to my own question. This isn't a rescue mission. This is about what Olivia can do for the Underground.

"Is that...dried blood?" I ask.

He pulls his hand from his face. "She didn't come nicely."

"Of course she didn't. You kidnapped her." I press my hand against my stomach. I feel sick. Sick that there's matching red matter under Olivia's nails. Sick that there's a bruise forming on her cheek. "Does Mikey know about this?"

He looks me right in the eyes. "Whose orders do you think we're following?"

The room spins, and black spots appear in my vision. I collapse on the pressure-sensitive tile. So Mikey's involved in this. Not just involved. He orchestrated the entire kidnapping. Is that why he sent us away? Maybe he wasn't protecting us after all. Maybe he just didn't want witnesses to his crime.

"He's just as bad as they are," I whisper.

"Don't judge him too harshly." Zed scrubs a hand down his face. "These are the casualties of war. Fates know, the chairwoman's not playing nice. If you don't want to live in her future, the one where Mediocres are executed, this is what we have to do. Show Olivia's vision to the world."

"I don't have it," she speaks up. "This vision you're looking for. The one I gave Callie all those years ago. I don't have it anymore."

"What do you mean? Where did it go?"

She ducks behind me. "Tell him, Jessa. Tell him what it's like being a precognitive. Different versions of people's futures flickering before our eyes. There's no one future, no single path. When Callie injected herself, she changed the course of our world. The vision of genocide I showed her disappeared from my mind. If we hadn't recorded it on a black chip, we'd no longer be able to access it. I have no idea where that black chip is."

I do. At least, I know who would know. Chairwoman Dresden.

"You're lying." Zed pulls an electro-whip from his belt.

"You have the vision. It's in your head. You just don't want to give it to us."

"That's not true." She tucks her face in between my shoulder blades. "Explain to him, Jessa. You're a precog, too. You understand."

I'm not a real precognitive, not in the same way she is. I don't see different versions of people's futures. I can access a vision only when the future becomes fixed. That's why my visions are limited to a couple of minutes in the future. That's why they're usually confined to physical events that don't involve independent free will.

But Zed doesn't know this.

"She needs to rest," I say. "Fatigue zaps the psychic abilities, and she can't access the vision right now because she's too tired. That doesn't mean it's gone forever." I have no idea if this is true, but it doesn't matter. It will appease Zed and buy us time. Time to talk to Mikey, time to get this all figured out. "Perhaps tomorrow morning, after she's had a chance to rest, we can try again." I turn to Olivia, gripping her hand. "Isn't that right?"

She nods.

He looks from me to her, his brow creasing. "Fine," he huffs. "We'll wait for morning. But tomorrow, you'd better have that vision."

He leaves the room, and I expel the breath caught in my lungs. Tomorrow, I have no intention of either of us being here.

24

Too bad Mikey has other ideas.

I lock myself in the first empty bedroom and connect with him through a secure interface. His holographic image appears in the room, and if I don't pass my fingers through his transparent body, I can almost believe he's here, sitting right next to me, his face lined with fatigue and his skin abnormally pale.

"Any more rocks?" I ask.

"Two." He shoves his hands through his hair, dislodging the piece of rawhide. "Both with dead rats. Each with messages worse than the last. It's been hours now, and the crowd's only growing. I have no idea where all these people are coming from."

So I was right. People from outside the compound are joining the riot. Thank the Fates they haven't migrated to the south woods, where we are.

Preambles over, I tell him how we stumbled upon Olivia and demand an explanation. He admits that he authorized the kidnapping—but reassures me that Olivia is not a prisoner.

"If she doesn't have the vision, she doesn't have it," he says tiredly. "The stealth copter needs to recharge, and then we'll return her to the secret location. No harm done."

"Oh, really?" I say, pacing the room. "You kidnapped a girl, Mikey. She has bruises all over her arms, dried blood under her nails. You don't think she's going to tell her mother?"

"No, actually, I don't," he says quietly. "We've been in contact with Olivia for a long time. And while she's not exactly with us, she's not fully with Dresden, either. Her role, as she sees it, is to see the future—not determine it. So she's avoided taking sides."

"Until you kidnapped her! Pretty sure that's going to jeopardize your already tenuous relationship."

His jaw firms. "Maybe. But she knew we were coming. She was waiting by the door when Zed and Brayden broke in."

I stop. Olivia said the same thing, more or less. She said she saw me in her future this morning. That means she knew the kidnapping was going to happen. The rough handling, the bruises. She saw it all. And yet, she came anyway. Why?

"It was a long shot, but one I had to take," Mikey continues. "Don't you see that? We need ammunition against the chairwoman, Jessa. The insurgents are demanding a war, and we need that vision of genocide to show the people. Without it, we'll never be able to win. I'd hoped we could get it from Olivia's mind. But if not…we'll just have to find some other way to access it. Perhaps this black chip she mentioned."

"But you'll let Olivia go home, unharmed?"

"You have my word."

My arms droop. He hasn't answered all my questions, but he's told me all I really need to know. Olivia will be safe. "What about Tanner and me? What do we do?"

"You might as well stay at the cabin for the night. The spiders will keep it hidden from the mob. You'll be safe there."

Olivia safe. Us safe. Ensconced in a secret cabin of the Underground. My stomach should be unfurling. I should feel relieved.

I don't.

The worst part is, that doesn't surprise me one bit.

I hover at the edge of the living area, my hair still wet from my shower. Hot water, scented soap. Being clean has never felt so good. But now that I've scoured off the mud, I have to deal with the sleeping situation.

Zed, Brayden, and Olivia are spread out across the three rooms off the hallway. Which leaves Tanner and me crashing on the living area floor. The entire room's been outfitted with computer terminals and long tables. There's not even a couch. Ordinarily, roughing it wouldn't be a problem. I slept in the wilderness for six years; I can sleep anywhere. But there're two of us. And only one thin mattress.

"Come in," Tanner says, turning his deep, glinting eyes to me. "I'm not contagious. And even if I were, you've already been infected by my mice."

Blushing, I walk into the room. I could be stiff and angry. The last time we talked, on a personal level, I'd stalked away from him. But so much has happened, with Zed, with Olivia. It seems silly to put up a wall between us, when all my other allies are far away.

He's sitting on the edge of the mattress. His skin is flushed red, as though he scrubbed extra hard. He smells like…honeysuckle and lime. I smell like that, too. There was only one soap in the shower.

"Did you talk to Mikey?" he asks.

Good. Business. I can handle business. "Yeah. He said we should stay here tonight, and tomorrow, when the copter's recharged, they'll take Olivia back."

"You trust him? After all this?"

I chew my lip. The knowledge of the kidnapping sits like a heavy stone in my heart. I'm not sure I know Mikey anymore—if I ever knew him. And yet, he's not the enemy here—Dresden is. I may not approve of his methods, but Mikey is on my side. He's looked after me all my life. I have to believe he has my best interests at heart.

"Yes," I say quietly. "I think I do trust him."

Tanner opens his mouth, as though to argue, and closes it again. "Good enough for me," he says, and I know that it costs him to relinquish control. Looks like we're both doing our best to get along.

I lie down at one end of the mattress. If I were any closer to the edge, I'd fall off. Tanner takes the mirror-image position on the other side, so that we're facing each other. There's at least three feet of space between us, but it's not enough. I'm too aware of him. Of the water droplet rolling down his temple. Of the way his cheek presses down into the pillow. If there were an entire room between us, he'd still be too close.

"How's Olivia?" he asks awkwardly.

"Asleep, last time I checked on her. But her rest isn't peaceful. She moves around like she's lying on concrete and can't find a comfortable position."

I ease onto my back. This brings me a foot closer to him, but at least I don't have to look at those soft lips anymore. "I can't believe she's actually here. I've imagined her so many times. Wondered how she's grown up and what she's thinking. I never dreamed I would finally meet her here, like this. Under these circumstances."

"She thought of you, too." He props himself on his elbow,

and I realize he must've known her, since they both grew up in the TechRA building. "She liked to pretend I didn't exist, but I was the only other kid around TechRA, so she'd be forced to talk to me sometimes. She was always bragging about her friend Jessa. How pretty you were, how talented. How you had powers just like hers, and how the two of you would grow up to rule the world."

He laughs, and it's as superior as always. But now, for some reason, instead of the arrogance, I hear the warmth behind it. "Of course, I was being fed my own visions of the future," he says, "so I didn't believe a word of Olivia's bragging. Except for how pretty you were. That I could see for myself."

I sigh. It's like he can't help himself. "You're flirting again."

"No, I'm not," he says seriously. "I was always a genius, you know. Even at six, I knew which girls to pay attention to."

I peek at him. The line of his lips is as straight as his brows, and the air feels heavy, stuffed with something I can't identify. Our eyes catch—and stay locked together. We're still more than two feet apart, but somehow, this encounter feels as intimate as the times when he held me, pressed against his chest.

Dragging my gaze away, I roll over, showing him my back. And yet, as I drift to sleep, the corners of my mouth tilt up. Just the slightest bit.

25

My cheek is crushed against a soft, cottony fabric, stretched over something warm and hard. It should be uncomfortable, but I cuddle closer, wanting more of that sensation against my neck and torso. I wrap my arms all the way around the muscular column. I don't know where they get their pillows around here, but this one is strangely magnetic. You couldn't pull me off if you tried. I rub my face up, up, up… and then, what feels like sandpaper scrapes against my skin.

I freeze. Oh dear Fates. I'm not hugging a pillow after all. That's Tanner's chin. And Tanner's chest.

My eyes fly open, and my breathing becomes quick and shallow as I take stock of the situation. Our legs are tangled up underneath the blanket, and his arms are locked around me. His mouth is blowing hot air against my ear, and my pajama top has gotten twisted around in my sleep, so that my bare stomach is pressed against his.

I swallow hard, and my heart pounds drumbeats against my rib cage. In our sleep, we've somehow gotten more intimate than we've ever been. More intimate than I've ever even dreamed. I should pull away. Put the proper amount of distance between us. He's asleep. There's no way he intends to be curled up with me like this. No way he'd like it if he wakes up and finds us in this compromising position.

He doesn't like me. To flirt and play games with, maybe. For real, no. I need to get out of his embrace before I make an even bigger fool of myself.

But I'm helpless to move. Paralyzed to break this up the way I'm supposed to. As magnetic as he was as a pillow, he's even more irresistible now that I know what I'm hugging.

Just another minute, I tell myself. *It's not like I got us into this position on purpose. One more minute while I figure out what to do.*

But then he shifts, and his face nuzzles down until his lips are pressed against my neck. His hands slide up the small of my back until they are nestled between my shoulder blades. He groans and rolls over, pulling me on top of him.

That's when he opens his eyes.

"Jessa?" he asks, his voice hoarse with shock.

Blushing, I try to slide off him, but his hands tighten around my waist, holding me in place. "I'm sorry," I blurt. "I woke up and found us like this. Neither of us was to blame. Just us moving around in our sleep."

I pull away again, and this time, he lets me move off his body. Before I can retreat to my side of the mattress, however, he grabs my hand and rests his forehead against mine. We stay like that, both of us breathing heavily.

After what seems like an eternity, he lifts his head. "I'd better go sleep in the eating area," he says in a strained voice.

"You don't have to do that. There's nothing to sleep on in there." Even my ears feel hot now. I bunch up the blanket so that it forms a line down the middle of the mattress. "Here, now there's a barrier between us. We won't cross it, I'm sure."

He stands, tucking his pillow under his arm. "Jessa, I never intended to play games with you," he says, his voice quiet, his eyes dark and unreadable. "You're worth far more to me than that."

My mouth opens, and the breath gets caught in my lungs. Before I can decide if I've heard him correctly, his bare feet are already padding away.

I dream of screams. My mother's whimpers in the middle of the night. My own six-year-old bellows when FuMA strapped me to a chair. The silent scream that ripped through the universe, crumbling up the fabric of time, when Callie stabbed the needle into her own heart.

And then there's another moan, one that is long and low and desperate, one that resonates deeply inside me. There are some terrors, once imprinted onto your memory, that you can never unsee. Some experiences so destructive no amount of evil will surprise you ever again.

I open my eyes. There it is once more, that moan. Not a dream, then. It's real. And it's coming from Olivia's room.

I look at the empty space next to me and remember that Tanner is sleeping in the eating area. Doesn't matter. It may be better for me to go alone, anyhow. I creep toward the room. My every nerve is on high alert, and little pops of energy dance along my scalp. This isn't going to be good. It can't be.

Easing open the door, I see Zed advancing toward Olivia, an electro-whip wound around his wrist.

"Give me the vision," he snarls, in a voice I barely recognize as human.

"Zed?" I say quietly so I don't startle him. "What are you doing?"

He turns, and I stumble backward. This...this isn't Zed. At least not the Zed I know. The one who would hold me upside down by my feet and tickle me, the one who skinned animals to provide for a community but never uttered a harsh word to anyone. His eyes are as wild as the prey he trapped, and his face is rigid with grief.

"What is it, Zed? Is it...Eli?"

His face crumples. Right in front of me, his features melt like hot wax and drip to the floor. His grief is so large there's no room for anything else. No reasoning, no speech, no movement.

My stomach bottoms out. I don't need any psychic abilities to know what happened. Eli is dead. They couldn't save him in intensive care.

"He...was my...air," Zed gasps. Each word rips its way out of him. "I have...nothing...left to...breathe."

Tears drip onto his face. Such small bits of moisture for such a large man, and yet, each drop gathers in my lungs, suffocating me. You don't need an ocean in order to drown. Sometimes an inch of bathwater is all it takes.

I close my eyes. That adorable orange-eating boy. Not even four, and already his feet were almost as big as mine. He had his father's size and his mother's passion. He would sit by Laurel for hours as she wrote her poems, on real parchment paper with a feather dipped in walnut ink. "When I grow up, I want to tell stories just like Mommy," he would say. She would smile and ruffle his springy curls.

Now, the only stories he will ever tell are in other people's memories.

When I wrench open my eyes, I'm looking right at Olivia. This is her chance to run, but she's just as transfixed as I am. She reaches out a hand and touches Zed's wrist.

He snaps up his head, and the whip shakes in his hand.

"You will give us the vision." His face deepens to the color of a bruise, and a pulse throbs at his temple. "You'll show us, or you'll be sorry that you are alive."

He grabs her hair and yanks, and I see the long, slim column of her throat.

Zed, stop! I say in my head.

But my mouth doesn't move. I feel the hand of Fate pushing against me, clamping my lips closed. What in space? I take a step forward, and it's like I'm moving through a medium denser than mud. What's happening?

And then I get it. This is Zed's future memory. The one that sent him to Harmony fifteen years ago, the one that's haunted him every day—every minute—since the moment he received it. The one where he beats a woman to a bloody pulp.

This is the moment Zed's memory comes true.

26

The hand of Fate is strong. So strong that it captures anyone who comes within her reach, compelling us to live our futures.

That's why it's so hard for me to move. That's why the words are stuck in my throat. Because this moment is Zed's future, not mine. Only he can change it.

Doesn't mean I can't help him.

I fight, kick, and claw against the current of time. My limbs remain frozen. I grit my teeth and dig my nails into my palms. Nothing.

Fate can go to Limbo and back. She sent an entire community into the wilderness. She makes Angela wake up every morning, terrified. She killed a little boy.

With every last bit of strength, I wrench out of Fate's grasp and regain control of my body.

"Zed, no!" I grab his arm. He shrugs me off but lets go of Olivia's hair. She scuttles backward like a beetle.

"It won't bring him back," I say, so that his attention will stay on me — and not the girl cowering on the floor. "You can do whatever you want to Olivia. It won't make what happened un-happen. It won't even punish the right people. Olivia had nothing to do with the mob. She wasn't even there."

"This isn't about punishing Olivia. It's about stopping Dresden," he spits out. "We need to show Olivia's vision of genocide to the world, so the people won't follow Dresden. We need to take down this madwoman before she…kills… anyone else." His voice cracks, and I threaten to crack along with him.

But I can't fall apart. Not yet. "This is your future memory. Don't you recognize it? This is why you ran to Harmony. Because you saw a vision of your future self beating up a girl." I breathe shallowly, repeating back to him the words he told me over a pot of peppermint tea, while baby Eli napped in a nearby bassinet. "We're here, Zed. The future. The moment you would've done anything to avoid."

"No. This isn't my memory." He shakes his head violently. "The girl in my memory was naked. She's wearing pajamas."

"Because I gave them to her." I shift so that I'm standing right in front of him. "Don't you see? The decisions of the people around you can make small changes in your memory. Minor details like clothes and hair. But you're the only one who can stop your future from occurring."

He tries to push past me, but I step to the left, blocking him once again. "Think of Callie. She changed her future. Maybe, like her, your future self sent you this memory so that you would make a different decision."

His shoulders droop. The hand holding the electro-whip falls. When I'm sure he's not going to rush Olivia, I move to the side. "Look into her eyes, Zed. Tell me that's not her. Your future. Your nightmare. Your opportunity."

"I…I didn't recognize her. What I remember most about my future memory is my own rage. She was just a girl, battered and covered in bruises." He drops his face into his hands, the electro-whip jabbing his forehead. "What have I done?" he moans.

"Nothing yet," I whisper. "This is your choice. You can live your fate or you can change it."

His breathing slows, and he lowers his hands. "You're right." He looks at Olivia, his eyes traveling over every bruise and every mark, many of them made by his own hands. He winces, and I know the image will be seared into his soul forever.

"Forgive me," he says, his voice thick. He hands me the electro-whip. "I'll...tell Brayden. We'll get the stealth copter ready. It should be charged by now. We'll take Olivia home. I'm sorry."

And then he runs out of the room.

Seconds pass. I take a shuddering breath. The world just changed in ways I can't fathom. Zed stopped his future. Like Callie, he picked our world off its trajectory and moved it onto a different path. Shouldn't we hear something? The sky breaking, tectonic plates moving? Maybe the heavens themselves cracking open?

But no. Time marches on, as steady and unceasing as before, and if I hadn't witnessed Zed's decision, I never would've known anything was different.

Is this what will happen when I defy the vision to be Dresden's assistant? Will the world continue to spin, none the wiser?

I walk toward Olivia. She huddles in the corner, and a part of me breaks. I was too late. I said I wouldn't let them hurt her, and here she is, traumatized with the prospect of torture. She's been secluded for years, never interacting with others, but never harmed, either. Who knows how she'll respond to this brutality?

When I touch her shoulder, however, she looks up, expression fierce. "Will he do as he says?"

"I think so." I flip the switch on the handle, and the electro-whip hums to life. Shuddering, I turn it off again. "He wouldn't have given me this weapon if he still intends to hurt us."

She sags against the wall. "You give me a headache, Jessa Stone."

I blink. "Excuse me?"

Her eyes flash. They are as black as space, with a few scattered specks. A reflection of the stars—or maybe time itself. "Literally, you make my head ache. You have so many paths laid open before you, so many paths you could choose to take. Every single one of your futures flickers before my eyes." She presses her fingers against her forehead.

"I don't understand."

"You see, when each of us is born, we have an infinite number of paths we could potentially take," she says. "With every decision we make, the number of paths narrows. Until, at the end of our lives, there is only one path left. Usually, by the time a person reaches sixteen, only a handful of major arteries remain. But you—you still have dozens. Maybe even hundreds. It could be a sign of power—or it might mean nothing at all."

"You see all my futures just by looking at me?" I ask, awed. "How do you live like that?"

Her expression clears. "It's hard. That's why my mother had me secluded. Not only to protect her—because Fates know, her enemies would use my powers against her if they could—but also to protect me. If I had to live out there, interacting with all those people on a daily basis, their potential decisions, their potential worlds would crush me.

"I've learned to build walls," she continues. "So I don't see into the future unless I want to. But when I look at you, the pressure is so intense, I can't help but let your futures in. You have so much potential, so much power. You've already altered the course of the future with Zed. You could change it even more. You could bring back your sister. Or not. It all depends on the choices you make."

My heart thumps against my chest, so hard I can almost feel my bones splinter. "You know how I can revive Callie? Tell me."

"Oh, I can't. Not because I'm being coy or evasive but because these futures are tricky things. The various paths flip through my head so rapidly. It wouldn't be fair to pick out a single one."

"Who cares about fair?" I grip her forearm, my fingernails digging into her skin. "She's been lying in a coma for ten years, Olivia. When she could've been here. With us."

Her face is pinched, her neck stiff. She holds herself tightly, as though her body might fall apart if she relaxes. "You're right. I don't care about fair."

"Then tell me."

"I've seen what a single word, a single action can do." She wraps her arms around herself. "I've seen how a single decision can lock us onto a certain path. Knowing the future is a large burden to bear, Jessa. I learned long ago that I can't try to influence it."

She stares over my shoulder, not at the room but at memories only she can see. "When I was a kid, I used to try and stop the bad things. But I couldn't. Over and over again, the action I took to prevent the future was the very thing that caused it." She moves her shoulders. "Do you get it, Jessa? I see the future, but I'm powerless to change it. I know too much. My knowledge influences my decisions so that I can't possibly make the right one. But you can. That's why I came here today. That's why I let them kidnap me. I knew you were in this future, and I had to talk to you."

I shiver. This isn't about Callie, but something bigger, something outside the small circle of people I care about. Again. First, it was Mikey, then the chairwoman. And now Olivia. They all want me to care about a larger political agenda, and I just don't.

Then, I remember something Tanner said. "When we were kids, you told Tanner that you and I were going to rule the world. That wasn't just talk, was it? You actually saw us. You saw a vision where it actually comes true."

"One of many possible futures," she says. "How you choose is up to you."

I shake my head. "Is this about the vision your mother showed me? If this is a trick to get me to become her assistant, it's not going to work. Like you said—I make my own decisions. I'll never take her side. Never."

"This isn't a trick," she says simply. "I'm not my mother."

At that moment, I hear voices from the hallway. Zed's, Brayden's, and Tanner's. Any minute now, they'll come inside. Any second now, they'll take Olivia back from where they stole her.

"You can't leave me like this," I plead. "What if it were your sister lying there? I know you don't have a sister, but you can imagine it. I know you've seen enough futures to know how it feels. Please, Olivia. Tell me. How do I bring Callie back?"

She shifts her eyes, focusing them on my face.

"Do you remember the nursery rhyme we used to sing in the T-minus eleven class, during the Outdoor Core?" she asks. "How do you stop the beast? Take away his food, he'll feed off the air. Cut off his head, he grows another one with hair. How do you stop the beast, Jessa?"

I wrinkle my forehead. "I don't remember the punch line.

Is this supposed to tell me what to do?"

Something flickers in her eyes. She opens her mouth, and I lean forward, determined to catch every word. But the door bangs open, and Zed strides into the room. My shoulders droop. It's too late; he's come for her.

And then, her words float out, so softly they might be from my imagination.

"Ask yourself why they have Callie. Think about why they've kept her alive all these years."

27

The blades of the stealth copter whirl, emitting that low, almost soundless hum. The resulting wind blows in our faces, knocking around Olivia's hair and making her look younger than she is. Someone I'd want to protect.

In a couple of minutes, Olivia will get in the copter. I haven't seen her for the last ten years, and I may not see her for the next ten.

"I used to be so jealous of Callie and you," she says. "Every day, she'd come to the T-minus eleven classroom to pick you up, and every day, she'd hold open her arms, and you'd fly right into them. I thought if I had a sister, maybe somebody would hug me, too."

"Your mother didn't hug you?" I ask, but I already know the answer. We're talking about Chairwoman Dresden here. The icicle queen herself.

"We didn't have that kind of relationship."

What kind? The mother-daughter kind?

But of all people, I should know that blood doesn't necessarily mean love. Being a mother doesn't mean you won't abandon your child when she has to run off to the wilderness.

I wrap my arms around Olivia, and her shoulder blades jab into my hands. "Take care of yourself, Olivia."

"Come with me," she says impulsively.

I laugh, but the sound dies in my throat. "Where? To your hideout? Or your mother's house? I'm not sure either would be appropriate."

Brayden and Tanner hop out of the cockpit and approach us. I haven't seen Zed since he ran from Olivia's room. I hope he's with Laurel. I hope they're able to find comfort in each other.

"Are you ready, Olivia?" Brayden asks. Everything about him appears sheepish, from the cap he holds against his chest to the freckles sprinkled across his face.

She nods, giving me one last searing look. A look that says so much—I just wish I could understand what. She climbs into the copter. Moments later, the sleek black machine rises into the air, as nimble as a bird. And then, it is gone.

The sky is streaked with color that is both intense and soft, like a tangerine smeared across a painter's canvas. The sun glows near the horizon but has yet to make an appearance. So peaceful, so calm. Not at all indicative of the bloodcurdling violence that roils underneath. Even now, I can hear distant shouts. Close my eyes, and I can see the body of a frail little boy, marked by too many footprints, destroyed by too little thought.

I shiver, and Tanner puts his hand lightly, carefully on my shoulder. "We need to get off the compound. The rioters will be awake soon. They might be feeling more reasonable this morning, but I'm not betting my life on it."

I nod. The grate that leads back to the metal pipe lies a dozen yards away, in the middle of the copter landing pad. I have on clean clothes now. They don't fit—my pants are rolled twice at the waist; my shirt's tied in a knot—but they're clean. I'd hate to get them filthy again, but little Eli no longer has that choice, does he?

Little Eli would probably give anything to be crawling around in the muck.

I blink back tears. Even all-knowing, not-fazed-by-anything Tanner squares his shoulders. And we descend into the sewer once again.

Later, we emerge free, if not clean. The pipe empties into a river, and we wade from the exit toward the shore. I take my time, dunking my head under the water, scrubbing at my hair and face. The Harmony compound—and the rioters inside—are far away, separated by a sturdy wall. For the first time in the last twelve hours, I feel like I can breathe again.

Still, we crawl behind a bush, into a little clearing blocked by oversize tree trunks and shrubbery, and stretch on the ground. The air is warm; the hard, packed dirt is even warmer. If we're going to be stuck outside, at least for the next few hours, at least the weather is nice.

My stomach sloshes around. The next few hours? How long do I have to wait before I go home, anyhow?

Tanner won't be returning to the Harmony compound, that much is clear. But what about me? Has my association with him tainted me so badly I'll never be able to go back?

Of course not. The mob will settle down. They won't be as prone to violence. They'll understand that I'm not to blame— that neither of us is responsible for the invention of future memory.

Even as I think the words, I remember a rock with a

bloody rat pinned to it. I picture Eli's body, at the bottom of an uncaring stampede.

I know, deep at the core of my being, that even if I go back, the compound will never be "home" again.

I turn toward Tanner, my cheek against the dirt. He's already looking at me. Something in his expression makes me feel like he knows what I'm thinking—has always known what I'm thinking—even though he doesn't have telepathy.

If only I could read him so clearly. His eyes are opaque, his expression closed. Sure, he told me about the torture from his childhood. But when it comes right down to it, how well do I really know him? I'm past holding his status as a scientist against him, but he has secrets he's keeping from me. Information he's learned by being one of Dresden's underlings.

He wants my sister to wake up. That much is clear. Is that enough for me to trust him?

Olivia's words float through my mind. *Ask yourself why they have Callie.*

I swallow hard. "Why has TechRA been keeping Callie alive?" My words are slow and halting, as I try to work it out in my head. "It can't be cheap. They had to maintain her muscles, supply her body with oxygen and nutrients, when there's very little hope of her ever coming back. Why would they do that?"

"You know why," he says, his eyes fixed on my forehead. "They were desperate to discover future memory, and the link between the two of you was the best chance they had for an answer."

He's lying. After all this time, I'm finally able to pick up on his tells. That bored, eyes-glazed-over look I assumed meant he was too good for me? Really, it's because he can't—or won't—meet my eyes.

"That's not why. Up until I held her hand and sent her that

memory, you thought the Sender-Receiver bond between us
was severed. Come on, Tanner. Be straight with me."

He sighs, and his features waver in and out of the sun's
rays, which are broken up by the jagged leaves. "You're right.
That's the line I've been taught to say. Dresden swore all of
us to secrecy, and if you know her at all, you know she can
be quite convincing. But I'm sick of keeping secrets. Sick of
being under Dresden's control. You deserve to know about
your sister, and I'm going to tell you. No matter what she
does to me."

My skin tingles; my breath catches. The energy in the air
around us swirls, concentrating on this boy, this moment. I
have the feeling I'm about to learn something big, something
huge. Something that will push my world off its orbit, and life
will never be the same again.

"Your sister has another ability," he says slowly. "Her
Receiver ability—the one she shared with you—was just her
preliminary ability. She has a main one, as well."

I blink. "What are you talking about? Most psychics
develop their preliminary ability when they're toddlers.
Callie's Receiver ability didn't manifest until she was
seventeen."

"Because you weren't around. Think about it. You're
the Sender; she's the Receiver. One is useless without the
other. You were supposed to have been born ten years earlier.
Because you weren't, she couldn't become a Receiver until
you became a Sender. Her preliminary ability laid dormant
until it manifested in you."

Cold air hits the back of my throat, and I realize my mouth
is hanging open. Deliberately, I close it. "What's her main
ability, then? I never saw one. Neither did Mikey or Logan.
At least, they never mentioned one to me."

"She can manipulate memories." His eyes fasten onto

mine. "She can change parts of a memory so that it looks like something new. Take a red ribbon and turn it blue. Latch onto an image of her little sister and sculpt it into a man with crooked teeth and a mole on his chin."

I frown. "How do you know this?"

"We didn't, not until we had her in a coma and under our care. Over the past decade, we scientists have probed every part of her brain, excavated every bit of her memories. That's when they saw what she was trying to do with her future memory. Instead of killing you, she was trying to change it so that she killed her future cheating husband." He shrugs. "Who knows? If she'd had more time, maybe she would've succeeded."

My brow creases further. "That wouldn't have really worked, would it? Even if she changed the memory, that doesn't mean she could change reality. I mean, who is this guy with the crooked teeth and the mole? Does he even exist?"

"No one knows. But Dresden's convinced the only reason Callie was able to change her future is because she has this ability."

"No." I shake my head sharply, and the wet strands of my hair whip around my shoulders. "Callie changed the future because of her force of will—and inspired so many people because of it. Angela, Zed." *Me*, I think but don't say out loud. It's because of Callie that I don't have to resign myself to a future as Dresden's assistant. "We know that we can shape our own futures. By her example."

"Honestly, I don't know. The research into this area is murky, but it's what the chairwoman believes. And she wants the ability for herself."

My head jerks back. "You mean she wants the ability to manipulate people's memories?"

He nods.

I press my fingertips against my head as the full extent of his meaning sinks in. Of course she does. That's why she's so obsessed with manufacturing fake memories, even the innocuous kind. In a world where future memory exists, this ability would give Dresden unprecedented power. Power so staggering it takes my breath away. She could show people exactly what she wanted them to see. She could manipulate the entire world to her liking.

Even worse, in a future that executes Mediocres, she alone would get to decide who is exceptional. She alone would get to determine who lives—and who dies.

I look at Tanner. He doesn't know about the vision of genocide. He doesn't know what the woman for whom he's been working is capable of. He merely thinks she's a power-hungry leader—but it's time he knows the true extent of her evilness.

It's time I tell him. Everything.

28

tell Tanner about the vision of genocide. The one that made my sister stab herself in the heart, the one our world is in danger of becoming now that future memory has been invented. The one that Chairwoman Dresden showed me. The one that revealed I would someday be her assistant.

I even tell him this part, something I never thought I would share with anyone. Because he gave me his secrets, and maybe it's time I gave him mine. Because Dresden's been controlling not just him but also me.

By sharing the vision with me, Dresden reinforced my sense of shame. She made me hide from the people closest to me. She cut me off from those who could've helped or at least supported me.

Not anymore. I'm done being ashamed of something that hasn't even happened. Something, if I have anything to do with it, that will never happen.

When I finish, I realize Tanner's face has turned parchment-paper pale. "I didn't know," he whispers. "Nobody ever told me."

"Most people don't know," I say. "Just the members of the Underground. That's why Zed was trying to torture the vision out of Olivia—because he wants to show the world. Mikey always said if we wanted to be believed, we had to wait until the timing was right. I guess he thinks that time is now."

"That's why the people are rioting. That's why they're so upset."

"Yes," I say softly. "They know what the invention of future memory might mean for our world."

He shakes his head, over and over again, like he can't believe it, and then he crawls away from me and lets loose a gut-curdling scream.

I blink. I expected him to have a strong reaction—but not this strong. Hesitantly, I put a hand on his back. It vibrates under my touch. "Tanner, are you okay?"

He flings his body up, knocking off my hand. "No, I'm not okay. I'm never going to be okay again. I...I've been assisting Dresden my whole life." He bangs his head against the trunk of a tree, harder and harder.

Shocked, I grab his shoulders. "Stop it, Tanner! You couldn't have known her end goal." I wrench him around to face me. His skin is split across his forehead, and a trickle of blood drips down his face. "You've been trained to be a scientist since you were six. You were doing only what you were raised to do."

"I knew she tortured me. That should have been enough. But I told myself she wasn't all bad. I told myself she did what she had to do for the good of society. I had no idea she was actually evil." His eyes beseech me to understand. "I'm so sorry. Please forgive me."

"I do." It's true. I never thought I'd say this, but for once, I can separate the vocation from the cruelty. Tanner may have the same occupation as the people who strapped me down, but he's not like them. He studies science for the pursuit of knowledge; they twist it to serve an evil master. He's an innocent pawn in Dresden's schemes, as innocent as I am. He's been tortured and traumatized ever since he was a little kid, and I...I don't want him to suffer anymore.

I wrap my arms around him and murmur in his ear. The way my mom used to before I left civilization. The way Callie used to when my mom was at work. I don't have much experience comforting others, but the words come easily, naturally.

"It's okay. You're okay. Everything's going to be okay."

I think of another boy, much younger, who was hurt at too young an age. Grief floods my heart, making me sicker than any motion-coaster. For Eli, it's not okay. Neither I nor anyone else will be able to comfort him ever again.

I hold Tanner tighter, until his breath slows down and evens out. There's not much I can do to change his past, but I can give him this moment.

I can give him right now.

"You've worked so hard, Tanner," I murmur. "Made so many discoveries, so many strides in research. You have so much value in our society. Unlike me."

I freeze. Crap. The last two words slipped out accidentally. But maybe he won't notice. Maybe he'll be too distraught to think about anything beyond himself.

But he does. He sits up and pulls out of my arms. "How could you think you don't have any value?" he says in a low voice. "You are so loved. By Mikey, Angela, everyone in the Underground community. As an outsider, I see this so clearly."

"That may be, but they love Callie more," I shoot back and then sigh. I didn't mean to do this. I didn't mean to shift the attention to me. But now that the words are here, hanging in the air between us, I can't just leave them. "That sounds bratty, doesn't it? I swear to you, this isn't about sibling rivalry. I don't care that they put my sister on a pedestal because I put her there, too. It's about whose life should've been saved."

Pressure builds behind my eyes, and I blink, trying to push the hurt back inside. Trying to keep the hot liquid from boiling over. "Callie knew one of us had to die, in order to prevent the vision of genocide she saw. And she unilaterally made the decision to sacrifice her life in order to save mine," I say, trying to explain the truth inside me. The knowledge I've always understood and lived with. "But she made a mistake. Everyone knows that, even if they don't say it. If they were given a choice, they would've chosen her instead. They wish she had saved herself instead."

"No," he says, shaking his head. "I refuse to believe it."

"Don't you see? Everybody who cares about me loved her first. My mom. Angela. Even Ryder. He didn't know her well, but he grew up hearing stories about her. Feeling the force of her legacy. If they care about me at all, it's because she loved me. Because I'm her little sister."

"That's not true,'" he says slowly. "I care about you, and I never knew her."

I give him a scathing look. "You don't care about me. You've told me so enough times."

He grabs a stick and digs in the dirt. Back and forth, back and forth. The rhythm is soothing, even mesmerizing. I wrap my hands around my knees. If it meant I never feel this ache in my heart again, I'd lose myself forever in the motion of that stick.

I assume we're going to drop the subject, but then he looks up at me. "This is…hard for me," he says haltingly. "I know I've sent you mixed signals. I know I pushed you away. I even said you weren't my type, for Fate's sake." He shakes his head, disgusted. "I'm surprised you didn't see through *that* in a nanosecond." He pushes the stick through the dirt a few more times. He's now dug a rut six inches deep. "The reason I did all those things was because...the opposite is true."

I wrinkle my brow. "What do you mean?"

"I like you too much." The words tumble out in a rush. "As soon as I came up to you at the hoverpark, I felt...this thing. This sense that I had known you before. That you had meant a lot to me. I know, I know. It sounds crazy, and I swear, nothing like this has ever happened to me before. It freaked me out. When I brought it up, you brushed off the feeling, so I knew it was all in my head. I knew you didn't feel the same way."

He tosses away the stick, replacing it with his hands in the dirt. "Believe me, when you grow up the way I did, an orphan nobody wants except for the brilliance of your mind, you learn how to build walls. I guess that's why I kept trying to push you away. That's why I made that absurd statement about you not being my type, when nothing could be further from the truth."

My heart's pounding so loudly it's about to burst out of my chest, but he scoops up two fistfuls of the earth as though he doesn't notice. The dirt trickles through his fingers. "I was just trying to protect myself, Jessa. I never meant to hurt you. The last thing I wanted was to make you feel worthless."

He reaches a hand toward my face and then hesitates. Maybe because his fingers are dirty. Maybe because he's not sure if I want this particular touch. Just a few minutes ago, my arms were wrapped all the way around his body. He was halfway across my lap. But that was different. That was comfort, while this is...something more. Something crazy and wonderful and real.

I grab his hand and bring it to my cheek, dirt and all.

Closing my eyes, I just experience his fingers against my face. This boy. I should feel like such a brat, complaining about not being loved for the right reasons, when he hasn't been loved at all. But he doesn't make me feel bratty. He makes me feel...worthy. By being here. By being me. I don't have to redeem myself in some way. I don't have to prove I deserve my sister's sacrifice. I just have to...exist.

I swallow hard. No one's ever made me feel this way before. The feeling is too big, too much. It's so large it might swallow me whole. Part of me wants to give him everything. And that scares me more than Limbo itself.

When I open my eyes, he's looking at me. And in his eyes, I see a girl who is stronger and braver and more beautiful than I could've ever imagined.

"I'm going to kiss you, Jessa," he says in a strained voice. "Not because I'm trying to fulfill our fate. Not because you happen to be right here. But because I want to, more than anything else in the world right now."

I lick my lips. "I want that, too."

And we don't talk again for a very long time.

29

Later, someone shakes my shoulders, and I jerk awake.

"We fell asleep," Tanner says, dark circles rimming his eyes. "We have to get to Callie. She needs you to send a memory every thirty-six hours to maintain the bond. It's been…" He taps on his wrist com. "Twenty-nine hours."

I sit straight up, my grogginess evaporating. Maintain the bond. That's just a pretty way of saying: keep her tethered to this world—and alive. But there's no need to panic. Not yet. "Seven hours. That's plenty of time. The TechRA building can't be more than a few miles away."

"Yes, we should be fine." But he gnaws on his cheek, as though there's something else he wants to say.

"What is it, Tanner?"

"I have a bad feeling," he says, and the words hit me like a slap. Tanner doesn't operate on feelings. He relies on data and analysis and logical conclusions.

"Dresden's finally gotten what she's wanted for so long," he continues slowly. "Things are going to change. I'm just not sure how."

"Let's go to Callie, then." The anxiety saturates my veins and begins to seep into my muscles, my nerves. "We have to make sure she's safe."

We move through the streets, as quickly as we can on our own feet. The bullet trains are shut down; the moving sidewalks are still. Instead of showing the latest news, the holo-screens plastered against the skyscrapers play on a loop the footage of Chairwoman Dresden's announcement. What's more, every other holo-screen is dented, as though metal sculptures or wooden benches have been hurled at them.

"ComA's issued a lockdown on Eden City." Tanner scrolls through his wrist com as we move from the shadows of one building to another. "The rioters have spilled into the city, ripping up park patches, destroying government property. So there's an enforced curfew until they can figure things out."

I see movement in my peripheral vision and pull Tanner behind the corner of a building.

"Did you see that?" I pant. Either my heart's racing—or it's his. I can't tell with our chests pressed together like this.

"ComA patrols." His lips barely move, and the words are the slightest breath against my mouth. "With electro-whips. Searching for curfew violators. We can't let them see us."

I nod, not daring to speak. We huddle in the shadows until they pass.

In halts and sprints, adrenaline-pumping runs and heart-pounding waits, we make our way to the TechRA building. ly, we arrive and proceed to the subterranean corridor without incident.

Without incident—but with a whole lot of emotion. Perspiration dots my upper lip and gathers at the nape of my neck, only to cool once it hits the chilly air. I peek over my shoulder for the thirty-seventh time. The hallway is sterile, empty. Even the stretchers that once lined the hallway are no longer present. The purple and green lights blink at me in the dimness.

I wish I could've changed out of my grubby, dried-out clothes, but stopping by my house was out of the question. As was swinging by Tanner's apartment in the nearby scientific residences. Every extra second we spend outside means an extra second we might get caught. We can't let that happen, not when we need to get to Callie.

Five hours and counting. Plenty of time, and yet, I feel each minute sliding into the next like sand dripping down an hourglass.

"Hurry." I grit my teeth to stop them from chattering. "The sooner I can send that memory to Callie, the better I'll feel."

"On it." He positions himself in front of the retina scan, lining up his eyes with the aperture. And stays there. Four seconds, six seconds. What's taking so long?

"That's weird," he murmurs. "It usually beeps to indicate the scans match."

Panic sprints up my throat. "Is something wrong?"

"Probably not. The maintenance bots were in here earlier this week. Maybe they upgraded the security system, and there's some sort of glitch." He moves to the next station and sticks his finger into the slot, so that the machine can take a sample of his blood. "That's why we have these back-up security systems."

His finger is pricked, and his face is scanned. He speaks into a microphone. But none of these results in that elusive beep.

He looks at me. I look at him. I realize all of a sudden we aren't alone.

Small cameras nestle in the ceiling, each one covered by a round, reflective eye. At this moment, every single "eye" is trained on us.

"Tanner?" I whisper, my mouth as dry as the air. "Why are all those cameras pointed at us?"

Before he can answer, sirens blare and the purple and green lights flash, filling the entire hallway with chaos.

Fike, fike, fike. They've caught us.

30

The sirens scream, drilling my ears with noise. I want to curl into a ball until it stops, but I can't. I have to reach my sister.

I grab the door handle and jerk, putting my entire body into the motion. It doesn't budge.

Abandoning the door, I take off down the hall, whipping my head back and forth. I need another entrance. Another way in to Callie.

There! A heating vent, covered by a grate. These vents have been good to me. They've taken me all over the TechRA building. Of course, the Underground has vetted all the ones I've used, but this one will work. It has to.

I grab the grate and pull. It comes off, and dust bellows out, choking me. I double over, coughing, and Tanner runs up to me.

"We've got to get out of here!" he yells. "We've got to—"

The door at the end of the hall opens, and half a dozen guards spill into the corridor.

Too late.

One of them grabs my arms, shoving me to the ground,

while two others point their Tasers at me—one at my temple, the other at my chest.

I'm unarmed, I want to say. *Just a girl, rendered helpless by a cough. It shouldn't take three of you to contain me.* But of course I don't. Even if they could hear me above the noise, they wouldn't listen.

Two more guards approach Tanner and flank him. But they don't restrain him. They don't wrench his arms behind his back. They don't force him to his knees.

Why not?

The question worth a lifetime of credits, and maybe a couple of Meal Assemblers to boot.

I try to catch Tanner's eye in all the commotion, but he either doesn't see me—or he won't.

The door opens again, and Chairwoman Dresden strides inside, her icicle heels slapping the tile, her smile shoving blades into my heart.

She waves her wrist in front of the security system, enters a code, and the alarm shuts down. Finally. We can hear one another talk again, but I'm no longer sure that's a good thing.

"You're so predictable, Tanner. I knew it was only a matter of time before you brought her back," Dresden says. "I didn't realize it would be so soon after my announcement, however. The riots are still going strong. A curfew is in place. But you couldn't wait any longer to betray me, could you, darling boy?"

"This has nothing to do with you," Tanner rasps. "I have to take Jessa to see her sister. She's the only connection Callie has to this world, to this time."

Something I can't read flickers in Dresden's eyes. "Yes, I know. Even though you never bothered to tell me. I had to find out from other people, scientists who are more loyal than you." She tilts her head. "Always so earnest, so idealistic. Even as a little boy, you thought you could save the world.

But what did I tell you when we took you in and trained you to be our hope for the future? You must be loyal to me—or people will die."

I gulp. What is she saying? Does she mean she'll kill Callie to punish Tanner? Will she kill me? No way. She's allowed both of us to live for the last ten years. She needs us. Doesn't she?

I may be confused, but Tanner doesn't have any trouble understanding her meaning. His shoulders droop, and his head lowers. Right before my eyes, he transforms into a six-year-old boy again. "I'm sorry, Chairwoman. It won't happen again."

"Damn the Fates right, it won't. I won't allow it." She snaps her fingers in the air. "Take them away."

"Wait a minute." I yank my arms, and the guards yank back, turning my body into a tug-of-war rope. "Where are you taking us?"

Dresden's smile gets wider and colder. A few more degrees, and it'll shatter in a million pieces. "You're going to isolation, of course. But don't worry. You won't be there long." She checks her wrist com. "A mere four hours and fifty-three minutes. Then you'll be free to do as you wish once again."

My blood turns solid. Four hours and fifty-three minutes. The exact amount of time I have remaining to send Callie a memory and tether her to this world.

"You can't mean that." I dart a look at Tanner, but he refuses to meet my eyes. Dresden can't possibly understand what she's saying. "I need to get close enough to touch Callie, for only a few moments. I need to send her a memory. It's the only way to keep her alive."

She turns to me, her eyelids at half-mast. "I told you already. I understand all of this, no thanks to my traitor boy. Your sister was valuable to me once upon a time. But now we've wrung her brain dry, and keeping her alive is costing

ComA too many credits."

"No." I lunge forward. "Please, Chairwoman. I'll do anything you want. You don't even have to bribe me. I'll sit in that chair. I'll let the scientists study my brain. For as long as they want. I won't even complain. I promise."

She flickers her eyes over me. "You had your chance, Jessa. You turned me down, time and time again."

"Please!" I'm begging now, but I have no choice. I need to make her change her mind. "I'll come work for you. I'll be your assistant. That's what you want, isn't it? That's why you showed me the vision. So that I could make it come true."

Her nostrils flare. "Do you think I'm stupid? I've seen how you really feel about me. Why would I want an assistant whom I can't trust? When you come to me, for real, you'll have to give me more than just words, Jessa. You'll have to show me, with actions, that you've changed. Irrevocably. You'll have to prove to me, once and for all, that you're on my side. Until then, don't bother negotiating."

She spins on her heels, but Tanner grabs her sleeve.

"Don't do this, Chairwoman," he pleads. "Callie's given you so much. Because of her brain, we were able to discover everything."

"She also took everything from me." Her voice rises, filling the hallway as thoroughly as the sirens. "I got back only what was originally mine."

The room's spinning; my forehead's burning. I can barely process what they're saying. But something Tanner says doesn't seem right. Something makes me focus in on his words and replay them in my mind.

"What do you mean, she let you discover everything?" I look from Dresden to Tanner. "I thought you weren't able to learn much by examining her brain."

Dresden turns to me, her eyes wide open. I guess she's

no longer bored. "You mean he didn't tell you?"

"Tell me what?"

"A few days ago, Tanner accomplished what I was beginning to believe was impossible." Triumph rings through her voice. "He discovered future memory and put our world back on track."

No. He couldn't have been the inventor. He was with me when Dresden made her announcement. He was just as surprised as I was. Wasn't he? Or is Tanner a bigger actor—a bigger liar—than I ever suspected?

I won't believe it—I won't—until I hear the words from his lips. "Tanner? Is she telling the truth? Did you invent future memory?"

For the first time since Dresden appeared, he lifts his head and meets my eyes. "Yes. I did."

The air tangles in my throat. Before I can figure out how to breathe again, Dresden steps forward. "Tell her how you discovered it," she says, her voice too gleeful, her expression too smug. "Tell her what—or, should I say, whom—you used."

It hits me then. The guards grab my elbows to keep me from pitching forward, but it doesn't matter. I'm free-falling anyway. I'm detached from my body, spinning in space, unable to tell which way is up.

The memories. He used the memories I sent into Callie's mind to keep her alive. I'm the Sender; she's the Receiver. Together, we were the key to the invention of future memory. The scientists were supposed to study our genetically identical twin brains. By observing the way messages were passed between us, they were supposed to derive a key insight that would lead to the invention of future memory.

But Callie changed everything by stabbing a needle into her heart. By making it impossible for me to send memories into her mind…until a week ago. When I did exactly what she sacrificed her life to prevent.

Callie lies in a coma, the last ten years of her life a black hole. Three lives—mine, my mom's, and Logan's—have been irreparably harmed. For what? This?

We've come full circle. I left civilization and came back again. I followed a maze and walked straight into a trap I never saw coming. One that plops me back into the world we thought we'd left behind.

"You tricked me," I whisper. "You told me to send my sister a memory. You said it would save her life."

"It did save her life," Tanner says miserably. "At the time I made the suggestion, that's all I was thinking about, I swear. But the monitors were already set up to record her brain activity, and when you sent that memory, it captured the transmission. What was I supposed to do? Here was all this data, right in front of me. Data that was ripe for analysis. Data for which I've been searching my entire life." He reaches a hand toward me, but one of the guards slaps a cuff on his wrist and pulls it down. Doesn't matter. I wouldn't let him touch me anyway.

"I couldn't resist, Jessa. For the sake of science, I had to see. I'd already laid the foundation with my mice. The messages you sent to Callie provided me with the final missing piece of the puzzle. They gave me what I needed to invent future memory."

"For the sake of science, you betrayed me," I say, my voice hard, my heart harder.

"I told you. I didn't know what the discovery of future memory meant." His eyes beseech me. The cut in his forehead reminds me. "Please. You believed me. You forgave me."

My soul cements until it is thick, solid concrete. "I don't forgive you anymore."

31

We are led to a small, square cell. Plain walls, no furniture.
It can't measure more than ten feet by ten feet.

One of the guards shoves me toward a wall. He has a five
o'clock shadow tattooed onto his laser-smooth cheeks, and he
stops in front of the complicated security panel by the door.
"You're in here for four hours and forty minutes. Let's round
it up to five hours, just to be safe." He keys in the parameters,
and a red digital clock appears in the air. "Once the timer
counts down, the doors will open and you'll be released. Until
then, make yourself cozy."

He laughs at his not-funny joke and leaves the room. The
door closes behind him.

A second later, I'm attacking the metal surface,
dropkicking the doorknob, punching the security system.
Pain lances through my hands and feet, but I keep hammering.
My sister's out there, and I won't be locked in here. I won't.

Parts of the panel break off and dangle in the air. The
hologram clock wavers and disappears. My hands are slick
with something wet and slippery and red, and then a pair of

arms wraps around my torso and pulls me away.

"Jessa, you're bleeding," Tanner says. "Why don't you—"

I throw his hands off me. "Don't you ever touch me again."

"I'm sorry." His eyes are like black holes in space, with their own gravitational pull. I could tumble into them so easily—but I've learned my lesson. I fell into them once, and I won't make that mistake again.

"This isn't the way I wanted things to work out," he says in a low voice. "Believe me, I never wanted to hurt you or Callie."

"Funny. I've heard you say that before." I gasp at the air. The oxygen leaks out of my lungs the moment it arrives. "Too bad I can't overlook the end result this time. Because of you, my sister is dead once again."

"Jessa, I—"

I clap my hands over my ears, and liquid smears into my hair. More blood. "Don't talk to me. Not now, not ever." I crawl into the corner, making myself as small as possible. Getting as far away from him as possible.

I can't do this. I can't talk to Tanner. I can't listen to his excuses. I can't sit here and exist. Not when this is happening again. I barely survived the first time. If Callie is taken from me once more, I will shatter.

"She never came back to you." Tanner's voice floats above me. "Her body is here, but her mind continues to skip through time. Even if you could have maintained the bond, there's no telling if she would've ever come back."

"Are you trying to make me feel better—or yourself?"

I lift my head just in time to see his face crumple. He sags against the wall, sliding lower and lower until he joins me on the floor. "I'm sorry, Jessa. You have no idea how sorry I am. I didn't know this would happen, but you're right. I never should've betrayed you in the first place. This is my fault."

I collapse into sobs. Because it doesn't help me to hear

his apology. Sure, it gives me someone to blame. It gives me a target for my anger. But hating him doesn't bring back Callie.

I want to rip the security system from the walls. I want to wrap the past around Tanner's and my necks, pulling and squeezing until one or both of us passes out. I want to stomp on Fate's face and dare a thunderbolt to come into this cell. If it strikes me, so much the better, because then I won't have to feel this pain anymore.

I don't know how long I cry. I don't know when my lungs give out. Eventually, I'm aware of the cool, hard concrete against my skin. Of my throat scraped raw and of the dried tears stiffening my face.

Tanner lies parallel to me, close but not touching. When I look at his face, he blinks, slowly, drowsily, as if he's been watching me for a good long time.

And then, I feel it. The bond snaps. A severance so clean and thorough I know there's no hope of resurrecting it. The bond that's been with me ever since I was born, connecting me to my sister. The one Angela convinced me that I imagined, the one that became stronger than ever when I sent that memory into Callie's mind.

The bond that connects Callie with our time.

I get on my hands and knees, but I can't rise any farther. Like a newborn calf, my shaky limbs won't support me, and I crash to the floor. "She's really gone now. She's dead." As I say the words, the meaning crashes over me.

The. Abrupt. Stark. Finality. Of. It. All.

I can't breathe. My lungs fold in on themselves, over and over. I can't think. My mind detaches from my body and goes whirling into space, searching, seeking, chasing my sister through time. I can't feel. My nerve endings blow up—and die. Like Callie. Like every good thing left in this world.

Tanner scoops me up and settles me on his lap, cradling

me like a baby. A few thoughts flash across my brain. I hate him. He's my enemy. He killed my sister.

At this moment, I'm too broken to care.

"I know it feels hard right now," he murmurs. "I know it feels unbearable, like you'll never survive. That's how I felt, too, when my parents were killed. I didn't think I could go on. But I did. Time passes. You take one breath and then the next. The moment disappears, and the next one arrives, and you're still here. There's honor in that. Simply enduring."

I close my eyes and keep them closed. Because that's what life without Callie feels like.

Dull. Dark. Dead.

32

The hologram clock is no longer in the air. The big red numbers no longer count down. I destroyed that security feature with a single slam of my fist. Eventually, though, the time runs out, and the door slides open. We are free to go.

I stare at the open door, and if a shred of my soul remained, I might've laughed. Just like that? We're held prisoners for a few hours, my sister dies, and now, we can roam the hall as we please. Go home, if we have any place left to call home.

Clearly, we're not going to do that. Clearly, we have some place else to go first.

I turn and meet Tanner's eyes.

"Her body might not be there anymore." His voice is low and cautious, as if too heavy a tone might break me. "Dresden probably dispatched someone to dispose of her as soon as the bond was severed."

"I have to see." The tears cling to my eyelashes like goopy mascara. "In case she's still there, I have to pay my respects. That's something Logan and I never got to do before. I need to do this now."

He nods, his face soft. "Of course you do. Let's go."

I follow him out of the cell, and we retrace our steps back to the subterranean corridor. I shouldn't let him lead me anywhere. I should spit in his face. He betrayed me. He killed my sister.

But my rage has disappeared into the same dimension as my laughs. *He didn't mean to hurt you*, a voice inside me says. *Tanner Callahan isn't a murderer. All he's guilty of is being an overly enthusiastic scientist. It's Dresden who's evil. Not him.*

I rub my temples. I can't…think…right now. I can't untangle my triple-knotted emotions. I'm too…tired. I wish I could close my eyes and sleep for a million years. And I will, as soon as I say good-bye to my sister. For the very last time.

We walk to the secured door. For a moment, I'm dizzy with déjà vu—but this time, when Tanner scans his retinas, there are no flashing lights and no blaring alarms. There's only a reassuring click that grants us access into the room.

He holds open the door, momentarily blocking my path with his arm. "Are you ready for this?"

I take a deep breath. "Don't…come in with me. I need a few minutes with her. Alone."

"I'll wait right here. If you need anything, just call, okay? I'm not leaving here without you."

And I'm not leaving here with him. But I don't have enough energy to argue, so I nod wearily and go inside. As before, the darkness swallows me, but there's a light gleaming from the far corner of the room. The very last pod in the very first row. My sister's body.

Preston must already be here. Tanner told me the machines are programmed to alert him when Callie's vitals enter dangerous territory. He was probably with her when she passed.

It is a comfort—albeit a small one—that Callie wasn't

alone in her final moments.

I approach the lit-up pod. I'm still a dozen yards away when my skin prickles. My pupils dilate. Every part of my body is on high alert. Something's wrong.

Preston sits, with his head bent over my sister's body. But his hands aren't clasped together, and he's not praying to the Fates or otherwise. He's not mourning her.

Instead, his hands are on her pulse, as though he's checking it. I don't understand. I whip my head to the machines, and there's her heartbeat, steady and sure.

What? I stumble backward, my world on a merry-go-round that won't stop, won't slow. It just spins faster and faster until I might fall right off this dimension. How can this be?

My sister is still alive.

33

My mind whirls, so fast and hard that my jaw aches. I grip my head, but it's not computing. My sister, alive. How? How? How?

I try to wet my mouth, but there's no saliva. "I don't understand," I croak. "How come she's not dead? I felt our bond sever. I *felt* it."

Preston lowers my sister's wrist. The impossible has happened, and yet he looks neither relieved nor joyful. Instead, his brows are creased, and his lips are tense. If I'm reading his eyes correctly, I'd say he's…scared. But that can't be right. Why would he be afraid?

"I told you Callie could only latch onto someone whose genetic thread was a psychic match." His voice is soft, and I shouldn't be able to hear him, not as well as I do. But the room is a cavern, and every word, every syllable pierces into my mind. "Your thread was the best match, since the two of you are twins. But there are other genetic threads. Other possible matches. Maybe they aren't ideal, but in a pinch, they'll work."

I blink. "You mean my mom was here?"

"No, she wasn't."

My lungs contract. My mom is our only living relative. Our only genetic match. Unless…unless…

"There's a third child," I say breathlessly. "Another embryo we didn't know about. I have another brother or sister?"

I rise onto my toes, about to take flight, but he shakes his head. "No, Jessa. You have no other siblings. Your mother only ever had two embryos in her womb, and you and Callie were it."

I crash back down. "Who is it, then?"

"I…" He looks up, as if the answer's etched into the ceiling.

I freeze. He's always seemed familiar to me, although I've never been able to place him. This must be the reason.

Quickly, I cross to the computer terminal, understanding but not. I've watched Tanner enough times that I know exactly how to curve my fingers around the keyball. Exactly what sequence of keys to press.

A holo-monitor appears in the air, one that measures the patient's psychic powers. Green dots throb in the shape of a horizontal figure — Callie. Next to her, much weaker orange dots pulse in a vertical shape. Preston. A string of lights connects the two figures. It's not as thick or layered as my thread was — but it's there.

"You," I say breathlessly. "It was you. You saw her body failing, so you offered her your psychic thread. She latched onto you."

He hesitates and then nods. "It wasn't my first choice for any of us. You have to understand that. This wasn't the way it was supposed to be. But when it became clear that you wouldn't get to her in time, it was either this or let her die." He looks up, his eyes glistening with unshed tears. "I could never let Callie die. So long as there is breath in my body. No matter what I have to sacrifice."

He loves her so much. More than as a subject or a patient. As much as my mom or Logan or me. Still, I don't understand. I don't know who he is. "But why? Why does she mean so much to you? Who are you?"

He comes around the stretcher and tentatively picks up my hand. His fingers are warm and firm. They wrap around my knuckles the way a nest cradles a bird's eggs. I'm reminded of the secret communication between Callie and me, how she would squeeze my hand three times to let me know that we were safe.

And then, he looks straight into my eyes. "Jessa, I'm your father."

34

My long-lost father. Preston. One and the same? No way. What kind of game is he playing?

I tug away my hand, and a sound escapes my lips, so short it doesn't even qualify as a laugh. "Don't be ridiculous. You're not my father. You're barely older than me."

"I'm thirty-one," he says gently. "That makes me fifteen years older than you."

"That makes you Mikey's age. Four years older than Logan. Four years older than my sister. So let's not discuss this any further." I back up a few careful steps. I don't know who he is, but based on what he's saying, he might be unstable. "Mom never talks about my father, but Callie used to. She told me all sorts of stories because she wanted me to know him, too. He wasn't some kid. He was this great scientist who time-traveled to the future and got stuck there—"

I cut off and look at him. Really look at him. Before I left civilization, my mother used to wear a hologram of my father around her neck. I haven't seen the locket since I've been back. Maybe the reminder was too painful after her entire family was wrenched away. I don't know. I do have a fuzzy recollection of my father's picture. The jet-black hair, the smooth brown skin, eyes that come to a crease at the corners. Could it be? Oh. Dear. Fates...

"You time-traveled here? To this future?"

He nods. "Just a few months ago, I said good-bye to your mother and four-year-old Callie." He rubs his forehead with long, slender fingers that might've held a yellow stub of a pencil, once upon a time. "She was such an angel. That soft curve of her cheek, that button nose. I could watch her sleep for hours. In fact, I did, because she got in the habit of sleeping in our bed. I would wake every morning with a foot in my face." He looks at me. "You didn't exist yet, but, uh, I bet you were a cute baby, too." There's a pause, as awkward as it is long. "I, um.... I'm sorry I missed it."

I can't believe this. I wouldn't believe it, except he's right here, right in front of me. With the hands I've heard so much about. With the eyes that peer back at me when I look in a mirror.

"So it actually worked," I say wonderingly. "Everyone assumed that bits and pieces of you were stuck in different times. Your head in the pre-Boom era, and your heart in the next millennium. But that's not the case. You're here, and you're whole and intact. Who knows about this? Tanner? Mikey?"

"You're the first person I've told."

"But why?" I ask. "This is huge! Whatever experiment you did in the past, it worked. TechRA would go crazy over this technology."

"That's precisely why I haven't said anything," he says slowly. "This discovery is so big, we have to be careful who we tell—and how. If the information gets into the wrong hands, there could be complete chaos. We could mess up the space-time continuum. It's not a decision I want to make alone, so I was going to wait until I returned to my present."

"Except you never came back." My voice is stiff. I can't help it. If he's telling the truth, then not only is he my father, but he is also the man who deserted us. "Mom's been pining for you for twenty-three years."

"I always planned to return." His Adam's apple moves, and he walks back to the stretcher, back to Callie. Maybe he feels safer with someone who's not awake. Or maybe he just feels more comfortable with the girl he considers his true daughter. "From your mother's perspective, it would've seemed like minutes after I left. She was never supposed to have time to miss me."

"Well, she did. And so did Callie," I say, my anger building. "I was only six back then, and I wasn't supposed to know any better. But I was old enough to notice when the conversation stopped, when the air felt so heavy it pressed down on my shoulders. I noticed when I woke up in the middle of the night and I heard sobbing. I didn't know if it was Mom or Callie, but does it matter? You broke both their hearts."

He drops his face into his hands, and his shoulders vibrate in a strange, seizure-like way.

Oh Fates. He's crying. This man—the father I've never met—is crying. Is his heart broken, too?

My anger shivers and then pauses, like someone's frozen a frame of a hologram. "Just go back to them," I plead. "There's still time. There's always time. Maybe Callie will still end up here, like this, but at least she would've had you for a few years." I lower my voice. "You could've helped Mom get through the loss of her firstborn."

"I can't," he says helplessly.

"Why not? You could just tell a couple of the other scientists. Whoever you trust the most. I'm sure they'll help you figure out a way to go back. If you love Mom and Callie, you would try."

"You don't understand. It's not the mechanics that's the problem. I know exactly *how* to go back. But it's precisely because I love them that I can't." He picks up Callie's hand, but he doesn't need the physical touch to prove their connection. Behind him, on the holo-monitor, the string of lights joins their bodies. Unarguably. Irrevocably. "Shortly after I arrived in this time, I learned that my precious Callie was lying in a coma. I learned about the existence of another daughter: you. Most importantly, I heard about your absentee father, the one who had gotten himself stuck in another time."

Behind him, the string of light glows brighter. Its circumference grows thicker. "You can imagine how shocked I was. I had every intention of going back to my time, and I couldn't imagine what had gone wrong. Still, I was determined to return. I didn't want to leave Callie like this, however, drifting endlessly through time. My plan was to stay a few months, anchor her firmly to the present, and then go back."

He holds out a hand to me. As if called by a magnet, I go to him, so that the three of us are connected, hand to hand. But I don't look behind me. I can't bear to see what's not there—the absence of any psychic thread binding me to either of them.

"You showed up and entwined yourself with Callie, and she was stable, more stable than she'd been in the last decade," he continues. "I thought this was my cue to return. I'd been gone six months, and I missed your mother. I missed little Callie. I wanted to go back and be with you from the beginning, from the day you were born. But then, you didn't come to rejuvenate your bond, and Callie was fading, fast. I had no choice." His face crumples, and lines of grief spread around his eyes and mouth.

That's when I get it. I get why he looks so sad; I get why he's aged beyond his years. "Callie. She's the reason you have to stay. She's the reason you can never go back."

"Yes," he says softly. "Now that she's transferred her bond to me, she and I are inextricably wound together. If I leave this realm, if I go back to my time, our bond will be severed. And she'll die."

35

The next morning, I wake on a thin mattress on the floor in Preston's apartment. Another mattress, another floor. I should be used to it by now. But I miss my bed. I miss my hoverboard. I miss Ryder and even my mom.

Not that I'm uncomfortable here. The warmth from the heated floorboards seeps through the padding, and the hum of the life-support machines soothes me. Like crickets in the woods, it acts as background noise to lull me to sleep. More importantly, the hum means that there is a life to support.

I rise onto my elbow and look at the bed next to mine. A stretcher, more accurately, surrounded by a dozen blinking machines. Callie.

She's alive, but we couldn't leave her in the cavernous room with the other dreaming bodies, not when Chairwoman Dresden thinks she's dead. She had ordered Preston to take away Callie's body, and he obeyed—just not in the way she expected.

Tanner helped us move Callie to my father's apartment, just a few doors down from his in the scientific residences. He helped us set up the life-support equipment. He would've stayed and helped even more—but after taking one look at my face, Preston sent him back to his apartment for the night.

"Hey, sis," I say. "It's fun spending the night with you again."

The greeting simultaneously makes me laugh and tear up. When I was a kid, I used to beg her to stay with me the whole night through, to curl her body against mine on the single mattress. Because I was scared of the dark—and also because I just wanted to be close to her. Those are my favorite memories. The two of us, whispering in the night like best friends and contemporaries, not sisters who were eleven years apart.

In retrospect, I realize that Callie was probably just pretending we were equals. What counsel could a teen like her want from a kid like me?

Still, it was nice of her to pretend. I grab a tissue from the compartment set in the wall and dab at my eyes. Fate is cruel. Her reach is long, nearly all-encompassing. I thought she was mean enough when she showed Callie a vision of her future self killing her little sister. But now, she's wielding her power even on those who skip through time, attempting to avoid her.

My poor mother. For the first time in years, my heart shifts, melting some of the frozen bars encasing it. I judged her so quickly for everything she did to me. Never once did I attempt to understand her. Her true love left for an adventure through time—and never came back. Can I fault her for clinging to the hope of his return—even at the expense of her child?

Yes, I think emphatically. The old resentment rises, but then it floats away like pollen on the breeze. I'm no longer mad at my mother. I just feel sorry for her.

I change into a TechRA uniform Preston filched from the supply closet and pad into the eating area. My father's already there, preparing coffee in the Drinks Assembler.

"Good morning," he says. Even those two words sound stilted, like he's not sure how to handle our relationship now that I know about it. He hands me a mug, keeping one for himself, but they feel more like life preservers. Objects we can each hold onto while we navigate these unknown waters of father and teenage daughter. "Sleep well? Were you, um, scared sleeping next to Callie's unconscious body?"

"Nah. Callie couldn't scare me, even if she were a zombie or a ghost." I wrap both hands around the coffee mug. I'd wrap my legs around it, too, if it were big enough. "Thanks. For letting me stay. You didn't have to. I mean, we don't really know each other." Fates. Why is this so hard? Preston is my father. My *father*, even if we only just met.

"Of course. You can stay with me anytime." He clears his throat and then clears it again. But no amount of guttural searching will uncover words that don't exist.

We both sip our coffees. I desperately try to think of something to say. We have an entire lifetime to catch up on—and yet, my mind remains stubbornly blank.

"I talked to Mikey last night," Preston finally says in a rush. "The riot's dying down, but tempers are still strong. A ring of people has staked out his house, complete with collapsible tents and portable meal assemblers, barricading him in so that he can't go to work."

I drink the last bitter dregs of the coffee, struggling to figure out how I feel. I should feel sorry for Mikey, but he hid Callie's existence from me. He authorized Olivia's kidnapping. He keeps more secrets than a safe. His intentions may be good, but he's no longer the man I used to know. Maybe he never was.

"You can stay here until it's safe," Preston continues. "Even beyond that, if you'd like."

"Are you sure? I don't want to impose. I could go

somewhere else—"

"Jessa, I'm your father." We both freeze at the words. He's said them before. I just thought them a few minutes ago. But this time, in this context, the utterance takes on a different meaning. It no longer refers to the biological relationship but to a social one. An emotional one. A relationship for which I'm not sure either of us is ready.

"I'm your father," he says again, more firmly this time. "You'll always have a home with me. Besides, where would you go? Next door, to Tanner's?" His voice rises. "He's a good scientist, I'll give you that. As my assistant, he would be trusted with my life. But as my daughter's suitor? You are not to spend a single minute alone in his company, you hear? I've seen the way he looks at you."

"First of all, he's not my suitor," I say tightly. "He might've pretended to be, but it's not true. It was all for show. And second, are you seriously going to try and tell me what to do? You haven't been in my life for sixteen years, Preston! You weren't here when I had to escape to the wilderness. You weren't here to help me negotiate my arguments with Mom. You haven't earned that right."

His jaw firms. "You're still my daughter."

"Only in name. Only through blood." I stop, my breath coming in large puffs. "I'm sorry. It's not your fault. None of us were to blame."

He looks at me, his eyes pulling down at the corners. My heart aches. I wish he'd been the first one to hold me after I was born, his tears wetting the receiving blanket. I wish he'd made sand turtles with me at the beach. I wish he'd placed me high on his shoulders, so that I could feel like I was taller than the world. But he didn't. He won't. And we both have to live with that.

"Don't worry," I say, my voice softening. "I don't even want to talk to Tanner, much less touch him. My virtue is perfectly safe as far as he's concerned."

The coffee mug stops halfway to Preston's lips. "What did he do?"

"What didn't he do?" I retort. "He invented future memory. He endangered Callie's life. He betrayed me." Now that I've had a full night's rest, now that I'm no longer shattered by the thought of Callie's death, the anger rushes to the surface again. "I trusted him, and this entire time, all he cared about was using me to advance his career."

"I don't know." He plunks down the mug. "I'm not a fan of those looks he gives you, but I think he truly cares about you."

Maybe he does, the voice inside me says. *Think how gentle he was when you fell apart. Think how he looked into your eyes and told you his feelings overwhelmed him.*

I push away the voice, confused. I'm pulled in so many directions, I don't know what to think. I don't know how to feel.

I do know this: I'd rather put my energies into the man who is inextricably twined in my life. "I don't want to talk about Tanner. I want to talk about you." I take a few tentative steps toward Preston.

I may not know him, but I want to. I want to understand him, his thoughts, his feelings. I want our relationship to be real, not just in name but also in meaning. Time, as we both well know, might be even more fleeting than the scant number of minutes we do have.

"I'm sorry you've been handed this fate," I say. "It can't be easy."

His eyes widen, and all of a sudden, his cheeks are wet, as though the tears have sprouted from his skin. "Don't misunderstand me, Jessa. I would do anything to keep Callie alive, and I'm happy to be here now, with you. But I can never have my family back. I don't get to grow old with the woman I love. I don't get to see my little girl—I mean, both my little girls—grow up. My future is your past. You've both been through incredibly tough times, and I wasn't there to help you."

I swallow hard, even though I know his tears are not for me. Have never been for me. He's including me in his regrets to be polite, but I heard his slip-up. His concern is for his little girl. His Callie. The one who existed when he left home.

"She didn't blame you," I whisper. "Did you know she used to tell me stories about you? Over and over again, so that she wouldn't forget. So that I would know you, too." I smile, but the tears I won't shed coalesce in a lump in my throat. I knew him, but he didn't have a clue that I was alive. "She loved you so much."

"I love her. And it helps to have both of you here, in the present, even if Callie's not awake." He sits and studies his hands, those long, beautiful fingers that figured so prominently in Callie's stories. "But it kills me to leave your mother behind. The thought of never seeing her again is like a machete to my heart."

"Why can't you see her?" I sit down, too. Not across from him but next to him. As though we can make up for our emotional distance with physical proximity. "She's right here, a few miles away. Once the riot settles, we can both go over there."

He coughs. Must be choking on saliva, since he hasn't drunk any coffee in the last few minutes. "I can't do that," he rasps. "She wouldn't want me, and it would just be painful for both of us."

"Why wouldn't she want you? She never remarried. She said she'd already married her soul mate. Any other relationship, by definition, would be less. I mean, I know it's weird, 'cause she's so much older than you…"

"You think I care about that?" he says fiercely. "I fell in love with Phoebe. She will always be beautiful to me, no matter what her age is. She will always be the love of my life."

"Don't you think she feels the same way?"

He moves his shoulders, so lost, so lonely. A single traveler, bobbing helplessly in the sea of time. "To me, only a few months have passed. I'm just as in love with her as I've always been. But for her, twenty-three years have gone by. Twenty-three years where she thinks I abandoned her. Where she believes I prioritized another time, another place, over her." He shakes his head slowly. "I just don't know how she'll feel."

"You'll never know until you try." Awkwardly, I place my hand on his arm. "Will you at least think about what I said?"

He covers my hand with his. No longer uncertain. No longer hesitant. "Now that you've brought it up, I won't be able to think about anything else."

36

Thirty minutes after breakfast—congee with salty egg and black chicken from the Meal Assembler—Tanner vibrates the floor and waltzes in.

I frown. Preston's in the study with Callie, checking her vitals, so it's up to me to play hostess. "It's Saturday. This isn't a TechRA lab. What are you doing here?"

Okay, so maybe that wasn't the most welcoming greeting ever. It's the best I can do.

He slowly takes off his jacket—uninvited—and slips out of his shoes—unasked. His hair is back to its silky state, falling over his eyes, and his muscular chest is hidden beneath a black thermal shirt. The fact that I was pressed against his chest not too long ago makes me frown even harder.

"Preston filled me in last night. About everything." Tanner's tone is neutral. He could be talking about the weather or a new record for his wind sprints.

I bristle anyway. "Haven't you ruined enough lives? This isn't your business."

"It is, actually. I'm Preston's research assistant, and now

that he's linked to the subject, literally, he can no longer be an impartial observer. I'm here to double-check his findings and run some data streams, so that we can tweak the experiment if necessary."

I flush. "That's my sister you're talking about. Not an experiment."

"This experiment happens to be saving Callie's life. Preston requested—and I agree—that we make it our top priority. I'm prepared to put my full attention on the matter. Unless you prefer I don't?" He raises an eyebrow.

He's talking like a scientist again, and I hate him for it. At least I think that's hate I'm feeling. Sticky, all-encompassing, black-tar anger. I have so many reasons to hurl plates at him, so many reasons to pound my fists against his chest—and hope like Limbo it hurts. But with all these reasons, why do I only feel like I want to cry?

I shoot to my feet before he can sense any weakness. "Do what you have to do. Just don't expect me to thank you for it."

"You wouldn't thank me for saving your sister's life?"

"Not when you endangered it in the first place." I leave the room without a backward glance. If Preston wants a host for his guest, he'll have to come out and play one himself.

I retreat to Preston's sleeping area. It's the only unoccupied room in the apartment. Maybe I shouldn't be in here without his permission, but he is my father. If only in name. If only across time. I normally wouldn't dream of invading his privacy, but today, my desire to get away from Tanner outweighs my civility.

The room is simple, the furnishing basic. Holo-screens on the walls. A retractable bed with a temperature- and pressure-modulated mattress. A washer-closet that launders clothes when you hang them up and close the door. But no personal trinkets, no customized holos. Nothing that would reveal that this room belongs to Preston instead of someone else.

It doesn't surprise me. I don't think travelers can transport physical objects. That's why Mikey's trying to figure out how to push prosthetic limbs through time.

All of a sudden, other questions pop up, one after the other, multiplying like weeds. Why did he come here? Once he arrived, what did he do? Who did he talk to? How did he get clothes? Shelter? How was he assigned a position as a scientist, much less the lead on Callie's case?

I wander around the room, trailing my fingers over the furniture. Maybe someday I'll get the chance to ask him. Maybe we'll sit, away from this chaos, unconcerned with riots and saving lives, and I'll teach him how to build a fire—a real one, not the kind you turn on with the flip of a switch. A fire like the ones we had in the wilderness. We'll roast marshmallows on a stick—the closest I get to cooking manually—and he'll tell me his life's stories. Our relationship wouldn't be strained or awkward, and it would be like we were actually father and daughter.

He would love me the way he loves Callie.

The thought knocks the breath out of me. Is that what this is about? Am I...jealous of my sister? Maybe I am. It wasn't easy growing up in the shadow of her greatness. It would be nice to be loved just a fraction of the amount that she's loved. That's all.

I turn to leave. I shouldn't be here. Tanner's had plenty of time to join Preston, so the eating area should be clear.

As I walk to the door, a corner of the wall screen catches my eye. The digital square cycles through Preston's favorite feeds—a calendar, an update of the weather, the latest news, and then a static screenshot.

I peer closer—and my breath catches. I recognize that screenshot. It's from a news article about a hoverthon I'd organized a year ago to raise credits for shelter dogs so they wouldn't be donated to TechRA for research.

Preston not only looked up the article, but he kept it as one of his favorites. Why? Was he researching me to figure out if he could trust me?

Or maybe he was telling the truth. Maybe he cares for me, just a bit.

Little bubbles pop in my chest like I'm a can of carbonated soda. But the fizz doesn't hurt, and I'm not uncomfortable. Instead, I'm smiling as I cross the threshold.

Maybe there's no reason to be jealous after all.

37

The first thing I hear when I walk into the hallway is: *Beep. Beep. Beep*.

My heart stutters, and the smile crumbles from my face. I've heard this noise before, just over a week ago. Callie's vitals have entered the red zone.

Forget not intruding. Without a second thought, I run to the last room down the hall, where Preston and Tanner are working. Where Callie's body lies.

I throw open the door. "What happened? Is Callie okay?"

Preston stands next to her stretcher, attaching a bag of clear liquid to her IV stand, while Tanner's fingers fly over the keyball.

"I was afraid of this," Preston says, his hands trembling on the bag. "I hoped and prayed I was wrong, but I can't keep pretending anymore. My psychic thread is similar enough to bond with Callie's, but it's not a match. I can't feed her connection the way you could." His voice becomes more garbled with each word, until it sounds like he has marbles in his mouth. "I can't keep her alive."

I grip the railing on the stretcher. "What are you saying?"

Tanner puts down the keyball and swipes a hand across his forehead. "Her heart's beating too slowly. The meds will speed it up for now. But it can't last. We need another solution."

The *beep, beep, beep* switches off, and my eyes fly to the holo-monitor. Sure enough, the medicine's done its work. Her heart rate has returned to the normal range.

For now. It can't last.

"Easy," I say, my heart pounding fast. "Just transfer her bond back to me." But even as I say the words, I know it can't be that simple. Preston and Tanner wouldn't look so serious otherwise.

My father shakes his head, and my heart sinks.

"I was able to connect with her only after your bond was severed," he says. "It was touch and go for a few minutes. I thought I'd lost her. Nothing but extreme luck allowed her to reattach to me after she'd been floating untethered in time. She's so much weaker now that if we tried the same maneuver again...well, I think her death would be all but certain."

Each sentence pushes down on my shoulders. "We don't have another solution. That's been our problem all along."

Tanner and Preston exchange a look. "That's not quite true," my dad says slowly. "Tanner's had a brainstorm. Something nobody else had considered."

I want to roll my eyes. Great. Here comes Boy Genius to solve the problem nobody else can. But if he can save my sister, I promise I'll never be annoyed at him again. No matter how superior he is.

"It should work, in theory." Tanner pushes the hair off his forehead. "But it's never been tried. If it fails, the risks are great."

"The risks are even greater if we don't try." I push down the panic that's climbing my windpipe. The breath rolls across

Callie's body in waves, and her skin is so translucent I can see the veins in her eyelids. "We could lose her."

"Agreed. Which is why we're willing to consider the experiment now when we weren't before." Preston looks at his assistant. "Do you want to explain?"

Tanner straightens his spine. "Like I told you before, we need to find a way to signal her brain. In our world, we think of time linearly. Yesterday is followed by today is followed by tomorrow. But Callie's mind zooms around with no idea of past or present or future. We need a glowing beacon she can't ignore. Something to say, 'Hey, Callie, over here. This is the present, this is the now.'"

He takes a deep breath. "If Callie can recognize the present, if only for a moment, her mind will have something to latch onto. It will synchronize her with our time, and she'll wake up again."

"So how do we signal her?" I ask.

"That's the problem. She's been in a coma these past ten years, so by definition, she doesn't have any memories from this time—at least, that she's aware of. But then, I got an idea when we were talking about Callie's ability to modify memories. When we were, um, lying down in the clearing." His eyes flicker to me for the tiniest moment, and my face burns. *When we were wrapped around each other as though we would never let go*, he might as well have said. "Callie has no memories of the present. So I thought, why don't we manufacture one?"

I will not look at him. I will not. "What do you mean?"

"Yeah, I know. It sounds crazy. Hear me out. We time-travel to the past, as close as possible to the moment her mind left synchronous time, when her synapses are firing at lightning speed. We lay a foundation there. We take a childhood memory that's lived in her mind for so long that it's turned into fact. A nursery rhyme, maybe, or a jingle her mind will automatically complete. And then we change it, twisting it in such a way that her mind will register that something's not right."

He peeks at me, as if to see if I'm still with him. "We come back to the present," he continues. "We use the modified nursery rhyme, the one we planted in her head, as that glowing beacon. We jolt her mind, like it was jolted only one other time in her life. And then we pray to the Fates that it's enough to stop her mind from zooming. To make it pause long enough for us to reel her back to the present." He puffs out a breath of air. "What do you think?"

I look from one scientist to the other. From the boy who could've meant something to me to the man who was, once upon a time, everything to my sister. Their expressions are identical. Serious. Hopeful. Waiting.

"There's one problem," I say. "We don't have a time machine."

"We do, actually," Preston says. "The same one I used more than two decades ago. The one that's been boarded up and abandoned. It's still there, in a cabin in the woods. I've been working on it these last few months in preparation for what I thought would be my return. I ran the final test a week ago. It works just as well now as it did twenty-three years ago."

"Still, it seems complicated," I say slowly. "Dangerous."

"Yep." Tanner nods vigorously.

"Very much so," Preston agrees.

"Countless things could go wrong when we play with time. Look at Preston. Whoever travels to the past could get stuck there—or worse."

The scientists nod. "You're absolutely right," Tanner says. "The risks are off the charts."

I take a deep breath. "Okay. When do I leave?"

38

"Wait a minute. Who says you're going?" Preston steps forward, tripping over the IV stand. Nimbly, Tanner catches the bag before it yanks the tube out of Callie's hand and hangs it back in place.

"Of course I'm going." My mind was made up the moment I understood the plan. "Who else would you send?"

"Me," Tanner says, sticking out his chest. "It was my idea. I should be the one to go."

The anger inside me flares to life. I should be grateful he's willing to risk so much to save my sister. And I am. Sort of. But a bigger part of me—the part that's still reeling from his betrayal—snaps.

"You don't know her. You don't care what happens to her. You just want full and complete credit for this theory. You'll probably write up the results for your core thesis." I curl my hands into fists. "Well, you know what? This isn't one of your lab experiments. Nobody's interested in your ego. We're not sending someone who's completely indifferent to Callie's welfare."

He raises his eyebrow. "If this is just about impressing the admission officials — which it isn't — then you should want me to go. Nobody wants to get into uni more than I do. Besides, I understand the physics of time travel. I'm the one most likely to be successful."

"Doesn't take much scientific expertise to recite a nursery rhyme," I retort. "Callie is way more likely to remember my words ten years later. I'm her sister, remember. Her twin."

Preston claps a hand on both our shoulders. That's when I realize I'm facing Tanner, my hands on my hips, my feet a shoulder's width apart. The universal battle stance. I'll throw down with him, right here, right now, if that's what it takes.

"This would be a moot point if I could go, being a scientist as well as Callie's father," Preston says. "But I can't. The moment I leave this time, my connection to her would be severed, killing her instantly and defeating the purpose of the trip."

He pauses, as though carefully choosing his next words. "May I say, Jessa, that Tanner has a point? I agree that Callie's more likely to absorb what you say, but should something go wrong, he's more likely to figure out how to come back to the present."

I back away, so that his hand falls from my shoulder. "You just don't want me to go."

"True. Selfishly, as your father, I can't bear the thought of losing either of you."

"Dad, you don't understand." The name slips out, and we both go still. I didn't do it on purpose; I wasn't trying to be manipulative. But now that the endearment is out there, now that I have his attention, I'm not going to squander it.

"Callie changed the future in order to save me," I say. "All my life, I've wondered if I was worthy of her sacrifice. Well, here's my chance to prove it. She gave up her life to save mine, and now, ten years later, I have the opportunity to give her life back to her. Please, Dad. Give me this chance."

He gnaws his lip, and I hold my breath. Neither Tanner nor I can do anything without his permission. Preston's the one who's traveled through time. He essentially invented the technology, at least in North Amerie. If one of us is going back to the past, we need the father of time travel guiding us.

Preston exhales. "How about a compromise? What if you both go? Both your arguments are valid, and although it's twice as risky to send two of you, I think it's twice as likely your mission will succeed. What do you say?"

Tanner and I eye each other. If this were about only me, I wouldn't go to a Meal Assembler café with him. But there's nothing I wouldn't do to save Callie, even if it means working with the boy who betrayed us both.

I nod reluctantly, and then Tanner nods, too.

"Great," Preston says, but he doesn't sound great. Instead, his voice cracks, and beads of sweat gather on his forehead. "The next thing we have to do is…uh, contact your mother."

"Mom?" My eyebrows climb toward the ceiling. "What does she have to do with anything?"

"You know what." He swallows a few times before he can get out his next words. "Twenty-three years ago, I asked your mother to act as my anchor. You see, time travel is so difficult because space and time need to be precisely coordinated. The earliest travelers flung themselves into time without thought to location—and perished in the deep reaches of space because the Earth was continuously moving. We can solve that problem, however, with an anchor. Someone who's resided in the same place, from the target date of your travel to the present, so that she's psychically attached to the location."

He twists his fingers together. "Your mother has lived in the exact same spot since I left her. Let's hope she's continued the practice of recording her memories every night, so that she can recall a particular date. If so, I'll be able to send you to any day you'd like in the last twenty-three years."

So that's why he's so nervous. That's why he looks like he's about to faint.

"You'll have to see her again," I say. "In order for this to work, you and Mom will have to come face-to-face."

"Yes. I'll have to see Phoebe again." A fine tremor runs through his body as he says her name. No matter how hard I try, I can't figure out if her name is a prayer or a plea.

Probably both.

39

"Come on, Mom. Where are you?" I mutter the next morning, spinning on my heel to march down the apartment once more. "Don't tell me you've changed your mind."

I had a holo-conference with her last night, filling her in on the day's events. She already knew about Olivia's kidnapping, but when I told her about how Dresden locked me up and I thought Callie had died, she cried along with me.

"She's not dead," I gasped. "I want you to know that. She's stable, at least for the time being. But I thought she was. Mom, they were the most horrible hours of my life."

"Of course it was, dear heart. Of course it was." She reached out her arms to embrace me. We were on a holo-call, so of course I couldn't feel her. But I closed my eyes and pretended I did.

But then came the hard part. The part when I had to tell her about Preston.

With halting words, I laid out the facts, as clearly and simply as I could. When I finished, she had become so still I could've mistaken her for a powered-off bot.

"Say something," I pleaded. "Please."

"He's still thirty-one years old? Is he...well?" Even her voice sounded like a bot's, flat and unemotional.

"Yes. Worried about you and Callie, but otherwise well."

"That's good." Her voice got softer and softer. She was shutting down.

"You can't pretend this isn't happening, Mom. You have to see him. And soon. You're the only way we have of saving Callie."

She didn't say much for the rest of the conversation. Didn't move much, either. But I got her to agree to come to us in the morning. She also confirmed she had been recording her memories every day for the last twenty-three years, without fail. The sights, sounds, and smells. What she thought, how she felt. As complete a record as possible of that moment in time. She did it, every single night, although she never mentioned it. Not once.

I begin my hundredth trek across the apartment. Everything is proceeding according to plan—if you ignore my mom's faint voice and my dad's uncontrollable jitters. Even my stomach flops around like a fish on land.

And then, the floor vibrates. Someone's here.

But it's Tanner and not my mother who walks through the door. "Your mom's in my apartment. She wants to talk to you."

"What about?" I ask automatically. Some mothers and daughters talk every day. Not us. Our talks—the real ones that involve actual thoughts and genuine emotions—are more like the once-in-a-comet variety.

"She didn't say. But she's not budging until she sees you."

Nodding, I look over my shoulder. Preston's nowhere to be seen. The door to his sleeping area is sealed shut. I have the bizarre feeling I'm playing matchmaker. For my parents. Who are separated in time by more than two decades.

I take a deep breath. "Okay. Lead the way."

...

When I walk into the spare room of Tanner's apartment, my mother is sitting in front of a mirror. A box of black data chips lies on the table in front of her—one chip for each year since my father left.

Her hand trembles as she dabs the concealer under her eyes. Most women in Eden City get their blemishes removed—but not my mom. She's always been proud of her age. When I was little, she would tell me bedtime stories using the lines on her face.

"These were the lines that were born when your father left," she would say, pointing to the wrinkles around her mouth. "And these lines formed in the first year of your life." She would indicate the three crow's feet that radiated from her eyes. "You made me laugh and laugh, my darling bunny. With your little expressions, your little hands. You filled me with so much joy I almost forgot to feel sad." She would pull me close, the conclusion of the story a whisper across my cheeks.

Now, she holds the eyeliner applicator to her face—for those women who opt not to tattoo—but her hand shakes so much the machine won't lock and draw a straight line. After three times, she slams down the applicator. "What am I doing? I'm fifty years old. I'm not going to be able to hide that fact. I don't want to hide it. I shouldn't have to." She closes her eyes and inhales deeply, quickly. Breaths to refill a rapidly dwindling supply of oxygen rather than to maintain the even flow of life.

"Mom." I move forward and pick up the applicator. "You look beautiful."

I position the applicator over her eye. The machine beeps,

records an image of her eye, and then draws a precise, perfect line along her lash. I repeat the process with the other eye.

"Thank you," she says in a tone I've never heard.

That's when I realize in all the years since I've returned, we've never had a moment like this. Our natural mode of communication was arguing, and I never spoke to her without rolling my eyes or yelling.

Shame spreads through me. I resented her for staying in civilization, for refusing to move to the Harmony compound with me. And now, because she did, we might be able to save Callie. At the very least, I owe her an apology.

"I'm sorry, Mom," I say in a low voice. "I was so mad at you for abandoning me, but now, I'm so grateful you made that decision. So grateful." I look into the mirror, searching for her eyes. When I find them, hers fill with tears.

"That was the only reason I could've let you go. I want you to know that, Jessa. It wasn't because I was waiting for your father to return. It was because I was hoping this day would come. The day that Callie's life depended on me staying where I was."

My breath catches. "You knew? This whole time, you knew we would come to this point in time? But how? Did you receive a message from the future?"

"Something like that." In the mirror, she moves her shoulders. "So much time had passed, I'd almost given up hope. Now, I'm so glad I didn't."

I turn her to face me. For this conversation, I don't want anything between us, not even a reflective surface.

"I didn't know the exact circumstances, but I was told in no uncertain terms that someday, I would need to act as an anchor to save my daughter's life." Her voice scrapes every bit of sinew and emotion from my heart. "I had to do it, Jessa. I had to save Callie's life, even if it meant sacrificing your welfare."

"Why didn't you tell me?" I whisper. "Explain the situation so I wouldn't have been so mad? So I could understand a little bit?"

"I couldn't. You were so young, but more than that, I didn't want to mess up the future chain of events. Fate is a tricky thing, Jessa. If you knew, I was afraid things wouldn't have unfolded the way they were supposed to. I was afraid I would jeopardize Callie's life, after everything we've sacrificed to save her."

"I was so cold to you." I duck my head, not looking at her. Not looking at my reflection. "All these years."

She cups my chin and tilts it up. "I don't blame you. Rightly or wrongly, I did abandon you. No matter the reason, I did it, and I have to suffer the consequences of that action. I knew what I was doing, Jessa. I knew exactly what my choice entailed, and I would make the same decision again." She tries to smile, but her eyes won't obey. "Doesn't mean I'll ever forgive myself. That's why I was always so restrained with you. I knew you hated me, and you had every right in the world."

I hug her, wrapping my arms around her neck, probably messing up the makeup I had just so carefully applied. "Oh, Mom. I don't hate you. I love you. I always have. I just didn't know how to show it." I pull back and look at the fine lines decorating her face. How many of them did I put there? "This wasn't easy for either of us. I'll forgive you if you forgive me."

She laughs, and it's like a flashlight cutting through a tunnel of sludge. Hope slicing through a world of despair. "I would take years of you yelling at me for a moment like this."

The tears push at my eyes, but they don't come out. Instead, they drop inside me, splattering onto my soul. "I'm sorry, Mom. I should've tried harder."

"It's a two-way street, Jessa. I should've tried harder, too." She reaches out and fixes my collar, even though it doesn't need fixing. "Especially because I knew you would forgive me someday."

"How?"

"Your future self told me." She gives me a stunning smile, one I haven't seen since I've been back in civilization. "She told me it was never too late for love."

I smile back. "She's really smart. Just remember that when you see Dad."

She stiffens, and the happiness drains from her face. "Is it time already?"

It was time twenty minutes ago, but I don't mention that. "Yes."

"How do I look?"

"Beautiful." I help her to her feet, turning her from the mirror. The only image I want her to see is the one reflected in my eyes. "You look like the woman Preston loves, no matter what age he is. No matter what age you are."

She doesn't believe me. I can tell from the flush of her cheeks, from the straightness of her spine. She looks like a woman about to go into battle, not like one about to be reunited with the love of her life.

"Let's do this," she mutters.

I follow her out the door. The riots continue outside, and I'm about to journey to the past to save my sister. But at this moment, I only want what every little kid wants: my parents together and happy once more.

40

My mother was in front of me, but somehow in the short walk down the hall, I overtake her. The closer we get to Preston's apartment, the slower she walks. It's as though she's trying to prove the old scientific joke: If she goes half as far with every step, she'll never arrive.

I look over my shoulder and give her a fortifying smile, but she's beyond encouragement. Her arms are crossed tightly, and her every step is accompanied by a labored huff of air.

"It's okay, Mom," I say. "You're not facing a monster. It's just Dad."

Dad. The name rolls off my tongue more and more easily. Yes, he's only fifteen years older than me, and yes, he's a time traveler from the past. But he's still my dad. The same age gap exists between Ryder and his adopted father, Mikey. Families come in all shapes and sizes. They're formed in countless ways—including time travel.

Only one question remains. Will my mom and dad be able to accept each other?

I walk into the apartment. Preston has emerged from his sleeping area, and he sits on the couch, twisting his necktie. I cover my mouth to hide a giggle. Twenty years ago, the height of fashion was to dress like our pre-Boom ancestors, including this unfortunate accessory. Most of the men eliminated ties from their wardrobe years ago—but not Preston. He's so cute. And if he twists the tie any harder, he'll rip it in two.

His head snaps up as we enter the room. On his face, I see hope and yearning, anticipation and fear. But the instant he glimpses my mom, every other emotion drops away, and sheer joy radiates from his every feature, his every movement.

"Phoebe," he whispers, and I'm no longer uncertain about what her name means to him. It is a prayer, pure and simple. My mother is his every dream come true.

He crosses the room in four large steps. He stops in front of her, and the air shivers with indecision. But then he grins, as if to say: *Forget that. I've been waiting too long for this moment.* Picking her up, he spins her around, in what is clearly one of their patented moves.

My mom is crying now, tears rolling freely down her face. He sits down and arranges her carefully on his lap, kissing her cheeks, right at the spot where the tears drip, as if he is ingesting her very essence.

"I've missed you so much." She lays a hand on his cheek. "You're the same, the exact same."

"As are you." He turns his head, so that her fingers are against his lips.

She opens her mouth like she's about to argue. *I could tell you stories with the lines on my face*, her parted lips seem to say. *In fact, I did. For the daughter you never knew was born.*

Instead, she closes her mouth and leans her forehead

against his, enjoying the present in the way only a person who has been ravaged by time can.

My heart full, I back out of the room, slowly, silently. In the future, they will have problems to work out, insecurities to smooth over, misunderstandings to unravel. But for now, in this moment, love is timeless.

41

When I return to Tanner's apartment, it's been transformed into mission headquarters. Baby Remi naps in a portable cradle that inflates with the touch of a button, and Mikey stands in front of the wall screen, circling and crossing out equations while he rocks the cradle with his foot. After a couple of days of being barricaded in their house, the Russells got fed up and snuck out the same way Tanner and I did. It must not have been easy to haul Remi through the tunnel, but they managed.

He nods at me as if nothing's wrong. From his perspective, nothing is. He's the same as he always has been. I just never knew exactly who he was until now.

I move farther into the living area. In the center, Tanner and Angela are studying blueprints of the TechRA building from ten years ago. My heart flips. This is really happening. We're really going back to the past.

Angela looks up from the holo-doc, blowing a strand of hair out of her eyes. "Glad you're here, Jessa. We have a lot to discuss with you."

"We can't transport nonessentials back through time," Tanner pipes up. "Which means we can't travel with our clothes."

"Wait—what?" My voice rises in a high-pitched squeak. He can't possibly have said what I thought he said. "Did you say we have to go back to the past…naked?"

"Yep," he says, his tone way too cheerful. "Just be glad we don't have to shave our heads. Your father did that when he traveled here—and when he arrived, he realized the hair on his body had passed through time unscathed. From Mikey's research with the prosthetic limbs, we've learned that so long as an item is sufficiently bonded to your body, it will remain intact through time travel."

I barely hear the rest of his explanation. I'm still stuck on the naked part. That means he'll see me…I'll see him… Damn the Fates. Can a wormhole open up and swallow me now?

"Don't worry, dear heart," Angela says. She taps a section of the blueprint, and it zooms in on a hallway. "I'm sure Tanner will be a gentleman and promise not to look. Won't you, Tanner?"

"Nope." If possible, his tone gets even brighter. "We're traveling through time—a journey very few scientists have taken. I need to pay attention. I'm not going to close my eyes over a false sense of modesty. Besides, I'll be naked, too. Jessa has my full permission to look."

He smiles at me, an obnoxious grin that makes me feel like I'm holding onto a live wire. *No.* I clamp down on the feeling. My skin might tingle, and my core might heat up—but that's my body. That's a chemical-based reaction. It has nothing to do with how I really feel.

"My parents are going to be in the room," I say evenly.

"And they remember what it's like to be young and in love."

"We're not in love." Outraged, I move forward, even

though I know he's just trying to get a reaction out of me. Bad move. The step brings me within a few feet of his chest, and the memory of my cheek pressed against him sears through me. "We don't even like each other."

His eyes flash. "You're entitled to your feelings. But don't presume you know how I feel."

"Why? Because I'm too stupid to understand the mind of the great Tanner Callahan?"

"No," he says quietly. "Because you matter too much for me to pretend what we had was nothing."

For a moment, all we hear is the squeak of the baby's cradle. And then even Mikey stops rocking. Silence blooms. So thick it nearly chokes me. So loud I'm certain Remi will wake. It winds into my heart and infiltrates my lungs, and damn the Fates, it hurts.

There's nothing I can do about the silence. Because nothing will take back Tanner's betrayal. Nothing will return our relationship to what it was shaping up to be. Instead, I drop to my knees by the cradle and place a soft kiss on Remi's cheek. The baby stirs, stretching her arms in a tiny, impossibly cute imitation of an adult, and continues sleeping.

"You may disagree on your feelings for each other," Mikey says, his mild tone indicating he's staying far from the topic, "so long as you are in agreement about one thing. Leave the past alone."

Huh? I sneak a glance at Tanner, and his raised eyebrows mirror mine.

"What do you mean?" he asks. "We have to travel to the past. That's the entire mission."

"You have to complete the mission, true." Mikey taps on the wall screen, and the equations disappear. "But it is vitally important that you leave as little a trail as possible. One flap of a butterfly's wings can cause a hurricane on the other side of the world. The killing of a single moth in the prehistoric era can set the world on an entirely different trajectory. A single action, no matter how small, may cause ripples that extend far into the future."

He takes a deep breath. "Our world developed the way it did because of the events in our past. Change one of those events, and you'll change our present. Now, most of these ripples are minor. They'll fade away long before they reach our time. But certain events are so big, so determinative of our world now, that changing them could alter everything."

His gaze pierces me, and my heart flutters. Clearly, he's trying to tell me something with life-or-death importance.

"Let me be perfectly clear," he continues, when neither Tanner nor I respond. "Do not try to save Callie. Do not try to prevent her from injecting herself. It happened. And because it happened, this is the world we live in. These are the children that populate that world."

As if on cue, Remi starts wailing, her tiny fists pummeling the air. Angela rushes over and lifts the baby to her shoulder.

Mikey spreads his palm across his daughter's back. "Do you understand what I'm saying? When you return to the past, you will be tempted to save Callie. You must resist. Her action was huge; she changed our entire world. If you try to change it back, if you try to stop her from stabbing the syringe into her heart, you will erase the lives of all the children who were born in the last ten years. You will risk Remi's very existence."

Angela gasps. "You wouldn't do that, would you, Jessa? You wouldn't take Remi away from me, even if it meant you could save Callie. Right?"

I look at the baby on her shoulder. At the chubby cheeks, the perfectly formed lips parted in an *O*. I reach for her, and Angela slowly hands her over, as though she's loath to part with her daughter. Especially now.

The second the warm, delicious weight of Remi settles against my chest, the moment I feel her silken-flower skin, the instant I smell that clean baby-fresh scent, I know. This life is precious. It is exquisite and unique. As are the lives of the millions of other children born in the last decade. I'm not at all interested in extinguishing those lives. I'm not remotely similar to Chairwoman Dresden. I will never, ever be her assistant.

If I had any doubts, they're erased right here in this moment.

"You have my word, Angela." I brush my chin against the soft down on the baby's head. "I would travel to the end of time to keep her safe."

"Thank you," Angela whispers. I pass the baby back to her, and for a moment, all four of us watch Remi sleep. The most uneventful pastime in the world—but somehow the most meaningful.

Angela lays Remi back in her cradle and shuffles to the holo-doc. "Now get your butt over here and memorize this blueprint."

42

Twenty-four hours later, the air whispers across the nape of my neck. My robe is cinched tightly around my waist. I've gone over the events of that ill-fated day so many times I've got the entire schedule memorized down to the minute.

Logan's been telling me stories for years about what happened on Callie's last day. But I had to be sure. I couldn't leave anything to guesswork. So I holo-called Logan and asked him to run down the day's events again, making up some story about how I wanted to memorialize the day in my journal.

I'm as ready as I'll ever be. Besides, I'm used to going on adventures. Sure, this will be the first time my escapade takes me across time. The first time I'm without my usual sidekick, Ryder. But this is nothing new for me. In fact, you could say all my other exploits were just a preparation for this one.

Doesn't mean my heart's not trying to race out of my chest.

"Relax, Jessa," Tanner says. He's wearing a similar robe, and I can see his bare collarbone. "Preston says it's more difficult to push a stressed body through time."

I roll my eyes. I was there, right along with Tanner, when my dad gave us those instructions. In fact, that's precisely why we're waiting in the mudroom. My dad doesn't want us to go into the living area of the cabin, where the time machine is located, until the very last moment. Something about not wanting to elevate our heart rates.

Too late.

I press my hand against my chest. "Gee, thanks for the reminder. Have any brilliant ideas on how to make me more relaxed?"

"As a matter of fact, I do." He shifts closer, his eyes as bright as solar flares.

I can't help it. My mind knows I'm mad at him, but my body automatically leans closer, too.

"You're freaking out about us seeing each other naked for the first time," he says, his tone placid and reasonable. "So I say we go ahead and take off our clothes, in the privacy of this room. Without your parents looking on. Without something as heavy as a mission hanging over us. Then you won't have anything to be nervous about. Am I right?"

I blink. He can't possibly be serious.

He puts his hand on the knot of his belt and begins to loosen it.

Oh. Dear. Fates. He is serious.

"Wait," I screech, lunging over to him and holding his robe closed. "That won't make me feel better at all."

"It would make me feel better," he whispers.

My hands are on his chest, so I can feel his heart sprinting. In a race, it would rival mine. His lips are inches away. If required, I could reproduce their shape on a holo-screen. His hot breath mixes with mine, and if I lean forward just a little bit, we'd be kissing.

"Will you ever forgive me, Jessa?" Tanner asks, breaking the spell. Bringing me back to myself. "I messed up. I failed to see the bigger picture." He moves his shoulders, as helpless as the little boy who lives inside him, the one who lost his parents and was raised by an institution. "I was doing the only thing I knew. The only thing I was taught. Everything for the sake of science. Progress is life, and life is progress. That motto was hardwired into me when I was a kid, and so, I invented future memory without thinking about the consequences. Without thinking about your sister or the future. I know better now, and I'm sorry."

I take a breath and slowly release it. A part of me weakens, that soft underbelly of my soul that has yet to be scarred by tragedy. That part wants to hold him tight because we're in this life together, this sucky, sucky life where people die and the chairwoman rules.

Tell him you forgive him, that voice inside me pleads. *You're about to leave on a highly dangerous trip through time. Hasn't your father's example taught you anything? You may never get this chance again. Tell him now.*

I let go of his robe and take a step back, gathering my courage. "I…forgive you. I believe you couldn't have known. I know you didn't mean to hurt me. But you did, and that means we can't pretend it never happened. We can't go back to before."

"I wouldn't want to," he says softly. "Our mistakes are as much a part of our lives as anything else. We have to embrace them, to learn from them in order to grow. I don't want to go back, but I'd like to start over. Could you give me another chance? Pretend we're just now meeting each other? I promise I'll be less obnoxious this time around."

I look at him, this boy who's been in my class but whom I really didn't know for years. He infuriated me from our first conversation at the hoverpark. And yet, with each passing day, he peeled away the layers of his confidence and arrogance, bit by bit, to show me his true heart. Would I forget everything I've seen just because he made a mistake? In a world where we can't change our past without significant consequences, would I throw away our future?

Fike, I've made mistakes, too. Just ask my mom. And yet, she continues to love me.

I take a deep breath. "I'll try," I say. That's the very best I can give him at this moment.

43

A rail suspended from the ceiling runs down the center of the living area. A thick metal arch hangs from one end of the rail, nearly as wide as the room. On the other end, my dad stands in front of a computer terminal, his hands dancing over a keyball, while my mother reviews a holo-doc of her notes. In the center of the room is a glass platform with two sets of footprints imprinted on the surface.

That's where Tanner and I are supposed to stand.

Sweat breaks out along my hairline, and I tug at the neck of my robe, trying to get a little air circulation. And my heart rate? Just as Preston predicted, it's climbing off the charts.

"How, uh…how exactly does this time machine work?" I ask.

Preston looks up, two parallel lines creasing his brow. "What do you know about the Einstein-Rosen bridge?"

I exchange a shrug with my mom, the other non-scientist in the room. "Nothing? Lovely name, though."

"Wormholes," my dad says patiently. "What do you know about the physics of wormholes?"

"Are they a kind of tunnel?" I wrinkle my forehead, trying to remember the cartoon drawings from my intro-level physics class. "If space were a two-dimensional surface, the entry point would be a hole, which leads to a three-dimensional tube emerging at a different hole along the flat surface. Except every dimension is increased by one." I try and once again fail to wrap my mind around the concept. "That's where the teacher lost me."

"That's the gist of it." He presses a button on the terminal, and the time machine comes to life. The arch moves forward a few inches, clanking and groaning against the rails. "When the arch passes over you, it will send you down a wormhole that will allow you to emerge in a different time. The anchor—in this case, your mother—ensures that you will surface at the right location and moment. So long as you and Tanner are touching, she'll serve as his anchor, too."

As if to demonstrate, the arch continues to creak forward, and a loud whir fills the room.

Preston raises his voice. "I know that's a simplistic explanation. I know you're capable of understanding more. But the machine's warming up, and I need you and Tanner in your places." Hesitantly, he lays a hand on my arm. "Maybe, when you get back, I can walk you through the details. What do you say?"

I meet his eyes and know he's asking for more than a rain check. Implicit in his question is the promise that I'll come back. The promise that he'll still be here. And the fervent hope that this is the beginning—and not the end—of our father-daughter bond.

I leap into his arms for a hug he's clearly not expecting, and after a moment, he wraps his arms around me tightly, so tightly, as though he never wants to let me go. "I never knew you were born," he says, and I almost can't hear him above the increasingly loud noise of the machine. "But that doesn't make you any less my daughter. Sometimes, the biggest holes in our lives are the ones we aren't aware of. Come back to us, Jessa."

He releases me, and my mother's next. She grabs my hands, and hers are clammy and cold. "Dear heart, I know you love your sister. I know you want to save her at all costs. But please, if the choice comes down to it…save yourself."

"But Callie's the good one. The one who deserved to live." An ache rises from my throat to the backs of my eyes. "She's the one we all wished had survived."

"What?" Her eyes, her mouth, her face go rigid with shock. "Jessa, what are you saying? How could you believe that?"

"I've always believed that."

"No, Jessa. No. You're so wrong. Or maybe I'm the one who was wrong." She pulls me into an embrace, her hands gripping my back. Something hot and wet drips onto my shoulders. Tears. She's crying. Over me?

She leans back, and her eyes are devastated, but her jaw is clenched. "Now you listen, and you listen carefully," she says fiercely. "I don't know what I did to give you that idea, but I have never felt that way. Not for one second. Do you hear me? You are just as worthy, just as loved as Callie. The two of you are twins, but the only thing identical about you is my love for you."

I blink. And blink. And blink. "It's almost worth going on this mission just to hear you say that."

She breaks down then, sobbing on my shoulder. "Then I should've said it sooner. I'm so sorry, dear heart. So sorry."

I wrap my arms around her, and we stand like that for an endless moment. Making up for all the hugs we didn't share in the last decade. My father approaches and embraces us both. I look at him over my mom's shoulders, and his eyes are wet.

"I'm sorry, too," he says hoarsely. "Sorry I wasn't here when you needed me."

I sniff. "I was fine, Dad."

"That's when a girl needs her father the most. When she doesn't even know it."

And then, the time machine emits a particularly loud groan, and we break apart. I glance up to find Tanner watching us, his eyes wistful, his smile sad. With a pang, I realize no one's here to see him off. I have both my parents, and he has nobody. And hasn't for a very long time.

My heart squeezes. I can do more than just try, damn it. I can show him I'm here for him, even if it's for only this moment. Leaving my parents, I walk to him and offer my hand. "Come on. Let's go back to yesterday."

He stares at me, his mouth closed. He may have already said everything that needs to be said. But I haven't.

"Whatever happens…I do want to start over," I say. "I don't want a single mistake to erase the future. So…my name is Jessa. And I would very much like to go to the past with you."

There's more—so much more—in my head, in my heart. But those feelings have yet to coalesce into words, and I'm not ready to share my half-formed thoughts.

"My name's Tanner. And I would go anywhere with you. You just have to say the word." He takes my hand, and the contact is both jarring and familiar. I simultaneously feel like I've entered foreign territory—and have come home.

We walk to the platform and stand on the footprints. We keep our hands intertwined and face each other. Already, I can feel the zip-pull-prick of the currents flowing around us.

"Looking good, you two." Preston takes his position behind the keyball, and my mother puts on a helmet made of thin metal strips and slips under the doughnut screen.

She injects a black chip into the terminal. In a moment, the memory she recorded of that fateful day will play across the screen, and she'll remember as hard as she can.

"On my count," my dad says. "Three…"

Letting go of Tanner's hand, I slide the robe off my shoulders. It falls to the platform, and cool air swirls around my naked breasts and stomach. Tanner mimics my movements. Despite his earlier joking, he looks directly, unwaveringly into my eyes. We join hands once more.

"Two…"

The currents nipping at my skin pick up speed and whirl wildly around us. I feel like we're inside a tornado, but there's no physical force. The vibrations skim along my skin, invisible gossamer threads that circle my legs, covering them, before moving up my torso, my neck, my mouth. I stare into Tanner's startled eyes, but I can no longer talk. The threads creep up our faces, and I can no longer see or smell.

"One…"

There's an impossible ringing in my ears. My body shoots out of itself, as though the molecular cells are trying to outrun their container.

And then…nothing.

44

My senses slowly return one by one. I feel the cool tile under my feet. Smell the burned remains of dinner left too long in the Meal Assembler. Hear the low, constant hum of com units before they went noiseless. Taste the sharp, acrid flavor of fear.

I open my eyes and see Tanner. Dark hair, bright eyes. Broad shoulders and well-defined pecs. Smooth, nicely muscled…and naked.

I jerk up my eyes before I can look any lower.

Oh Fates. That means I'm naked, too. Yanking my hand out of his, I glance around wildly and snatch up an afghan hanging over the back of a recliner. My mother's recliner. The same water-filled chair on which I rock on the nights I've been invited to dinner. Except…there's no scratch on the center cushion.

I wrap the blanket around myself and take stock of the room. It looks just like my mom's living area, with a few small differences. There's only one wall screen instead of four, and it is smooth and whole, minus the chink in the corner from the lobster cracker that flew out of my hands last Return's Day. The revolving photo frame cycles through images of Callie and my six-year-old self, and the floor is regular old linoleum tile. My mom didn't upgrade to the pressure-sensitive flooring until I was fourteen.

"So it worked?" I lick my dry lips. "Are we in the past?"

"One way to find out." Tanner wanders to the computer terminal next to the wall screen, completely unselfconscious with his nudity.

I flush and train my eyes on the ceiling. I'm not going to look. It would be the height of hypocrisy when I asked *him* to promise not to look. There's no way I'm going to—

I look. Just a tiny peek, really. Enough to see his very fine and very bare bottom.

I grab another blanket, march across the room, and hold it out. "Could you please cover yourself?"

His lips quirk. "That's kind of you to offer. But I'm perfectly comfortable—"

"Just take it!" I squawk.

The smile widens, and he rolls into the blanket. Which brings him inches away from me. Damn the Fates. He's covered up, all right, but now he's standing in very close proximity. Naked. With nothing between us but a few loops of yarn.

His eyes flicker down—and I *know* he can't see anything. I know that. But heat zips along my body, filling every cell and pore until I'm pretty sure even my toes are blushing.

"Jessa?"

Father of Time, even my name sounds suggestive on his lips.

"Yeah?" I mumble. What would I do if he tried to kiss me right now? Would I push him away? Or would I let his mouth linger for just one delicious moment...

"Should we go see what date it is?"

Oh. Right. Of course.

I gather up my afghan, and we shuffle to the terminal. He tucks the blanket firmly around his waist, and a few flicks of the keyball later, the wall screen changes from a waterfall to a calendar.

There it is. The date blinks out at me—ten years in the past. The date of Callie's supposed death.

"We did it," I whisper. "We time-traveled to yesterday."

"More like yester-decade." He stares at me for so long that my stomach begins to turn slow, precise somersaults.

"What is it?" I bring my free hand to my face. "Did the time travel warp my features? Am I missing a nose or an ear—"

"Not at all. You look as beautiful as always. It's just..." He stops, and I gape at him. He's never called me beautiful before. He did say I was "pretty" when he was talking about Olivia and the past, but the comment that stands out in my mind is when he described my looks as "atrocious" in the sewer.

But now, he glosses over the compliment as if it's a given. "There's something I want to show you."

He glides his hands over the keyball, and the calendar shrinks to a corner of the screen. An instant later, a ComA-approved biography of Tanner Callahan appears on the wall.

"The Father of Future Memory," the title proclaims.

I frown. "I don't understand. Is this your father?"

"No, it's me. Read the biography. You'll understand."

I skim the paragraphs. It summarizes Tanner's childhood accurately, as far as I know. His birthplace of Eden City, the early and uncanny aptitude for the sciences, the demise of his parents, a list of his academic accolades. But then, the biography veers into events that have yet to occur, detailing his experiments at uni, his marriage and offspring, the significant and wide-ranging discoveries he made in his forties. The text is even accompanied by an image of a middle-aged Tanner, one with laugh lines and a squarer, fuller jaw.

"The bio talks about you as if you're an older man." My eyes drift to the calendar in the corner. "But you must be, what? Six years old, just like me? Did they get this information from a future memory?"

"Nah. I mean, Olivia had some foreknowledge, but even she couldn't tell for sure what the future held. They just made up the whole thing." He steps toward me, and his knees brush mine through the blanket. "You see, back then, er, I guess I should say *right now*, FuMA had a very keen interest in making everyone believe that future memory had already been invented. It was how they got their legitimacy. They needed people to believe that they couldn't change their futures. Imagine how much chaos would ensue if people found out future memory hadn't even been discovered yet. Thus, they needed an inventor, a Father of Future Memory." He spreads his arms out, making the blanket shift precariously on his waist. "They picked me."

It hits me then. Of course. His name was in the stories Callie used to tell me—in particular, the one where she got her name. I can't believe I didn't make the connection until now. According to Callie, our father named her after the greatest inventor of their time. Callie Ann for Callahan.

Tanner Callahan.

He gestures to the photo of his older self. "They could've extrapolated a better picture. I'm much handsomer in real life, don't you think?"

I ignore his comment. "Let me get this straight. You knew from the time you were six years old that you were destined to discover future memory?"

"I knew the future legacy they had created for me," he

corrects. "The future they hoped would come true. From that moment, I was determined to fulfill their prophecy." He takes a deep breath, and his chest brushes against my hand clutching the afghan. "Especially after what happened to my parents."

I swallow. "Was this around the time they died?"

Instead of answering, he swipes his fingers along the keyball, and a news vid pops onto the screen. "The chairwoman made sure this was recorded. She told the reporters that my parents were important dignitaries. But really, I think she just wanted a visual reminder to hold over me. To make sure I stayed in line."

Silently, we watch the short clip.

An older couple waves at the camera and then kisses a little boy—Tanner, I realize with a pang. I'd recognize those dark eyebrows anywhere. In the background, the TechRA building spears into the sky, majestic and imposing.

The couple climbs into a self-driving vehicle—a silver-plated spherical pod—and the car takes off. But something's wrong. The pod veers wildly back and forth. An instant later, it slams into a building and bursts into flames.

I gasp, bringing a hand to my throat. A voice-over tells us that the FuMA-issued vehicle had malfunctioned and the inhabitants, Deacon and Brenna Callahan, special guests of Chairwoman Dresden herself, died upon impact.

The clip ends, and Tanner restores the wall screen to its placid waterfall. Still, I can see the flames licking up the sides of the pod.

"Were those...your parents?" I ask, even though I already know the answer.

He nods, pulling the blanket around his chest as if he's suddenly cold.

"The car was FuMA-issued," I continue. Dresden's statement replays in my mind: *You must be loyal to me...or people will die.* I wondered if her words were an idle threat; I wondered if anyone actually died. But I was too distraught at the time to pay much attention.

Now, my chest feels tight, and my mouth tastes of bile. I don't want it to be true—I can't bear for it to be true. But the logical conclusion gets right up in my face and refuses to disappear.

"Did Dresden have anything to do with the malfunction?" I whisper.

He looks at me then, and his eyes are so empty, so bleak that the breath is squeezed from my lungs.

"She warned me," he says in a low voice. "She said if I didn't quit my whining about going home and seeing my parents, she would punish me. I was property of ComA now, and I had to learn that the most important priority in my life was science. If I continued to be distracted by other things, she would make sure my life was rid of all such frivolity."

My mouth drops. "She killed your parents so you would focus on your experiments?"

He nods once. But once is all it takes. One "accident" is all it takes to shape a child. One command is all it takes to extinguish two lives. One leader is all it takes to chart a world's course into madness.

"That's what I meant when I said that science was all I ever knew." He rubs the back of his neck. "At first, I fixated on my projects out of fear. My parents were the only ones who loved me, but they weren't the only people in my life. Olivia was my playmate, even though she never admitted to liking me. And there was MK, who watched us both. They weren't family, but I didn't want to see them hurt.

"After a while, my obsession became habit. I started believing what they told me—that I would become the greatest scientist of our time. I wanted that. For myself, but also for my parents." A muscle twitches in his cheek. "I thought that if I accomplished everything the chairwoman wanted from me, if I became the Father of Future Memory, not just in name but also in fact…then maybe I could redeem myself for my parents' deaths. Maybe I could make sense out of the senseless."

"Oh, Tanner." The lump in my throat grows so big it might choke me. "Your parents' deaths weren't your fault. It was the fault of a madwoman who will do anything to get what she wants."

"I know that here." He points to his temple. "But it's much harder to convince myself here." He spreads his hand over his bare chest.

Don't I know it. That same guilt pushes me to do the same thing. Something so big and important that it will redeem myself, once and for all.

For Tanner, it was the invention of future memory. For me…I don't know yet. Saving my sister will bring me close, but it won't get me all the way there. Whatever the answer is, I have a feeling it's rooted here. In the past.

"Your younger self," I say. "The six-year-old Tanner. He's there now, isn't he? In the TechRA building. That's where he lives, right?"

He blinks, as if the fact just occurred to him. "I suppose so. Just like your younger self is there now."

"Are you going to try to see him tomorrow?"

He shakes his head. "I don't see what good can come of it."

I agree. I'm not even sure why I asked, other than the fact that it seems strange that our younger selves will be somewhere in the building. Completely vulnerable to the future that lies ahead of them. I want to grab both kids, wrap them in my arms, and keep them safe. But that's never been an option.

"Come on." I stand. The afghan slips over my shoulder, but my nudity no longer seems relevant. Even when Tanner's gaze flickers down, for the briefest moment, to my bare breasts. "Let's go find some clothes before my mom comes home."

45

Five minutes later, I'm wearing one of Callie's school uniforms, a lightweight silver jumpsuit that zips up the front. Tanner instructed me to be quick—and I'm glad. Otherwise, I might've been tempted to sit on Callie's bed and imagine the last time she slept there. To play some of her holo-vids, which no doubt feature manual chefs separating eggs or whipping up soufflés. To shove my hands underneath the mattress to see if anything's hidden there.

That last thing I actually do. And I'm not sorry because I find something. I carry the object back to the living area, where Tanner's waiting.

"What do you have?" he asks as I come into the room. He has on a pair of my dad's old scrubs—pale blue, soft cotton, with multiple pockets for scientific instruments.

My heart lurches. Just a tiny bit. Tanner would be the first to tell you he looks good in everything. In this instance, he's actually right. With the contrast of the pale fabric against his tanned skin and the way the shirt settles on his shoulders, he looks adorable.

"I found a book of poems." I lay it gingerly on the table. It's a real book, a physical book, with a cracked binding and tissue-thin pages. Even at this time, real books were rare; in my present, they're damn near nonexistent.

Opening the book, I find a brilliant red leaf, dried and crumbling, pressed between the pages.

I suck in a breath. I've seen leaves like this in only one other place. Logan's house. Because he doesn't have an ample supply of books, he presses them under other objects. A wooden fruit bowl, a fluffy bath rug, warrior statues made out of bolts and washers. I used to make a game out of finding his stash of leaves. But not once has he ever explained what the leaves were for. Or whom they were supposed to represent.

All of a sudden, a memory flashes across my mind. I am crouching in the dirt with Logan, rolling leaves into roses. It was Callie's Memory's Eve. The day before she disappeared from our lives. The day before everything changed.

Reverently, I trace my finger along the veins. "I think this leaf has something to do with Logan and Callie's relationship."

"You should put it back," Tanner says, a muscle throbbing in his forehead. "That book has nothing to do with our mission. Remember what Preston said about altering the past?"

"It's just a book," I protest. "What could it hurt if I look at it?"

"Put it back. The flap of a butterfly's wing may cause a hurricane on the other side of the world. We can't know."

He's right. I'd forgotten, but I won't let it slip my mind again. Closing the book, I hurry back to Callie's sleeping area and slide the book under the mattress, where it belongs.

When I return to the living area, Tanner raises an eyebrow. "Did you place the book at the same angle as how you found it? Did you make sure the entire leaf was tucked safely inside?"

"I don't know." I bite my lip. Now that I think of it, I'm

pretty sure a corner of the leaf was sticking out of the book. "But what difference can it make? Preston said only the big events, with far-reaching ripples, would have an effect on our present world."

"I'm sure you're right. But maybe you'd better fix it, just in case."

"Fine. I'll go back and—"

The front door rattles. Tanner and I freeze. How can it be time already? By Preston's calculation, we should've had an hour before my mom returned from the Russells' living unit, where she welcomed Callie and Logan back to civilization and watched them eat spaghetti squash.

An hour couldn't have passed already. It couldn't.

And yet, the door opens, and my mother walks into the room—at least, my mother as she was ten years earlier, ridiculously young and just as lovely.

"Callie! How in space did you get here before me?" She crosses to me, smelling like vanilla. She doesn't smell like this anymore. I can't remember the last time she smelled like this. "Weren't you supposed to sleep over at the Russells'? You should be in bed. Big day tomorrow. And did you cut your hair?"

She picks up a strand of my hair—and I see the moment that it hits her. This is not her daughter Callie but somebody else.

Her eyes widen, and she takes a careful step back. "You're not Callie."

"No, I'm not." I take a deep breath. "I'm your other daughter. Jessa."

"Impossible. Jessa's six years old. She's been taken away by FuMA, and Callie's going to rescue her tomorrow…" She lifts my chin, and my features hit the light. "Dear Fates, you look just like her."

"We're twins, you know. Eleven years removed. But now that I've traveled from ten years in the future, we're practically the same age."

Her jaw drops. "Time travel? You can't mean…" Again, her words die. Because she knows better than most that time travel exists and nothing is impossible. "Jessa?" she whispers, her voice hoarse with wonder and fervent, desperate hope. "Is it really you? From the future?"

I nod. Tears spring into her eyes, and she jumps forward to wrap her arms around me. "Oh my baby Jessa. Look how you've grown. Look how pretty you are." She pulls back, drinking in my face. "That means it worked. Callie was successful. I knew she could do it. I knew she could save your life. If anyone is strong enough to fight Fate—and win—I knew it would be her."

"Yes." I can't tell her the truth. That my sister was successful, but not in the way she imagines. That Callie did manage to save my life—but at the expense of her own.

She grips my hands. "I've missed you so much."

"I've been gone for only a few days," I say, referring to my six-year-old self.

"My heart breaks every hour, every minute that you're not with me," she says, her voice trembling, her eyes searing into mine.

I frown. Who is this woman? It's certainly not my mother, at least not the one I've known for the last four years. That woman is more restrained; our conversations are much more stilted. She would never pour out her heart like this—and assume her affections will be accepted without question.

Oh Fates. This was the woman she was before tragedy struck. This open, affectionate woman is my mother before both her daughters were ripped away from her.

I close my eyes and take shallow, openmouthed breaths. It

is almost too much to bear. I would rip apart my very soul if I could save her from the pain she's about to endure. But I have to think of Remi. Remi and all the children born in the last decade. I can't go around changing the past because of them.

Oblivious to my distress, my mother winds an arm around my shoulders. "Now who is this young man?" She gestures at Tanner, and he smiles angelically at her. But angelic for Tanner still looks like the devil, and my mom's hand tightens on my arm, as if to say: *What are his intentions? Should I be worried?*

"His name is Tanner Callahan," I say. "He's a scientist, and he accompanied me on this trip to the past."

She frowns, and I remember that she's familiar with the ins and outs of time travel. "Naked?"

"Your daughter's quick with the afghan," he says earnestly. "I tried as hard as I could, but I caught only a glimpse."

My mom tries to frown, and then smiles, and then frowns again. "Tanner Callahan," she repeats slowly. "Any relationship to the Father of Future Memory?"

Of course she knows his name. Everybody did in this time.

"People say I look just like him," he says, eyes wide and innocent. "Except Jessa. She thinks I'm way hotter."

My mouth drops open. "I do not!"

"You didn't say it. But I could tell you were thinking it."

"Mom!" I turn to my mother, hoping she'll put Tanner in his place. But she doesn't even bother to hide her amusement now.

"He has a point, dear heart." She smiles broadly at him. Hmph. Figures she would like the cocky scientist type. "But I can't officially sanction you flirting with my daughter, Mr. Callahan. So would you mind if I steal Jessa away? I don't have much time to get everything packed."

"Go right ahead," he says with a broad, identical smile. He sits on the recliner, crossing his hands behind his head.

"I'll be here."

Looping an arm through mine, my mom guides me down the hall and into her room. It's not until she pulls a suitcase from under the floorboards that her words sink in.

"Pack?" I ask. "Pack for what?"

"To go with you and Callie to Harmony, silly. Surely you must know that. Since you're from the future..." She trails off. "Oh no. You're from the *future*. We don't make it safely to Harmony. Something goes wrong tomorrow, doesn't it?"

I blink. Wait a minute. Doesn't she know she's supposed to stay and act as an anchor? She said she'd received a message from the future. I assumed it was a future memory. But what if it wasn't? What if it was...me?

No, that can't be right. I wasn't here all those years ago. But I was. I am. She said that my future self told her that I would forgive her one day. That time is now, and now is then.

I clutch my forehead. Dear Fates. I'm so confused.

Well, one thing's for sure. She can't know how the future will turn out. She'll try to stop Callie, and little Remi will be as good as gone. Vanished without a trace. As if she never existed.

"You're the one being silly." Summoning all of my acting ability, I plaster a smile on my face. "Everything turns out just fine. Look at me. I'm standing right here, aren't I?"

"Thank the Fates for that. You scared me, dear heart." Reassured, she moves to her closet and taps a button. The clothes rack begins to rotate, and she grabs her shirts as they pass.

I lick my lips. I have to find the right words for this next part. I have to convince her to stay, or this very moment won't ever be possible. "It's just that...you can't come with us to Harmony tomorrow."

She grabs a dress that's about to turn the corner. "What are you talking about? Of course I'm going. You don't expect me to let my girls go to the wilderness by themselves, do you?"

"Mom." I grab her shoulders and tug her away from the closet. "You have to trust me. You can't go to Harmony."

"Why? Callie can take care of herself, sure. But you're six years old, Jessa." She pulls herself to her full height. "You must be mad if you think I'm going to let my six-year-old run away from civilization without her mother."

I exhale slowly. Maybe if my breaths are even, my words will be, too. "You have to stay exactly where you are because you're the anchor."

She blinks. "Is this about your father? Because if it is, you can forget it. I want him to come back as much as anybody. You know that. I love him more than anything in this world. Except for two people. You and Callie." She lifts her chin. "I'm sorry, but Preston's just going to have to stay stuck in a different space-time. I will not send my six-year-old to the wilderness with just her sister. And that's final."

Heat pricks the backs of my eyes. I didn't know. I didn't know she wanted to come with me. I didn't know she tried this hard.

"It's not about Dad," I say hoarsely. "It's Callie. She's sick in the future. Really sick. The only way to save her is for me to come back here to this time. She has a condition called Asynchronicity."

As quickly as possible, and without giving away that she's been in a coma for the past decade, I explain how Callie's mind is not in sync with her body. In order for her to find the right time, I continue, I need to plant a seed here in the past, so that we can trigger it in the future.

When I finish, my mom limps to the bed, her dress crumpled in her hands. She stares at the material like she doesn't recognize it. "Will that actually work?"

I move my shoulders. "It's the only hope we have."

She is silent for so long I think she might've passed out. But when I peer closer, I see a single tear rolling down her cheek before it plops onto the dress.

"What about you, Jessa?" Her voice is low and anguished, as if her very limbs are being ripped away. "Oh, my baby. Who will take care of you?"

"Callie will," I lie. I crouch on the floor in front of her, so I can look up into her face. "You know what a good sister she is. These last six years, she's been like a second mother to me." I catch her eyes. Time for truth now. The most honest truth I know. "Mom, you have to trust me. If there's any chance of the three of us being together in the future, any chance at all, then you have to do this. You have to let me go."

She holds my gaze for a moment and then nods. The dress slips out of her grasp and falls to the floor.

"So you'll do it?"

"What choice do I have?"

The breath I didn't realize I was holding rushes out of me. "You can't tell Callie, okay? Say whatever you have to, but she can't know you're staying here to save her in the future. It will mess up everything. Please, Mom. You'll do that, won't you?"

"For Callie, and for you, I'll do anything." She holds out her arms, and I fly into them. We hug, for the last time in the next six years. I close my eyes. The wool of her sweater scratches my cheek, and the light, fresh scent of vanilla surrounds me. I know I'll remember this moment forever. No matter what time I'm in.

"Over the next few years, I'm not going to be very nice to you," I mumble into her neck.

"Oh dear heart, that's to be expected."

"It's not just teenage brattiness, okay? The six-year-old me thought you abandoned me. And she holds it against you. I'm sorry, Mom. So sorry."

She pulls back, wiping away my tears with her thumbs, even as the moisture springs up in her own eyes. "You don't have to apologize. What have I always told you? I will always love you, no matter what."

"Just remember what I said. Please. It's never too late for love. Over the next few years, when I say terrible things to you. Remember that I don't know."

"I will," she says. "I'll know in my heart that you love me. Even if you don't know it at the time."

46

The building glints in the early morning sun, looking remarkably like the skyscraper of our future. The same tall spirals, the row after row of reflective windows. The only difference is FuMA was bigger and more powerful than TechRA at this time. So, even though it was already shared between the two agencies, everyone called it the FuMA building.

Tanner and I walk nonchalantly to a side door, a lightly trafficked entrance that faces the woods. We're wearing the navy slacks and white short-sleeve shirts that constitute the FuMA uniforms. He has a mustache attached to his upper lip, and we're both wearing wigs provided by my mom. Hopefully the disguises will suffice to let us pass as employees.

At this moment, somewhere in this very building, the seventeen-year-old Callie and Logan are walking around, searching for a precognitive to give them answers about the future. It was hard enough for my mom to sneak them in with the laundered sheets, so Tanner and I are on our own.

"Are you sure this is going to work?" I whisper, even

though we're the only two people around.

"It should." Tanner strokes his mustache like it's a pet. It must tickle or something. He can't keep his hands away. "My fingerprints have been in the system from the time I was five. Yours were entered a few days ago, when FuMA processed you as a lab subject. It's the only biometric that doesn't change in ten years. That's why we're at this entrance, where there's no voice or face recognition."

I lick my furnace-dry lips. "And you're sure we have security clearance to enter the building?"

"Your mom checked. Our clearance gives us access to all the upper floors." He smooths the synthetic hair over his lip again, and I realize he's nervous, too.

So many things could mess up. The time travel could've altered our fingerprints. Or maybe somebody will check the logs and realize that the six-year-old Tanner Callahan and Jessa Stone have no business wandering around the building together. But it's the best plan we've got.

"You go first," I tell Tanner.

"If anything goes wrong, run to the woods and find Potts's cabin. He'll let you hide until it's safe to go back to the time machine."

I nod. I don't know if Potts still lives in his cabin in my present, raising his bloodhounds. But I've heard all about him from Logan's stories.

Tanner squares his shoulders and presses his fingertips on the sensor. Eternal seconds pass, and an awful feeling washes over me. We've been here before, with his fingers on a sensor. And it did not end well.

But then, the sensor beeps, and my shoulders droop. At least one of us is in.

Holding my breath, I mimic his movements. One…two… three…four seconds. *Beep*. Oh, thank the Fates. I lean forward and air-kiss the sensor.

Tanner watches me with a strange expression on his face. As though he's thinking of another time, another place. When we kissed on the shore by the river.

Or maybe that's just wishful thinking.

Blushing, I hurry forward. He falls into step beside me, and we travel down the halls, trying to look like we know where we're going. I thought the building would feel familiar. I thought that I would experience déjà vu or that old memories would flash across my mind. But so much has changed. I see only the skeleton of the TechRA building I know now, and any memory I have is from the future not the past.

A few employees pass us, but they do no more than glance at us as they hurry on their way. Our disguises must be working.

Following the map in my head, I stop at the apex of two hallways, at a window ledge stuffed with potted plants.

I pinch a pointy green leaf between my fingers, and a crisp, woodsy smell fills the air. Logan told me about the plants. The entire building is full of them. People in my time don't have the same yearning for the natural. Maybe, ten years later, they're simply accustomed to the metal sculptures.

I point down the corridor on my left. "Logan and Callie should be coming down that hallway in a few minutes. Along with a skipping Olivia."

Tanner knows the plan, of course. He helped me form it. But it helps me to say the words out loud. To remind myself what I need to do. "A FuMA employee carrying a plant will come around the corner, crash into Olivia, and the pot will go flying. Soil, ceramic pieces, and green stems will fly everywhere."

My throat works, but there's nothing to swallow. "That's my cue. In the middle of the chaos, I'll walk by and say the jingle—our version of it. Callie might not register it, but her subconscious will. When she hears our version again in the future, she'll remember."

At least, we hope. But I don't say that part out loud. No need to put my pessimism into the universe.

"She's been primed," Tanner says. "Your mom confirmed."

That's the other part of our plan. This morning, when my mom went to see Callie, she played the correct version of the jingle on her wrist com. If Callie noticed the background music at all, she would've just dismissed it as an advertisement from my mom's newsfeed. But now, her subconscious will be primed to receive a jolt when it hears the tweaked version.

"After they leave us, they'll go to William's office. See Olivia's vision of the genocide. And then, Callie will go see the younger me—and jab herself with the syringe." Goose bumps erupt on my arms. I shouldn't be this anxious. These events I am detailing are in the past. They already happened. Yet being in this time means they'll happen all over again.

"You're not going to try to stop her, are you?" Tanner asks.

"Of course not. We've been over this. I wouldn't risk Remi."

He nods slowly. "Keep that in mind when you actually see her."

At that moment, little Olivia appears at the end of the hallway, her messy braids flying. And then, around the corner comes Logan…and Callie.

At the first sight of my sister, my knees turn to water. I sway forward, and all of my carefully laid plans fly out of my head. She's here. She's here, and she's alive. She looks so young. So much like me.

My muscles bunch; my blood sings. Every nerve in my body urges me to spring forward and tackle her. All I have to do is move, and I can save her. I can keep her alive. She never has to go to William's office, never has to see that vision of genocide.

She did everything in her power to save me. Shouldn't I do the same? I can stop all of this. Right here. Right now. I just have to move.

"Think of Remi." Tanner is suddenly in front of me, gripping my arms. "Sweet baby Remi. She's innocent, defenseless. Would you rob her of her chance at life?"

I take a shuddering breath, and rationality seeps back in. I can't do that to Angela. I can't even do that to myself. I'm not the master of the universe. I don't get to decide who dies and who lives. Who exists and who vanishes without a trace.

That's when I understand why my dad suggested that Tanner accompany me. It's not because he's a scientist. It's to stop me from doing something I'll regret forever.

"Where's the employee?" His voice interrupts my thoughts. "The one who crashes into Olivia. Shouldn't he be here by now?"

I look down one hallway. And then the other. He's right. There's no sign of anyone.

"Don't worry, he'll come," I say with a confidence I don't feel. "Mustached man, carrying a plant. He has to. This is the past. It already happened."

The seconds tick by. Olivia skips farther down the hallway. And still, he doesn't show up.

Tanner grabs a plant off the window ledge. "Do you think we're supposed to hand him one of these as he passes?"

I peer down the hallway, and then I look back at Tanner. Down the hall, and then back at Tanner once more.

Tanner, who holds a plant with broad green leaves. Tanner, with his mustache flopping over his mouth like a caterpillar.

He looks so much like a FuMA employee. If I didn't know better, I would think he actually was one.

I freeze. My lungs turn into blocks of ice. Oh. Dear. Fates. "It was you," I whisper. "It was you all along."

He raises his eyebrows. "Huh?"

"Don't you see? Nobody's coming. It was always you. You were always the one who crashed into them. The mustache. The plant."

"I don't understand—"

"I don't, either. But you've got to get out there before the past gets messed up."

I shove him, and he careens around the corner. Not a moment too soon.

Olivia slams into him, knocking him to the ground. The pot flies out of his hand, smashes into the wall, and breaks into a million pieces.

The ceramic remains scatter across the floor. A trail of soil leads like bread crumbs to the broken plant stalk.

Just like the memory. Callie's memory from the future. Before her future self killed me in the vision, she walked past a scene exactly like this one. Logan told me about it so many times that I can see it in my head. Just as it's playing out in the present.

Seventeen-year-old Logan runs up to Olivia and helps her to her feet. "I'm so sorry, sir," he says to Tanner. "Are you okay?"

Tanner's mustache twitches. It looks like he's vibrating with rage, but he's actually freaking out. We never planned this. He doesn't know what to do, what to say.

"I-I don't have time to deal with this," he finally sputters out. "I'm late for a meeting."

"Don't worry, sir," Logan says, so polite, so in control, even as his Adam's apple bobs. "We're interns here. We'll call a bot to clean it up."

Callie comes up to Logan's shoulder. Tanner stares at her. It's one thing for him to talk to a younger Logan. But for him to see Callie, alive and well, when he's seen her only in a coma, is clearly throwing him.

Please, Tanner, I plead. *Don't let them suspect anything is off.*

Tanner blinks and seems to pull himself together. "Out-of-control kids," he says under his breath. "Irresponsible child-minders. You'd think, with all of FuMA's resources, they'd get someone more appropriate to watch the chairwoman's kid."

He strides down the hallway and disappears around the corner.

Callie turns to Logan. She doesn't see me, and I face the window, where I can watch her reflection. The scared eyes, the trembling fingers. I want to gather her in my lap and hug her. The way she used to hug me, with my knees poking into her chest.

"That broken pot was in my memory," she whispers. "It looked just like that. The trail of soil, the bright green leaves. My memory's coming true."

This is my shot. This is when I need to walk past them and mutter the jingle. They're so absorbed in each other that their conscious minds will never notice.

But I can't. The hand of Fate presses down on me, locking me into place. The same hand that tried to stop me from interfering with Zed's memory. As much as we are bound by our future, we are also bound by our past. The loop of time fixes us into place.

Logan takes her hand. "Knowing the future doesn't take away your free will. Only you can decide what you will do. We've come so far, Callie. Let's finish this."

I squeeze my eyes shut because there's only one conclusion

to this day. One finish to this chain of events. And neither of them is going to like it.

"I'm scared," my sister says.

"Me, too," Logan replies.

I mouth the same sentiment in my head. *Me, three.*

47

"What in Fate just happened?" Tanner asks a couple of minutes later. Logan, Callie, and Olivia have disappeared to fulfill their fate—at least, the one of their own making. We're ensconced in a supply closet. My fingers won't stop shaking.

"It's like when I talked to my mom." My voice trembles. My teeth clack. I might as well be standing at the epicenter of an earthquake. "I'm the one who convinced her not to go to Harmony. This entire time, she had a visit from my future self. We're part of the past, Tanner."

He inhales sharply. I'm falling apart, but this...this development is pulling him back together. Turning him into the person with whom he's most comfortable. A scientist.

"This supports Preston's theory," he says thoughtfully. "There's a debate among the scientists. Many of them believe that Callie proved the many-worlds theory of time travel, that her decision not to kill you shifted us onto a different, parallel path. But Mikey refused to accept this. He insisted that time isn't linear—that instead, it is an infinite loop. Thus, it would be possible to travel to the past and talk to your younger self, without any paradox about how your two selves could exist at the same time.

"Preston suggested both theories could be true. Time is an infinite loop *and* there are many worlds." He drums his fingers against his cheek. "Do you understand what I'm saying? Callie picked up our world and plopped us onto a different path. But now that we're on that path, we're in an endless, continuous loop."

I press my fingers against my temples, struggling to wrap my head around it. "So we were always here. We were always part of history."

He steps backward, and his elbow knocks into a tray of black data chips. I'd thought we were in a supply closet, but upon closer examination, I realize every last tray contains black chips. There must be thousands of black chips in here. Maybe even millions. We must've stumbled into some kind of memory bank. How many future memories were received and recorded before my sister messed up the system?

I shiver, and Tanner runs his hands along my arms. Even with the synthetic hair over his mouth, he is ridiculously attractive. Almost without thinking, I reach out and straighten his mustache. My fingers linger on his mouth, and I can feel his hot breath against my hand.

For a moment, we stand perfectly still. My heart pounds a bass line in my ears.

"Were you able to say the jingle to her?" he asks. Each word moves his mouth against my fingers. I like it. I want to keep my hand there, and if we were anywhere other than the past, maybe I would.

Reluctantly, I pull down my hand. "No. I was frozen to the spot. I probably could've moved. I could've broken through the resistance of Fate, but I didn't. It just wasn't the right moment."

"When else?" he asks. "It's not like we have a lot of opportunities left. Olivia shows them the vision. Callie walks down the hallway. She stabs herself."

My eyes widen. "That's it. That's when I'm supposed to say the jingle. After Logan and I jump down the laundry chute. Before the people who inject the antidote arrive. There will be a few precious seconds when she's drifting in and out of consciousness. I can go to her then."

"Any idea who injects her? Her file claims she was given the antidote at the two-minute mark. Enough to save her mind but not her body. But it never says *who* administered the antidote."

"It's got to be that guard, William. Right?" I wrinkle my brow. "Or maybe my mom?"

"Negative. Your mom had no idea Callie was even in a coma until a couple of weeks ago, and Mikey and I have quizzed William hard. He insists he had nothing to do with the antidote."

It hits us both at the same time. I feel like all the oxygen has been sucked out of the air. "Oh Fates, Tanner. What if it's us? What if we're the ones who are supposed to give her the antidote?"

He nods rapidly. "It makes sense. That's the part we never understood. Nobody else even knew they were there. How could they have gotten her the antidote so quickly? It's got to be us. Especially since we've been a part of everything else."

"But we don't have an antidote," I screech, whipping my head wildly around the closet, as though expecting one to materialize. But we're still in a memory bank full of black data chips. No syringes filled with red liquid anywhere. "We can't use the one Callie had because she smashed it on the floor. If we attempt to intervene, we'll change the course of history."

"I have an idea." Tanner checks the wrist com my mom

lent him. "We have fifteen minutes before Callie walks down that hallway. There's time, but we have to hurry."

Abruptly, he turns and walks out of the closet. I scamper after him. "Where are we going?"

"To get the antidote." He strides down the hall. I take two steps for every one of his. "The system hasn't changed much in the last decade. If the formulas are still kept in the dispensary, then I know exactly where we can find another antidote."

We pass the shattered ceramic pot, the trail of soil, the broken plant stalks. My steps falter, and I stop. The mess is still here. Nobody's cleaned it up. Nobody will until after Callie walks down this corridor again.

Tanner looks over his shoulder. "Coming?"

I nod and hurry after him. And pray to the Fates he knows what he's doing.

48

Two flights of stairs and three corridors later, we walk into a chilly, oversize refrigerator. The dispensary. Thirty degrees cooler than the rest of the building, housing racks and racks of needles in every color of the rainbow. And many more colors that never existed in nature. Cotton-candy pink and fluorescent yellow and neon green. Everywhere I look, I see needles. The racks extend from floor to ceiling and are stacked ten deep. I feel like I'm in one of Eden City's virtual theaters, staring into a set of reflecting mirrors that go on forever.

Tanner walks to the computer terminal, scans his fingerprints, and begins tapping on the keyball. "Good thing I've studied Callie's case half my life," he mutters. "I have her entire file memorized. I know the name of the antidote: Formula X9453. I even know her dosage."

I wrap my arms around myself. It's so cold I can see my breath in the air. "Are they going to wonder, a few days from now when they inspect the records, what a six-year-old was doing dispensing this antidote?"

"Yes." His fingers pause, for an infinitesimal moment, over

the keyball. "I turned out okay."

"Wait a minute." There's something in his tone, something both raw and resigned. Something that makes the hair stand up at the back of my neck. "You know what happens. You know what happens to your six-year-old self because of this."

He curls his hands into fists. "Got it. The formula's located in row AA, rack 9.14."

He starts to walk down the dispensary. I grab his shoulder. "Don't change the subject." I need to know what happened to him. It may be in the past; there may be nothing I can do to change it. But I need to know. "What did they do to you? As a result of your fingerprints just now."

He stops moving, but he won't look at me. "You know what they did, Jessa. The same thing they did to you, except mine lasted longer."

My heart drops. "This? This is why they tortured you for six months?"

He doesn't answer, but he doesn't have to. The look in his eyes scares me. If you sliced it up, you would see layer upon complicated layer. Of things too dark and dreary to discuss on a flimsy platform five stories up. To discuss anywhere, really, except right here. Right now.

"How did the torture stop?" I whisper.

"I finally convinced them I had no idea how my fingerprints got logged in the system. Which was true. I really didn't know, not until this moment." He shrugs, and even that small movement looks painful. "When they started scraping me off the ground every day, because I was too spent to hold myself up, they concluded I was telling the truth. They came up with a couple scenarios, equally far-fetched. In one, somebody succeeded in impersonating me and breaching the virtually un-breach-able FuMA security system."

"And the other?"

His lips curve. "A future Tanner travels back in time and breaks into the dispensary. Totally out there, right? Strains the imagination, doesn't it?"

I try to smile, too, but I can't. What his six-year-old self is about to endure robs all the smiles—real and fake—out of my heart.

"Tanner, I'm sorry."

"Let's not talk about it." He resumes walking around the room. "Come on. Let's find the antidote and get out of here."

He stops at the appropriate row and presses a button to rotate the racks, stopping at the ninth one. He counts down fourteen trays, and there they are: a dozen glass tubes with a red formula swimming in the barrel. The antidote.

He removes one tube and places it into a machine on the far wall. He taps in the proper dosage, and the machine automatically fills a syringe.

I lick my lips. "Is one enough? What if something goes wrong?"

He hesitates. Removes the syringe and checks the safety cap. Puts the needle in his pocket and looks around the room. And still makes no move to prepare a second syringe.

That's when I get it.

"They punished you more for a second syringe, didn't they?" I ask. "Of course they did. The more formula that's missing, the angrier they're going to be. Forget I said anything. One antidote is sufficient."

He takes a deep breath. "No, you're right. We came all this way. We're not going to mess everything up just so I can have a few less torture sessions. We'll take two—"

"Tanner. No. We don't need it. I was just being paranoid."

"We don't know what we need. In the past, I was punished for taking two syringes of formula. So we'll take two now." He taps the machine, and a second syringe is filled. He holds it out to me. "Here, you'd better keep this, just in case."

He meets my eyes, and I tumble into their depths. My heart expands until it fills my rib cage, until it presses against my lungs. I can't breathe for fear that it might pop. I don't know how I could've ever thought he was a jerk. How I could've thought him arrogant and selfish—when the opposite is true. Tanner Callahan is the most selfless boy I've ever met. I don't know if he can change the future, but he's picked up my heart and moved it to a different plane. No matter how this turns out, my life will be changed forever, knowing what he's done for my sister. Knowing what he's done for me.

I take the needle from him.

And then, the door whooshes open and somebody walks into the room.

49

"Oh, good. I was hoping someone would be here." A commanding voice floats into the room, colder than the air. Colder, even, than icicles.

I stiffen. My back is to the door, but I don't need a visual to confirm her identity. Just our luck. Chairwoman Dresden.

"A little help, please? I have an important meeting to attend."

My heart gallops out of my chest. I exchange a we-are-so-screwed look with Tanner, and then he smooths his fingers over his mustache and shuffles forward.

She's not focused on me. At least not yet. I walk to the last rack and pretend I'm terribly busy cataloging something. Anything.

Since my face is so similar to Callie's, she'd recognize me in an instant. Tanner's got ten additional years and a mustache. He just might survive her scrutiny.

"Are you new?" she demands. "I don't recognize you."

Or not.

"Yes, ma'am. Just started last week." His voice trembles,

but that's to be expected. Dresden would be suspicious if one of her employees *wasn't* afraid of her.

"Fine, fine." I hear, rather than see, her hands waving in the air. "I have a standing order. You'd better get it memorized because I'm not going to put up with your incompetence every week."

The computer hums, as if Tanner just booted up the terminal.

"You fool." She's an entire room's length away, but I swear I can feel the drops of her spittle spraying my back. "My prescription's not in the system. What about 'privacy' do you not understand? Hmm? How exactly did we hire you?"

She utters a long-suffering sigh. "You there! In the back. Help us out before your friend here loses his job."

I turn a quarter of the way, showing as little of my face as possible. My heart's returned to my chest, but it doesn't do me any good, wheezing about like that. "Yes, Chairwoman?" I ask, my voice faint. "Tell me what you need, and I'll be happy to get it for you."

"The amber formula," she snaps. Each syllable could slice glass. "Row D for Dresden. First rack, first tray. Because it's me, these syringes are pre-filled. Give me a week's worth. And if you can't calculate that in your tiny brain, that's seven needles."

"Yes, ma'am." Tucking my head down, I hurry to the proper row. Oh, fike. How did Tanner operate these racks? Holding my breath, I push the number one on the keypad, and the glass door slides open. Thank Fates. I take out the first tray and remove seven pre-filled syringes.

Now what? Do I just hand her the needles? Put them in some kind of container?

Luckily, Tanner is by my side with a glass rack. He arranges the amber-colored syringes inside with a deftness I wouldn't have been able to improvise, and hands the rack to Dresden. All without her getting a good look at my face.

I retreat to the end of the dispensary, peeking at Dresden out of the corner of my eye.

She places the rack into a solid carrying case, obviously designed for this very purpose. "Listen. You're new here, both of you, so it's worth repeating the rules. Nobody knows I was here. Nobody knows what you gave me. One word to anyone, and your careers, your lives are over. Understand?"

"Yes, Chairwoman," Tanner says.

She shifts her laser-sharp glance to me, and fear climbs up my throat like magma up a volcano. "Yes, Chairwoman."

"Good." She spins on her heels and stalks away.

For a moment, we don't speak, breathing in the chilled air, giving our hearts a chance to settle down.

"What on earth was that about?" I finally ask. "Why all the secrecy? What were those needles?"

Tanner reads the label underneath the tray. "There's no description here, just a code. If she's injecting herself daily and renewing her order every week, she's got to be treating something. Is Dresden sick?"

"I don't know." Even as I say the words, I remember how she walked into the transport tube in my bedroom. I thought it was funny at the time, but maybe she wasn't just being clumsy. Maybe it has to do with this ailment.

Clearly, something's going on with Dresden. Something that started ten years ago, in this time. What, I have no idea.

Chances are, however, it has nothing to do with our mission.

"We need to go." I wrap my hand around the syringe in my pocket. "Before we're too late."

He nods. Moving quickly, we walk down the hallways, heading toward a room numbered 522, where my younger self and sister are waiting.

50

Déjà vu hits me the moment we turn onto the right corridor, and it's no gentle stream. It's an ocean wave crashing into my legs, almost knocking me down.

The same linoleum tile. The same stinging scent of alcohol. Those IV stands jumbled in the corner, that diamond niche cut into the wall. Even the third panel of lights in the ceiling blinks on and off.

Just like I remember. Just like yesterday.

My palms go slick with sweat. My heart beats in my throat like an extra tonsil. Every muscle in my body screams, *Run!*

This is where my darkest fears formed. Where I relived memories that weren't mine. Where they shaped me into the person that I am, for better or for worse. Definitely worse.

Helpless. Worthless. Every "-less" that ever existed.

I sway, and Tanner wraps his arm around my waist, holding me up. Our eyes meet, and I don't have to say a single word. He knows. Perhaps more than anyone else, he knows exactly what I'm feeling right now.

"They tried to…persuade you here?" he asks gently. Ha.

That was their word for it. Persuasion. As if calling it by another name could disguise the torture they were actually performing.

"Yes." The word is faint, so faint that it fades away into the silence, and I can't be sure if I've actually said it.

"They tried to defeat you back then. But you won't let them win now."

It's the exact right thing to say to bring me back to myself. I'm not six years old anymore. They don't have control over me the way they used to.

"Okay. Let's do this." Squaring my shoulders, I push him into a relief room. "Ten years before our present, a few months before this time, the Underground strategically placed spiders all over the building, which gave them secret access through the air vents. That was how Logan broke Callie out of Limbo."

"And how you broke into my lab."

Fike. I hoped he wouldn't remember. "Well, lucky for us, I have the location of every spider memorized. So my vandalism days were good for something." I crouch by the toilet and try not to touch anything, even though the entire room is sanitized after every use. "See the panel behind the toilet? That's our access point."

He sighs. "Why do all my adventures with you involve crawling through sludge?"

"We won't go near the sludge. I hope. I'll go first." I take a deep breath and crawl straight into a seemingly solid wall, emerging in an air duct on the other side.

I wriggle forward to make room for Tanner, who appears a few seconds later.

"You're not claustrophobic, are you?" Fates, I should've asked earlier. They tortured him for six months. Who knows what other phobias those nightmare memories induced?

I sense, rather than see, the shake of his head. The only

illumination comes from the light filtering through the air vents. "Nah. They didn't get a strong enough reaction the first time, so they stopped giving me the memory of being buried alive."

I grimace. "How efficient of them."

"You're telling me." He taps his wrist com, and a blueprint of the building—identical to the one we've been studying—is projected in front of us. "According to this, we go up the ladder, crawl straight for thirty feet and then left for another thirty. Her room should be right below us then."

I nod. Since he's in front, he climbs the ladder first and enters the horizontal air shaft. It's wide enough for both of us, but we crawl single file. For the next few minutes, my only visual is the soles of his hovershoes.

Before the last turn, he pauses. "Remember." His voice floats back to me. "If we get separated, meet me at the cabin where the time machine is housed. Doesn't matter how long it takes. I'll wait for you."

"Why would we be separated?"

He starts crawling again. "You never know. I just want to be prepared."

Before I can formulate my next question, he stops at an open air vent and scoots to the side. I crawl up next to him, wedging my shoulders against his, and we both look through the slats into the room below.

A little girl lies in a narrow hospital bed.

Me. Jessa. When I was six years old.

51

lie on the bed, my head propped on some pillows. There are white sheets all around me, and a white teddy bear with a red bow sits on the windowsill.

I fidget, turning left and then right. Looking at the closed blinds and the bear. Drumming my feet against the mattress. Clearly bored to death.

I don't know how right I'm about to be.

The other me, the one who's sixteen and perched in the air shaft, shudders. "I…I can't see this," I whisper to Tanner. "I've relived this moment hundreds, maybe thousands of times in my memory. I don't know if I can live through it again in real life."

He wraps his hand around my wrist. I don't know if he's restraining or supporting me. Either works. Pain snakes up my arms, and I look into his deep, bottomless eyes, scaring even in the dim light.

"One second at a time," he says. "All you have to do is exist, from one second to the next."

His next words are unspoken, but I can read them clearly

in the creases of his forehead. *If I can survive six months of torture, then you can get through this.*

I only have time to nod, and then the door opens. Callie comes into the room.

I freeze. It's here. The moment that changed all of our lives.

Every rational thought flees, and all of a sudden, I'm struggling, pushing, shoving. Doing everything possible to wrench out of Tanner's grasp.

"Think of Remi," he growls in my ear.

I know these words should mean something. I know this name belongs to someone important to me. But right now, the words are nothing but noise. The only thing I want is to get into that room. To stop my sister from what she's about to do.

I struggle harder. He winds his arms around my torso and clamps his legs around my knees, locking me in place. My pants hike up, and my leg scrapes against a seam in the metal shaft. His hands clasp around my waist, his grip digging into my skin. I fling my head back and arch my spine, but it's no use. I can't get free.

A burst of laughter pierces my consciousness. Callie's laugh. It is high-pitched and hysterical. And shuts off an instant after it begins.

"Callie! You came!" I hear her voice. *My* voice, but so young, so strange. Like the voice you hear on a holo-mail. The voice that could never be you—but is.

"Of course I came," my sister says.

Tanner loosens his hold on me, and I look through the vent to see Callie pick up little Jessa's hand.

I want to nail my eyelids closed. Anything not to see this scene from a new perspective. Anything not to have another angle to my nightmare.

But I'm as helpless to look away as I was to stop my sister ten years ago.

"How are they treating you?" Callie continues.

"The food is gross," the younger me says. "And they never let me play outside."

"When you leave, you can play as much as you'd like." Her voice cracks, and so does my heart. "I love you, Jessa. You know that, don't you?"

Tears geyser through my body, filling every space, every cavity with hot, stinging liquid. *Please, Callie. Don't do this. It's been so hard without you. We'll find another way. Just don't leave me. Please.*

"Forgive me," Callie whispers. Her arm whips through the air, and she plunges the needle into her chest.

A hole rips in my own soul, and I open my mouth to scream long and loud and lost.

Before I can make any noise, Tanner's hand slaps over my mouth, turning me to face him. I resume my struggle. I don't want this. I need to see what's happening below. Need to live the worst moment of my life all over again. But he presses his forehead against mine and his eyes swallow my despair.

The door clatters open. I hear Logan's voice. "No, Callie. Don't do this. Don't—"

Tanner's eyes pierce into mine. *This is the past*, they tell me. *We are here now. You will survive today because you survived it yesterday.*

"What have you done?" Logan pleads. "Oh dear Fates, what have you done?"

The tears spring from my soul, spilling onto my cheeks, dripping onto Tanner's face.

Callie's response comes more from my memory than from anything I actually hear. "This is the only way," she says. "The only way to save Jessa. The only way to save the future."

Those were the last words I heard her say as a child.

Fates help me, they will not be the last words I hear now.

Tanner eases back, and I look into the room, my vision blurry with sorrow.

Below, Logan cries like somebody reached into his chest and ripped out his soul. The little girl who is me is hysterical, ripping tubes out of her arm and flinging away the bedsheets. "What happened? Get up, Callie. *Get up*."

Logan lays Callie's body on the floor and places a kiss softly, reverently on her lips. He straightens, tears streaming down his face.

"Jessa." He catches my younger self as I claw off the last tube, lifting me up before I can reach Callie's body. "Do you remember me? I'm a friend. Your sister's friend."

"Of course." My younger self calms momentarily. I remember those arms. I remember how safe they made me feel. "You're the boy from the park. We made roses out of leaves together."

Little Jessa flails, trying to get down. Logan continues to hold me, as if he knows that if I touch my sister, I'd never let go again.

"Callie needs to rest," he says hoarsely. "And we need to get out of here. Before they come back."

"Who?" Little Jessa asks.

"The bad people. You want to get away from the bad people, right?"

"Yeah. They locked me in a nightmare cage. And they wouldn't stop, even when I begged them."

"We're leaving," he says. "They're never going to hurt you again."

"What about Callie?"

"Callie can't come with us right now." His face crumples for half a second. Then, as I watch from above, he puts his mask back into place, feature by feature.

My six-year-old self doesn't notice. But I do.

"This is what Callie wanted," he continues. "She wanted those bad people never to hurt you again. Can you do this for her?"

Little Jessa nods. In three large strides, Logan crosses the room and wrenches open the laundry chute. He deposits my younger self inside and then climbs in himself. The flap bangs shut. And then they're gone.

Leaving Callie's body lying inert on the ground.

52

We have less than a minute to act.

"Come on," I say to Tanner, the sadness gone, the adrenaline kicking in. "We have to hurry."

Moving quickly, the steps familiar from my multiple lab break-ins, I remove the vent and stow it in the air shaft. Next, I lower myself feet first through the opening, dangle for a moment from the ceiling, and then drop onto the floor.

Unlike the labs, this room isn't armed with motion sensors. If it were, Callie and Logan would've set them off long ago. Tanner drops beside me, and we go to Callie's body. Without missing a beat, he takes the antidote from his pocket, finds a vein in her wrist, and injects the syringe.

Or, at least, he tries to. Callie jerks at the last second, and the red formula ends up all over the tile, mixing with the antidote she smashed on the floor.

My heart stops. "What happened? How did she move?"

"The formula must still be working through her system," he says shakily. "It's a good thing we brought the second needle."

I shudder. We came so close to leaving behind that second needle. So close to failing our mission. So close to not reviving my sister.

He swallows hard and holds out his hand. "The syringe?"

"Yes, of course." I fumble in my pocket and give him the needle.

He takes a deep breath. And injects my sister once again.

This time, the syringe goes in. This time, Callie inhales sharply, her entire upper body rising off the ground. Her eyes flutter open halfway. They stare at me, unfocused, and begin to close again.

I slide my arms gently under her torso and pull her onto my lap. "Callie. It's me, Jessa. I need you to listen to me. I have something very important to say."

A puff of air escapes her mouth, and her eyes open all the way. "Jessa," she breathes. "My twin. My half. My soul."

The tears rise in my throat. I want to sob and rage. I want to shake her, to throttle time. She changed her future, all right, but it shouldn't have been like this. I should be lying there, not her.

Never her.

I take a shuddering breath and force the emotion back down. There simply isn't time.

"Listen to me, Callie. Your life depends on it." I wait, reviewing the nursery rhyme in my head. The one I skipped rope to during the Fitness Core. The one Olivia posed to me before she got on the stealth copter. The one with which my mother primed Callie this morning.

When my sister's eyes focus on me, I take a deep breath and say:

"How do you kill the beast?

You take away his food, he feeds off the air

You cut off his head

He grows another one with hair."

And then, I change it. I change it into something that will resonate with her. Something that will make her zooming mind pause. Something that will yank her back to the present.

"How do you stop the chairwoman?" I enunciate each word, making sure she doesn't miss a syllable. "You become her friend and change the system from within."

That's it. Just a few words different from the original, but I hope it's enough. It has to be enough.

"Remember that, Callie. Oh, please. Remember that."

She nods. Her hand twitches, as if she would like to bring it to my face, but she is weak, so weak. It's a miracle — in the form of a red liquid antidote — that she is awake now.

"I would do this again," she says. Her voice is so soft that I have to read her lips. "In every life and every world, I would choose to save you. Every single time."

The tears spill from my eyes. There's no stopping them now. If not through my eyes, the liquid would escape through any available opening — the pores of my skin, my open mouth. Some way, somehow, these tears are finding their way out.

So this is her Fixed. She doesn't know the terminology, of course, but this is what she means.

"I love you, Jessa. They'll never be able to take that away from me."

I grip her hand. "I love you. So much. I'll never be able to tell you how much."

Her eyes close, and carefully, I lay her on the floor. They'll find her soon enough. When my younger self ripped the tubes from my arms, it would've set off an alarm. The medical assistants will be here shortly to check on Little Jessa. They'll find Callie, and they'll do what needs to be done to keep her alive. My work, here in the past, is done.

I look around the room, searching for Tanner. It's time for us to go home.

There's only one problem. He's not here. Sometime during my last conversation with my sister, he disappeared.

53

don't understand. He was just here. Where could he have gone? Why would he have left me now, of all times?

Unless...this was what he intended the entire time. His words in the air shaft come rushing back. *If we get separated, meet me the cabin where the time machine is housed.*

Why would we get separated? I asked.

He didn't answer.

Why? What could he possibly want to do here in the past, without my knowing?

The answer comes to me, and it pitches me forward, slamming my knees hard against the tile. Other than saving Callie, there's only one possible thing that could interest him about this past.

His younger self.

My heart thunders. My throat dries. My gut alternates between screaming and weeping. This isn't right. He's not finding his younger self to say "hello." He wouldn't have been so secretive. He's looking for his younger self in order to *do* something to him. I have no idea what, but it can't be good.

I need to find him. Now.

I race into the corridor. I don't know what I'm doing. I don't know where I'm going. Tanner's the one with the security clearance, not me. He's the one who knows his way around the computer systems. He's my only contact. So what do I do? Who can I get to help?

There's only one possibility, really. Someone who will help me without asking too many questions. Someone whose approximate location I know.

The six-year-old Olivia.

Tucking my head, I skip down the stairs and walk toward the spot where Tanner crashed into Olivia and sent a plant flying. According to the blueprint I memorized, William's office isn't far from here. Hopefully, even though Logan came tearing after Callie, Olivia is still with the FuMA guard in his office, resting after receiving that horrific vision of the future.

I pass our point of interception, but I don't see any ceramic pieces on the floor. No trail of spilled soil, either. Which means enough time has passed for someone to clean up the mess.

Please, Olivia. I break into a jog. *Please still be with William.*

I careen around the corner, making a beeline for the first block of glass-walled offices. Oh, thank the Fates. They're here. I press a hand against my chest, breathing hard. Olivia is sitting in a lounge chair, and a man with russet hair tipped with gold holds out a cup to her, urging her to drink from it.

They both look up, startled, when I burst through the door.

"Callie." The man I assume is William jerks to his feet, the cup slipping through his fingers. "Is everything okay? Logan was so worried. He seemed to think somebody might get hurt."

He thinks I'm Callie. Good. I have on a FuMA uniform rather than the silver jumpsuit she was wearing. My wig's also a slightly different color from hers. He doesn't notice. Why would he? What's more likely — that I'm a time traveler from the future or the girl he just saw a few minutes ago?

"I'm fine. Everything's fine." Are our voices similar enough? William doesn't blink, so they must be. "I just need to talk to Olivia. Privately. Is that okay?"

He picks up the cup and sets it on a tray next to a white candle. "Of course. She may be in shock after receiving that vision of the future. It'll be good for her to talk to you before we take her back to MK."

Without another look, the guard ambles out of the room.

But Olivia is not so easily fooled. She tilts her head, her eyes flitting from the too-brown wig to the new set of clothes. "You're not Callie. You can trick him, but you can't trick me. You're the one I see in my future. The one who helps me. I thought it was Callie at first. That's why I showed her the vision. But it's not. It's you."

I crouch in front of her, so that our eyes are closer to being level. "My name's Jessa," I say slowly. "Like your friend Jessa. Exactly like her, except ten years older. I'm from the future."

She nods. The realization passes through her eyes. The knowledge settles in their depths. She doesn't freak out. She doesn't cry or scream. She is the most composed six-year-old I've ever met, but maybe that's because she's lived decades, maybe even centuries in the future. She bears the weight of human experience on her thin shoulders.

"I need your help," I say. "I came here with a friend. You know him — or at least you know him as he was in this time. His name is Tanner Callahan, and he lives in these buildings. FuMA is training him to be a scientist."

"Of course I know Tanner," she says primly. "But I don't play with him 'cause he's a boy."

"Can you...take me to him?"

"Sure. I know exactly where he is. He spends all his mornings in one place."

I help her out of the lounge chair and, thank the Fates, she seems steady enough on her feet. We stop by the room next door, the other half of William's office.

He's picking helmet contraptions off the floor, from where they must've been knocked down. "Are you taking Olivia? I don't want her going anywhere unless it's back to MK. You and Logan better get out of here. Especially now that we know what the future holds." He shakes his head, his face almost translucent next to his red hair. "That vision was damn scary. Jeesh. No wonder the chairwoman wants to keep it under wraps."

"You have my word I'll get Olivia back to MK." I cross to him and take his hand. I don't know him, but he helped my sister. For that, I'll always be grateful. "Things are about to get…crazy. You've helped us enough. I don't want to get you in more trouble by telling you anything else."

He nods, and I know this is nothing new for him. As an Underground sympathizer and a FuMA employee, he's used to operating on a need-to-know basis.

We leave. Olivia walks next to me sedately. No jumping. No skipping. A completely different girl than the one who ran down these halls earlier.

"Olivia, are you okay?" I ask softly. She might be the most powerful precognitive of our time, but she's still a little girl. One who just saw a vision of her mother condemning her to death.

"My mother doesn't love me."

"I'm sure she does," I say automatically and then wince. I know no such thing. I don't know if Dresden is capable of loving anyone, even her own daughter. "I mean, in her own way, she must." Fike. Am I making things better or worse?

"That vision…" Her voice is so young, but the knowledge in her tone is beyond her years. Fates, it's beyond *my* years. "It doesn't have to be the future, you know. It's only one of many possible paths. We still have time to change it."

"I know." The words are heavy with all the tears I still have left to shed. "When Callie left you, she came to my room and injected the syringe into her own heart. She thought it would save our world from genocide."

"No. I've seen the future. I saw the girl who changes everything. And it's not Callie. At first, I thought it was, since you two look so much alike. But I was wrong. You're the one who saves our world."

My mouth goes dry. "You mean because I came back here to the past? Am I successful? Does Callie wake up ten years from now?"

"I don't know. That wasn't part of my memory. That's not what I saw."

I'm almost afraid to ask. "What did you see?"

She turns to me, her eyes as luminous as the stars, as the galaxy, as time itself. If I look closely enough, I'm certain I'll be able to see my future. Everyone's future.

"I can't tell you much," she says. "When you know too much, too early, the future has a way of not coming true. But I'll say this much: I see you next to me. We are fighting."

Every cell in my body goes still. This is what the future Olivia told me as well. "Who are we fighting? And why?"

She presses her lips together, and I know it's useless to pry. She's already told me everything she's willing to say. We walk the next two corridors in silence, and then Olivia stops at a closed door.

"Here we are," she says. "Tanner should be inside, playing with his mazes and mice. That's all he ever does."

"Thank you. Do you know how to get back to MK?"

She nods.

"Will you promise to go straight there?"

She nods again.

And that's it. Any moment now, she'll leave, and I won't see her for the next ten years. But I don't want to let her go like this. Knowing her mother doesn't love her. Believing she's alone in the world.

I take her arm. It's so skinny, so frail. Once upon a time, I had arms like this. "Olivia, wait. I'm your friend. You know that, right? No matter what time or place I'm in, I'll always be your friend."

She nods a third time, her eyes wider than usual, and scurries down the hallway.

I take a deep breath and face the door. Whatever the older Tanner Callahan is doing, I'm about to find out.

54

open the door—and not a moment too soon. The older Tanner has a little boy in his arms, and he's half carrying, half dragging him toward a spinning spherical blade. The kind used to cut through wood. A tool you would need to construct mazes out of planks of varying sizes. A whine fills my ears as the blade slashes through the air. Just as easily as it would slice through human skin.

The boy kicks and screams as though his life depended on it—and maybe it does.

I run up to them and grab Tanner's arm. "Tanner! What are you doing?"

He flicks my hand away like it's an insect. "This kid is stronger than I remember being," he pants.

"I don't care who you are," the boy screams. "I don't care if you are me. You could be Father Time himself, and I still wouldn't let you hurt me."

"Pay attention, you little brat," Tanner says, his voice strained. "This is for your own good. It's a bit of pain for a lifetime of remembrance."

He grabs the boy's hand—his younger self's hand—and tries to force it toward the spinning blade.

My heart lurches. Dear Fates. I step between them and the spinning blade. "Tanner, stop! Explain to me what you're doing."

He looks up, his eyes so wild I almost don't recognize him. "If anyone would approve, it should be you. I'm giving myself a reminder of what's important."

He pushes his younger self to the floor and digs his elbows into the boy's back. "I'm the cause of future genocide. I invented future memory. I take full responsibility, and that's why I'm going to fix it." He sucks in a breath, winces as if it hurts, and then sucks in another one. "If I cut off some of my fingers, then I'll change the course of our future. When I grow up and see that severed mouse's leg, I'll know not to do what I did. Not to invent future memory. We'll shift to another path. The riot won't happen. Callie's life won't be in danger. Chairwoman Dresden will continue to be stymied."

"We can't change the past." I grip his shoulders. "You're the one who keeps reminding me. Remi—"

"Will still be born," he interrupts. "If you saved Callie, the ripples would extend to everyone close to her, which includes Mikey and Angela. But my ripples will die long before it touches any of you. None of you even know me at this time. We won't even live in the same city for six more years. Whether or not I'm missing a few fingers won't affect any of your lives one iota."

"You don't know that," I whisper.

His jaw tightens. "The payoff is too great. I have to risk it." He gets off the boy and, with renewed energy, hauls him up and once more tries to force his hand to the blade.

My mind spins, working through his logic.

If he's right, future memory wouldn't be invented. Callie

would still be bonded to me. Dresden would have to find another way.

And Tanner...Tanner would be missing a few fingers. He'll bear the scars for the rest of his life. Add to this the torture that's about to come, and it will rock him to his very core. It will change him.

The Tanner Callahan I know—the one I'm beginning to love—might as well be dead.

The blade touches skin, and the little boy's scream pierces the air.

"No!!!" I throw myself at them with all my strength, knocking them away from the blade.

Tanner hits the ground, and I wrench his younger self from his arms. I pull the little boy, who is full-on hysterical, onto my lap.

"Not like this." I kiss the boy's forehead, wetting the too-familiar black hair with my tears. "Callie already injected herself to keep future memory from being discovered. And then you invented it anyway. Don't you see? No matter what we do, science will find a way. You told me yourself. We can't stop science any more than we can stop the beast in the nursery rhyme. How many more lives do we have to ruin before we understand that?"

The older Tanner pulls his knees to his chest, his shoulders vibrating violently. "I can't be responsible for genocide. I can't be the cause of that and live with myself."

"No," I say with all the force in my soul and body. But he's not listening to me. As lost as he is in his own guilt, he doesn't hear.

So I turn to the little boy on my lap. "You are not responsible, do you hear me? The only one who can be blamed for Dresden's actions is Dresden herself. None of this is your fault. Not the world you live in and not your parents' accident."

"Do you really think so?" The boy stares at his hand, where blood is blooming from the cut in between his fingers. "If I had listened more, if I had behaved better, maybe the chairwoman wouldn't have gotten so angry. Maybe she would've punished me instead of them."

I grab a roll of gauze from a nearby table and wrap his finger as best as I can. "There was nothing you could've done. You did the best you could, and your parents would've been so proud of you. I'm proud of you." I tie the gauze, hoping it holds long enough until a real medical assistant sees him. "You're not responsible for the world, Tanner. Just try your best, in everything you do, and I promise you it will be enough. You may feel alone here, so alone. But I promise you that you will be valued. You will be loved."

He buries his face in my neck. "You're nice. Are you an angel, just like my mommy?"

I swallow hard. "Something like that."

"When I grow up, I want to marry you." The fabric of my shirt muffles his words.

I laugh through the moisture wetting my eyes. "Why don't we work on being friends first?" I wrap my arms around the little boy, and I glance up to find the older boy watching me. I can't read the expression on his face, but that's nothing new. I've never been able to tell what Tanner is thinking. But for the first time, I know what's in my own heart.

So I look straight into his eyes and tell him. "You stay the boy you were meant to be. I wouldn't change a thing about you. You hear? Not. A. Single. Thing."

55

Too soon, we have to leave the young Tanner. Everything in me wants to bundle him up and take him back to the future with us, where he won't have to suffer through six months of torture. Where he won't grow up alone and unloved. Where he'll be safe. But I can't. Time is a loop, but it doesn't flow in both directions. If I take the six-year-old Tanner to the future with me, I'll break that loop. The Tanner who is by my side now would disappear.

This is the way his path unfolded, and I have to let time follow its natural course.

We are quiet as we find our way out of the building, sticking to the less trafficked corridors. Once we emerge outside and go into the dense vegetation of the forest, he turns to me, the dappled sunlight decorating his face with shifting shadows.

"I told you once that the only reason I survived the torture was because an angel came into my life," he says. "She held me in her lap and told me that I was valued. I was loved. That's the only thing that kept me going when the pain got to be too much. When I would've done anything to get it to stop."

He takes a few quick breaths. "Over the years, her features have blurred. Until I was sure of only one thing: She was beautiful." He breaks off, dropping his face so I won't see his eyes. So I won't see his heart. A full thirty seconds pass as he struggles to compose himself. And then he lifts his head again. "Today, I find out that my angel was you. That's why I thought I had known you in a past life. That's why I reacted so strongly at the hoverpark. From the moment I met you, I've felt like I was in love with you. The feeling didn't make any sense to me, so I tried to push it away. But now, I know that nothing makes more sense in the world. It was you, this entire time. It's always been you."

He tugs me forward, and I trip over a root. I stumble against his chest and look up into his eyes. He begins to lower his mouth to mine. Our noses bump. His lips graze instead the skin by my ear.

I smile. Our entire relationship, Tanner has been cocky and smooth. Well, he's awkward now, and I love him all the more for it.

"Let's try that again," he whispers, cupping my face with his hands.

This time, our mouths connect solidly. I kiss him like I've never kissed anybody before. It's not just our lips that are touching. Not just our tongues, not just our chests. I feel like our very souls are meeting. And it doesn't matter if we're in the present or the past. It makes no difference if we're in this world or another one.

There's only one true Jessa and one true Tanner. And we're here. Together. Now.

He pulls back a fraction of an inch. "I love you, Jessa," he says against my mouth. "You saved me."

"I love you." I weave my fingers together behind his neck.

"And you were the one who saved me."

And he did. I've spent my life engaging in stupid pranks that didn't amount to anything. Trying my hardest to avoid anyone's political agenda. When my true goal was always in front of me. I just never understood it until he showed me what was important.

Him. Our love. The people in our lives.

We've been going about this all wrong. Callie, Mikey, the entire Underground. We thought we could prevent genocide by preventing the invention of future memory. When future memory was never the culprit. It was always Dresden who was to blame. Dresden who is the enemy.

There's only one way to kill the beast.

He gives me one last kiss and then squints at the sky. The sun is blazing overhead. "I hate to say this, but we need to get going."

I nod and rub my thumb over his knuckles. There, where I never noticed it before, is a scar between his ring and middle finger. In the exact spot where a whirling blade might cut. "Was this always here?" I ask.

He holds up his hand, and mine along with it, and considers the scar in the sunlight. "As long as I can remember."

"Our lives have always been intertwined," I say. "We just never knew it."

"I want our lives to stay intertwined," he says somberly.

"Me, too."

He lowers our hands, and we begin to walk through the woods, picking our way around the brambles and thorns. I don't know how much longer my hand can stay fused in his.

All I know is this: I don't want to let go. Not for the rest of this time and all of the next one.

...

I open my eyes. I'm standing on a metal platform. Naked once again. Disoriented one more time. I blink at the metal arch. Hear the creaking groan of one of the most powerful generators of our time. And register that the boy I value above all others is across from me. Also naked.

My mom and Preston descend on us.

"You're okay," my mom sobs, wrapping her arms around me. "You're back here with me."

I embrace her for a long moment, closing my eyes. My hands begin to tremble as it sinks in. I did it. I went to the past—and returned, safe and sound.

My mom pulls back, handing me a robe. Out of the corner of my eye, I see my dad helping Tanner get dressed.

"Did it work?" my mom asks. "Did you go to the past?"

I slip my arms through the sleeves. So strange, but from their perspective, only a brief time must have elapsed. "What did you see?" I ask.

Preston helps Tanner on with his robe. "The metal arch passed over you, and there was this tornado of energy. For a few seconds, the wind was so strong we couldn't see your bodies at all. And then the arch passed over you again, the wind died down, and here you are." He looks at us expectantly. "Well? What happened?"

"We went to the past," I say slowly. "We saw Callie. We completed the mission."

All true, those lines. But it's such a gross understatement of what actually happened it feels like a lie. Those sentences capture nothing about Tanner's past. They skim over how it felt to see my sister again, what I learned about my relationship with my mother. They leave out my insights about my purpose in life.

Only a few seconds have passed, and yet, I'm an entirely new person. A person who bears little resemblance to the old Jessa Stone.

There'll be plenty of time later to fill in the details. Or maybe not. Maybe those things don't need to be spoken, shouldn't be shared. Maybe what has passed should stay in the past. Maybe Tanner and I are the only ones who were meant to remember yesterday.

I reach out and take Tanner's hand. Whatever happens next, I want it to be with him.

My mother places her hand over our connected ones. Of course she knows there's more. She was there for part of it. But I've also learned she's nothing if not patient. She's been waiting for ten years for this day, after all.

"I'm so glad you came back to me," she says simply.

I try to smile. "Was there ever a doubt?"

Something flickers in her eyes. Hope. Nothing but an ember, really. Her family has been torn apart for so long. A husband stuck in the future, a daughter she believed was dead. Another daughter who spoke to her with only resentment. She's on the verge of having her entire family back again—but she knows better than to hope.

And yet, it seeps in anyway. Hope is the flame that will not die, no matter how much tragedy tries to smother it.

"I need to see Logan," I say hoarsely. "I need to tell him about Callie. He has as much right as we do to be there by her side. Whether or not the jingle works, whether or not she wakes up, he should be there when we try."

Instead of readily acquiescing, as I expect, my parents exchange a look. One that makes my stomach free-fall to the floor.

"What is it, Mom? What. Is. It?"

"We didn't want to tell you earlier," she says slowly. "We didn't want it to interfere with your mission. But Mikey came to me this morning. And he said…" She moves her shoulders helplessly. "Oh, Jessa, he said Logan was going to propose to his new girlfriend today."

My heart stutters. "Well, did you stop him? Did you explain what we were going to do? That Callie might come back to us?"

She stares at the floor, and my father places his hands on her shoulders. "We couldn't. Mikey insisted we didn't interfere, and he has a point. Even now, we have no idea if our crazy plan will work. We don't know if Callie will wake up. It wouldn't be fair to knock Logan's life off-kilter now that he's moved on."

"This isn't about fair." I remember the way Logan crumpled when my sister's eyes closed. The way he put himself back together so that he could take me to safety.

In that instant, I know Mikey's wrong to keep this from Logan. He might mean well. He might be trying to protect his brother. But Logan has already lived his pain. So did Tanner. They both became the people they are because of their experiences.

I wouldn't erase the Logan I know any more than I would change Tanner. Any more than I would blight Remi out of existence.

"I'm telling him," I say, looking from my mom to my dad to Tanner. Daring them to disagree. "It's the right thing to do."

56

I run. My feet fly over the ground, and my arms whip against the bramble and brush of the woods. The air whistles in and out of my lungs, and a stray branch slashes my forehead. I don't bother to stop or even wince. I have to find Logan.

Dear Fates. Don't let me be too late.

Logan wasn't at his house. He left Mikey's—where he confided his intention to propose—hours ago. But I know him. There's one place to which we both escape when we need to think. A place where the sky is our ceiling and the water is our floor. The place where we both feel closest to Callie.

I have to believe that for a decision this big, he would come here first.

Please. Let me be right.

I crash through the woods, heading toward the cove where the lake juts into the land and the trees spread their leafy fingers overhead. I skirt around a fallen moss-covered trunk, and there he is. Sitting on one of two side-by-side stumps that always seemed tailor-made for us.

The sun is warm on my skin, and the air smells of fresh

pine and damp earth. This is what the outdoors—what home—always smells like. And yet, my hands are slick with sweat, and my heart thumps in my throat.

I walk to the stumps. My shoes crunch on small sticks, and Logan looks up. Deep circles rim his eyes, and the lines on his face seem to have multiplied. I may have traveled a decade into the past, but in that same time, Logan looks like he's jumped forward ten years.

"You did it, didn't you?" I say, my knees weak. "You ejected Callie from your heart."

He drops his head. "I guess you heard. Every day, Angela and Mikey were on my case. To move on. To let go. To live. This is me, trying to do that."

I close my eyes. This is my fault. I should've told him as soon as I learned about my sister. I shouldn't have listened to Mikey. I shouldn't have waited. Because now, we can't go back to yesterday. Even if Callie wakes up, what's done is done.

Oh, engagements can be broken. But not for someone like Logan—someone whose word means everything. He's loyal, steadfast, unflappable. That's why he is so loved. That's what makes him who he is.

Everything inside me compresses into a tight, dark ball. I'm too late.

I open my eyes, just in time to see his face change. The lines smooth out; his expression turns calm and placid. There's nothing he can do about the bags under his eyes, but right in front of me, he mutates from a man plagued by tragedy to one who is solid and steady—to the Logan I've known all my life.

The transformation is subtle, and I might've missed it if I hadn't watched him from a certain air shaft in the past. But I recognize the shift now. I see how, all of his life, he puts on a mask for me. To protect me.

"I love you, Logan," I say quietly. "I always have, and

that will never change. You were my savior, my protector. You were the only one who loved Callie as much as I did. But I never appreciated what you went through. How hard it must've been for you to keep it together and take care of me, when you were just a kid yourself. How you had to put your own despair below mine. But you did it."

He traces the tip of his shoe in the dirt. "In the beginning, I did it for Callie. All she wanted was for you to be safe. When she couldn't protect you anymore, I took the reins. Because I loved her." He tilts his face to the leaf-covered sky. The one that's always there, always whole, no matter how broken we are underneath. "But pretty soon, you wormed your way into my heart, too. You were a cute kid, you know. It's easy to see why she loved you so much."

"I never talked," I say, flushing. "Remember how you would all be laughing and joking, and I'd be in the corner, sulking?"

"Not sulking." He picks up my fingers and squeezes them. "You were just taking it all in. Besides, you didn't have to talk or tell jokes for me to accept you. I love you simply because you're Jessa. The sister of my heart."

I take a deep breath and then another one. The tears line my lungs, and every breath brings a little more moisture to the surface. This man. He's done so much for me. Given me so much. Cruel or not, he deserves the truth.

Haltingly, I tell him everything. How I discovered Callie was still alive. How Mikey convinced me to stay quiet. Our wild plan to save Callie and our journey to the past. How I saw a younger him save a younger me.

When I finish, it's so quiet I can hear the wind rustling the leaves. The crickets chirping their beginning-of-summer song.

"Say something," I beg. "Are you mad?"

His eyes flash. "Am I mad? Ten years ago, my life was

destroyed. My heart was ripped out, and every time I hoped it could be put back, I was shot down. Encouraged to forget about Callie and move on. Now you're telling me there's a possibility she might come back to us?" He shakes his head wonderingly. "I should want to tear time apart that you kept this a secret for so long. But all I can feel is amazed. I might get to listen to her laugh again. To hold her hand. To see in her eyes how my touch affects her."

"But isn't it too late? You're engaged. You're no longer free to love her."

"No," he says. "I'm not."

My heart—and time itself—stops. "You told Mikey this morning you were going to propose to Ainsley. When I got here, you said it was a done deal."

"I meant I made the decision to propose," he says. "I didn't actually go through with it."

He takes something out of his pocket. At first, I think it's a ring, but then I see it is a plant bracelet. Thin green stalks woven together and preserved in some kind of sealant so that it holds, even after one year—or ten. "I had every intention of proposing to Ainsley today. But as I was leaving my house, something caught my eye. Something bright and red. The corner of a leaf."

He slips the bracelet on his wrist. "I don't know if you know this, but when we moved back to civilization, your mom gave me Callie's old books. The physical ones. There weren't many, just a few cookbooks and a thin volume of poems by Emily Brontë. I kept them on a shelf, and today, as I walked past, I saw a bit of red sticking out of the book of poems. I don't know why I never noticed it before. When I opened the book, a bright red leaf came fluttering out. Just like the ones I used to give her when we were kids."

I can hardly breathe. That was me. Logan never noticed

the corner of the leaf before because it wasn't sticking out before. When I went to the past, I put the slim volume back where it belonged, but I left a corner of a leaf poking out. Tanner was so worried that my one small action would change the future—and it did.

Maybe everything does happen for a reason. Maybe our paths roll out exactly the way they're supposed to unfurl.

"I knew right then that I couldn't go through with the proposal." The mask slips from Logan's face, and he shows me exactly who he is when he's not trying to protect me. A man who hurts...and loves. "I knew this was a sign telling me to wait for something, anything." He swipes his hand over his eyes. "Maybe I have more precognition than I thought."

"Maybe so." I stand and hold my hand out to him. "Come on. Let's go wake up my sister."

57

"Are the doors locked?" my father asks the next morning. "The shades drawn? Com units off?"

"Yes," I say. We're back in Preston's apartment, and we're as ready as we'll ever be. More ready than even he suspects.

My head's fuzzy. My limbs ache. I haven't slept for twenty-four hours because I've been busy making arrangements for my secret plan. A plan no one knows about except Tanner. But sleep is overrated. Just ask Callie. She's being doing nothing but sleep these last ten years.

"You're sure Dresden doesn't know?" My father wheels on Tanner. "You swear you didn't let anything slip in a conversation, in a report?"

Tanner holds up his hands. "Not a word. I swear to the Fates."

"She can't know about Callie, you understand?" He paces the living area, leaving angry red footprints on the pressure-sensitive tile. "She thinks Callie's dead, that her body's disposed of. If she discovers I snuck her out, it will blow my cover—everyone's cover. We'll no longer be the docile Underground under her thumb but the secret rebellion plotting to overthrow her. It will ruin everything."

My mom puts her hand on his arm, and he stills. "I'm sorry." He drops his forehead onto her shoulder. "I'm just nervous."

It's amazing to see the connection between them already. It's like they picked up where they left off twenty-three years ago. And that connection will only continue growing. Even if Callie wakes up today, even if his bond with my sister is no longer needed to connect her to the present time, Preston's not going anywhere.

"I've already lost you once," my mom said fiercely to him yesterday. "I'm not going to risk losing you again. The past has already happened. Jessa survived it, and so did I. So let's just leave well enough alone. If you go back, there's no telling what the world will look like." She lowered her voice. "No telling how worse off Callie's condition could be."

Preston couldn't argue. Even though I know it kills him to lose twenty-three years with us, he didn't want to risk losing our family, either. Not when we're about to be reunited once again.

I tear my eyes from my parents and look around the rest of the room. We're all here, gathered outside the room where Callie's body lies. Mikey and Angela, with little Remi in her arms. Logan. Ryder, my best friend, who comforts me just with his presence. Zed and his wife, Laurel. Brayden. Tanner. My mom, my dad, and me. We're the people who mean the most to Callie. We also happen to be the leadership of the Underground and the first fugitives Dresden would chase if —and when— she learns the truth.

After all, nothing stays a secret from Dresden for long. Tanner told me they're already looking for Callie's body. It's been four days since we snuck her out of that cavernous room, and it's only a matter of time before they find her.

But Preston doesn't know that. And now's not the time to tell him.

We troop into the next room and arrange ourselves around Callie's body. My sister lies on the stretcher, breathing evenly, gently. Lost in the sea of time. Her eyelids are closed and her limbs are loose and limp. She has no idea we're about to yank her back to the present.

"Step away," I say to the others. "Give me space."

Sweat soaks my hair, and my heart drills a hole through my chest. We've got more than one shot at this, but the first time has the greatest chance of success. With every repetition, the jingle will become less strange. Less likely to jostle her mind. Callie will begin to absorb the jingle into her consciousness, and then it will feel like every other memory to her. Floating and aimless.

Everyone takes a big step back except Logan.

As we previously discussed, he stands across from me. I hold one of Callie's hands, and he holds the other.

I square my shoulders, and the air around me seems to vibrate. Or maybe that's just my trembling nerves. I send a quick prayer into the universe. And then I speak:

"How do you kill the beast?
You take away his food, he feeds off the air
You cut off his head
He grows another one with hair.
How do you stop the chairwoman?
You become her friend
And change the system from within."

Her eyes twitch. As if she's trying to open them. As if she's struggling to remember how.

I suck in a breath. The only other time this happened was when I sent her the memory. That means she hears my words.

That means she has a reaction.

"The jingle did its job," my father says softly. "It triggered her mind. Her mind has stopped zooming, and it's trying to figure out where to land. Now, it's up to the two of you. Let her hear your voices. Bring her back to us."

Logan brings her hand to his chest. As we planned, he's going first. "Come back to me, Callie. Please. Wake up."

I shoot him a look as if to say, *Is that all you've got?*

He shuffles his feet. I know he's uncomfortable. He's been shut down so often whenever he talked about Callie. He's had to put so many priorities ahead of his grief. He's not used to speaking so openly.

"Give her your heart, Logan," I murmur. "That's why you're here."

He nods, swallows. And begins again.

"Callie. Calla Lily. My heart, my red leaf. I've been in love with you since I was twelve. Since you leaned back in your chair, craning your neck to see the sun. I knew from that moment you were the girl for me. You're good and kind and brave. More importantly, you love deeply and unconditionally. You don't hold anything back." His voice breaks, and he lowers his face over their hands. "You…you destroyed me, Callie. I understand why you did it. You wouldn't be who you are if you hadn't. But you've been lying there for ten years now. I continued living, but your absence is the constant in my life. It greets me every morning and accompanies me to bed every night. I can live without you. I know that now."

His voice grows stronger in both volume and depth. It pierces all the way through me. "But I don't want to. I gave you a leaf to remind you of the sun, Callie. But you are my sun. Without you, my world is dark, and it's time for you to come back to me again."

I stare as hard as I can at her face. Is that another twitch?

Yes, it has to be. A definite flutter of her eyelashes. She's trying. Father of Time, she's doing her best to get her eyes open.

Come on, Callie. You can do it. Wake up. Wake up. Wake up.

And then, miracle of miracles, it happens. Her eyes creak open. They shut again immediately. But they open once more, squinting against the dim light. They dart around the room a few times, a hummingbird lost in flight, and then they settle on me.

My world tilts. Flips upside down, turns inside out. If I weren't holding onto Callie's hand, I might slide right off this plane into a different dimension. Is this moment really happening?

It is.

"Jessa?" her voice rasps. It's little more than a whisper, and it isn't any wonder. She hasn't spoken for ten years.

My eyes are wet and blurry, and I don't know if I'm crying, or if she is, or if it's the very air that's weeping. "It's me, Callie. I'm here. And so are you. So are you."

The others get in line, and one by one, they each have their moment with her. She recognizes all of them, even my dad. And then, it's Logan's turn. They don't say much, but they don't need to. Their love is apparent in the graze of his knuckles against her cheek, in the way their gazes latch onto each other's and refuse to waver.

My heart is full to the point of bursting. I'm crying and laughing. I hug my mom and kiss Tanner and toss baby Remi into the air. I've experienced joy before, but nothing like this. Nothing even close to this.

I know, without a single, slightest doubt: I've never been so happy in my life.

58

ater, I'm in front of Callie once again. Holding her hand
once again, while the others talk to one another in small
groups. My sister lies against her pillow, exhausted. The
machines kept her muscles from atrophying, but she's not
used to sitting and breathing on her own.

Still, there's a reddish tinge to her cheeks that wasn't
there earlier. The light in her eyes completely overwhelms
the fatigue in her face, and her breath, while short, has the
unevenness associated with life.

I check my joy. My job here isn't done. I didn't get to say
the speech I prepared, and maybe that's just as well. It won't
preempt what I'm about to do now.

"I have something to say to you, something everyone
should hear," I tell Callie, raising my voice to get the others'
attention. My throat is tight; my heart, the one that so recently
expanded like a balloon, feels even tighter. "For a long time,
I believed I should've died instead of you. I felt unworthy of
your sacrifice. You gave so much—not only to me but also to
the rest of the world. You gave us back the belief in ourselves,

in our own free will, in the control we have over our futures. 'Remember yesterday' became our rallying cry. Remember Callie. Remember what she did to change her future. If Callie could do it, then we can, too."

I take a deep breath. This one comes from deeper than my lungs. It comes from the very center of my soul. "While I appreciate what you gave me, while I honor and love every bit of who you are, I've come to realize that you made a mistake. That's okay. Because every mistake brings us closer to the right answer."

I let her hand slip through my fingers, and I back away. Ryder and Angela part as I crowd into them, giving me a clear path to the wall screen. And the security panel next to it.

"How do you stop the chairwoman?" I flex my hand. My fingers are shaking, but I don't need steadiness for what I'm about to do. "Not by taking your own life. Not even by cutting off the fingers of a little boy. You can't stop the chairwoman by delaying the invention of future memory. First, because science won't be delayed forever. And second, because future memory is simply a tool. You can't stop a monster by taking away her tools. You have to get into her brain and you change her, and if she's unmalleable, then you have to change her organization."

My back bumps into the wall. And there it is: the red security button, at the top left corner of the panel. The one with a direct line to PuSA, the Public Safety Agency. The one that alerts the authorities of a traitor in our midst. Every ComA employee is urged to install one in his or her home, and every apartment in the scientific residences has one.

"I used to believe I was unworthy, but not anymore. Everything that's happened has led me to this moment. When I finally prove my worth to you."

My eyes drift to Tanner, and he gives me a single, precise

nod. He's the one who helped me hide all the equipment. He's the one who knows about and believes in my plan.

Quickly, before I can change my mind, I flip open the glass cover and push the button. "You have exactly six minutes to get out of here before PuSA arrives. Run through the woods and jump into the river. I've hidden canoes on the other side. There's enough dry food and equipment in them to last you several months in the wilderness. Medicines for Callie, formula for Remi. Everything you could possibly need to make your lives comfortable. It's time for you to go on the run once more."

The anger, the rants, the cries explode instantaneously.

"What are you doing?" Logan roars. "Callie's still weak. She's in no shape to travel."

"Remi's just a baby," Angela wails. "She might die out there in the wilderness."

"I didn't think you had it in you," Ryder bites off. "In all our years of friendship, I never pegged you for a traitor."

I cover my ears. No. Not him, too. My closest friend. He knows me better than I know myself. I'm not going to see him for a long, long time. I can't bear for this to be the last words I hear from him.

But what can I do? Even if I block my hearing, I can still see the kaleidoscope of their accusations. The slashing anger in Ryder's cheeks, the twisted rage in Mikey's lips, the burning betrayal in Angela's movements. My mother looks worried, my father confused. Each expression cuts me, deeper than my skin. Deeper even than arteries and veins. I hurt, I hurt, I hurt. I didn't know I could hurt so much.

This is the core of my nightmares. This is the vision I swore would never come to fruition. Their hatred. My betrayal.

Well, it's coming true now. Except it's worse. Worse than waking up screaming in my bed. Worse than recognizing the birthmark on the waist of the chairwoman's assistant. Worse even than facing myself in the deep of night and knowing that the only solution is to betray my family.

Because I knew what was coming. And I still chose to do it.

So the vision will come true after all. I will become the chairwoman's assistant. Just not for the reasons that I thought.

I'll become her assistant not because I'm on her side. But because this is the only way I know to stop her. The only way I can get her to trust me. The only way I can insinuate myself onto her team and work my destruction from within.

She said she needed actions, not words. Well, this is the only action I can think to take. If I'm right, then maybe I'll save the world. Maybe I'll obliterate this future of genocide, once and for all.

If I'm wrong? Then I will have suffered the hatred of everyone I love for no reason at all. Tanner's been through worse.

The room spins around me with their anger, with their flurry of motion. Hate me or not, they must save themselves. They must get away before PuSA breaks down these doors.

My knees go weak, and I stumble. Tanner catches me an instant before I hit the floor. Looking into his eyes, I know that at least he is on my side—will always be on my side.

No one else pays attention to me. I'm beneath their notice now.

All except Callie. She is the only one who is still, while the others race around, struggling to prepare in five minutes for a trip that might last five months or more. She is the eye of a storm that's been raging for the last ten years, and she watches me with the deep love and generosity only a sister can feel.

"Forgive me," I whisper, repeating back to her the words she said to me so many years ago.

"Always," she says, and with that single word, she gives

me strength. Hope that I will be brave enough and worthy enough to face what's to come. To do what I need to do to defeat the chairwoman.

Callie believes in me. For now, and for always, and that means everything.

Of course, it shouldn't surprise me that she alone would be the one to understand. It was the jingle that woke her up, after all.

end of book two

Read on for a sneak peek of

SEIZE TODAY

Chapter 1

Across the control room, technicians stand at their com terminals, their hands moving busily over keyballs as they monitor the memories being transmitted from the future, right at this very moment. Right in this very building.

It's like we've gone backward in time, to the way our lives used to be eleven years ago. Once again, every seventeen-year-old in North Amerie is ushered into a government building on his or her birthday. Once again, the teens are instructed to open their minds in order to receive a memory from their future selves. Once again, these visions serve as an all-knowing guide for the recipients — and as a guarantee for everyone else: employers, loan officers, even prospective spouses.

It's as though Callie Stone never stabbed a syringe into her chest, as though the invention of future memory was never threatened. As though I didn't go into isolation for the last decade.

Nothing might as well have changed...except for one

thing. Jessa and I are now part of the system.

I look across the room at Jessa Stone — Callie's sister and more importantly, my ally. She wears the same crisp navy uniform as me, but hers has three golden bars across her shoulders to indicate that she's the personal assistant to my mother, Chairwoman Dresden.

It's been six months since Jessa betrayed her family in order to gain my mother's trust. Six months since my mother asked me to come out of my cabin in the woods, where I had sequestered myself for ten years, so that I could follow Jessa around and determine her loyalty.

I didn't want to. Isolation is safe. Isolation doesn't bombard you with a million people's futures, with tragedies that you're helpless to change. But I set Jessa on this path. I convinced her that she would be the one to stop my mother's future plans of genocide. Of course, Jessa believes that the Chairwoman is the ultimate bad guy, that she's nothing but pure evil. I don't agree. I *know* my mother. I've lived a thousand of her alternative visions, and I'm absolutely convinced she's got her reasons for making such bad decisions. They may not be *good* reasons - they may not justify or excuse anything – but in her mind, she's doing what's right.

I don't tell Jessa any of this. I doubt it would go over very well. But after dragging her into this situation, the least I can do is be her shadow.

That's what the FuMA employees call me when they think I'm not listening — Shadow. It makes sense, I suppose. I'm the strange girl who spent ten years by herself in the woods. I'm the meek employee who trails after Jessa from room to room, never acting and barely speaking. It's what I do best, what I've always done best: observe.

It's just too bad that I finally have a nickname from someone other than Tanner, and it turns out to be "Shadow."

Jessa wanders over to me. "Want to take a break?" Her tone is so warm that I can almost convince myself that she likes my company. That we're not simply forced to work together. That she's actually my...friend.

I peek at grown-up Tanner, the third FuMA official in the room and the only other person who knows our true mission. "In fifteen seconds, Tanner will be joining..."

...*us*, I finish in my head. Ugh. Again? Six months ago, right when I rejoined society, I picked up this terrible tic of dropping the ends of my sentences. Not on purpose. My therapist at the Technology Research Agency, the one my mother forces me to see, thinks it's because I secretly think that my words are unimportant, that no one could possibly be interested in what I have to say. I don't know if she's right, but it's a habit I've been trying—without much success—to break.

It's only because these are the first words I've spoken today, I reassure myself. I'll be better once I get a little warmed up.

"You think?" she murmurs, eyes brightening. "He's in the middle of a session. He can't just drop everything."

Five seconds...four...three...

Sure enough, Tanner glances up from his terminal and then swaggers toward us. Instead of a navy suit, he wears a white lab coat over his black thermal shirt and cargo pants—his unofficial scientist's uniform. Reaching us, he kisses Jessa on the cheek.

Almost without realizing it, I curl my shoulders forward and I back up one step, two steps, three steps, until I'm standing behind an empty com terminal.

"You're so predictable," Jessa says to Tanner.

"Well, of course I'm predictable." The black hair flops over his forehead. "You're standing with the only true precognitive of our time." He flicks a glance at me—or at least, what he can see of me, since I'm mostly hidden by the metal structure. "She can see my future!"

"Correction," Jessa says mildly. "She can see the many different paths your future could take. She has no more knowledge than anyone else which path you'll actually choose." Her lips curve. "But it's nice to have proof that you can't resist me."

"*You* can't resist *me*." He grabs her waist, tickling her, and she shrieks with laughter.

I drop my eyes to the floor and try to make my body even smaller. Not because I want Tanner for myself—Fates, no. I've known him since before he knew how to make his hair lie flat. But because when I look at them, my chest aches.

This is what I want. What I've always wanted. Someone to love, and someone who loves me.

But for some of us, love only exists in a few measly twigs in the branches and branches of our possible destinies. I'm not like Jessa. I don't know how to open my heart to someone. Maybe I don't even have a heart. The only affection I've ever known is from a phantom mother who doesn't exist in this timeline. And my father? I don't know if I ever had one. Even as a child, I heard the snickers and gossip about the Chairwoman's test-tube baby. Who would blame the world for finding me unlovable?

Not me. Not in a single one of my futures.

"So, what's your excuse for interrupting your work?" Jessa asks.

Tanner sobers. "I actually have one this time." He untangles himself from her but keeps a hand on her hip. "We've had another case. The third one this week. Like the others, the girl's fine when she's receiving her future memory. But afterward, she's confused. Mumbling to herself, walking into walls. Talking to people who aren't there." He moves his shoulders. "I don't know how to explain it."

I frown. Tanner Callahan, boy genius and the freaking inventor of future memory, admitting that he doesn't know something? Must be serious.

"Let's go talk to her," Jessa says. "Is she still in the recovery area?"

He nods, and the three of us troop down the hall. Well, to be more accurate, the two of them troop, and I drift behind, not wanting to intrude. Jessa looks over her shoulder, gesturing for me to join them. I flush and quicken my steps but continue to trail behind them.

We enter the recovery area. The patient is in the third partitioned section, staring blankly at the walls. She wears her black hair in two braids, and her left hand lays palm-up on the table, a freshly inked hourglass tattoo gleaming on her wrist. Presumably, underneath the tattoo, a black chip containing her future memory has just been implanted.

A hologram floating in front of the partition displays her name. Danni Lee.

Jessa crouches down and takes her free hand. "Hi, Danni. My name is Jessa Stone, the Chairwoman's assistant. Can you tell me what day it is?"

Danni's eyes focus not on Jessa but on a spot over her shoulder. "They say I live my life like a moth to a flame— attracted by bright lights and exciting moments," she says dreamily. "They say this will be the death of me, since the life of a moth who flies too close to the fire will soon be extinguished."

"O-kay." Jessa glances at Tanner. He shrugs, as if this was exactly what he expected, and sinks down next to her.

"Are these bruises from today?" He examines the marks on Danni's shins. "How did you get these?"

"But I ask you: is this bad?" Danni continues. "Would you

rather live a long, uneventful life, or seize the moment and leave this world in flames?"

My stomach feels like these very same moths are flitting inside. Danni's not registering a word we're saying.

Jessa stands and gestures for Tanner and me to follow her out of the room. Danni continues to mumble about moths, and a nurse enters and injects her with an amber-colored syringe.

I don't want to leave her like this. I don't. But reaching into her future tells me that she'll soon recover from her symptoms and return to her regular routine.

"The bruises are from walking into a chair today," Tanner says, reading her hologram file. "If her symptoms are like the others, she'll return to normal after a few hours."

We step back into the hallway. "But where did her symptoms come from?" Jessa asks. "They didn't have these problems ten years ago, when future memories were processed as a matter of course. Is something different about the way memories are being received today?"

"That might not be true," Tanner says, his steps slow, his words slower. "They might've had this problem ten years ago."

"What do you mean?" she asks.

"The amber-colored syringe that the nurse was injecting into Danni's arm. Look familiar?"

She gasps. "Oh dear Fate. You're right."

We continue walking, both of them lost in their thoughts. I have no idea what they're talking about. I should probably just ask, but my jaws seem to be fused shut, once again. No doubt they've forgotten I'm here.

As I try to work up my courage, Tanner turns to me without prompting. "You know Jessa and I time-traveled to the past, right?" He rubs the skin between his ring and middle finger. "Well, we saw your mom. Even back then, ten years ago, she was medicating herself. She had a standing order for a formula, seven doses every week." He pauses. "It was amber, just like Danni's."

I frown, but I don't say anything.

He shrugs, as though he's read my mind. "It could be some kind of pain-killer Or maybe she and Danni are being treated for the same disease."

"There's more." Jessa's voice is gentle—too gentle. "I saw your mom walk into a door last night."

My mouth finally opens. "And I stubbed my toe on a..."

...*cleaning bot*. Fike. Not only did I drop the last part of my sentence, but the words I did say came out too fast, too loud. For years, I only talked to myself and the chipmunks, so I have little practice with voice modulation. I swallow hard, order myself not to break off mid-sentence, and try again. "Being clumsy's not a crime." Great. Now my words are so soft I doubt either of them heard me. At least I completed the sentence.

"That wasn't the first time I've seen her be clumsy," Jessa continues, unfazed. "When she came by my cottage, to show me the vision that I would be her assistant in the future, she almost crashed into a transport tube."

I lift my eyebrows, since nonverbal movements are an easier form of communication. Jessa's "evidence" doesn't prove anything other than that my mother might need new retinal implants. And yet, cement fills my veins.

I had no idea about the syringes. Not the first clue that my mother has a condition that reaches back ten years. For a moment, the old nightmares come back to me, the ones depicting a time that's dreary, desolate, *desperate*. People fading away. Our world stitched together by a single thread that's unraveling, unraveling, unraveling...

No! I slam the door to that vision shut and reinforce it with a fortress wall, brick by brick. No. I refuse to grant entry to those images. I refuse to let them rise to the level of conscious thought.

Ten years ago, I was teetering on the edge of madness, from seeing too much and too far into our possible futures. My mom whisked me to a cabin in the woods so that I could work on building the mental walls that would protect me.

She must've done something to herself, too, because shortly before my isolation, I stopped being able to reach into her future.

Gone was the phantom woman who loved me. Gone were the different versions of Marigold Dresden who rocked me and held me tight. Gone were the alternate realities I used to comfort myself. Maybe it was silly to mourn the loss of a woman who didn't exist, but I did.

And I never forgot her.

"Olivia, are you okay?" Jessa asks, concern etched in her lovely teardrop eyes.

I take a shaky breath. Nausea roils through my stomach, and a thousand knives jab into my brain. But I erected my mental walls just in time. I'm safe, for the time being.

"I'm fine," I mouth. My words don't rise to the level of audible hearing, but Jessa's been around me enough that she should understand what I'm saying.

Before she can respond, the head technician, Bao, flies out of the control room. "Miss Stone, I don't want to interrupt," he bursts out. "But we've got a late arrival who's just about to receive his future memory. And I think it's one you'll want to see."

Interview with the Author

Brenda Drake: We're celebrating the paperback release of Pintip Dunn's *Remember Yesterday*. Since we're such great friends, Pintip agreed to let me torture her with some questions about the series (yeah, she's brave). So, are you ready, Pintip?

Pintip Dunn: I guess? *bites fingernails*

BD: I'll go easy on you, I promise. Jessa and Callie are such close and loving sisters. They would sacrifice everything for the other. Is there a relationship like that in your life that inspired this one?

PD: Oh, that is easy! Jessa and Callie are directly inspired from my relationship with my little sister, Lana. She is twelve years younger than me, and we've also been extremely close. I like to tease her that in this series, I get to act out my fantasies of killing her. But the truth is, *Forget Tomorrow* is about how much Callie loves her little sister—and the lengths she would go to in order to protect her.

BD: I really loved Logan in the first book, but Tanner completely stole my heart in *Remember Yesterday*. Is there a character that surprisingly gripped your heart while writing this story?

PD: Can I say...all of them? Ha!

BD: No. You must choose. Think of it as if they all were in a burning building: which one would you rescue first?

PD: What? You are so evil. Why are my characters being burned alive??

BD: You're the one who likes to kill your characters. Now: answer.

PD: Such a dictator. Well...I cried my eyes out writing this book (more than I've bawled for any other book) and most of the tears were for Tanner, Jessa, her mom, and her dad. So I guess Tanner and Jessa are my answer. But oh, Callie and Logan have never relaxed their grip on my heart. Book Two also introduces readers to the grown-up Olivia and Ryder, but you don't really get to know them until Book Three. I love this couple, too.

Oops, I think I accidentally listed all of them. And I'm gushing. How embarrassing. Is that allowed, to gush about my own characters? I feel like that parent who is ridiculously proud of her children.

BD: I gush over your characters, so you definitely can.

PD: And I gush over yours! I mean, Bastien! I could write an entire letter about him—a love letter, that is. Oh wait, that interview's coming later...

BD: Speaking of love, Tanner loves to show up at all the wrong moments and it flusters Jessa. Do you have a so-want-to-not-be-here-but-want-to-be-here moment from your teen days?

PD: Hmmm, I'd have to say my freshman year of college. I wanted so *much* out of life, and I wasn't yet confident in who I was, and it was just a very emotional time for me. Still, I think it was the most fun year of my life. I became best friends with the people who lived in my hallway (and we're all still super close today), and I ended up marrying one of them.

BD: You so lucked out there. I don't think you could ever write a better hero than your hubby. Okay, I know this will be hard, but I have to know. Are you Team Logan, Team Tanner, or Team Ryder? And why?

PD: This is really hard. They are so swoony in each of their own ways. I love how devoted Logan is to Callie, even a decade after they first fell in love. I love how Tanner and Jessa have a connection beyond what even they know. And I love how Ryder is exactly the right person that Olivia needs. But if I had to pick one...it would have to be Tanner. He's so cocky and arrogant and broken, and I know this will sound weird, but I fell even more in love with him after writing Book Three.

BD: On that note, we can end the interview. Thanks for talking, Pintip. It was so much fun! Everyone else, go grab all the books in this series. *wink*

Brenda Drake is the *New York Times* bestselling author of the Thief of Lies series. Visit her online to learn more about her books: www.brenda-drake.com. And look for a continuing interview between Pintip and Brenda in the back of the paperback of Brenda's *Guardian of Secrets*, coming soon!

ACKNOWLEDGMENTS

This is the third time in a year that I've had to write acknowledgments for a novel. While my comments may feel repetitive, my gratitude is just as heartfelt.

Thank you to my amazing agent, Beth Miller, for your continued guidance and advocacy. I'm so glad I have you on my side!

My brilliant editor and publisher, Liz Pelletier, has helped me shape this story with her astute insight. Thank you, from the bottom of my heart, for your continued belief in this series. Thank you to Madison Pelletier for being one of my earliest readers, and thank you to the entire team at Entangled—and in particular, Melissa Montovani, Stacy Abrams, and Heather Riccio—for turning this story into a book.

L.J. Anderson, the cover is just breathtaking. Thank you. My gratitude goes to Rebecca Mancini for placing the Forget Tomorrow trilogy with my foreign publishers. Thank you to Lucy Stille, my film agent.

Thank you to Editions Lumen, in France; Record, in Brazil; and Pegasus Yayinlari, in Turkey, for bringing the Forget Tomorrow trilogy to your respective countries.

I would like to thank RWA for awarding Forget Tomorrow with a RITA® for Best First Book, an honor beyond my wildest dreams.

GRAB THE ENTANGLED TEEN RELEASES READERS ARE TALKING ABOUT!

BLACK BIRD OF THE GALLOWS
BY MEG KASSEL

A simple but forgotten truth: Where harbingers of death appear, the morgues will soon be full.

Angie Dovage can tell there's more to Reece Fernandez than just the tall, brooding athlete who has her classmates swooning, but she can't imagine his presence signals a tragedy that will devastate her small town. When something supernatural tries to attack her, Angie is thrown into a battle between good and evil she never saw coming. Right in the center of it is Reece—and he's not human.

What's more, she knows something most don't. That the secrets her town holds could kill them all. But that's only half as dangerous as falling in love with a harbinger of death.

27 HOURS
BY TRISTINA WRIGHT

Rumor Mora fears two things: hellhounds too strong for him to kill, and failure. Jude Welton has two dreams: for humans to stop killing monsters, and for his strange abilities to vanish.

But in no reality should a boy raised to love monsters fall for a boy raised to kill them.

During one twenty-seven-hour night, if they can't stop the war between the colonies and the monsters from becoming a war of extinction, the things they wish for will never come true, and the things they fear will be all that's left.

I am indebted to Danielle Meitiv for her genius brainstorming of this book and to Meg Kassel and Kimberly MacCarron for their insightful comments. Thank you, as well, to Brenda Drake, Vanessa Barneveld, Denny Bryce, and Stephanie Winklehake for your friendship and constant support. Special thanks to all of my writing groups—and a shout-out to Katie Robinson for her stunning photographs.

Thank you to my family, the Hompluems, the Dunns, and the Techavacharas. I could write pages about what you mean to me—but let suffice it to say, I love and appreciate all of you so much. I have the best family in the world. I believe that with every ounce of my being.

To Antoine and my three beautiful children: you are ALL my favorite. I feel blessed every day to be a part of your lives. And finally, thank you to my wonderful readers. I hope you enjoy Jessa's story just as much as Callie's!